PRAIS

CAUGHT

"*Caught Up in You* is Roni Loren's best book to date. An angsty backstory made beautiful by a hero who doesn't know how perfect he is. Don't miss this Ranch treat!"

—Carly Phillips, *New York Times* bestselling author

FALL INTO YOU

"Steamy, occasionally shocking, and relentlessly intense."

—*RT Book Reviews*

"Fast-paced and riveting with clever plot twists . . . Loren brings her characters to life in an enticing and passionate story."

—*USA Today*

"Sexy suspense done right . . . It's hot, it's sexy, full of alpha dominant goodness, and a thrill of a story."

—*Under the Covers Book Blog*

"The best of the series." —*Fiction Vixen Book Reviews*

"An erotic romance with heart and serious heat."

—*Romance Novel News*

continued . . .

MELT INTO YOU

"Quite a ride. The story is heartfelt and pulls you into the relationships with the characters. *Melt Into You* takes the traditional version of romance and twists it so that the idea of three individuals in a relationship seems perfectly right."

—*RT Book Reviews*

CRASH INTO YOU

"Loren writes delicious, dark, sensual prose . . . Multidimensional characters, a very complicated relationship, and suspense combine to make *Crash Into You* unique and emotional—an impressive debut from Loren."

—*USA Today*

"Revved up and red-hot sexy, Roni Loren delivers a riveting romance!"

—Lorelei James, *New York Times* bestselling author of the Blacktop Cowboys and Rough Riders series

"Hot and romantic, with an edge of suspense that will keep you entertained."

—Shayla Black, *USA Today* bestselling author of *Ours to Love*

"A sexy, sizzling tale that is sure to have readers begging for more! I can't wait for Roni Loren's next tantalizing story!"

—Jo Davis, author of *I Spy a Dark Obsession*

CAUGHT UP IN YOU

RONI LOREN

HEAT BOOKS | NEW YORK

THE BERKLEY PUBLISHING GROUP
Published by the Penguin Group
Penguin Group (USA) Inc.
375 Hudson Street, New York, New York 10014, USA

USA I Canada I UK I Ireland I Australia I New Zealand I India I South Africa I China

Penguin Books Ltd., Registered Offices: 80 Strand, London WC2R 0RL, England
For more information about the Penguin Group, visit penguin.com.

This book is an original publication of The Berkley Publishing Group.

Library of Congress Cataloging-in-Publication Data

Loren, Roni.
Caught up in you / Roni Loren.—Heat trade paperback edition.
pages   cm
ISBN 978-0-425-25992-4
1. Erotic fiction.   I. Title.
PS3612.O764C38   2013
813'.6—dc23
2013009590

PUBLISHING HISTORY
Heat trade paperback edition / August 2013

PRINTED IN THE UNITED STATES OF AMERICA

10   9   8   7   6   5   4   3   2   1

Cover photograph: Abstract Tulle © Coka / Shutterstock.
Cover design by Rita Frangie.

To my grandfather, Ron,
who buys my books but (thankfully) doesn't read them.
Thank you for always being such a supportive force in my life.
I'm proud to be named after you.

ACKNOWLEDGMENTS

First, a giant hug of appreciation to my readers. Your support and excitement for these books are the very things that allow me to keep writing them. I'm forever indebted. I heart you all.

As always, thank you to my husband, Donnie. I wouldn't want to live this life with anyone but you at my side. You're the best man I know.

To my son, you always know how to make mommy smile even when I'm so stressed I can't see straight. You with all your beautiful quirkiness and smarts helped inspire the hero in this book. Never think you need to be anything but yourself.

To my parents, thank you for always being there for me no matter what. I love you beyond words. And particular thanks to Mom for always listening to me ramble about whatever is going on in my day. You keep me sane and grounded.

To my editor, Kate Seaver, thank you for all your guidance and support. I knew Kelsey and Wyatt's story would be a unique challenge. Your feedback was invaluable.

To my agent, Sara Megibow, thank you for your unwavering enthusiasm and support. You are a great business partner, cheerleader, and friend.

To all of the team at Berkley and Penguin, thank you for doing so much to champion my books.

To all the wonderful writers I've met over the past few years, you amaze and inspire me. And a special shout-out to my NTRWA friends for being such an amazing group of welcoming and supportive women.

And finally, to my go-to girls for when I need to vent, squee, or just have a fun chat: Jamie Wesley, Julie Cross, Dawn Alexander, and Gen Wilson. And to Taylor Lunsford for always being willing to beta read for me.

ONE

"You know, picturing someone naked this early in the morning isn't good for your health."

Kelsey LeBreck leaned forward to get a better view through the kitchen's pass-through, smirking at Nathan's jab but not tearing her gaze away from her subject. "Hush and keep flipping his eggs."

But of course her co-worker ignored that command. "I mean, think how long you'll have to wait before you can get home to your vibrator and imagine Mr. Tall, Dark, and Loaded rocking your world. You're going to be so pent up and distracted, you'll screw up everyone's order."

"I do that anyway." *Except his. Never his.* Though, that wasn't really an accomplishment, considering he always ordered the same thing.

"Yet you still get better tips than Chandra."

"I'm charming that way." And desperate. When that tip meant the difference between being able to pay for a tank of gas instead of riding the bus, she could channel so much sunshine and sweetness, even the grumpiest customer couldn't be mad at her for long.

"Are the muffins ready to go in yet? Darryl's going to be here any minute and you know how he gets if shit is late."

"Working on it." Kelsey blindly stirred her muffin batter as she watched Wyatt Austin adjust his glasses, fold his newspaper just so, and then spread out a stack of documents on the table in front of him. He had a way of moving that was somehow graceful and efficient all at once. Like he'd figured out the most streamlined way to do each and every thing so that he could fit the maximum amount of work into every minute of the day.

And maybe he had. God knows his schedule was more predictable than the sunrise. At six fifteen every weekday morning, he would walk in the cafe with his newspaper tucked under his arm and his own travel mug of coffee. He'd sit at the same table in the far corner, the one that provided him both a view of the television on the wall and the least amount of glare for his laptop screen. She knew that only because she'd finally asked him one day why he chose that booth all the time. When she'd joked that he sat there because it was her section, he'd just offered that enigmatic smile of his—one that had promptly made her forget the last order she'd taken from the table before him.

"You need to stop torturing yourself," Nathan said from behind her, the sizzle of the griddle playing soundtrack in the background. "From what I've heard, the suit doesn't date. And he's not gay either. Believe me, I'd be the one serving him eggs and sausage if he were."

She snorted and finally looked back at Nathan. "Sausage? You're going with that one, really?"

He held his arms out to his sides and gave her a come-on-how-could-I-pass-that-up look.

"How do you even know this stuff? And you, with the fetish

for skater boys, would go after Wyatt Austin, CEO-in-training? Please."

"I love the shit out of that strong, silent type. They're usually crazy good in the sack. Like they're saving up all that intensity just for you." He shrugged and turned over a row of bacon with his spatula. "And money never hurt anybody. I'm not above being a kept man."

"You're a top."

"And so are you, baby girl. But that hasn't stopped you from your mad, passionate love affair with Mr. In Charge."

She sighed and turned back to her batter, grabbing a ladle so she could scoop it into the muffin tins. It *was* a mad, passionate love affair. He was the absolute perfect boyfriend for her right now. Delicious to look at, panty-dampening to fantasize about, and completely and utterly unattainable.

Nathan set a plate next to her and slid the egg white omelet and two slices of turkey bacon onto it. "Order up. Now, if you're not going to give up on this crush, why don't you take this plate over there and ask the guy out?"

She spun to face him, muffin tray in her hand. "Did you forget to take your meds today? I'm a waitress and wannabe baker. His family owns an entire company."

"So the fuck what? He has more money than you. Big deal. Doesn't mean he's better than you. In fact, he'd be a damn lucky bastard to get a date with you. Hell, I'd take you out just to get these secret muffin recipes of yours."

She handed the pan to him, picked up Wyatt's plate, and kissed Nathan's cheek. "Thanks, hon. But if I've learned one lesson in life, it's that fantasy is always better than reality."

He gave her a sly smile. "But fantasy can't have breakfast in bed with you the next morning."

No. But it also couldn't break your heart.

Or break *her*.

Kelsey turned on her heel and pushed through the kitchen's swinging door. Time to serve breakfast to her imaginary boyfriend.

———

Wyatt sipped his coffee and flipped through the reports he'd printed out last night. The profit margin was still in decent shape, but their client numbers had suffered a significant dip over the last two quarters. Their competitors Merrill and Mead were doing some mighty fast talking and had stolen two of Austin and Associates' top clients—two clients who Wyatt had been making a shitload of money for. So God only knows what Tony Merrill had promised them to get them to leave. Or maybe Merrill was outright spewing lies about A&A. That'd be his style. The whole thing was giving Wyatt a twitch and a headache.

"Egg white omelet with spinach and cheddar and two slices of turkey bacon, extra crispy."

Wyatt looked up from the papers, momentarily startled at the interruption. *Damn*. Usually he made a point to watch Kelsey's swaying walk over to his table, and he felt a pang of disappointment over missing the morning highlight. That walk and smile were a big part of the reason he'd started driving four blocks past his building to eat breakfast at the Sugarcane Cafe.

His brother, Jace, had introduced him to the place and to Kelsey a few months ago, and Wyatt hadn't been able resist the temptation of being served by her each morning ever since. The woman could make that retro blue-and-white diner uniform look as sexy as high-end lingerie—not that it had stopped him from picturing her in the latter anyway. "Thank you, Kelsey. This looks great."

"My pleasure. Anything else I can get you, Mr. Austin?" She smiled with a head tilt that made her blonde ponytail swing behind her.

He'd imagined very, very naughty things involving that ponytail one too many times. *Cool it, Austin.* "Tell me about the muffin du jour."

She leaned over and grabbed the discarded sweetener packets he'd used in his coffee, inadvertently giving him a glimpse of the golden curved flesh peeking through the collar of her shirt. "Of course. Thinking of breaking tradition and ordering one today?"

He raised an eyebrow.

She shook her head, but there was humor glinting in those blue eyes. "It's fresh raspberry made with a touch of vanilla and a citrus-infused simple syrup poured over the top to make them extra moist and tart."

"Sounds delicious."

"But you don't want one," she said, confirming his standard answer before he could give it. "You know, one day I'm going to bake one that sounds so enticing, you're not going to be able to help yourself."

"Is that right?" he asked, fighting a smile. Truth was, he didn't eat sweets that often. He kept his diet as regimented as his schedule. Discipline in all things. But he loved hearing her describe her food and watching the pure pride that starched her shoulders and brightened her eyes.

"Yep. It's a personal mission of mine," she said resolutely, her hand on her hip.

"What is?" he asked, leaning forward onto his forearms, holding her gaze. "To tempt me?"

Her eyes held his for a long beat before they shifted away. She pressed her lips together, smoothing her gloss. "Um . . ."

He realized too late how low his words had come out, how laced with innuendo. He quickly straightened in his seat, dragging his attention back to his work in front of him. *Too young. Too sweet. Too messy.* "Bring me one of those muffins, Kelsey."

There was dead air for a moment, as if she were righting her thoughts, then she said, "Oh, of course. Right away, sir."

But when she turned on her heel to go, a soft curse passed her lips. She spun back around, and he looked up to find her wearing a please-don't-hate-me expression. "What's wrong?"

She peeked back toward the kitchen. "I forgot. They won't be ready for another fifteen minutes. I got in a little late from my overnight job and didn't get them started on time."

He frowned. "You work an overnight shift and then spend all morning here?"

"I only do the other job a few nights a week," she said hastily. "Usually the timing works out, but there was an accident on the interstate this morning and . . ."

He held up a palm, silencing her. "I'm not worried about muffins not being ready, Kelsey. But I am wondering when you find time to sleep and take care of yourself. And frankly, I'm a little concerned that you're driving a car and working in a kitchen with no rest. That's dangerous."

Her gaze darted downward, a pink tinge washing over her cheeks. "It's fine, really. I'm used to crazy schedules and don't really need a lot of sleep."

"And both jobs are necessary?"

She looked back at him, and he could see her lingering embarrassment over the conversation. He should be polite and let her off the hook. Her personal business was her own. But the thought of this vibrant girl working herself to the bone to get by wasn't sitting well with him.

"I'm saving up for culinary school. This job pays for the basics. The other goes into my school savings."

"I see."

"Excuse me," a nasally voice called from a few tables over. Snapping fingers accompanied the annoying interruption. They both turned. A pinched-mouthed woman had her bony hand in the air, trying to get Kelsey's attention and beckoning her like she was an errant puppy. "I'm out of coffee."

Wyatt sent the woman a quelling look, and she quickly looked down at her cream-cheesed bagel with a *well-I-never* huff. He brought his attention back to Kelsey. "Go ahead and take care of your tables. God forbid anyone has to wait a second for something. And let me know when the muffins come out."

"Yes, sir," Kelsey said, clearly relieved to be released from the conversation.

And though he was always at his desk by seven sharp, he lingered over his omelet today, taking the time to enjoy the hum of conversation around him and the sight of his favorite waitress doing her job.

Kelsey checked on him once and brought fresh coffee, but in between that, she was a nonstop machine of smiles, banter, and serving prowess. Even when she got something wrong, Wyatt watched in fascination as she won the person over to her side. Hell, she had one older man smiling and apologizing to *her* when she served him oatmeal instead of cheese grits. He'd patted Kelsey's arm and joked that his wife must've put her up to it since he was supposed to be cutting back on calories anyway.

It was like watching a master-level demonstration in social sparkle. If he had to make all that small talk and feign interest in all these people's woes and requests, he'd lose his fucking mind. But Kelsey seemed to thrive on it, like she fed off the energy in the diner. She was magnetic to watch.

By the time she made her way back to him with the fresh-out-of-the-oven muffin, his reports and laptop had gone untouched. She set down the plate and laid a fresh napkin next to it. "Hope it doesn't disappoint after all this time."

"Oh, I have no doubt it will have been worth the wait," he said, watching her instead of looking at the muffin.

"Anything else I can get you?"

A hotel room and an hour of your time. Maybe two hours. Or a weekend. But he shook off the tempting thought. Yes, he came here every day to enjoy the presence of his pretty waitress. But he'd always done it with the knowledge of look but don't touch. Like enjoying a fine piece of art. Meant to be observed, appreciated, even turned on by, but not meant for consumption. Beyond the fact that she was probably at least a decade younger than his thirty-seven years, Wyatt had learned to steer clear of the ones who nudged that old, buried desire that lay sleeping in the recesses of his past. And Kelsey didn't just nudge it; she fucking assailed it.

"No, this will be all. Thank you."

"Enjoy." She gave him a bright smile and sauntered off, the walk just as impressive from the reverse angle. He liked that she moved around with the confidence of a woman who knew she drew attention from the opposite sex and was okay with that—no apologies or self-consciousness. She wouldn't be the type to insist on doing it in the dark.

Awareness stirred below his belt as he imagined peeling her out of that uniform, tasting that pink-glossed mouth. He shifted in the booth. God, he needed to make some time to get laid. His body was reacting like a fucking teenager drooling over the head cheerleader. Ridiculous. Ever since his colleagues-with-benefits thing had ended with Gwen two months earlier, he'd been working too much to seek out anyone else. But if he didn't set something up soon, he was going to have to stop coming here and putting temptation in front of himself.

He watched Kelsey maneuver toward the front of the restaurant as he broke off a piece of the muffin and put it in his mouth. Wow, that was good. Moist and still warm and not too sweet. The balance of flavors was complex enough to stand up in one of those frou-frou bakeries where they charged you six bucks for a pastry. No wonder the girl wanted to go to culinary school.

He was no chef, but he recognized skill when he tasted it. And she was wasting that in some hole-in-the-wall cafe.

Not your business, his mind warned him.

Wyatt glanced at the clock on the wall. He hadn't shown up this late for work in longer than he could remember. His assistant was probably all aflutter, wondering if he was dead on the highway or something. Mr. Routine had deviated. Call the press! His phone was on vibrate in his laptop bag, but he had no doubt there'd be messages.

But right when he was about to pull his gaze away from Kelsey and grab his cell out of his bag's pocket, she halted mid-step, panic freezing her features. Wyatt followed her line of sight to the man who'd walked into the diner. Stocky and spiky-haired with a mean set to his mouth, the guy looked like a human version of a hyena. Kelsey turned quickly toward the kitchen, the tray in her hand wobbling, but the hyena had already locked his sights on her and was making his way in her direction.

A cold feeling crawled up the back of Wyatt's neck, his protective instincts going on full alert. This man meant trouble. Without moving his attention away from the guy, Wyatt gathered his papers and laptop and tucked them in the bag, preparing in case he needed to intervene.

Kelsey was on a hasty path to the kitchen, but before she could slip behind the counter, the guy laid a hand on her upper arm—a grab, really—and leaned next to her ear to whisper something. For a casual onlooker, the gesture would probably appear friendly, like someone she knew giving her a message. But even from behind, Wyatt could see her body go ramrod straight, could see that she didn't want this person near her. He had the instant urge to break the guy's nubby little fingers for daring to touch her.

She nodded stiffly and set her tray down on the counter. The guy nudged her toward the back end of the restaurant. She ventured a quick glance toward the kitchen as she took a step away from the counter, but the kid manning the griddle didn't seem to notice anything was going on. Wyatt was already on his feet though, heading in that direction. He didn't want to make a scene if this was, perish the thought, a lovers' squabble or something. But he'd learned to follow his instincts in business and they never let him down, so he wasn't going to distrust them in a situation like this.

The man was moving at a casual pace, but he was clearly guiding a reluctant Kelsey to the back exit. Wyatt let them stay a few steps ahead, so he wouldn't be noticed. But if the two slipped out the back door, he was going to have to get involved. No way was he letting that punk get Kelsey alone in the alley.

"Mr. Austin! Wait!"

Wyatt turned, the instinct to respond to his name automatic, and the other waitress was waving a hand at him and holding his bag. "You forgot your things."

"Put them behind the counter for me. I'll be right back." He quickly turned back toward the exit, but the heavy door was already closed. "Fuck."

No longer caring who saw him, he jogged toward the door and shoved it open, blinking for a second so his eyes could adjust to the sunlight. "Kelsey."

A small gasp.

He turned to the left to find Kelsey pressed up against the dirty wall and hyena-man looming over her, his arms braced on each side of her. Trapping her.

"It's all right, man. Go back inside. I'm just having a little chat with my girlfriend," the guy said, his easy tone not matching the spark of menace in his dark eyes.

Red leaked into Wyatt's vision. "Get your fucking hands off her, or we're going to have a problem."

"Oh, really, GQ? What are you going to do?" He moved one

hand off the wall and grabbed a knife from his waistband. "You going to choke me with your necktie?"

Kelsey's gaze darted to Wyatt's—but where he expected to see fear, he saw rage. He had only a split second to figure out she didn't plan to stand by and let him handle things. "Kelsey, d—"

But before he got his words out, Kelsey jerked her knee upward, hitting the guy square in the nuts. The howl of pain echoed down the alley as the guy doubled over, and Kelsey ducked and juked left out of trajectory. Acting on pure adrenaline, Wyatt launched himself at the guy linebacker style, going straight for the arm wielding the knife, and slammed the guy's hand against the wall. The knife clattered to the ground, but the guy swung at him with the other fist.

The punch landed against Wyatt's jaw, almost knocking his glasses off his face, but the pain barely registered because the desire to maim, torture, and annihilate was burning like a bonfire in him. This scumbag had threatened Kelsey. Sweet, beautiful Kelsey. He grabbed the guy by the throat and smashed him against the wall again, using the extra inches of height he had on the guy to his full advantage. "You want to hit me again, asshole? Try it. Swing at me and give me a reason to choke you."

Hyena's eyes flooded with challenge. "Empty fucking threat. You know that bitch piece of ass isn't worth getting a lifetime in jail."

Wyatt's grip tightened. He'd never thought himself capable of killing another person, but in that moment, he would've enjoyed ridding the world of this trash. He bared his teeth as he pressed just a little harder against the guy's windpipe. "Oh, really? You're going to count on that? I have lawyers so good that I could choke you right in the middle of the fucking restaurant and be lauded in the papers as a hero. So don't. Fucking. Tempt. Me."

The guy's eyes bugged a bit at that, whether from the threat or the pressure on his throat, Wyatt didn't care. Hyena wet his lips, and his voice came out hoarse. "Fine. Just let go, man."

Police sirens wailed in the background, echoing against the buildings.

Wyatt eased the pressure and smiled. "I'll be sure to do that. In a minute."

The guy closed his eyes, sagging in Wyatt's grip.

An hour and an ice pack later, Wyatt sat on the back steps outside the restaurant, watching as the last cop car pulled away. He'd asked them to make sure to not release details of the event. The last thing he needed was the press picking this up. His father would love that. Kelsey, who'd been standing at the end of the alley, turned around. She had her arms wrapped around herself and carried a hollow look in her eyes.

When she got close, he lowered the ice pack and saw the tears that shimmered in her eyes. "I am so sorry, Mr. Austin. Is it bad?"

He set the ice pack aside, pushed himself to stand, and dusted off his slacks. "Please, I think we've moved on to the stage where you can call me Wyatt. And I'm fine. I'm more worried about you. Did he hurt you?"

She shook her head and a thousand responses seemed to touch her lips in rapid time, her mouth twitching. But after a few too many failed attempts at speaking, she simply flung herself at him, stunning him with a hug. His arms went out to his sides as if they'd forgotten the proper response to being embraced, and he looked down his body at the woman he'd so often imagined touching.

"Thank you," she whispered into his shirt.

God, she was warm. And her scent . . . Who'd have ever thought bacon and maple syrup could smell so goddamned perfect on a woman? The thought that anyone would want to harm her had his rage firing up anew.

Unable to hold back any longer, he gave into the urge and

wrapped his arms around her, holding her against him as she let the adrenaline and the emotions drain out of her.

The back door of the restaurant cracked open, and the kid from the kitchen peeked out, concern weighing heavy on his boyish features. He'd come outside a few times to check on Kelsey, and Wyatt had instantly liked him. "You okay, baby girl?"

Kelsey stepped out of Wyatt's embrace with an apologetic smile and swiped at her face. "I'm fine, Nathan. Thanks for checking on me. And for calling the cops."

"I've only got an hour left on my shift. Want me to give you a ride home after?" Nathan asked, looking between her and Wyatt.

"I—"

"I've got her," Wyatt said, cutting her off.

Kelsey's head whipped around. "Mr. Au— Wyatt, you don't have to do that."

"You worked all night and you've had a hell of a morning. You don't need to be waiting around here. I want you in bed."

Nathan's eyebrows disappeared beneath his shaggy bangs.

"Resting," Wyatt clarified.

Kelsey actually gave him a half smile on that one, some of the color coming back into her cheeks. "Yes, sir."

He should've told her to drop the sir. But for reasons he'd rather not examine at the moment, he wasn't in a hurry to stop hearing that little gem roll off her lips.

He pressed his hand to the small of her back to lead her back up the stairs, reciting in his head: *Too young. Too sweet. Too messy.*

TWO

Kelsey stared out the side window of Wyatt's BMW, trying to get her skin to stop crawling and her heart to stop its attempt to bust out of her chest. When Howie Miller had stepped into the restaurant, it was like being yanked back eighteen months—her life rewinding and then hitting the play button at the shittiest part.

Well, almost the shittiest part.

She'd been so careful. Had picked up and moved her whole life to a completely new area. She'd even registered her apartment and all her utilities under another name. And the cops had said they would never reveal that she'd been the informant. But the look in Howie's eyes when he'd pushed her against the wall had said he knew exactly whose information had put his brother in jail. If Wyatt hadn't followed her out there and distracted him . . . She didn't even want to think about it. In that world, being a snitch was a capital offense. And Howie had looked more than ready to mete out her punishment.

Wyatt, who'd been quiet for the last few miles, glanced over at her. The lingering anger over what Howie had done hovered there in the tense lines of his face and his grip on the wheel. He looked as if he wanted to beat up the guy all over again. "What did that punk want with you? I'm guessing it wasn't a random attack."

"No, it wasn't," she said, turning back toward the window, wishing she didn't have to have this conversation with Wyatt. Wyatt, who only knew her as the chatty waitress and his brother's friend. Nothing else. None of the ugly stuff. She'd hoped it could remain that way.

"Was he an ex or something?"

She grimaced, the idea making her stomach turn. "God, no."

Wyatt blew out a breath like that was the best news he'd heard all day. "Then what?"

She glanced down at her hands, fiddling with the silver bracelet she'd treated herself to when she'd celebrated her first year sober. That day had felt like such a fresh start, like a new life was there for the taking. But apparently the dregs of her past were determined to stir up and muddy everything again. "I helped put his brother in jail a while back. He wasn't supposed to know it was me, but I guess he figured it out and was coming to pay me back."

"Christ," he said under his breath as he took the turn toward her apartment complex. "Thank God he's going to be behind bars now, too."

"Yeah, we'll see how long that lasts," she said dryly.

Wyatt flexed his fingers against the steering wheel again, those big, beautiful hands of his knotted with tension. "You need to file a restraining order on him when you get home. Just to be safe."

She had to fight back the scoff that wanted to jump out of her throat. Restraining orders were worth about as much as the ink used to sign them. In her experience, they usually just served to instigate the person further—like waving a flag at a crazed bull. "Sure. Will do. My building's the one there on the right."

"You're humoring me," he said, displeasure coloring his tone as he swung the car into a parking space.

"I'm sorry," she said, letting her head fall back against the seat, exhaustion setting in now that the adrenaline had left her system. How long had it been since she'd slept? She couldn't quite remember. "I'm not trying to be flip. I just—everything was going so well and now I have this to deal with. I want to throttle that asshole." She opened her eyes, staring forward. "Is it supposed to be this hard to live a drama-free life?"

She caught his smirk in her peripheral vision. "Some people would call drama-free boring."

She turned her head toward him. "Boring sounds *amazing*."

He smiled fully now. His jaw was still a little swollen from the punch, but that didn't reduce the impact of the expression. God, he was gorgeous when he let that grin slip through, lighting up all those dark features and revealing the dimples hidden beneath. He smiled so infrequently that it felt like a gift each time it happened, like she'd won some secret contest.

She stayed where she was, enjoying the close-up view of him too much to look away. But in the small space of the car, the ocean blue of his eyes darkened behind his glasses the longer she sat there, his humor morphing into something decidedly more intense. Heat seeped through her in a slow roll, the playful fantasizing about her fictional boyfriend becoming more of a desperate itch for the real thing.

Wyatt reached out, his large palm cradling the side of her face. "You're too young and too sweet to have so much history in those eyes."

She wet her lips, her cheek tingling beneath his touch. "I'm not that young, Wyatt. Or that sweet."

He stared at her, that blue gaze boring into her with the precision of surgeon's knife, and she thought he was going to lean over and kiss her. She wanted him to. Even though she knew it was a ridiculously bad idea, knew that the minute she crossed that boundary with him, she'd be just another woman he'd bedded. She was well aware of the score with guys like him. Had tripped down that path a few too many times in the past. Wealthy men didn't date women like her—they entertained themselves with them.

But all Wyatt did was brush a thumb over her mouth, swiping the moisture she'd left there, and then lowered his hand with a softly expelled breath. "Come on. I'll walk you up. You need rest."

She blinked, the loss of his touch like a cold wind against her face, and tried to drag herself back to reality. "Oh. Um, don't worry about that. I'll be fine."

But he was already opening his door. "I'll feel better if I see you safely inside. I rarely get the opportunity to feel chivalrous."

She laughed, breaking some of the tension that'd been thrumming through her body from the imagined almost kiss, and pushed her door open to climb out. "Is there a white horse to ride up the stairs?"

"Nah, he's in the shop." He offered a little bow and a bent elbow. "Will my arm suffice, fair lady?"

She tilted her chin up in her best imitation of haughtiness. "I guess that will do."

He smiled and took her hand, linking it around his arm. "Lead the way."

If Wyatt had any opinions about her modest apartment complex and its peeling paint or sagging stairs, he kept the judgment off his face. She knew he'd probably never spent a night in anything with less than five-star accommodations, but she wasn't going to bother being embarrassed about where she lived. She'd worked hard to get her own place on the decent side of town and even if it wasn't much, it was hers.

She guided him to her door and reluctantly released herself from his hold to slide the key into the lock. There was a note taped above the doorknob, and she suspected it was the landlord telling her rent was a day overdue. She grabbed it and turned the knob, stepping inside.

She expected Wyatt to follow, but when she turned around, she found him leaning against the doorjamb like a vampire who needed permission to cross the threshold. "You can come in if you want."

His mouth lifted at the corner. "Probably better I don't. Leaving the car was hard enough."

So she hadn't imagined the almost kiss. She set her purse down on the breakfast bar, debating whether or not to push the issue. Even nudging a toe down this road was a bad idea. But she couldn't help herself. The question that had been hovering in her mind ever since that first week he'd started coming to the restaurant spilled out. "Why do you come to the cafe every morning? Jace told me where your building is. It's not convenient."

He crossed his arms over his chest. "Because I like you."

She absorbed that for a second, the matter-of-fact way he said it. The answer didn't shock her exactly. He wasn't one of those guys to throw lines at her and shamelessly flirt, but she could tell when he looked at her that he wasn't just concerned about getting her attention for a coffee refill. However, mixed in with that subtle interest, she always sensed some underlying layer of distance. Like he was watching her from the other side of bulletproof glass. "So why didn't you kiss me in the car?"

He pushed himself off the doorframe and stuck his hands in his pockets. "Same reason."

"Right." At least he was honest. Message, loud and clear. If they slept together, she would never seen him again. "You don't date."

"No, I don't. Not very dateable, I'm afraid."

"Sure, with the good looks, your own company, and the penchant to save waitresses in dark alleys, women must run away in horror," she teased. "Come on, you know you could have your own season of *The Bachelor* and fill Texas Stadium with the contestant casting call."

His curving lips had an edge of resignation to them this time. "Women like me on paper. But the reality isn't as bearable. I work from seven in the morning to past ten most nights. I'm a control freak in all aspects of my life. And my social graces leave a lot to be desired."

"Meaning, you can be an asshole."

He shrugged, unapologetic. "My tolerance for others is limited."

She had already gathered that about him. The glare he'd sent that customer who'd interrupted them today could've bent the silverware. "Yet you visit me every morning."

"You're exceptionally tolerable," he said, stepping inside finally and picking up the note that must have fallen to the floor when she'd set her purse down.

His comment and having him only a pace away from her—in her apartment, alone—had her thoughts disintegrating for a moment. To stop herself from moving even closer and embarrassing herself, she went for the safety of humor. She tilted her head and batted her eyelashes in her best southern belle impression. "Oh, Mr. Austin, you say the sweetest things. You should write poetry."

He chuckled and handed her the paper, his hand lingering against her fingers for a few extra seconds. "I'll see you tomorrow, Ms. LeBreck. Try to stay out of trouble until then."

"Will do my best." The loss of the skin-to-skin contact left her feeling even more alone than she had a minute before. She looked down, unfolding the paper in her hand to have something to do besides grabbing the lapels of his jacket and taking the kiss for herself. "Thanks again for everything today. I'm really sorry you had to get inv—"

Her words stuck in her throat like a wad of taffy as she stared down at the drawing on the page—a very familiar, distinctive *D*.

"Kelsey?" Wyatt's voice filled with concern. When she didn't respond, he came toward her. "What's wrong? You've gone white."

She closed her eyes, a wave of nausea and raging anger rolling through her. A firm hand grabbed her elbow, steadying her. She took in a deep breath through her nose, trying to keep the temptation to lose her shit at bay. She'd been here before. She could handle it.

Of course, before she could've taken a shot of whiskey and smoked a cigarette. But neither of those options were available anymore. This time she was on her own in every way.

"He came here first," she said, her voice sounding flat.

Wyatt took the paper from her fingertips. "Who? Miller?"

She nodded, trying to regain her internal composure so that Wyatt didn't notice how she was running around and screaming on the inside. "I need to get out of here."

"Wait, what?" Wyatt asked as she pulled away from him.

"Miller's part of a much bigger operation—the D-Town Players." She headed toward the closet on the far side of the living room and yanked it open, a plan trying to form in her swirling brain. How long had they been standing here talking? What if someone was already heading this way? Where the fuck was her suitcase? "That note is letting me know they know where I live."

"Fuck, Kelsey," Wyatt said, lines deepening around his mouth. "How involved is this? Is it some sort of street gang?"

She shook her head, squatting down to move a few boxes at the bottom of the closet. "They're much more organized than that. I don't exactly know how big it is. I was never privy to that." She dragged her overnight bag out of the back corner and turned around. "I just . . . dated some prick who was a drug runner for them back when I was too stupid to know better."

She watched the distaste cross Wyatt's face, and her heart died a little. One of the things she loved most about her brief times with Wyatt was how he looked at her like she really was the sweet, innocent thing he believed her to be. Like she was something precious and fragile. Unlike everyone else she knew, he hadn't looked at her through the filter of her past and all the mistakes she'd made when she was using. Or through the even darker glass of being a victim. Only a handful of people knew what she'd endured at the hands of her mother's murderer last year. But once someone knew, that was all the person saw—assault victim. Now streaks of that ugliness were tainting the bright little bubble of space between her and Wyatt.

"Where are you going to go?" he asked, shutting the front door behind him and bolting it. "My company has corporate apartments we rent. You can stay in one of those if you need a place."

She shook her head. The last thing she wanted was some handout. "Thanks, I appreciate it, but I can stay at my sister and her fiancé's place."

That was a lie. She wasn't going to put Brynn and Reid at risk on her behalf. Not again. Reid had taken a bullet the last time he'd rescued Kelsey, and her sister had almost ended up dead. But Kelsey couldn't tell Wyatt where she was really heading. He'd already found out enough of her secrets today. The last thing he needed to know was what she did as her night job.

Wyatt frowned, obviously not thrilled with that plan, but he nodded. "Pack your bag, and I'll drive you."

"I have a car downstairs. I just take the bus some days to work to save money on gas."

"Then I'll follow you there to make sure you're safe."

She opened her mouth to argue, but what was the point? In truth, having someone watch her back as she left the apartment wasn't a bad thing. The D-Towners were probably just trying to scare her, but she also knew they were capable of a lot worse than that, so she wasn't going to take any chances. "Thanks. Guess you probably shouldn't have stuck around for that muffin today. You'd be tucked safely in your office by now none the wiser, making people their millions."

He shook his head. "Best decision I've made in a long time. The millions will still be there tomorrow."

And now, because of him, she would still be around, too. "Thank you, Wyatt. Really. I'm so—"

He held up a hand. "If you apologize one more time for something that is absolutely not your fault, you're going to see my mean side."

The threat shouldn't have sent a hot shiver through her, but it did. The image of the quietly intense executive losing some of that nothing-phases-me exterior called to her in a way she couldn't even define. The feeling was foreign, frightening. The fact that he'd shut down the possibility of them sleeping together was probably a very, very good thing, even if her hormones hadn't quite jumped on board with that plan yet. "I'll be ready in a few minutes."

"I'll be here." Wyatt sat down on her loveseat, pulled out his cell phone, and started scanning through emails as if he'd wait forever if that was how long she needed.

She stood there watching him for a few moments longer than necessary, knowing that this would probably be the last time she'd have him this close. Sure, she'd be able to hide out for a few weeks, but this wasn't going to go away anytime soon. She'd thought she'd escaped undetected the last time, but clearly they'd discovered the role she'd played in Raymond Miller's downfall. And if D-Town was determined to hurt her, she wasn't going to be safe anywhere near their territory.

She let out a long breath and turned her back, heading toward her bedroom. Wyatt didn't know it, but their fictional love affair was about to come to a quick and quiet end.

Because she was going to have to leave her life here in Dallas. And leave him.

THREE

Wyatt leaned back in his desk chair, scanning the report on his computer screen and only half-listening to his father prattle on. Wyatt didn't have the patience for a Bill Austin lecture on a good day, much less this morning. After showing up at the Sugarcane Cafe for the second week in a row to find no Kelsey, Wyatt had left with heartburn and a bloodstream full of frustration.

Her co-worker, Nathan, had been like a fucking Navy SEAL with his ability to withstand interrogation. Wyatt had prodded the guy up one way and down the other trying to get information about Kelsey, even offering to pay Nathan for the information. But all the cook would reveal was that she was safe and that he didn't know where she was, which was bullshit of course. That kid knew exactly where she was.

He admired the guy for being protective of his friend, but the not knowing was like a thorn burrowing into Wyatt's brain. The whole situation was out of his control and that was completely unacceptable. He hadn't been able to concentrate for shit since he'd last seen her. He'd even driven by her sister's house like some lame stalker to see if her car was there. It wasn't. And when he'd knocked on the door to the house, no one had been home.

Then this morning he'd come in to find a message from the cop who'd handled the alley incident, letting Wyatt know that the asshole had made bail. Kelsey's attacker was out there, roaming the streets like nothing had fucking happened. Our brilliant legal system at its best.

"Wyatt, you were supposed to handle this," his father barked. "You can't just say no to big-time clients because you feel like it."

He huffed his annoyance. "I was busy this weekend. And I don't eat deer, so why would I waste time shooting one?"

His father made that frustrated noise of his, like the hiss of trapped steam leaking out of a pipe. "Wyatt, you—it isn't about the deer. You know that."

Wyatt minimized the screen and turned toward his father, bored with this conversation already. He had bigger things to worry about than some self-important client getting his pride hurt over a declined invitation. "I bet the deer would beg to differ."

His dad's palm landed on top of the desk, a soft smack but pointed nonetheless. "This isn't a joke."

Wyatt closed his eyes and rubbed the bridge of his nose beneath his glasses. "Didn't say it was."

His father tugged at his necktie and tightened it again, obviously trying to regain his trademark Bill Austin composure. "Dirk Billings wants to trust the guy handling his fortune. He wants to feel connected to him. Like buddies."

"And sitting for hours in a wooden box with guns and cheap beer to shoot something I don't even eat is going to accomplish this?" Wyatt shook his head and straightened the papers on his desk. "If he wants trust, he needs to look at my record and talk to my other clients. If he wants to feel connected, I'm more than happy to schedule regular phone calls or meetings to go over his portfolio. I spent last weekend analyzing the numbers from last quarter. We have some quirks in there that don't make sense. That's what I needed to spend my time on. Not hanging out in the woods doing tick checks with a windbag."

The thought of being caught in a deer stand, making chitchat with a guy who thought the South should've won, was Wyatt's personal version of hell. He'd end up turning the gun on his client instead of the wildlife. That wouldn't be good for the company image.

His father's skin went ruddy, his hold on his anger obviously dwindling. "Ignoring this part of the business is not going to work anymore, son. Merrill and Mead are giving that level of personal service to their clients. They're stealing them away from us with good ol' boy wining and dining. Or golfing and hunting as the case may be. Those imbeciles don't have anything on you when it comes to the financials, but if you don't learn how to play the nicey-nice game, we're going to keep losing big fish. You want that jerk you graduated with to woo away all of our clients?"

Wyatt's jaw clenched at that thought. Tony Merrill had been an arrogant prick in graduate school, and time had only seemed to enhance those attributes. Wyatt had received a jovial email a few months earlier from Tony thanking him for sending over one of his best clients. *Jerkoff.* "When their net worth starts going down because Tony doesn't know his ass from an alligator, they'll return."

"They're not coming back, Wyatt," his father said quietly. Too quietly. Wyatt had feared that lethal tone when he was a kid. It usually meant fire and brimstone were coming.

"Don't panic, Dad." Wyatt turned back to his computer to click open the next page in the report. "You've got the Carmichael retreat at the end of the month. And you always come back with new clients from that. You handle the ass kissing and spouse charming, and I'll keep their business here with the results I can get them."

His father shifted in his seat and cleared his throat. "I'm not going to be able to attend the retreat this year."

Wyatt's hand stilled against his mouse, and he spun his chair back toward his father. That retreat was a must. Business leaders killed to get invitations to the exclusive trip put on each year by real estate tycoon Edward Carmichael. On the surface, it was billed as a relax and unwind trip for executives and their spouses. But that casual, guards-down atmosphere was where deals were made and partnerships were formed. "What are you talking about? That retreat was responsible for three of our biggest new clients last year."

"Your mother has threatened divorce. So we're going to a thing," he said, giving a near imperceptible shrug.

Wyatt stared at him, the words not quite making sense at first. Divorce? His parents had never had what anyone would call a loving relationship. His dad wasn't an easy man to live with and had cheated more than once. But he and his mom had always seemed to have a mutual agreement to stay together—like a polite business arrangement. "A thing?"

"Some counseling vacation." He scoffed and tightened his tie again. "As if that could be called a vacation. All that touchy-feely hippie bullshit. But she's going to leave me if I don't go with her."

"Jesus, Dad."

His father waved a dismissive hand. "Don't start the pity party. It'll be fine. I think your mother just had some white light moment when she had that heart attack and is getting loopy on me. We'll do this, I'll buy her something nice, and we'll move on. We always do."

Not with that attitude. But Wyatt kept the comment to himself. If his mom wanted to make a run at a happier life, he wasn't going to begrudge her that.

"Which is why I'm going to need you to handle the retreat and *not* fuck it up."

Wyatt was still reeling from the previous news, but of course his father wasn't going to linger on anything non-business related for long. "Me? I can't go on the retreat. Who's going to handle things here why you're out? I'll just cancel it this year. Carmichael will understand."

A muscle twitched in his father's jowl. "No. He won't. We'll be cut right off the guest list for the future. I've been working on getting that family's accounts for years and I'm this close. One rebuff and it's gone. Plus, Tony Merrill will be there. If we cancel, we may as well hand our clients over to him with a bow around their necks."

Wyatt leaned back in his chair, rubbing his head, the thought of attending a Carmichael retreat curling dread in his stomach. Wyatt had never been, but he knew it wasn't anything like the business conferences he attended. This was a schmoozing trip. No workshops, no meetings, it was all about rubbing elbows and kissing ass.

And Wyatt didn't kiss ass.

"I'm not going on some trip to tell people how fucking fantastic they are. I'm not a salesman."

"You will, and you better become one fast." His dad pinned Wyatt with a hard look. "You are supposed to step into my shoes when I retire. But if I dropped dead tomorrow, you'd be woefully unequipped."

Wyatt could only stare back at him. "*Unequipped*? What with the doctorate, the decade of experience, and a record that could lap anyone else here?"

"If this business was one hundred percent numbers, no one could even attempt to challenge you. Not even me. You're brilliant, Wyatt. But half the job of being a CEO is selling yourself, the image of the company, and generating new business. It's politics. For people to trust you with their money, they have to want to work with you, to *like* you."

Wyatt clenched his teeth, having flashbacks from his high school years. He'd won a lot of awards, but the popularity contest was one he'd never had a shot in.

"You need to show me you're capable with this part of the business. Otherwise, you're starting to make me wonder if you're the right person to take over the top spot when I step down."

Wyatt's fingers dug into the arms of his chair, cool steel in his voice. "Excuse me?"

That position had been decided since Wyatt's first IQ test in grade school. Like an Olympic athlete, his whole life had centered around getting groomed and trained for this role, especially after his father had realized that his other son, Jace, had absolutely no interest in taking over the family business.

Wyatt thought of all the things he'd turned down, walked away from, or not tried because he was on this path. Because he was the "good" son, the heir apparent. All the hours and blood and sweat he put into this company. Now that role was up the air?

"My first responsibility is to this company," his father said curtly. "You know I've never given you anything simply because we share DNA. You've earned everything you've gotten so far. But now you need to earn this. If I don't think you're the best candidate, I won't hesitate to give it to someone else. Eric has been in line for it for years and has as much experience as you do."

"You've got to be kidding me."

"Look at my face," his dad said, using the same words he used to say to Wyatt when he was a child. "Does this look like my kidding face?"

Wyatt made a sound of disgust. "You're a cold-hearted sonofabitch sometimes."

"I am. That's what gives me my edge, son. If I made decisions based on emotions, you'd have grown up in some shithole in the suburbs. This is a weakness of yours, and my future CEO can't afford weaknesses."

"I got it," he snapped, bitterness leaking into his words.

"Good." His father pulled a paper from the inner pocket of his jacket and laid it on Wyatt's desk. "That's a list of people going whose business we want to acquire. Do whatever it takes to get them."

Wyatt unfolded the paper and scanned the neat list of typed names. Some of the biggest players out there were listed of course. His father always aimed for the outfield. But Wyatt's gaze snagged on the name at the bottom of the page. "You've got to be fucking kidding me. *Andrew* Carmichael? If you think I'm going to go kiss Andrew's ass, you have an—"

"He's the biggest fish on that list now. Ed's health has been in the shitter lately, and he's handed over lots of responsibility to Andrew, including this year's retreat. Retirement is probably inevitable within the year. So you need to work the son. And you two used to be friends. Use that." His father straightened his coat.

"Friends? That's quite a revisionist history there, Dad." The guy had made grade school painful and high school a fucking nightmare.

"Come on. You can't still be hung up on stuff that happened so long ago. So he liked to pick on you. He was just threatened because you were smarter than him and got more attention."

Wyatt gritted his teeth. Childhood teasing he could've forgiven, but Andrew had upped the ante when they hit high school. When Wyatt had been chosen for a prestigious scholarship over Andrew, the bastard had retaliated by getting Wyatt's longtime girlfriend tipsy at an after-prom party and then fucking away her virginity on Wyatt's bed, making sure Wyatt walked in at just the right moment. Wyatt's one and only fist fight had ended with a naked Andrew knocked out in the middle of the hallway.

"I want him on our roster."

"There are other big players we can go after. We don't need him."

"We do and you're going to get him." His father stood and pulled out an envelope. He dropped it onto the desk. "Nancy in travel has already changed mine and your mother's reservations into your name. You need to let Nancy know who you're bringing with you."

Wyatt picked up the envelope and looked at his father. "Who I'm bringing?"

"This is a plus-one trip. Most of the events are for couples, so don't be the asshole who shows up solo. And for God's sake, don't bring that woman you brought to the charity ball. She had about as much personality as a shoehorn. You need someone who isn't going to be afraid to mingle and flirt. The prettier your date, the more the other guys will be interested in hanging around you two."

Oh, this was getting better and better. What was he supposed to do, call up the rent-a-girlfriend-for-a-week service? He worked fifteen-hour days and most weekends. Like he'd told Kelsey, dating didn't exactly fit into that schedule. He'd had a colleagues-with-benefits thing going for a while with a woman who worked in the building next door, but they'd stopped their Saturday night meet-ups a while back when she'd decided she needed more and had laid out an ultimatum for him. He didn't do ultimatums.

But regardless of his father's opinion, he would've been faced with the issue anyway. Because there was no way he was going to show up to this thing and face Andrew without some knockout on his arm. It was petty, but he didn't fucking care. "I'll figure it out."

"That's what I want to hear. Get to planning, son. You leave in a week." And with that, his father headed out of Wyatt's office, riding that high horse he so loved to be on.

Wyatt leaned his head back on his chair, tipped his glasses up, and ran a hand over his face. Part of him wondered what would happen if he stood up and walked out. Quit. The fact that his father would even consider giving someone else the CEO position was enough to tempt him to do so. He had enough money to live whatever the hell kind of life he wanted. He didn't need to be here.

But even the thought sent a gash of loss through him. He loved his job and fed on the play of numbers, on the win of making the right decisions, on the high of knowing he had the answers where others couldn't see them. This *was* his life.

If he walked away, what would be left? He didn't even know who he was outside of this place.

No, he needed to figure this shit out. The socializing aspect of business had always been his Achilles' heel, but it wasn't an unlearnable skill. At least he hoped it wasn't. He could figure out how to play the game. And if he had a beautiful woman with him who did have some social finesse, all the better.

And he had just the woman in mind.

That is, if he could fucking find her.

Wyatt picked up his phone and hit the speed dial.

"A call in the middle of a work day from the suit? Is the building on fire? Have zombies taken over the city?" his brother, Jace, asked, grin evident even over the phone.

"Is there such a thing as a work day for you?" Wyatt lobbed back. "Or do you just sit around while your staff waves you with giant fans?"

"Hmm, there's a thought," Jace said, something squeaking in the background. "I'm actually working very hard trying to get the lighting right on a display of high-end glass dildos. Important stuff."

"Clearly."

Jace chuckled. "So what's going on? I know you didn't call to shoot the shit."

"How do you know that?"

"Come on, Wy."

Wyatt frowned. Was he really that bad at the social thing?

Even with his brother? Probably. Yes. "Remember back when I helped you out with the Diana situation, and you said you owed me?"

"Of course."

"Well, I'm ready to take you up on that."

"Name it, brother. If it's in my power, I'll do it."

"I need you to help me find Kelsey LeBreck."

FOUR

Kelsey stared down at the sweat-glazed back of Hawk Nichols as he sucked in a deep breath, bracing for her next blow. She strolled around to stand in front of his prone form, making sure he heard her boots clicking deliberately along the cement floor of the dungeon room. She'd strapped him down on all fours along a padded spanking bench about half an hour ago, and he was already flying high. Keeping the braided leather cat in her right hand, she touched Hawk's fingers with her left. They flinched slightly, still warm. Circulation was good.

She had to watch it with this kid. The twenty year old was the star receiver on his college football team, so pain was part of his daily existence. And he craved the edge of being under her hand, the place the pain would bring him. But she couldn't trust him to call his safe word if she went too far. Once he slipped into subspace, the bulky athlete was as vulnerable as a kitten. She ran a hand over his damp hair, and he nuzzled her palm and moaned—the simple touch her reward to him for taking so much.

"You still with me, sub?"

"Yes, Mistress. Please," he whispered, his voice hoarse. "Please."

She knew what he was begging for. Her flogging hadn't gone to the intense place he needed yet. He was still hovering on the precipice, waiting to lose himself to it all. "You've done well tonight, sub. You know you'll be rewarded."

"Thank you, Mistress." His fists flexed and released, flexed and released, the need quivering off him. His cock hung heavy and hard between his spread thighs despite the boot laces she'd used to bind his scrotum and the base of his penis, and she knew he had to be desperate for relief by now.

She ran her fingers along his spine as she made her way around him. He really was a beautiful guy, though still a little lost. They were only separated by a few years in age, but she felt lifetimes older. Hawk had this unvarnished innocence that she doubted many had seen. Big and intimidating in looks, most people probably gave him wide berth and never looked deeper. But he was as gentle a soul as she'd ever met. A gentle soul who craved a bit of brutality.

His father, of all people, had dragged Hawk into The Ranch a few months ago when he'd discovered his son had been burning himself with candle wax while masturbating. One night, Hawk had used the wrong type of candles and had used them too close to his skin. He'd ended up with second-degree burns in hard-to-explain places, and his father had dragged the information out of him.

Most parents would've probably hauled the kid into a therapist, thinking he was sick and self-harming. But Hawk's father had been part of the scene in his past and, after talking with his son, had recognized Hawk's behavior for what it was. He'd made the kid promise that if he took him to a place where he could get what he needed that he'd never play like that alone again. The next week he'd brought Hawk to The Ranch and had plunked down the hefty membership and session fees without a blink.

Ever since, Hawk had been a weekly client for Kelsey, and she'd grown quite fond of him. Though, her heart still broke a little each time she saw the guarded look in his eyes. She knew that besides his father knowing, this was a big secret for Hawk. Even his girlfriend, who he seemed to adore, didn't know. Kelsey knew what it was like to keep those heavy secrets and wouldn't wish that on anyone.

But she couldn't fix that for him. She didn't have that kind of power. But she could at least give him this. She released Hawk's right hand from the leather cuff and drizzled warmed lubricant into his palm, then she squared herself up behind him, her heart picking up speed beneath the laces of her corset. She reached down and removed the bindings from the base of his cock. "You have permission to touch yourself, sub. But you're not allowed to come until you've taken all ten of my strokes. You understand?"

"Yes, ma'am," he said, his voice now shaking with anticipation.

Kelsey took a steadying breath. This was always the hardest part for her. She enjoyed the power and rush of being a top, but unlike many of her fellow doms, sadism wasn't in her blood. She didn't derive pleasure in giving pain for pain's sake. She administered the pain because it was her job, and her satisfaction came from giving a sub what he or she needed. And for Hawk, seeing him let go for a few moments, getting some catharsis, would make it worth it.

She raised her arm high and then, using all her strength, lashed Hawk's backside with the cat. The braided leather strips striped along his back and buttocks, the sound of leather meeting flesh filling the cavernous space and mixing with the thudding rock music she'd put on in the background. Hawk tried to rear up, the bench rattling a bit from his brute strength, and he moaned loud and long. His fist slid harshly up and down his cock as she landed the next blow.

She worked him hard over the next few minutes, her arm aching from the exertion and her skin going damp and prickly. Hawk jerked and writhed in his bindings, a caged beast on the verge of losing his fight for control. But the sounds he made were pure ecstasy, the intense pain launching him to that plane of nothingness he craved.

Kelsey landed the last hit and watched in fascination as her sub exploded at the precise moment she'd ordered, his body going stiff, his hips thrusting forward, and his release spilling over his fist as he fucked his hand. A man lost to himself and to the world for a few exquisite seconds. Freedom.

Beautiful.

For some ridiculous reason, she had the urge to cry. She dropped the cat to the floor and sank against the wall, sliding to a sit, exhaustion sapping her. She knew she should stay on her feet, stay in the position of power, but he couldn't see behind him, so he'd never know. She pulled her knees to her chest, her body throbbing and aching with unmet need, but not for Hawk. She never slept with her clients. She didn't even allow them to touch her. But seeing the intensity of another reach their sexual bliss often left her craving her own.

And tonight there was something even uglier pressing at her. Jealousy.

It wasn't an emotion a domme should feel toward her sub. She was supposed to gain her satisfaction from his submission. And Hawk had submitted beautifully tonight. But as she watched Hawk lying there bound, breathing hard, and blissed out, she felt the ugly emotion creep up.

"Lady K?" he whispered after a few quiet minutes, snapping her from her souring state.

"Yes." She pushed herself to her feet, turned down the music, and started unfastening the rest of his bindings. "You okay?"

"Yes, ma'am. Thank you." He cleared his throat. "I was just wondering, how long before the marks go away?"

She frowned and ran a gentle hand along the angry red stripes on his back. "You know I wouldn't leave you with anything long lasting, sweetheart. I'll never betray the contract we set up at the beginning. Do you need me to stop leaving even temporary ones? There are other things I can do that won't leave any evidence."

"No, please don't stop," he said quickly. He turned his head to find her, his eyes still a little glazed and his hair flopping over his forehead. "I like seeing the marks. Sometimes . . . sometimes I jerk off again later after a session while I look at the markings in the mirror." His face flushed at the admission. "But I'm . . . I'm going to see my girl tomorrow night."

Kelsey sighed. "Sit up for me, Hawk."

He followed her directions, and she handed him a towel to clean himself up and another to drape over himself.

Once he was covered and seemed to be coming back into his head, she asked, "Is this girl important to you?"

He kept his eyes down as he cleaned the evidence of what had just happened off his hand and thigh, shame obviously creeping in. Kelsey hated that, hated that he was still struggling so much with this part of himself, that the beast of guilt was such a relentless one. She wished she could just snap her fingers and take that hurt away from him. But she knew that road was going to be a long one for him.

"Yes, ma'am. I think I love her."

She sat down on one of the chairs by the wall and braced her forearms on her fishnet-covered thighs. "Look, hon, I know you're hoping I can beat this out of you, but that's not how it works. You need to consider that these desires may not go away."

His head dipped and his blond hair fell farther down his forehead, shielding his eyes.

"And I know there are people who manage to walk both sides of the line." *Like me.* "But living a double life is not a fun option.

Have you ever considered talking to your girlfriend about this? Feeling her out? You never know, she may be open to it."

He snorted and shook his head. "Christina is majoring in elementary education and barely even curses. We didn't sleep together until after we'd dated for six months. She's sweet and innocent and . . . she'd be repulsed by me if she knew."

"Maybe you're not giving her enough credit," Kelsey said gently.

He hauled himself to his feet and walked over to the hooks he'd hung his clothes on. He pulled on his boxers and jeans, then gingerly eased his *Got Beer?* T-shirt over his head, wincing when the material hit his back. "No disrespect, Lady K. But you don't understand. You live in this world. I don't. I *won't*. I want a normal life with a normal girl."

Kelsey tried to keep her expression placid, though the implication stung like little pieces of glass in her skin. *I don't want to be a freak like you.* "I see."

Hawk halted, his face falling, then he was crossing the room, getting to his knees at her feet. "I'm so sorry, Mistress. That . . . that didn't come out right. I say stupid shit sometimes." His expression turned earnest. "You know how thankful I am for what you do. I would never—"

"Shh," she said, caressing his hair. He instinctively lowered his head and gave her invitation to stroke him. She knew Hawk hadn't meant it to insult her. He was scared. And frankly, he was right. She didn't have a normal life and never would. This week had been proof positive of that. She couldn't even maintain an imaginary "normal" relationship without it getting fucked up. "It's okay. And you're right, I'm the last person who should be handing out relationship advice. I suck at them."

Hawk lifted his head, his eyes a little wide. Probably because it was the first piece of personal information she'd ever shared with him—or any client for that matter. She was usually good at keeping the boundaries clear when not in a scene. "Is it because of this? What you do?"

She smiled. If only it were that simple. "No, hon. Not because of this."

His lips parted as if he was going to ask more questions, but her look must've warned him off. He gave a little nod, bent all the way to the floor to kiss the top of her boot, then rose to his feet. "Thank you for tonight, Mistress."

"My pleasure, Hawk."

He gave her a shy smile, then before walking out the door he pulled something from his pocket and set it on the table by the door. Money.

A tip.

Even after all that happened this week, the simple gesture gutted her, cut right through her, letting everything spill out. She'd tried to have a real conversation with someone, and he'd paid her for it.

She didn't know what was more depressing—the blatant reminder that she was only a hired hand or the fact that she couldn't afford to turn down the cash. She leaned her head against the wall and tapped lightly.

But she wasn't left alone in her ruminating for long. The door squeaked open a few seconds later and Marc, one of the managers, poked his head in. "Hey, Kelsey. Grant said to send you up when you were done with your session. He set aside a few minutes to talk to you."

She blew out a breath and nodded. She'd made a request earlier to talk to her boss, but she hadn't expected him to free up time so quickly. She wasn't exactly looking forward to the conversation, but hopefully, this would solve her immediate problem. "Thanks. I'll be right up."

Kelsey sat in the cozy waiting area outside the office of Grant Waters, owner and operator of The Ranch, and tried to keep her nerves in check. She'd worked part time at the BDSM resort for the last six months and had experienced nothing but great interactions with Grant, but she still couldn't stop her knee from bumping up and down. The man was downright intimidating, and she knew what she was about to ask was outside the rules.

A few minutes later, the door on the other side of the room opened and filled with the impressive outline of the tall cowboy. His girlfriend, Charli, stepped out from behind him, a little flushed-faced and sending an apologetic smile in Kelsey's direction before turning back to Grant. She pushed up on her toes and gave him a quick kiss. "We'll finish this . . . discussion later?"

"Count on it, freckles," he said, tugging one of her red locks, his adoration for Charli like rays of warmth beaming off him. "Meet me in the barn when you get home from work."

"You got it, cowboy." A visible shudder went through Charli, giving Kelsey a good idea of what the barn would entail. Grant wasn't considered the Master of The Ranch for nothing. He hadn't played publicly since he'd gotten together with Charli, but Kelsey had heard stories of how intense of a dominant Grant could be.

And though she had a fair dose of jealousy over the couple in love, Kelsey couldn't help but smile for them. She'd met Charli when Charli had first come to The Ranch and had liked her instantly. And she knew both Charli and Grant had gone through a lot to get to this point.

When Charli turned around, she headed Kelsey's way and gave her a quick hug. "Hey, gorgeous, haven't seen you around in a while. We should grab dinner soon."

Kelsey returned the hug, standing up in the process. "Definitely. Give me a call."

Charli gave her one last pat on the arm and headed out, leaving Kelsey with Grant. That alone was a testament to how strong of a relationship the two had. How many women would leave their guy alone with a chick in thigh-high boots and a corset?

Grant nodded in Kelsey's direction. "Come on in, Kelsey. Marc said you wanted to chat."

"Yes, sir." She followed Grant into his office, the warm woods and stone of the room matching the rustic feel of the rest of the resort, and sat in the chair across from his desk. "I had a few questions about my position."

He settled in his large chair and adjusted the blinds behind him so that there wouldn't be a glare on her face. "Sure. Shoot."

She clasped her hands in her lap, trying to keep herself from fidgeting. "Some things have come up in town again, and I think the only way out of them is going to be to move away for a while."

His dark eyebrows lifted. "What kind of trouble, Kelsey? If you're struggling with your sobriety, there are things . . ."

"Oh, no, nothing like that," she said, her words rushing out. "This is old trouble that won't seem to go away. I think I just need to cut my losses and start over somewhere else. But I need to have more of a nest egg to do that. I thought maybe I could start taking on a few trainees to earn some extra money."

Grant frowned and leaned back in his chair, considering her in a way that made her want to bow her head. "The requirements for my trainers are very clear. Both sides of training are required. And you haven't done the submissive part yet. Believe me, I understand why you haven't been able to do that portion. After what happened to you last year, I can only imagine how frightening that could be. I wouldn't want anything to trigger those memories for you. But it wouldn't be fair or safe to make an exception. I need my trainers to understand and experience both sides firsthand."

"Right." She looked down at her hands, not surprised by the answer but disappointed. She'd tried to do the thirty-day submissive immersion twice now because being a trainer was more lucrative than being a part-time domme like she was now. But each time the day to start had gotten close, she'd cancelled at the last moment. And she hated that. Hated that her attacker still held any power over her at all. Davis hadn't been a dominant, he'd been a sociopath and rapist who'd held her against her will, beat her mercilessly, and tortured her for the three days he'd had her. She obviously knew that wasn't what submission entailed. Yet, she still hadn't been able to take that step with anyone.

Grant sighed and leaned forward, setting his chin on his clasped hands. "Kelsey, can I be honest with you?"

"Yes, sir," she said quietly.

"I hired you because you'd been through a lot, and I wanted to give you an opportunity to get on your feet. And I think discovering your domme side has helped you gain confidence that the men in your past had stolen from you. You've blossomed these last few months."

Warmth gathered in her chest at the compliment. "Thank you."

"But dominance is not your natural state," he said, his eyes meeting hers. "You're more than capable of being in that role, but I can tell you have to work hard at it."

She frowned, his matter-of-fact assessment like a bucket of cold water over her head. "I don't understand."

His too-keen eyes evaluated her. "After a session, you don't look satisfied or fulfilled. You look spent. And I know you don't use your membership benefits here. The only people you dominate are the ones paying for the privilege. You don't play with anyone for your own enjoyment."

She glanced away, focusing on a spot over his right shoulder. Truth was, as sexually pent up as she could get, she never had the desire to take up one of the submissive members on their offers.

She'd been abstinent since about a month after the attack. The first few weeks afterward had been filled with a backslide into drinking and far too many one-night stands. She'd been on a mission to erase the memory of that last person who'd touched her by having any and everyone in her bed. But after waking up hungover in some strange apartment, parked between a guy she'd picked up at a bar *and* his girlfriend, she'd hoofed it to her therapist and returned to The Ranch to ask for her job back. And thank God she'd done those two things. She didn't even want to think about where she'd be otherwise.

Dominance really wasn't about getting off for her anyway. It was a release of different sorts. It kept the hungry demons at bay— the whispers of old addictions, the threads of insecurity, the temptation to tumble backward and not feel. It centered her. "I just haven't found someone who interests me yet."

"Hmm," he said, obviously not buying that ocean-front property in Arizona she was trying to sell. "Or perhaps you've got a longer and more important journey left on the other side of the equation, and what happened to you blocked you from accessing that side of yourself. When you first approached me last year, before Davis, you wanted to do the submissive part first. It was what you were drawn to."

She shook her head. "I'm not a submissive, Grant. Men have controlled me all my life. I can assure you, I gain no satisfaction from being at someone's mercy."

"Or maybe you've met the wrong someones."

"Well, there's no fucking doubt about that."

He gave her a kind smile. "I could see if some of the clubs in Dallas are looking for part-time dommes, if you'd like. You could earn extra money that way, though their screening processes for members are going to be more lax so you may get some jerks in the mix."

She shook her head. The last thing she wanted were guys who thought dominatrix equaled prostitute. No way. As she sat there, frustration started to morph brick by brick into resolve. "No. I'm tired of this. Davis is dead and letting him haunt me means he wins. Fuck that. I need to try again."

Grant watched her for a long moment, then nodded. "I'll tell you what, darlin'. You find a dom you're comfortable with to complete the other half of your training and when you're done, I'll be more than happy to let you take on a few trainees or a small class. And if you do well with those, I'll even recommend you to The Plantation in New Orleans. They pay well and are looking for new trainers. It'd get you out of town and a place to stay rent free."

A ticket out of town and more money? It was exactly what she needed. "That would be amazing."

"Do you want me to ask Colby if he wants to take you on? Or maybe Kade Vandergriff? Kade's looking for a sub, though I think he prefers one who is going to submit to the full experience."

"No." She adored Kade, but didn't want to muddy the waters with a friend. She didn't need to take the training to that level to get the benefit. "I'd prefer to keep sex out of the training."

"Not a problem," Grant said, making a note on a pad on his desk. "I'll talk to Colby later and see if he's interested."

She wet her lips. Colby was a friend and a good guy. She'd assisted him in more than one training class, but the thought of submitting to him left her feeling hollow inside. However, the sooner she could get this done, the sooner she could put some real money in her pocket and get the hell out of town. "Thank you, Grant."

He gave a quick nod, though he looked more resigned than pleased. "Anytime, Kelsey. But please make sure you're truly ready to do this and that this is the job you want. I think you have potential to be a terrific trainer, but unless you feel a passion for that role, the position will drain you dry. A nice paycheck won't fill in the gaps."

She glanced away, her body feeling heavier in the chair than it had a moment before. The Ranch had been her saving grace after she'd recovered from the attack. It had provided her a job, structure, and a group of friends who had treated her like family. She loved the strange, alternative world that existed behind its gates. But despite the good people, the posh resort, and the luxury of the surroundings, she never felt more excited than when she was crammed in that tiny, hot kitchen at the Sugarcane concocting a new recipe and chatting with her customers. That was what put the froth in her coffee each morning. That and serving her favorite patron . . .

But that dream was going to have to be put on hold for a while. Culinary school would have to wait. Her life would have to wait.

Again.

Perhaps payment for former sins was never really done.

But at the very least, maybe she could put a vicious ghost to rest.

FIVE

Wyatt leaned back in the seat of his brother's car, plucked off his glasses, and rubbed his eyes, a blinding headache booming behind his lids. "Half of me is hoping you're fucking with me about this and that you're going to say 'just kidding' when we pull up."

Jace glanced over at him, wryness tugging at the side of his mouth. "Sorry, brother. 'Fraid not. But if you're going to give Kelsey shit about this, I'll turn around right now. Just because she's not as innocent and vanilla as you thought she was shouldn't make a difference."

"It's not that," Wyatt said with a tired sigh. "It just makes the favor I was going to ask her for a little more complicated."

"Why is that?" Jace asked, merging into the other lane and throwing a what-the-fuck glare at the interminably slow driver they were passing.

Because it made her even more enticing. Because the idea that the sweet waitress had a down and dirty side made his cock ache. Because the thought of her submitting to his will had old desires burning holes through a wall he'd erected a long time ago. "Because I don't . . . do this."

"You used to," Jace said pointedly.

"Don't start."

"No, I will fucking say what needs to be said, Wy," Jace said, irritation cutting through his normally laidback manner. "You think you can turn that shit off? That you can simply pack it away in a neat little box and pretend that isn't part of you? You may be able to convince yourself of that, but I saw you in action in college. Don't forget who brought me to my first play party."

"I didn't bring you. You followed me."

"And thank God I did because I might never have figured out what all the stuff I was feeling meant."

Wyatt shook his head and adjusted his glasses back in place. Jace was the one and only person in his life who knew Wyatt had been in a D/s relationship when he was in graduate school. But his brother also knew what had happened and should know better than to push him on this. "I'm glad you found your thing. But I have no interest in traveling down that road again."

"Right. Because I'm sure you find that scheduled Saturday night fuck very fulfilling," Jace said, throwing him a look. "Pick up dry cleaning, shop for groceries, screw fuck buddy of the month."

Wyatt scowled. "It's not like that."

"I bet you even put it on your calendar," Jace said, on a roll now. "Do you draw in a little heart there? Or maybe a happy face?"

Wyatt grunted, but had to wrestle back a smile on that one.

"Holy shit!" Jace said, his expression lighting like a dog who'd stumbled upon a favorite bone. "You *do* put a smiley face, don't you? You sick fucker."

He shrugged. "I *may* put a star."

Jace laughed hard at that, his eyes watering with the effort.

"And for the record, the woman I was . . . spending time with is not in the picture anymore. So no more Saturday night appointments." And really, Wyatt hadn't felt any regret over that. Their get togethers truly had become about as interesting as picking up his dry cleaning. He got more out of one morning at the diner with Kelsey than a slew of Saturday nights with Gwen.

"Fantastic. You're unattached and in lust with one of my favorite women. Perfect time to live a little and have some fun."

Wyatt stared out the window, watching the dark of night creeping over the fields. "No, it's not. Even if I wanted to try this world again, Kelsey deserves better than what I can offer. You know I'm not cut out to do all that relationship stuff. My life doesn't have room for that. I'll end up hurting her."

Jace smirked as he pulled off the road and took a left onto a half-hidden driveway. "And what makes you think *she's* looking for a relationship, genius? You're getting all noble and shit, but why would you assume all women are pining away for roses and a ring? Kelsey's been through a lot—much of which has been caused by men."

"What do you mean?" he asked, sensing Jace was talking about more than drug dealers being after her.

A flicker of regret passed over this expression. "It's her story to tell, not mine. But all I'm saying is that I doubt she came to work at The Ranch because she was searching for the One with a capital O."

Wyatt focused on the large cedar building looming in the distance as he absorbed Jace's words. Why *had* he assumed that? Maybe that wasn't what Kelsey wanted at all. He'd met those women out on a husband hunt all the time. Girls like that flocked to guys like him—ants to a Popsicle stick. They got wind of his money and position and were already building dream houses on the beach in their minds. He could smell it on them like over-spritzed perfume. He'd never gotten that vibe from Kelsey, not even a whiff.

"Maybe you're right," Wyatt admitted.

Jace leaned out of the car to press his finger to a machine at the entry gate, then turned back toward Wyatt. "I'm always right. I thought we'd established this by now."

Wyatt sniffed, so used to his brother's ego that he didn't bother to respond to it. "This whole plan might work out after all."

The gates in front of them swung open, and Jace pulled forward. "Oh, and one thing I forgot to tell you."

"What's that?"

He sent a sly grin Wyatt's way. "Your sweet waitress who I know you're weaving filthy slave fantasies about?"

Wyatt grimaced but didn't deny it.

"Yeah. She's a dominatrix."

"She's a—" Wyatt's head dropped back against the seat. "Ah, fucking hell."

───

Kelsey stripped down in the locker room and donned the standard black bra and panty set that most female submissive trainees wore at The Ranch. Colby had also told her to wear a basic leather collar for their first session. She knew why he'd made the request. He'd obviously sensed her reluctance to take the role even in their initial limits negotiations and wanted to put that psychological symbol in place early. And it'd been a powerful one. The minute she'd fastened the simple strip of leather around her neck, her heartbeat had picked up speed and her skin had gone clammy.

I can do this, Kelsey reminded herself.

Surprisingly, despite the trauma with Davis, fear wasn't at the forefront of her mind. She knew Colby wouldn't physically harm her. There wasn't even a doubt there about that. She was more knotted up about what this submission could open in her. She tried not to think of all the men she'd yielded to in her life. None of those relationships had been D/s based, but the blind trust had been there all the same. When she let her guard down, she could lose herself in a guy. Each time thinking *this* was going to be the one who didn't fuck her over. And time and time again, she'd picked the wrong guy to grace with that hope.

Growing up, she'd thought it was her version of rebellion against her mother's sour view of men. Her mom had told her and her sister to trust none of them, that men only did what was good for their dicks, their wallets, and their ego. But Kelsey had trundled along, reading her fairy tales and believing that she could create her own one day. And that silly girlish hope had only led her right down the path scarily close to the one her mother had ended up on. Kelsey had been used, taken advantage of, and belittled more times than she cared to remember. And now she was going to let another guy have control over her.

Even though logically she knew it was temporary and that Colby would rather cut off an arm before he ever hurt her, she was having trouble keeping her dread locked away.

She glanced at the clock and realized she had three minutes before she was due in the training room. *I can do this,* she repeated silently, and took a deep breath. In an hour, it'd be done. The hurdle crossed. All she needed to do was get past this first session, then it would get easier. Gathering up all the iron inside her, she straightened her spine, slipped on a silk robe and ballet flats, and headed out into the hallway. Reluctant or not, she wasn't going to dare to be late.

Once she made her way down the hallway to the training area, Kelsey let herself in, shucked the robe and shoes, and kneeled down in the middle of the quiet room. Colby had left a kneeling pad on the floor and had made sure the temperature in the room was comfortable. Both were subtle messages to her that he wasn't going to push her too hard this first time. But there was a blindfold sitting in front of the mat, proving that he wasn't going to be *that* easy. She slipped on the blindfold, sat back on her legs, and laid her palms up on her bare thighs. Now she waited.

───────

Grant Waters crossed his arms and eyed Wyatt before looking back to Jace. "Kelsey's in a training session right now."

"With who?" Jace asked. "Wyatt just needs to talk to her for a few minutes."

"And Wyatt isn't a member here," Grant said, ignoring Jace's question.

Jace groaned. "Come on, man. I signed him up for a membership a few months ago. You already have all his information and approved him back then. He just never took advantage of the gift. And you know I wouldn't send anyone in who I didn't trust to follow the rules. Wyatt knows how this works. He's the one I learned from."

Grant hooked his thumbs in his pocket, stared both of them down for a moment more, then softened his stance. "You're lucky we're friends, Austin. Because I would normally throw out a member for trying to pull this kind of last-minute shit."

Jace smiled his most winning smile. "Aww, is that your way of telling me you love me best?"

Grant shook his head. "Poor Evan and Andre. How they put up with your cocky ass is a wonder."

"They both happen to love my ass. And I, theirs."

Grant let out a long, God-give-me-the-strength sigh and cocked his head toward the big door on the far side of the lobby. "Kelsey's supposed to be working with Colby. If he left the viewing window open to the room, you're welcome to observe. But don't interrupt." He looked to Wyatt, his gaze all business now. "If you want to talk to her, you wait for the scene to be done."

Jace clapped Grant on the shoulder. "Thanks, man. 'Preciate it."

Wyatt shook Grant's hand and thanked him, but Wyatt could barely get the words out. *They could go watch? Fuck. That.* The thought of seeing Kelsey touch some other guy or worse, having that guy touch her, had a sick feeling gathering in Wyatt's stomach. No way would he be able to stand by for that.

He caught up with his brother as Jace walked through a door that led from the main lobby into a hushed hallway. The dark maroon walls and soft scone lighting gave Wyatt the sense of entering into some other realm. He leaned over to his brother, keeping his voice low. "Jace, I can't watch her with some other guy. I'll want to—"

Jace gave him a knowing look. "That bad, huh?"

"Fuck." Wyatt raked a hand through his hair, the wave of possessiveness more concerning than anything he'd felt about Kelsey thus far.

"Don't worry," Jace said. "I'll look in first."

Jace led him down another hallway and up a set of stairs until they ended up in a corridor lined with doors and windows. Jace walked ahead of him, peeking in and then waving Wyatt forward. "Come on, the rooms are soundproof, so no one can hear us."

The first two rooms were empty, the third had two men and a woman in it—one guy fucking the girl from behind, the other guy fucking him. All their faces were twisted in the throes of ecstasy, and the lack of sound gave the sense of watching some porn flick on mute. Wyatt had never considered himself a voyeur, but the scene was kind of hard to turn away from. All that flesh.

"You all right, brother?" Jace asked as he turned to see what Wyatt was looking at. He smirked. "Ah, nice. Don't think too hard on that one, though. I don't want you traumatized."

Wyatt looked back to his brother. "Why would I be— Ah, hell, never mind."

Jace laughed. "Come on."

Wyatt's brother had revealed to him a few months ago that he'd fallen in love with not just a woman, but his best friend, Andre, too. Wyatt had been happy for Jace even though he knew a three-person relationship would be a tough journey to walk. And he'd been around the trio, saw the shared glances, the affectionate kisses. It'd been odd at first to see his brother kissing another guy, especially when Jace had been such a womanizer all his life. But the three of them were all so easy together, so loving, that it'd quickly become normal to Wyatt. However, he'd purposely not allowed his mind to travel to what all that involved behind closed doors. There were some things you didn't want to imagine, and his brother having sex was one of them.

At the last door on the left, Jace peeked in the window and sent Wyatt a quick thumbs up. "Bingo. Found your girl."

"She's not my—"

"And you're in luck, brother. She's all alone. Looks like she's still waiting on Colby."

Relief sprung up in Wyatt like fucking daisies popping up around him. God, he was so damn screwed with this girl. "Can I get in?"

"Sure, the doors don't lock here. But if she doesn't want you in there, you'll need to leave." He nodded toward the other end of the hallway. "I'll look out for Colby and explain what's going on."

Wyatt glanced back over his shoulder, expecting the other man to appear any second. He didn't need to waste any time. Kelsey wasn't going to like that he'd tracked her down here, but he had to see her again. And he hoped he could offer her a solution to both their problems.

But as he walked by his brother and saw the view through the window with his own eyes, all semblance of rational thought leaked out of his head into a puddle on the floor. Kelsey wasn't in the domme position at all. She was kneeling quietly on a cushion with her head bowed and her long blonde ponytail hanging down her back, a blindfold covering those pretty blue eyes. A scant pair of panties curved over her slim hips, and her breasts were framed by a demi-cup bra that barely covered her nipples.

His cock nudged against his fly, all the blood in his body charging south. He'd imagined her so many times, what she'd look like stripped out of that waitress uniform. But the fantasy wasn't even in the same zip code as reality. She was absolutely, unequivocally breathtaking. And though he'd beat the urges down for so long, the old dominance inside him rose up like a phoenix from the ashes—ravenous and seeking.

He wet his lips. "How do you block out these windows?"

Jace frowned. "Don't go there, Wy. You're only supposed to be talking to her. If Colby comes down here and sees the window darkened, he's gonna come in."

"Then keep him busy." Wyatt turned the knob on the door and stepped inside, closing the door behind him before Jace could say anything else. Deadly quiet surrounded him, augmenting the little catch in breath Kelsey gave at the click of the door.

Her lips parted as if to call out to whoever was there, but then, apparently remembering her role, she clamped them shut. She shifted her position slightly, her nerves evident. Wyatt glanced back through the window to find Jace sending him a warning look, but Wyatt ignored him and caught sight of the switch next to the window. Wyatt smiled, gave Jace a little finger wave, and flipped the switch. Instantly, the glass darkened, eventually reflecting only Wyatt's image back at him.

He turned back around to look at Kelsey again, savoring the sight of her there on her knees. She looked so pristine, so lovely and lush. The stark overhead light caressed sun-kissed skin that called to be touched, tasted. A perfect gift perched there just for him.

No. Not for him. For some other guy, he reminded himself. The reality check made him flinch. This wasn't fair to Kelsey. She hadn't given her consent for him to see her this way. He cleared his throat. "Kelsey?"

She startled, her entire body stiffening. "Who's there? Where's Colby?"

Before he could respond, her hand went straight to her blind-fold, yanking it off.

He held up his palms. "Kelsey."

She blinked once, twice, then her eyes went round. *"Wyatt?"*

"Yes, I'm sorry. I didn't mean to burst in on you like this."

She glanced downward, as if remembering how little she was wearing, and scrambled to her feet. She reached for a robe on the bench behind her and wrapped it around herself with hasty movements. "What the hell are you doing here? How did you even get in?"

He stayed on the far side of the room, not wanting to make her retreat further. "I was worried about you, and no one could tell me where you were. I needed to see if you were okay. So I called in a favor to Jace."

"Goddammit. He shouldn't have told you anything." Her whole face was flushed now. Part of it was clearly anger, but he also sensed shame there, embarrassment. "I didn't want you to . . . This is not your business."

He frowned, rubbing a hand over his jaw and feeling like a jackass for putting her in this position. "You're right, it's not. I'm overstepping bounds all over the place, but I had to see you. And God, to see you like this . . ."

Her expression turned pained, and she looked away. "Right. Like this. Guess you can let whatever shred of respect you had left for me go now."

He took a tentative step closer, unable to resist the magnetic pull she always seemed to have on him. "Is that what you think? That I've lost respect for you? Kelsey, it's taking everything I have not to haul you off to a private room and tie you to something so I can spend the rest of the night showing you exactly how I'd like to respect you."

Her face whipped back his way, surprise morphing her features. "What?"

He peeked back at the closed door, hoping he still had a few minutes before being interrupted. "You're not the only one with secrets."

She stared at him for a long moment, and he could almost see when the awareness dawned.

"You're a dom," she said flatly, not looking at all happy about this conclusion.

The term sounded almost foreign to his ears, it'd been so long since someone had called him that. "I used to be."

She shook her head and looked to the heavens. "I should've known."

Wyatt crossed his arms. "But Jace told me you were, too. Why are you in here?"

All the starch seemed to leave her body as she knotted the sash around her waist and pulled the robe more tightly around her. "I'm trying to get promoted to a trainer so I can make more money. This is part of the process."

"How much money do you need, Kelsey?" he said, the possessiveness flaring up in him again. He'd be damned if he was going to let her turn her body over to some random guy so she could get cash.

She pinned him with a warning gaze. "I appreciate your concern, but don't get any charitable notions. I don't take handouts, Wyatt. I can handle this."

The door opened behind him, and he spun around to find his

brother with an I-told-you-so look standing behind a man who could only be Colby. The guy was as tall as Wyatt but built like a fucking lumberjack. And he looked mad enough to swing an ax Wyatt's way. "Kelsey, you all right, sweetheart? Or do I need to haul this fucker outside?"

Wyatt gritted his teeth.

Kelsey raised a palm. "It's okay, Colby. He's a friend of mine. And was just leaving. I'm sorry about the delay. I'll be ready for our session in a second."

Wyatt looked between the two of them. *The hell she would.* He stepped closer to Kelsey, thinking fast, altering his original plan. "I can offer you a job."

"Wyatt—"

"I'll pay you twenty-five thousand dollars for a week of work," he said, snagging a figure out of the air. "But you'll need to come with me right now."

Her lips parted in surprise. "What?"

"I can explain everything to you, but not here." He glanced at Colby and Jace, then back to her. "You don't have to do this right now. At least hear me out first."

Kelsey stared at him for a stretch of seconds, and he thought she was going to tell him to take his money and fuck off, but then she blew out a breath. "Fine." She peered past Wyatt. "Colby, I'm sorry, hon. I didn't mean to screw up your schedule. Can I take a rain check? I need to take care of something."

Colby shrugged. "Sure thing. Gives me a good reason to cut out early tonight. I had a long week at the day job anyway. Let me know when you want to reschedule."

Kelsey walked around Wyatt and pushed up on her toes to kiss Colby's cheek. "You're a sweetheart."

His lip curled. "You wouldn't have said that if you'd gone through my training session."

Kelsey smiled and patted his arm before peeking back over her shoulder at Wyatt. "Come with me. I have to change, then you can walk me to my cabin and we'll talk."

For the first time ever, Wyatt saw the glimmer of dominance in her own eyes, the sass. He was on her turf now and he sensed the confidence of that running through her. The sight should've warned him off. He didn't have a submissive molecule in his DNA. But somehow it only made him want her more.

"Yes ma'am," he said, the corner of his mouth lifting as he sidled up next to her, slipping a hand on the small of her back. "You're in charge."

For now.

SIX

Kelsey curled her legs under her in the arm chair, listening to Wyatt make his offer. She was still having trouble wrapping her mind around the fact that Wyatt Austin was here at The Ranch and in her cabin, chatting with her like they had some actual friendship. It was like she'd stumbled through some portal where fantasy and reality collided and morphed. But what Wyatt was suggesting was even more mind-scrambling than finding out that he used to be a dom.

"What do you think?" he asked after laying out his crazy proposal with stoic precision.

She strung together his last few sentences in her head, rewinding and digesting them again to make sure she was hearing him right. *Yep. Still crazy.* "So, wait a second, you want to pay me all that money to be your *date?*"

Small frown lines appeared around his mouth, like parentheses framing his dissatisfaction with that explanation. "Sort of. You would be posing as my girlfriend and accompanying me to events at the retreat."

Unbelievable. She would've never thought the man delusional. She reached up to pull the too-tight band from her hair, releasing her ponytail and some of the pressure building in her head. "Wyatt, have you met me? I'm a waitress who grew up in a neighborhood that cops were afraid to go to at night. No one's going to believe I'm some rich chick from out of state."

He leaned forward on the couch, bracing his forearms on his thighs, his features half in shadows in the lamplight. "Yes, I have met you. And what I see is a beautiful woman who can think on her feet and who has the ability to charm anyone in a room. I can get you up to speed on the finer details, the etiquette. And maybe you can help me, too, because God knows making small talk and schmoozing clients are on top of the list of things I suck at."

She arched a brow. "You can't be that bad."

"No. Trust me. The universe gave all of that skill set to my brother." His focus drifted to the hand she was using to finger comb her hair, his gaze tracking her movements with open appreciation. "I like your hair down. I never get to see it that way."

"Thank you." She clasped her hands in her lap, the memory of how he'd looked at her in the training room coming back to her. Even before she'd gotten over the surprise of seeing him standing there, her body had gone hot and needy at his blatant perusal of her form. Never had she had that kind of reaction to such a clearly dominant assessment. The rush of it had nearly knocked her on her ass.

But she couldn't let herself get distracted by the bone-deep attraction he always roused in her. This was dangerous territory. The suggested deal was way too reminiscent of how her mother first started her "career." Rich men making seemingly harmless offers. A night on the town, a few pretty things to wear, and a wad of cash to help a girl with her tough situation. What was expected in return was easy, right? Especially if the guy was good looking and charming anyway. Her mother had stepped into the trap of that fairy tale facade, and the sharp-toothed demons waiting on the other side had devoured her and spit her out, leaving her irreparably broken.

And though Kelsey didn't want to believe that this was the type of arrangement Wyatt was suggesting, she needed to ask the question. She cleared her throat. "What exactly would you be expecting for the money?"

"Precisely what I said."

She lifted her gaze to him. "But we'd be staying in the same room."

"Of course," he answered, looking a bit exasperated. "I thought that was clear."

She shifted on the couch, the answer stinging and anger welling. "So you think because I let men pay me to beat them, that I'd just take a check to fuck someone, too?"

For a second, he looked as if she'd thrown ice water in his face, then he grimaced. "Kelsey, no. Do you honestly think I'd expect sex in return for money?"

She shrugged, her heart still beating too fast. "You wouldn't be the first guy in my life to make that offer."

Or the tenth.

When she'd stripped at the club, the offers had come nightly. Luckily, even in her haziest days of drug addiction, she hadn't taken anyone up on it. But she'd be lying to herself if she didn't admit that she'd stayed with boyfriends much longer than she would've because they'd funded her habit. She bet if Wyatt knew all of that he wouldn't be sitting here wanting to parade her around his clients. He wouldn't want to be seen with her anywhere.

He dragged a hand through his hair, appearing to be truly pained that she'd ever been propositioned in that way, and met her gaze. "Look, I'm not good at lying. So I'm not going to sit here and pretend that I don't want you. That I haven't thought about you in exactly the position I found you in tonight. That sharing a room with you and *not* touching you isn't going to be a challenge. But nothing has changed since the day I didn't kiss you in the car. I'm not going to pretend to offer something I don't have to give just to get you in bed."

The stark honesty startled her, hitting some unfamiliar spot inside her. She wasn't used to guys straight-shooting with her. All her life, the men she attracted were the smooth-talkers, the snake charmers, the guys with the wink-and-a-smile promises. This man wasn't feeding her a line. If she took this money and stayed with him, he'd keep his hands off her no matter how much he wanted to do otherwise. She knew it without a shade of doubt.

But the question was, would she survive it? She hadn't slept with anyone in almost a year and for the last few months, the man sitting across from her had been playing the lead role in her fantasies. Fantasies that had scared her, had made her want things she hadn't been able to do with anyone else. Things she'd been dreading doing tonight with Colby . . .

"Thank you for being honest with me. And I know I can take you at your word," she said, her voice steady as resolve began building in her, crystalizing.

"You absolutely can," he assured, some of the darkness and tension lifting from his face, hope replacing it. "So you'll do it?"

Twenty-five grand would solve her most pressing issue with the snap of her fingers. She'd be able to move and get on her feet, find another job. One magical sweep of the money wand and it'd be done. Someone else fixing her problems for her again. The carrot danced in front of her at the end of that stick. And it looked mighty delicious.

But before she could reach out and take a bite, she thought back to her session yesterday with Hawk, the way she'd felt when he'd dropped that fifty-dollar bill on the table. Did she want to be bought by yet another man? Hired help? The little spark of pleasure she got when she was around Wyatt would be twisted and tainted once money got dumped into the mix. And that spark was the only pure thing in her life at the moment.

A menacing voice whispered in her head. *You're going to trust this guy, you stupid girl? You'll be all alone with him. He could hurt you, Kelsey. It could be a trap like last time. Why else would someone like him want trash like you?*

She swiped her damp palms on her pants and mentally gave Davis Ackerman's ghost and his ugly whispers the finger. "I'm not taking your money, Wyatt."

His mouth went slack. "What? If it's about sharing a room, I can get a suite with a sofa sleeper—"

She shook her head and held up a palm, halting him. "You may be able to survive sharing a room for all that time. But I won't."

He clamped his mouth shut, his brows quirking upward.

"I'm not exactly in the market for a relationship either, you know. I'm not searching for some guy from the castle on top of the hill to come save me from my poor, peasant life. Up until that asshole dragged me into the alley, I was pretty damn happy with where I was. And now I'm just pissed that I have to turn everything upside down because of him."

"I wasn't trying to imply that—"

"I'm not done," she said, shifting her feet back to the floor and leaning forward. "What I need is a job that pays more so that I can get away from this current mess and get back on track with my plans. And what I have to have in order to get that job is for a dom to put me through a month of sub training."

He scowled. "With that fucking lumberjack."

She smirked. Colby would love that nickname. "Maybe. Or maybe you and I could do an even exchange."

"An exchange?" he asked, his tone growing wary.

"I'll go with you to your retreat and be the best pretend girl-friend a guy could have." Before she could think too hard on it and chicken out, she slid off the chair and onto the floor, her knees hitting the cool wood and her heart trying to pound right out of her chest. "And you knock the dust off your dominance and put me through my paces for the first week or so of this. After that, you can decide if you want to finish my training or send me back to Colby for the rest."

He made some noise in the back of his throat, and she couldn't tell if it was a pleased sound or a horrified one. "Kelsey, I don't . . . I haven't since college."

She sensed fear there, resistance, but it was underscored by the pure need that flared in his irises. And that alone sent more heat through her than anything she'd experienced in years. "Were you any good, Mr. Austin?"

He closed his eyes, rubbing his brow bone, as if looking at her wasn't allowing him to think properly. "I mentored under the best. He told me I was a natural."

She didn't doubt it. The man reeked of power and control. And she had a feeling Wyatt Austin didn't do anything unless he could master it completely. "Why did you stop?"

His eyes snapped open at that, a veil sliding down between them, his whole demeanor going distant. "Things got too . . . intense. Kelsey, I don't think I can—"

She scooted closer, sliding her hands onto his spread knees. His reluctance only added more fuel to her resolve. He was scared, too. "It won't be easy for me either. It's been a long while since I've been with any guy. And giving over control triggers a lot of old fears in me. But with you, I feel like maybe I could do it. Like I want to try."

He looked down at her, conflicting emotions waging a battle in the set of his mouth, the clench of his jaw. He cupped her face. "You asking me this while on your knees in front of me is not even close to fair fighting."

She let a slow smile curve her lips. This was what she loved about being around Wyatt. He didn't see her as the fuckup or a trauma victim or even as a piece of ass. He saw her as a woman. He saw *her*. And the simplicity of that felt amazing, empowering. "A week away. We both get something we need *and* something I think we've both been wanting since the day you sat in my section. And at the end, I don't expect anything of you, and you don't expect anything of me. Clean finish."

He traced her cheekbones with his thumbs, and the simple sensation rocketed through her. She rarely let subs touch her, and never without permission. But even a brush from Wyatt had her swallowing hard. "I'd be taking advantage of your situation."

"Maybe I'm taking advantage of yours," she countered. "I'm attracted to you. I wanted you to kiss me in the car that day. And I've wanted you to act on those looks you throw at me in the restaurant. I was just afraid to make a move because I figured you wouldn't like what you saw behind the sweet, young waitress image you'd assigned to me."

He gave a rueful smile. "You *are* young. And I still think you're sweet."

"I'm twenty-five."

He groaned. "Christ. I'm more than a decade older than you."

"Like that matters." She let her hands slide farther up his thighs, growing bolder there at his feet. "And I promise you, I'm not as sweet as you think."

His gaze devoured her, and he pressed his palms into the couch cushions, as if it was taking everything he had not to reach out and pillage. "I wasn't an easy master. You need to know that. And if I open up that part of me again, I'm afraid I won't be able to keep it to a CliffsNotes version."

A shiver went through her, some strange cocktail of apprehension and anticipation stirring. She knew—really *knew* in the deepest part of herself—he would never harm her. She'd been eye-to-eye with evil before and could sniff out the stench of it like a dog. But seeing the honest worry in the lines around Wyatt's mouth and the tight hold of his shoulders had her wanting to curl into his lap and kiss away those fears. "You aren't a man who does things halfway. I wouldn't expect anything less from you in this arena either."

He regarded her for another long moment, then finally reached out for her.

"Come 'ere." He cupped her shoulders, his palms hot against her bare skin, and guided her off her knees and onto the couch, straddling his lap like it was the most natural spot for her to be. Like they hadn't been simply server and customer a few weeks ago.

He adjusted her, and the hard ridge of his cock pressed against her through the thin material of her yoga pants. She closed her eyes, overwhelmed for a moment with the feel of him, his heat, the heady masculine scent she'd only gotten teasing whiffs of before. God, how long had she imagined being this close to him? Moisture coated her sex, her whole body going into melt mode at the contact. And the feeling was *good*—so good—to just be turned on and hot for a guy. A taste of normal.

She forced her eyes open, not wanting to miss a moment of this. Up close, Wyatt was even more potent than she'd imagined, the blue in his eyes more intense, the curve of his mouth more sensual. Male beauty tucked behind dark-rimmed glasses and a stoic's disposition. His palms glided across her shoulders and over the straps of her tank top, then his fingers were threading in her hair. He touched her as if he were sculpting a piece of clay to create her form—a reverence and appreciation there that made everything in her want to break open. "Promise me you won't let me hurt you, Kelsey."

The words were so soft, the look in his eyes so stripped, that she lost her breath for a moment. She reached out and brushed the back of her hand along his stubbled jaw. "I promise." *You can't break the broken.*

With that last assurance, it was as if the tide he'd been swimming against reversed. His fingers tightened along her skull, and he brought her mouth down to his, his lips capturing hers in a soft but demanding kiss. Her body seemed to sigh into it, to surrender to the moment. But the second her muscles went lax, his tongue parted her lips, and all semblance of slow and easy fell away from them. Their tongues collided in a rush, hungry and seeking. Her hands began to roam, grabbing at his shirt, pressing against the hard, solid body beneath, wishing there were no layers between them.

All the pent-up months of wanting this man, wanting to know what he tasted like, what would please him poured into the connection between them. Everything went electric, like static coursing over her skin, heightening her senses. The feel of his hands against her scalp, the spicy scent of his cologne, the scrape of stubble against her face—it was all amplified.

This man lit her up.

And his kiss was as desperate as hers, his lips and mouth drinking her in, consuming her one stroke and nibble at a time. He arched his hips, grinding his cock against her sex and making her moan into his mouth. In that moment, she was ready for whatever this crazy agreement would entail, as long as she got to experience him like this. This untethered abandon. She rocked forward, curling her fingers into his dark blue polo shirt and holding tight, as he bit her bottom lip and then worked his way along the curve of her neck.

He lowered his hands to the curve of her hips, guiding her against him in a slow, undulating motion, his hard length teasing and tormenting her. The soft satin of her panties brushed along her now-slippery cleft, making her skin go flushed all over. When he grazed her collarbone with his teeth, she let out a pleading gasp. "Wyatt."

"I want you to come for me," he said, the heated command

hitting her like a branding iron, marking unfamiliar places inside her. "And then you won't be allowed to again until our trip. You understand?"

Fuck. The shift in him was so absolute, so gut-wrenchingly sexy, she could barely form her response. "Yes, sir."

He closed his eyes, as if inhaling and absorbing her reply. Then he moved his hand between her spread legs, cupping her sex through the thin cotton and massaging her clit with toe-curling accuracy using the heel of his hand. "I can smell your arousal, love. And you're wrong about one thing: You're definitely sweet. I can't wait to taste just how very."

Her head tilted back, the pleasure crawling up her spine and climbing out in a groan. It wouldn't take long. Even though she was more than adept at handling her own needs, she'd thought about Wyatt touching her for so long that she felt as if she'd been on the edge of this particular orgasm for months—one only he could give her.

While he continued the skillful rocking pressure between her thighs, his free hand traced up her sternum, brushing the inner curves of her breasts through her shirt, and then collaring her neck. She'd seen the move done a hundred times by doms in The Ranch's playspaces, but never before had anyone done it to her. An overwhelming wash of pure need went through her system, the press of his palm against the hollow of her throat slaying her. She closed her eyes against the dueling sensations of helplessness and blinding desire as he held her exactly in the spot he wanted her, not allowing her to escape his erotic torment.

"Come for me, Kelsey," he said, his voice like warm cider on a cold night. "I've imagined it one too many times alone in my own bed. I want to know what you sound like when you break open."

The words sent her body aflame. Images of him slipping his hand beneath the covers at night, taking his cock in his hand and thinking of her was a little too much for her stampeding hormones to handle. His grip tightened against her throat, and the hand between her legs became more intense and precise, her swollen nub pulsing now.

"Wyatt." His name was more plea than anything else. Every muscle in her body seemed to contract, bracing for impact.

"Let go," he said softly.

At that last whispered command, blessed release crashed over her, wrenching a sharp, keening cry from her throat. Her hips bucked against his hand, shamelessly seeking every bit of pleasure he was willing to bestow upon her, as she rode the wave of orgasm.

"That's it," he said, still holding her in place, though there was grit and strain in his voice. "So fucking gorgeous."

She shuddered hard, and her breath came out in ragged gasps.

"Good girl," he said softly, the two words holding pride, endearment.

And as if he knew the exact second where she couldn't take anymore, he moved his hand away and eased her against him, pressing her forehead into his shoulder as she panted her way down from her peak. His fingers caressed her back, tracing her spine. But the relaxing move didn't hide the fact that his erection was a prominent and insistent pressure against her hip.

"You okay?" he asked, brushing a gentle palm over the back of her head.

"I'm fantastic," she murmured into the curve of his neck. She shifted her weight, languidly reaching down to clasp the hard ridge of his cock through his slacks. "Now it's your turn, handsome."

He grabbed her wrist, not roughly, but firmly enough to halt her movement. Startled, she sat back to face him, and he brought her hand to his mouth, kissing the inside of her wrist. "Tonight was for you."

"But I want to make you feel good, too." And that was the damn truth. She couldn't wait to touch, to explore, to pleasure him. Her mouth watered at the thought of sliding down between his knees and taking that thick cock between her lips, to finally know what he tasted like.

"And that's not your decision," he said with a faint smile, though she could see he was more than tempted. His whole body was taut, tense—hungry. But he didn't move. "We've made a lot of agreements tonight. Big agreements. I want you to have time to think this through before I take it any further."

"You think I'm going to change my mind?"

He eased her off him, setting her against the arm of the couch and pressing a soft kiss to her mouth. "I hope you don't, but tonight has been a whirlwind, and our judgment may be a little fogged with desire at the moment. I know mine always is when I'm around you."

She smiled at that.

"We head out in a little over a week. I can be patient. I've waited this long to have you. Surely I'll survive a few more days."

She glanced down at this tented slacks, lifting an eyebrow. "You sure about that?"

He gave her a look that seemed to say *touché*. "I'm going to send a driver for you and a personal assistant to help you over the next few days. They'll make sure you're set up with everything you need for the trip." She opened her mouth to protest, but he gave her don't-even-try-it eyes. "And I don't want to hear any reports of you arguing with them about me buying things for you. This is an important business function and, as my companion, there will be an expected level of dress. It's my responsibility to provide that for you. If that feels wrong to you, you can give the stuff back after we're done."

She pressed her lips together and nodded.

"And you will come and stay with me at my home the Friday

before we leave. We need to come up with a plan, a story of how we met, the little details that couples know about each other."

"Okay." Nerves fluttered in her belly as the haze of pleasure mellowed and reality set in. She was going to have to really work hard at pulling this off so she didn't let Wyatt down in front of his colleagues. He was putting a lot of faith in her.

"And until then"—he put a knuckle beneath her chin—"you will not train with anyone, you will not pleasure yourself, and you will get some rest."

The authoritative tone sent a soft hum through her veins. "Yes, sir."

"And just so you know, I consider our arrangement, as temporary as it is, an exclusive one. I expect you to be faithful to me from now until the end of it. I don't share."

Her shoulders stiffened. Knowing that he was heading home turned on and pent up poked at her mind like bony fingers. Did he have some girl he saw on the side? He wasn't dating anyone, but she doubted a man like Wyatt was a monk. She hated the crackle of jealousy working its way through her, but she couldn't help it. "And you?"

The corner of his mouth lifted, as if amused by the question. "I would never disrespect you that way. The exclusivity goes both ways."

She released a breath she hadn't realized she'd been holding on to.

"And if you change your mind about any of this . . ."

She reached out and grabbed his hand. "I'm not going to change my mind."

He gave her fingers a squeeze. "'Til Friday, then."

"'Til Friday."

And with that, he gave her another gentle kiss and was gone.

The second the door closed behind him, the vacuum his absence left behind walloped Kelsey. It was as if all the warmth in the room had just disappeared. She grabbed the throw from the back of the couch and wrapped it around her shoulders. She'd lived alone for the last year and had enjoyed the solitude, but she had the instinctive urge to call after him. To ask him to stay here with her at the cabin. Something in her settled when he was close by.

And that terrified her more than anything had in a long time.

The last thing she needed was another addiction.

And Wyatt Austin was turning out to be a very, very tempting drug.

SEVEN

"You're going to *what*?" Jace asked once he and Wyatt were back on the highway heading toward Dallas.

Wyatt leaned against the headrest, his body still buzzing with unreleased energy and his better judgment starting to sneak back in now that his head was clearing. "I know. She should've just taken the money."

"Ha. That would've set up a nightmare of a trip. Her being on your arm all day as your girlfriend and then sharing your room at night, possibly your bed. You would've spent most of the trip jerking off in the shower to keep your hands off her. Sounds like fun for all."

It would've been tortuous. But at least it would've been safer. "I don't want to hurt her."

"So don't." Jace glanced his way, headlights from a car coming in the opposite direction flashing across his features. "I know it's been a long time for you, but you're still a master of self-control. You're not going to lose your shit and do something stupid. That's my style, not yours. You know how to do this. Pay attention to her signals, sift out what her needs are, and then push her to her edge."

Wyatt sighed and rubbed his eyes beneath his glasses. "I don't know if I'm as calm and in control as you think."

"Did you fuck her tonight?" Jace asked, shifting his gaze back to the road.

"No."

"Would she have let you?"

"Yes." And he'd wanted to. God, had he wanted to. "It wasn't the right time."

Jace gave a triumphant smile. "See. There you go. Proof positive you've still got it. Because believe me, not many men would walk away from a willing Kelsey LeBreck. That girl is temptation personified. I've seen male subs grovel at her feet for the mere privilege of serving her a glass of water."

"She got on her knees for me, man," Wyatt said, looking out the side window, almost talking to himself. "I was ready to say no, that there was no way I could do this, go down that road again. But seeing her there, I couldn't fucking stop the urge. The need to claim her welled up and took over. Orders started falling out of my mouth like I was possessed by some former version of myself."

Jace reached out and gripped Wyatt's shoulder, giving it a squeeze. "Welcome back to the dark side, brother. We've got cookies. Hope you enjoy your stay."

Wyatt turned his head, his tone deadpan. "You're not helping."

His brother laughed. "Come on. You've got a beautiful woman willing to play slave to you. And your business retreat issue is fixed. Embrace that. You've made this agreement. Now keep your word and stop stressing about it."

Wyatt sagged in the seat. His word. That's what he'd given Kelsey. And he didn't go back on a promise. Plus, if he was honest with himself, he was already in too deep to walk away. How

Kelsey had felt against him tonight, the way she'd melted under his commands had lit a fuse that wasn't going to burn out easily. Even the sound of her voice, those soft cries as she came kept replaying in his head like some song he couldn't shake.

He had to have her. And not only in his bed, but surrendering to his will, being *his*.

He prayed that a week would be enough, that he wouldn't get consumed by that need like he had with Mia . . .

Because if he stripped Kelsey of even one ray of the light that seemed to shine from her, he'd never forgive himself.

You're older now, more in control, he reminded himself. He wasn't some lovesick college student. This was a sexual arrangement, not a relationship. Kelsey was *not* Mia.

Yeah. Now to get himself to believe it.

"Bring me to your place before you drop me off at mine," Wyatt said, shoving the worries back into the dusty, dark corners of his mind and refocusing on the task at hand. He needed to take a page from Jace's book and live in the moment for a change.

"Okay. How come?"

"Because I'm going to need you to open up Wicked for a private shopping session tonight. It's time I use my investor discount, don't you think?"

Jace's grin was pure mischief. "I thought you'd never ask. Hope you've got an extra suitcase to bring on the trip, bro. Because you're about to get the kink hookup of the year."

⸻

Kelsey sat on a bench outside of The Ranch, her leg bumping up and down as she waited for Wyatt's driver to pick her up. She was suddenly having visions of those scenes in *Pretty Woman* where the stuck-up shop owners were giving Julia Roberts shit because they thought she was trash. Kelsey glanced down at her simple white sweater and jeans, hoping her outfit didn't scream "Imposter!" to anyone who looked too closely.

And what was Wyatt's personal assistant going to think? Would Wyatt have told him or her that Kelsey was some new woman in his life, or would he have told the person the truth? The latter made her stomach churn. She'd been on the other side of judgment in her life too many times to count. She should be used to it by now—the upturned noses, the whispered comments, the passive-aggressive remarks. But, though she was more practiced at her outward response these days, that kind of judgment still chipped away at her with painful accuracy.

So when the limo pulled up a few minutes later, Kelsey had gone into total mannequin mode—her smile stiff and her fingers clutching her purse like it held the Hope Diamond. But when the back door swung open and a petite, dark-haired woman slid out, all of Kelsey's anxiety sloughed off her and puddled on the ground, relief swooping in.

"Evan?"

"Hey there." Evan Kennedy smiled and hopped onto the curb to give Kelsey a quick hug. "You look so surprised. Wyatt didn't tell you who was coming?"

Kelsey squeezed Evan back before releasing her. "No. He said a personal assistant. That's all I knew. But man, am I glad to see you."

"Same here, sweetie. Wyatt asked Jace if he could borrow me to help you out with 'girlie' stuff." She did air quotes complete with an eye roll. "I swear. You'd think I was taking you out to buy your first tampons or something."

Kelsey laughed, so relieved to see Jace's girlfriend that the sound came out giddy. She and Evan weren't particularly close, but she'd gotten to chat with her a few times at The Ranch when Evan wasn't occupied with both of her dominants, Jace and

Andre. And Evan had never been anything but warm and welcoming toward her. "I hope I didn't take you away from anything important."

She waved a dismissive hand. "Hell, no. I photographed two weddings and a sweet sixteen party this weekend. I *need* a day away. Especially when said day includes riding around in a limo and shopping for you with someone else's credit card."

Kelsey smiled, even though the idea that Wyatt was buying things for her still sent uneasiness through her.

"Plus, Wyatt helped Jace and I out with a crisis last year, and I'd do just about anything for that guy. He's good people."

The driver came around the front of the limo with a polite smile. "Ready, ladies?"

Evan grabbed for Kelsey's hand to tug her toward the car, her delight evident. "Yep, whisk us away, Henry."

Both of them climbed inside, and Kelsey had to hold back her gasp at how luxurious the inside was. She'd been inside limos a time or two for bachelorette parties and such, but she could tell instantly by the buttery soft seats and the embossed A&A on the glassware that this wasn't rented. This one was owned. By Wyatt's company.

Wyatt owned a fucking limo, probably many, and one day would own an entire company. It wasn't news, but seeing it right there in her face definitely rocked her a bit. It was easy to normalize Wyatt when he was sitting in the cafe drinking coffee and reading the paper, imagining that he was just an everyday guy who happened to wear designer suits and have a big job. But Kelsey had never really allowed herself to think too far past that, to truly grasp that this man existed in a world of filthy, filthy wealth.

And she was about to enter into that universe to try to deceive it into thinking she belonged there.

She was way out of her depth. With this ruse. And this man.

She tucked her hands beneath her legs, sitting on them to fight the instinct to grab the handle of the door and hop right back out. This was why Wyatt had given her time to change her mind. He knew things would look different in the daylight. But she'd made an agreement and didn't plan on backing out now.

They rode into the city, Evan providing a steady stream of chitchat to keep Kelsey's mind from spiraling down into the pit too far. But by the time the driver had stopped in front of the city's swankiest shopping district, the concerns were starting to tiptoe in again like thieves trying to hijack her remaining resolve.

Evan directed Kelsey into the first shop, where a young brunette flashed them a perfectly practiced smile and led them to a private dressing area that had posh leather couches, champagne, and a tray of canapés set up for them. She motioned to the space like a Vanna White wannabe. "Mr. Austin let us know what types of things you'd need for your upcoming trip, Ms. LeBreck. So our stylist took the liberty of assembling some outfits for you to try on. He said you preferred classic lines with an edge of sexiness. Obviously, if these don't work, we can go through the store and pull some more looks for you."

Kelsey stared at the racks of dresses and outfits that lined the far wall of the room. Next to them, accessories were set out on a table, grouped by color and level of dressiness. She cleared her throat. "Um, thank you. I'm sure I'll be able to find what I need. This looks great."

The girl beamed as if she'd personally designed all the clothes in the room. "Would you like me to help you get started?"

Evan glanced at Kelsey, then back at the girl. "I think we're okay right now. But we'll call for you if we need any assistance."

The girl nodded and breezed out, leaving Kelsey and Evan behind with the clothes, champagne, and classical music.

Evan shook her head, watching the door close behind the girl. "I can't believe people actually get to shop like this."

"Seriously." Kelsey walked over to the rack of dresses, reaching out to feel the jewel-colored fabrics, the luxurious material gliding over her fingers. Handwritten price tags hung from each one, some costing more than her monthly rent. She grabbed one tag, running her thumb over the outrageous number.

"I can hear you panicking," Evan said, stepping behind her. "You okay?"

Kelsey peeked back over her shoulder. "You do mindreading on the side?"

Evan sent her a sympathetic smile. "Sorry. I live with two doms. I've picked up on a few things. You went all stiff."

Kelsey dropped the price tag and let a shimmery cocktail dress slide over her hand. It was all . . . so much. Too much. She headed to the side table with the champagne, but moved past the alcohol and grabbed a sparkling water instead. "I'll be all right. I think it's starting to set in that I'm actually going to do this."

"Which part?" she asked, her pale blue eyes showing true concern.

Kelsey took a long gulp of water. "How much did Wyatt tell you?"

She shrugged, a bit sheepish. "He didn't give me details, but I sort of relentlessly pestered Jace until he spilled the whole arrangement. Sorry?"

Kelsey shook her head, having no doubt how persuasive someone like Evan could be. "It's fine. I'm just worried that I'm in over my head and that the people at the retreat are going to see right through me." She leaned against the back of a settee, not having the energy to put up a front with Evan. "A year ago, I was spinning around poles and shaking my ass for tips—though I haven't quite shared that with Wyatt yet. So this is like a foreign country with people speaking a different language. I don't want to be humiliated, and I definitely don't want to embarrass Wyatt. Those people—"

"Are just people who happen to have more money in their bank account," Evan finished. She sat down on the couch, frown lines creasing her forehead. "I don't know how much you know about me, but I wasn't born with money either. I was a foster kid and was on the streets for a while. I also spent almost a year living with Jace and Wyatt's family when I was a teenager. So I went from nothing to the McMansion. And I remember never feeling so out of place in my life."

Kelsey sat down, the revelation shocking her. Evan always seemed so put together, so refined. She'd been a street kid? Then another thought hit her. She'd *lived* with Jace and Wyatt. "So you and Jace, back then?"

She smiled a little. "Long story. But what I realized pretty quickly was that money doesn't protect people from problems, it just hides them better from the public eye. Everybody is playing some role when out in society. And most are so busy keeping up their own airs that they aren't looking so closely at yours. So as long as you smile, make small talk, and act confident, you'll blend in."

Kelsey sipped her water. "You make it sound so easy."

She shrugged. "It can be. I think your bigger challenge is going to be once that hotel room door shuts with Wyatt. That's where you can't fake it."

Kelsey fiddled with the cap of her bottle. "It's only for a week."

Evan gave a conspiratorial smile. "Sure. Now let's get you undressed. So many outfits, so little time. And after this, we still need to get shoes, beach wear, and make a stop by the lingerie boutique."

"Lingerie?"

"Mmm-hmm. Lots of it. I thought Wyatt was Mr. Conservative. But based on the list he gave me, he's more like his brother than I thought."

Kelsey's skin heated at the thought of Wyatt selecting what

undergarments he wanted to see her in. "I have a feeling there's a lot more to Wyatt than anyone thought."

Evan's grin turned sly. "Scared of what you might find out about him?"

"Yes."

More scared of what she may find out about herself.

EIGHT

Wyatt sat at his kitchen table Friday afternoon and flipped through the profiles of the retreat attendees that his assistant had researched and compiled for him this week. He scanned each guest's business, hobbies, and personal causes. Hollis Myers: CEO of movie theater chain, plays a lot of cards (blackjack not poker), donates regularly to the American Cancer Society and the National Center for Missing and Exploited Children. Cam Berthelot: head of natural gas drilling company, enjoys deep-sea fishing, has a second home in Florida, and donates to the Red Cross. Belle Pritchard: owner of bridal shop chain and wedding planning business, big into supporting local small business owners, and donates to grassroots organizations and an LGBT legal defense fund.

Wyatt scribbled a few notes, but those were mainly for Kelsey. He knew some of these people already. And for the ones he didn't, his memory had always been photographic so he wouldn't need a cheat sheet after reading through the list a time or two. But the more each of them knew about the guests, the better shot they had at making relevant conversation and engaging them. People liked to talk about themselves; you just have to give them an opening and a topic. The hard part for him was always the talking-back portion. He didn't know how to fill space with airy chitchat. He usually ended up talking business, which made people's eyes glaze over, or he'd make some obscure movie reference and no one would get it. He'd learned early in life that keeping that shit to yourself was much wiser than getting that what-the-fuck-is-he-talking-about? look.

His cell phone rang, buzzing against the table and breaking through the silence of the empty house. The name of his driver flashed on the screen. He hit the speaker button. "What's going on, Henry?"

"Ms. LeBreck declined my offer to be picked up," he informed him with that to-the-point tone of his.

Wyatt glanced up from his paperwork, a sinking feeling in his gut. So he'd been right to worry. Kelsey had changed her mind. "I see. Did she say why?"

"I had informed her of your requested itinerary of dinner out and then a return to your home. She said she had a few errands to run first and wanted your address so she could drive herself directly. She was rather insistent."

Wyatt blinked. "She's still coming?"

"Of course, Mr. Austin. I just wanted to inform you of the change in plans. She didn't give me an indication of what time she'd be arriving. I didn't want you to be caught off guard."

Wyatt leaned back in the chair, more relieved than he cared to admit. "Thank you, Henry. I'll be sure to be prepared for her."

"You're welcome, sir. Do you need anything else from me this evening?"

"No, just plan to be here tomorrow to bring us to the airport."

"Yes, sir. Have a nice evening."

Wyatt hit the end button, took off his glasses, and ran a hand over his face before putting them back on. So Kelsey had decided to alter his prescribed plans from the very start. The move both perturbed and intrigued him. They hadn't made the formal transition into the D/s roles yet, but he'd tried to get her primed for the mindset the last time he saw her as well as with his very precise instructions on her shopping trip. He had no idea if her little rebellion tonight was an intentional statement of her independence or just a way for her to hold on to the last of her freedom before she surrendered to him.

He turned toward the triad of windows to his right and stared out over the expanse of his pool and backyard, anticipation rolling through him. Tonight was going to be a test of sorts. For both of them. If it went well, they'd leave for the trip tomorrow with a new confidence. If it didn't, he'd have to revert to the original plan and pay her to accompany him, no training or touching involved. Thunder rumbled through the quiet kitchen, pulling him back to the view. It'd been raining off and on all day, a cold front coming through. Now the clouds hung low overhead, blocking out the last rays of the afternoon sun, and the wind had begun to rattle the early fall leaves off the trees.

Maybe they'd be better off not going out tonight. Things looked like they were about to get pretty nasty outside. His gaze flicked to the clock on the oven. He grabbed his phone and scrolled through his numbers, looking for the one he'd recently added.

Kelsey answered on the second ring, road noise and pattering rain in the background. "Hello?"

"Where are you?" he asked, skipping past niceties.

"Uh . . . in the middle of a blinding storm at the moment. But if I followed directions correctly, I'm pretty close to your place."

He frowned, a clap of thunder outside his window signaling the start of the onslaught. "You should have let Henry drive you. I don't want you out in this."

"I'm fine. There's just a lot of water on this road all of a sudden, so I'm taking it slow. I can handle a little storm."

"Kelsey, if there's water on the road, you need to turn around. The neighborhoods around here flashflood easily with the lake nearby. There's no way to tell how deep it is."

"I think it's—" There was a strange whining sound in the background. Then a string of curses.

"What's wrong?"

"Can I take back what I said? I think my car just stalled out."

"Christ." He shoved his chair back from the table, almost toppling it in his rush. "Tell me where you're at. I'm coming to get you."

"Um, wait, shit, I'm not sure. I can barely see anything," she said, the pattering in the background now blending with the sheets of rain banging against his kitchen windows. "I think the next cross street ahead is supposed to be Briarpatch."

Hell, right by the golf course. That spot was notorious for flooding. "What kind of car do you drive?"

"It's a ninety-nine white Honda Civic."

"All right. Stay put for now. I'm only ten minutes away. If the water looks like it's rising, get out of the car and onto higher ground."

"Okay. I'm sorry. I didn't meant to—"

"Not your fault. Just hold tight. And keep your phone close." He hung up the call and strode toward the garage, grabbing a set of keys off the pegboard in the laundry room and pulling on a jacket. His car wouldn't be any better than hers in the water, but his housekeeper's son had been working on an old Jeep and had asked to store it at Wyatt's. The paint job wasn't done yet, but Wyatt knew the kid had gotten the engine in shape last month. If this helped him get Kelsey out of this situation safely, he'd buy the guy that paint job.

Visibility was still a challenge as he made his way off his property and toward the cluster of neighborhoods closer to the highway. The sky had gone a weird green-gray, and the automatic street lights were popping on even though it wasn't even six yet. He kept a hand on the wheel and called Henry to set up and handle a tow for Kelsey's car. Wyatt didn't want her sitting out there, waiting for someone to get her car.

It took him a little longer than he hoped to get to her. Other cars besides hers had gotten stuck, so he had to carefully maneuver around them, but luckily the water seemed to be staying at a manageable level. The rain let up a bit as he made his way down the road, and he spotted Kelsey's car in the right lane, the street lamp above her making the white car look orange.

He pulled up behind her and hopped out, the icy rain soaking him instantly. Kelsey was already opening her door before he got to her. She pushed an umbrella through the crack and popped it open, a bright pink spot in the haze of gray. She climbed out of the car, water rushing over her heeled boots, and grabbed the top of the car to steady herself.

He made his way over as quickly as he could, but he still had on his dress shoes from his trip to the office earlier today and the damn things had no grip. He motioned at her and raised his voice, fighting with the ever-rolling thunder. "Get in the Jeep!"

"All my stuff is still in here," she called back, taking a careful step in his direction and shutting the driver's-side door. "For the trip."

He made his way over to her, locking a hand beneath her elbow and breathing a sigh of relief that she was okay. "I got it. Let's just get you inside the Jeep first."

"I can help."

"And I want you out of this. Inside. Now."

She gave him the eye but held back another protest. She thrust the umbrella into his hand and now he could see the damn thing wasn't just pink but also had a pattern of little cupcakes all over it. "Take this."

"I don't need—"

"So all the stuff doesn't get wet."

"Fine." He took the umbrella from her and nudged her toward the Jeep, putting the keys in her hand. "Go. And turn on the heat."

As soon as he verified she was able to get herself through the water without stumbling, he opened her trunk and grabbed her suitcase, but there looked to be two grocery bags in there as well. Dammit. He couldn't get all of it. He slammed the trunk closed and hurried back to the Jeep, tossing the suitcase in the back, then sloshed his way back through the water for the sacks of groceries.

By the time he climbed back into the driver's seat, he was soaked, freezing, and trying hard not to shiver. He shrugged out of his drenched coat and held his hands up against the vents, but no warmth was coming out.

"I can't get it to heat up," Kelsey said, her voice vibrating with her own shivers. She wrapped her arms around herself, her blonde hair saturated and dripping onto her shoulders.

Crap. Apparently the kid had fixed the engine but hadn't gotten to the heating system yet. "We need to get back to the house."

"But my car . . ."

"I've already got someone on the way." He made sure nobody was behind them, then reversed and drove over the median to get to the other side of the road so they could head back. "We need to get home and out of these clothes."

She glanced his way, an eyebrow lifted. "Not wasting any time getting me naked, are you?"

He chuckled, glad she could still make jokes when her vehicle was about to float down the damn street. "Don't tempt me. I just walked around with a pink cupcake umbrella. I may feel the need to reassert my manhood."

She smiled and leaned forward to shrug her way out of her saturated jacket, filling his peripheral vision with an impossibly tempting view. He tried to keep his eyes on the road, but had a hard time focusing on safety or being a gentleman with Kelsey's now-see-through cream-colored blouse taunting him, the wet material clinging to her skin and molding over the swells of her breasts and her cold-stiffened nipples. Wyatt stopped for a red light and dropped any pretense of politeness to give her a long, assessing view.

She glanced his way, no doubt noticing the heat in his eyes, then looked down as if only now realizing what she'd revealed. Her hands moved to cover herself.

The flash of modesty endeared him, but he wasn't going to let her get away with it. Training started now. "Put your hands in your lap, Kelsey. No reason to hide from me. You need to get accustomed to me seeing your body."

She wet her lips and followed his direction, clasping her hands in front of her. He could see the pattern of her lace bra beneath the shirt now and the dark shadow of her areolas peeking through. The sight was enough to have his cock twitching and his good sense evaporating. He'd promised himself he wouldn't touch her until they negotiated limits. But he hadn't anticipated this kind of immediate assault on his noble intentions.

The car behind him honked, dragging him from the delicious sight. The light had turned green, and he had no choice but to pull forward. He cleared his throat. "Have you had any second thoughts about our arrangement?"

"No."

"Honesty, please."

She sighed. "Yes. But not in the way you think. I'm mostly worried about not being able to pull off a ruse."

"We're going to work on that some tonight. I think you're going to do better than you imagine, though. You're naturally charming, so people will be drawn to you. All we need to worry about are the little factual details that may come up."

"Right."

"Did you remember to bring your passport?" He'd been happy to hear she already had one on hand from a past trip to Mexico. Even with his connections, getting anything moving that quickly through a government office would've been tough.

She patted her purse. "Got it."

They rode along in silence for a while, the pounding rain and bad visibility a good distraction from the siren call of temptation winding through his mind. *Control.* This was about his self-control. He'd spent an extra long time in the shower this morning, stroking himself to release as he imagined the scene from Friday night, Kelsey tipping her head back and coming against his hand. He'd wanted to prepare himself so that he didn't jump on her like some horny pervert when he finally got her to his place. But the few minutes with her in the car had his blood heading south and desire pumping through him like he hadn't climaxed in a month.

Patience.

He took a left onto the long driveway that led up to his place. Kelsey bent forward, trying to peer through the rain-covered windshield. His house was barely visible through the haze of the storm and the trees that dotted his property. "You've got a lot of land around you."

"I like my privacy." He hit the button on the garage as he took the final turn up to the house. "In fact, you're going to be my first overnight houseguest. I usually don't like sharing my space."

Her brows lifted at that, and he realized too late that he probably shouldn't have mentioned that. "You should've said something. I could've come over tomorrow morning. You didn't have to invite me to stay the night."

He pulled the Jeep into the garage and cut the engine. "Yes, I did."

Her gaze followed him as he got out and walked around to her side to open the door for her. He could feel her question before she even voiced it. "Why?"

He offered her his hand, and she took it, her fingers still icy. "Because my home is the place for all of my most precious possessions." He helped her down from the Jeep and brushed his lips over her knuckles. "And you, love, are about to become the most important of them all for the next seven days."

He braced himself for her reaction—the implication of ownership a bit of a test. If she was going to truly give herself over to this and shed her domme role for the time they were together, he needed to get her head in the right place from the start. He was in charge. She was his to command. Wyatt had talked to Grant Waters earlier in the week to make sure his training would count for Kelsey's requirement, and Grant had warned him that Kelsey wouldn't feel safe if he didn't immediately prove himself worthy and capable of the role, that she would deftly manipulate a weak dom to hold on to her own control.

Wyatt wasn't one to take directives from someone else, but on that, he'd agreed wholeheartedly. He wanted nothing more than to have the full experience with Kelsey and to make her feel absolutely safe and protected in his hands. A distilled version had never been in his plans.

"You understand what you've agreed to, Kelsey? To be owned by me?"

Her lips parted slightly, and the shiver he felt go through her hand seemed to have little to do with the cold. She managed a nod.

Nice. She liked the idea, and her body was already reacting to him. He glanced down the length of her—the slightly smeared makeup, the lush set of her mouth, the clinging shirt. All of it put together was like some erotic dream come to life. He wanted to yank those boots and jeans off her and lick the rainwater from her skin, chase away that chill in the most decadent way possible, feel her heat up against his mouth. But in his cold garage before they'd discussed a single limit was neither the time nor the place. Mustering up every ounce of restraint he possessed, he set his hands on her shoulders. "Let's get you into a hot shower so you don't end up with pneumonia. A sick sub will do me no good."

"Yes, sir," she said, a little catch in her voice.

He stared at her for a moment longer, watching the slight glaze go over her eyes. He cupped the side of her head. Was it possible? Kelsey had declared that she'd never willingly submitted before. The word *willingly* had stuck in his gut like a rusty piece of metal—a grim clue about what exactly may be lurking in Kelsey's past. But right now, her whole demeanor suggested that she was already sinking a bit, going into that headspace where subs let go.

The achingly erotic sight squeezed the air from his lungs and vaulted his dominance straight to the surface—a demanding, pounding force that could no longer be kept on a leash. He needed her under his control. Right. This. Minute. He tightened his hold on her shoulders, battling with himself. But when she dipped her lashes and her muscles went loose beneath his fingertips, it was all the signal he needed. He wasn't sure about a lot of things between them. But in this moment he was sure of one thing—for whatever reason, she needed this as much as he did right now, needed him to take over fully. And God did he want to. Without giving her warning, he bent forward and hauled Kelsey off her feet and over his shoulder.

She let out a little yelp, the move apparently breaking her from the spell she'd been in. "Wyatt!"

"Hush."

"You don't need to—"

He gave her ass a smack, the sound of his hand against her wet jeans a little too enticing. He had to hold back from giving the other side a similar pop. "It pleases me to carry you. Are you going to deny me that?"

"No, sir," she said. "It's just, there are groceries and—"

"It's cold in here. They'll be fine." He shoved open the door that led to the laundry room and then headed into the darkened kitchen. The storm was still splattering against the windows, but he barely heard it as he made his way through the living room and up the stairs. His dress shoes squeaked against the wood, and he knew he was leaving footprints in his wake, but he didn't care at the moment. All he was concerned about was the woman who had her cheek pressed against his back.

Once they made it into his en suite bathroom, he set Kelsey on her feet. Her cheeks were flushed and her blue eyes wide, but he didn't sense any fear there. He reached out and turned on the shower to heat up the water. Then he was in front of her again. He clasped her chin, lifting her face to him.

"I need to discuss limits and boundaries with you, Kelsey. I want to know where your lines are so that I don't harm you. We need a safe word."

She nodded in his hand, and he released her chin.

"But right now I don't have the patience for that." He reached for the buttons on her blouse, pulling them free, and pushing the garment off her shoulders. The material hit the tile with a wet smack. "I've spent morning after morning in that cafe, talking to you, watching you, aching for you. I sit there getting no work done because all I can think about are the filthy, deviant fantasies I conjure up about you. You drive me to distraction, love. And I've spent one too many nights in this very shower, taking my cock in my hand and imagining it was you around me instead of my fist."

She closed her eyes, his name a soft whisper across her lips.

He reached for the waistband of her jeans, dragging her

against him, his voice low. "And what I'm about to do has nothing to do with training or our deal. I want . . . *need* to fuck you before I lose my goddamned mind. And I need to do it my way. So if you don't want that, say so. And if I do something you aren't okay with, tell me to stop. That's all the safe word you need right now. Even once we establish one, I will *always* listen to the word *no*. Do you understand?"

Something seemed to open in her expression, like a flower unfurling for the sun, and without a word, she met his eyes and worked the button and zipper on her jeans. The slow grinding sound of the zipper's teeth was one of the sweetest noises Wyatt could ever remember hearing. Then, her cold little fingers were encircling his wrist and dragging his palm down beneath the thin satin of her panties. Hot, damp heat coated his fingers, and he groaned.

"I'm all yours, Wyatt," she said softly. "I trust you. And you aren't the only one who's gotten off on fantasies about the other."

She reached out and ran her hand along the length of his erection, which was now prominent against his wet slacks. His eyelids went half-mast, pleasure at the simple touch vibrating through him like a sonic boom.

"Take off the rest of your clothes," he rasped.

"Yes, sir," she said, her voice heavy with her own desire now.

He slipped his hand from her and brought his fingers to his lips, tasting her arousal as he stepped back to take in the full sight of her disrobing. God, every little part of her was even sweeter than he'd imagined—her taste, the scent of her skin, the soft want in her eyes. He didn't deserve this, but hell if he wasn't going to enjoy the unexpected gift.

Her focus stayed locked on him, her eyes flaring as he pulled his fingers from his mouth, and she tugged her boots off. Then, without any hesitation or modesty, she stripped out of her jeans and panties and then unhooked her bra. The lacy scrap fell to the floor. She stood before him, gloriously naked, and lowered her lashes. Waiting. Submissive.

His.

As Wyatt stepped forward, he felt the last semblance of resistance disintegrate inside him, like a flame to parchment. The man he used to be, the one he'd locked away inside himself, rose up from the shadows of his past and grabbed hold of the reins.

Dominant. Determined.

And ravenous.

God help them both.

NINE

Kelsey watched the change come over Wyatt with a touch of awe, his cool reserve switching to something wicked, predatory—a heavy coat falling away and revealing what lurked beneath. His laser-blue eyes devoured every inch of her naked body, raking over her in a way that made everything in her tighten and ache. And, to her relief, no fear or hesitation welled up in her. All the worries that were present that night preparing for Colby were blessedly absent. Instead, her chilled bones began to warm as he stepped closer.

"Undress me," he said, his deep voice like a stroke to her skin.

"Yes, sir." She lifted her hands to find them shaking ever so slightly and carefully worked the buttons on his wet dress shirt. She'd already been shamelessly staring at the ripples and bumps beneath the thin material, but pushing the shirt open and seeing his naked chest had her tongue pressing to the roof of his mouth. *Sweet baby Jesus.*

As she suspected, he was honed and hard—the exquisite body of an athlete hiding behind the trappings of a businessman's attire. A dark smattering of chest hair tracked across his pecs and narrowed to a line down his abdomen, disappearing below his belt. She had the urge to lick his damp skin, to taste those flat nipples, and to trace that line downward. But he hadn't given her permission, and she knew the rules.

She traced her hands down to his belt buckle, slowly dragging the leather through the metal, enjoying the way his cock twitched behind the fabric of his pants. Soon he'd be inside her, laying claim to her. Her sex clenched at the image, her body begging for what she'd so long imagined. What would it be like to be at his mercy? To give in to his will? No longer feeling patient, she unfastened his button and pulled down the zipper, getting onto her knees and pushing his pants and boxer briefs down in one swift motion.

His cock bobbed free, long and thick and so fucking gorgeous that she almost couldn't stop herself from reaching out and caressing the sure-to-be-silky skin. She knew most women wouldn't describe a man's erection as such. But Kelsey couldn't help but appreciate the pure primitive beauty of Wyatt's arousal. Every part of him called to her.

"I like the way you're looking at me, love."

"May I touch you?" she asked, a little surprised by the breathlessness in her voice. Hell, she sounded like one of her subs, desperate and pleading. But she couldn't bank her natural reaction to him.

"Yes."

She rose up on her knees and took him in her hand, the heat of him almost searing her still-cold hands. He tensed a bit, and she winced, releasing him. "I'm sorry. My hands . . ."

He threaded his fingers along the back of her damp hair. "Then don't use your hands."

He guided her forward and she closed her eyes, dragging her cheek along the length of him, the smooth warmth sending a ripple of unadulterated desire through her. He loosened his grip on her, giving her free rein. She nuzzled the trimmed hair at the base of his cock, his masculine scent like a jolt of adrenaline to her own arousal, then she dipped down and ran her lips along his sac, earning a deep groan from him.

"Enough, love," he said, his voice strained. "I promise to give you full access to explore and taste as you please at some point. But right now, I need something other than your pretty mouth."

Reluctantly, she pulled away and lowered back to the floor to tug off his shoes and socks so she could remove his pants. He took her hand and helped her back to her feet, then tugged her against him. Steam rolled out from the top of the shower, cascading around them as he pressed a kiss to her mouth. The chill from their stint in the rain became more and more of a distant memory as his palms roamed her back and his tongue worked a slow, sensual dance against hers.

Rain pinged against the skylights, and time seemed to slow as he grabbed the back of her thighs and lifted her against him, holding her without breaking away from the kiss. His cock pressed against her belly, and her soft whimper was one of lost desperation.

He pulled back for a moment, his gaze tracing over her face, as if he didn't quite believe she was here in his bathroom, naked and wrapped around him. She knew the feeling. "Water's ready."

And so was she. He set her back on her feet and pulled open the shower door. Jets were blasting from more than one spot, and the main showerhead was directly over top—raining down like the storm outside. He guided her in, the water blissfully warm against her, and laid a gentle kiss on her lips.

"I'll be right back," he said. "Don't get started without me."

"Ha. I don't know." She turned into the water. "These showerheads look like they could be mighty effective. And you did make me wait all week . . ."

He grinned and smacked her ass with a sharp but playful blow that sent water droplets flying. "I assure you your patience will be well rewarded."

He slipped out of the bathroom for a few seconds, and she tilted her head back, enjoying the spray and steam, relishing the fact that she felt so comfortable here with him. All week she had built up tonight, worrying that things would be awkward or practiced or formal. Worried that their worlds were too different to ever come together on the same plane. Worried that all she'd endured last year would come rushing back once he slipped into the dominant role. But the minute he'd put his hands on her, all those anxieties had evaporated into a haze of *Oh, yes. This.*

Cool palms slid along her waist, startling her for a second. She opened her eyes and leaned back into Wyatt. "Everything okay?"

He kissed along her shoulder, working his way toward her neck as his hand reached out and adjusted the cascade of water to a more manageable level. "It's better now that I'm in here with you. Just wanted to make sure we had everything we need."

She glanced at the shelf of shampoo and soap and noticed that he'd added a foil packet and a bottle of lubricant. "How very thoughtful, Mr. Austin."

"Mmm." He grabbed the soap, sudsing his hands, then moved his palms along her ribcage in slow, methodical circles. His cock pressed against her back, a hot promise. "Is it wrong that I love hearing you call me that when we're like this?"

She tipped her head back against his shoulder as his hands made their way up to the bottom curves of her breasts. He dragged the slippery suds up and over her nipples, massaging and gently pinching. She groaned as a fresh wave of heat flooded her sex. "Wrong? No. Dirty? Maybe."

He chuckled, low and dark.

"And I have to tell you," she said, arching into his touch. "You're not going to need any lube if you keep doing this."

He pinched her nipples a bit harder, making them go dark pink and hard beneath the soap suds. "Is that right? You're that wet for me already?"

"I've been wet for you since I left you last week, sir. And even before then."

A low sound of approval passed his lips, and he traced one hand down her side, finding his way to the curve of her ass. He backed up a bit, sliding his hand between them and dragging the soap along her crack. "I don't think it's your place to tell me what I may or may not need to use on you, love."

Hot goose bumps tightened her skin as his finger found her sensitive back entrance, teasing lightly. Her knees went liquid, and she couldn't hold back the soft, achy gasp.

"See," he said against her ear, "our training time together is going to be about exploring you, finding out what buttons get you to make that noise you just did, what I can tease and reward you with. Plus, I've been thinking about this ass way too long to not touch it now that I have you here."

The tip of his finger, still slippery with soap, pushed gently inside, sending a wash of sensation across her nerve endings. Her clit pulsed in time with his ever so slight movements. Her hand went out in front her, bracing herself against the shower wall— both to keep herself steady and to stop her from relieving the pressure in her clit. She'd done anal play a time or two before, but the guys she'd been with had never had any finesse about it. And by some miracle, Davis hadn't violated her there. But somehow Wyatt had instantly distilled her most forbidden and indulgent hot spot. He moved his other hand between her thighs, gliding over her mound and providing adept pressure. Then he plunged the fingertip in her backside a little deeper.

She moaned hard then, yearning. She'd gone a week with no orgasm, a week filled with dirty, delicious Wyatt fantasies. And she'd gone a year without the real thing. She was feeling every bit of that deprivation now. Her other hand landed on the wall, fully braced now. Water sluiced over her as she rocked into Wyatt's dual touch. "Wyatt, please . . ."

"Come for me, Kelsey," he commanded, his voice harsh against her ear. "Show me how bad you fucking want it."

The effect was instant and overwhelming. She let out a sharp cry that bounced off the shower tiles and rode his fingers without care or concern for how wanton she must look. The orgasm was almost painful in its intensity, all the built-up tension bursting in one explosive moment. Her fingers curled against the hard tile and she called his name in a long gasping pant, rocking into the sensations, until her head sagged between her shoulders.

When her cries quieted, he didn't give her a second to even grab a lungful of oxygen. He shifted his hands and grasped her waist, turning her in the large shower until she faced the back wall, which was covered with jets he hadn't turned on yet. "Lean forward. Hands back on the wall. Don't move them unless I tell you."

She followed his order, flattening her palms against the tile, her chest still rising and falling with her quick breaths. Her head buzzed with half-formed thoughts, but she vaguely registered the sound of the foil wrapper over the sound of the water. A few more dials were turned and the overhead shower went off, but the jets in front of her came to life. Wyatt adjusted the knobs, lining her up until two smaller jets hit directly against her nipples. She arched with the awareness.

"Let's see how effective these really are, shall we?" he said, wickedness in his tone.

He adjusted one more lower knob and the spray of water landed right against her mound, a breath above her throbbing, sensitive clit. "Oh, Jesus."

"You don't get to come again until I do," he said. "You understand?"

"Yes, sir." But already she could feel the beginning of another orgasm building. The first a mere appetizer apparently.

His hands captured her hips, tilting her just so, and then he was spreading her, the tip of his cock pressing against her entrance. Her body attempted to resist—Wyatt was big and it'd been a long time for her. But when his stubble brushed over his shoulder and his lips tickled her ear with a whispered, "Open for me, love," all tension seemed to drain from her. He pushed forward, and her body melted around him like butter over flame.

"Ah, that's it, beautiful," he said, his voice pure appreciation. "Christ, you feel good."

She bit her lip, her eyes watering with the pleasure of it all and the feel of him inside her. The lights flickered above them, the storm still raging outside. But it was no match for the intensity of what was happening inside. Wyatt stayed still behind her, giving her time to adjust, but the lack of movement was ratcheting up her need to an almost unbearable level.

"Please," she whispered.

"Please what, Kelsey?" he challenged in that low, taunting tone. "Tell me."

She wagged her head like a restless mare, his stillness pushing her to desperation. "More, sir, *please.*"

"So pretty begging," he said, grazing her shoulder with his teeth and then sinking them into her neck. "You want to be fucked? Is that it?"

Wyatt thrust forward, burying himself deep and stretching her until his balls tapped her skin. A moan vibrated past her throat and her eyelids snapped shut. The sense of fullness was so fierce, so perfect, she almost came on the spot—the jets holding her on the brink already. But she clamped her teeth together and forced her eyes back open. *Focus.* She knew from being on the domme side that delayed gratification could be well worth it. The longer the tease, the bigger the payoff. But as he pumped forward again, she wondered if she had the strength to hold off.

She stared at the water sliding over the tiles, trying to cling to her last vestiges of self-control, but then the lights blinked and the room went black. She gasped in surprise, but Wyatt didn't falter. "Ignore it, love. I don't need light to make you feel good."

The walls of the shower flickered with the white lightning flashing through the skylights, the strobe light effect matching the disorienting feeling of having the man she'd so long lusted after pumping inside her.

"You know how many times I've thought of this, Kelsey? How long I've wanted you? How many times I've imagined taking you in the back of your restaurant, lifting up that sweet little skirt and having you just like this, bent over and at my mercy?"

The words landed hot on her, making her sex clamp around him, aching, begging. The picture he painted was one that could get her off almost by thought alone. *This* is what he'd been imagining when she'd served him omelets? Had she known that, she would've never been able to get through a shift without ruining her panties. She loved how dirty and deliciously deviant this seemingly buttoned-up man could be. "I would've let you, sir."

He gave a harsh grunt and gripped her waist hard, his fingers pressing into her skin with near bruising strength. Owning. Claiming. He thrust into her, rocking her into the shower jets. The bottom one was now hitting her clit with every forward thrust. *Wham. Wham. Wham.* Like some relentless hot tongue flicking at her in the dark. Pressure built low and fast, the stimulation making the ability to form thoughts go haywire.

"Hold on for me, Kelsey," Wyatt ground out. "I want you to go over with me."

"Yes," she gasped. "Please."

"Good girl. I want to feel you come all over my cock."

"God, yes," she moaned, her control slipping.

His pace increased and he fucked into her with abandon. Now she knew she'd have bruises on her hips. She didn't care. Bruise her. Brand her. Fuck her. He could do whatever he wanted right now. Her fingers had to be white against the shower wall as she pushed back against the onslaught of his erotic assault. Her nipples tingled in a constant state of arousal from the water, and every inch of her seemed to be glittering with bright need. Her body rocked against the shower spray, his cock pistoning into her, and her every molecule seemed to whirl and tighten. She wasn't going to be able to wait . . .

"Wyatt!" she cried out, her orgasm an unstoppable train of sensation and brute force.

A loud, rumbling groan tumbled out of him as he went over the edge with her, his cock swelling inside her and pulsing with his release. He rode the rocket launch with her, pumping inside her as unintelligible sounds passed her lips and her muscles began to shake with the power of it all. The feel of him, the water, the heat. Her head swam.

He banded an arm around her waist and swiveled her over and away from the jets, as if he'd known the exact moment when it all became too much for her. He held her against him, her back to his chest, his cock still inside her as she sucked in deep breaths, slowly finding her way down from all that intensity.

"Shh," he soothed. "You're okay, beautiful. Just take your time. I've got you."

The words were like warm balm to her twitching body. He slipped out of her, while still holding her upright, and tossed the condom to the shower floor. Then he led her back to the bench on the far side of the shower. He sat down and pulled her onto his lap, the steam wafting around them and the lightning still flashing through the skylights.

She curled into him, glad for the water and the dark. At least he wouldn't see that she was crying. Crying from relief, from physical exhaustion, and from the fact that she now knew there was no way she'd walk away from this unscathed.

This man could undo her.

This was gonna hurt.

TEN

Wyatt carried the bags of groceries they'd left in the car into the kitchen. He'd lit a few candles and put them on the island, but they barely provided enough light to work by. He peeked into the bags, confused as to why Kelsey had brought groceries with her. It wasn't like they could bring them on the trip. But maybe it had worked out after all because there was no option for going out to dinner now, and his cabinets were pretty bare. After their interlude in the shower, they needed more than granola bars and bananas to refuel.

The shower. He released a breath as he loaded the items into the darkened fridge. The night had not gone at all as planned. He'd promised himself he was going to handle this in a very calm and controlled manner. This kind of relationship, even if only for a week, was something that needed discussion, knowledge of individual limits, and negotiation. It had been irresponsible of him to just go after her like some overeager frat boy. But when he'd seen that haze of submissiveness fill her eyes, that doorway to subspace peeking open, he'd gone into conquering mode.

And she'd let him take over, given him leave to use her in exactly the way he desired. His own psyche's response to it had been potent and impossible to quell, the dominant needs in him no longer content staying buried. It had been so long since he'd allowed that horse out of the stable that everything had surged at once. Instead of easing her into it, taking it slow and letting them get used to each other, he'd charged forward like she'd been wearing his collar for months.

Physically, she'd responded beautifully to it, her body surrendering to him fully. But afterward, he'd sensed her closing in on herself. When he'd dried her off and wrapped a robe around her, her words had been lighthearted, but her expression had been shuttered. He'd pushed too hard too quickly, and she was retreating. He didn't like it. It was like a bright flag of challenge waving in front of him, taunting him. He wouldn't accept her shutting herself off from him. The training they were going to do had a big physical component, but the real heart of any D/s relationship was the psychological aspect. Without that, it was just playacting.

But this was partly his fault. He'd been the one to move too fast, sending her back behind her shields. So he wasn't going to push anymore tonight. They had things to discuss and plans to make anyway. He had seven days with her and possibly three additional weeks if they decided to continue the training when they returned from the trip. There'd be time to peel back those layers and find out what lay beneath.

A clicking sound from behind him dragged his attention from the refrigerator. Kelsey stood in the entryway of the kitchen in a pair of yoga pants and a long-sleeved T-shirt, the flashlight he'd given her in her hand. "There you are. I think I took a wrong turn at the bottom of the stairs. This is a big-ass house."

"I'm sorry. I should've put some candles in the living room to guide your way. Did you find everything you needed upstairs?"

"Yeah, thanks for bringing my bag up," she said, stepping

inside and giving him a once-over with the flashlight, sliding the orb of light down over his T-shirt and pajama bottoms and pausing at his bare feet. "Wow, you look different."

He started on the other bag of groceries, the corner of his mouth lifting. "I don't sleep in suits, you know."

"Well, one wonders."

He placed a block of cheese inside the fridge, then heard the electric whoosh of the power kicking back in. Lights blinked on above him, and the refrigerator hummed back to life. "Excellent."

He adjusted a few things on the shelf now that he could see where he was placing everything, but spun back around when he heard the gasp. Kelsey was still in the arched doorway, but her blue eyes were wide.

"What's wrong?"

"Ho-lee shit." She stepped inside, her bright pink top in sharp contrast to the all white room, and ran a hand along the granite countertops. "This is . . ."

"A kitchen?"

She gave him a don't-be-stupid look, and he lifted an eyebrow. He didn't get *that* look too often.

"I hate you so much right now," she declared.

"Okay . . ."

She walked over to the range and petted it like it was something precious. "Fuck, you have a *Viking*." Her head dropped forward as if she were praying at the altar of appliances. "And let me guess, you don't even cook."

"I'm . . . sorry?" Her accusatory tone seemed to indicate an apology was necessary. "I have a cook, does that count?"

"No." She raised her hand at her side, keeping her back to him, but silencing him all the same. "Give me a second. I think I'm sporting girl wood."

The laugh burst out of him, echoing up the vaulted ceilings. "Over my stove?"

"Shh."

But he couldn't help himself. "So if I ever need to get you in the mood, I should have kitchen catalogs on hand?"

She spun around with a smirk, but he couldn't help but notice the sharp little points now pressing against that fitted top.

He chuckled even harder.

"What?" she asked, pressing her lips together, obviously on the verge of a laugh herself.

He waved a hand in her direction, trying to keep his eyes from straying downward again, to no avail. "Nothing. Never mind."

"Oh, come on. What?" Then she followed his glance and saw what was impossible to miss. She crossed her arms over her chest, mock offense on her face. "Hey, it's cold in here. And my hair's still a little wet."

He nodded solemnly. "Uh-huh. Or you just got turned on by a range."

She harrumphed and snagged a bag of oranges he'd taken out of one of the grocery sacks, turning to the opposite counter and keeping those perky nipples out of view. "Hey, we all have our kinks, right?"

"Clearly. Makes mental note to bring a spatula and a wooden spoon on our trip to satisfy your kitchen fetish."

She made a noise that sounded suspiciously like a snort. *God, sexy and so fucking cute on top of it.*

"So what's with the groceries?" he asked.

She turned around and shrugged. "I had heard the weather was supposed to get bad and thought we'd eat here instead. Plus, considering the things we have to discuss, I figured a private setting may be better."

He leaned against the island. "You could've mentioned it to me. I would've have Ms. Murel prepare something for us before she left for the day."

The side of her mouth lifted. "I thought I'd cook for you. You know, as a thank you. And because I enjoy it and rarely get to do it for someone outside of the cafe."

"Oh." The idea warmed him in a surprising way, that she'd want to prepare something for him. He couldn't remember the last time someone not on his payroll had made a home-cooked meal for him. Even growing up, meals were always cooked by staff. "Well, I'd like that."

The smile that crossed her face brightened the whole room. "Good. You sit down then, and we can work out the stuff for the trip while I get things prepared. I'm going for simple since I'm starved and don't have the patience to wait for anything slow-cooked."

"Simple sounds great." He sat down on one of the stools at the island and pointed out where everything was as she set up her prep area.

Once she had the tools she needed and started chopping some of the vegetables for the pasta dish she was making, she got right down to business. "I know you want to talk about negotiating limits and such. But I don't think we need to spend a lot of time on that. I'm not a novice, so I know what those checklists look like. My main hard limit is that I'm not into verbal humiliation. I've been called enough names in my life. I don't want my lover doing it. Also, I don't want to be shared."

He frowned. "I would never do that, Kelsey. That's not my style."

She expertly sliced through an onion, her movements sure and efficient. "Good."

"How do you feel about pain play?" he asked, fascinated as she scooped the diced onion to the side and ran the knife through a pile of mushrooms with delicate precision.

Something flickered across her features. *Fear?* But she quickly covered it. "I can't handle canes, single-tailed whips, knife play, or face slapping. And nothing that would require me to take something stronger than aspirin the next day. I try to stay away from medications."

He nodded. He suspected there was much more behind those limits than she was letting on. The medication one was a pretty obvious tell—she was running from a drug dealer after all. But the expression that had crossed her face at the mention of pain play had a cold feeling gripping his gut. He wanted to ask her more about it, but promised himself he wouldn't push her anymore tonight. "Fine. Any other hard limits?"

"No. And I'm on the pill and have my medical reports with me. I also got yours this week. So if you want to skip condoms, I'm okay with that."

He steepled his fingers in front of him, considering her. He didn't go without condoms. Ever. He trusted that Kelsey was telling the truth about her birth control, but he couldn't take even the slightest risk that she wasn't. He'd seen how pregnancy could be used as a weapon, especially when one person was from a certain lot in life and the other wasn't. The thought was ugly, but he wasn't going to let the wildly enticing thought of being inside Kelsey bare make him stupid. "I prefer to use condoms regardless."

She glanced up at him, her gaze knowing and a little wry. She shrugged. "No problem. The safe words at The Ranch are *yellow* for a pause and a check-in and *Texas* for everything to stop. Are you okay with me using those?"

"Whatever is easiest for you to remember." He couldn't help but notice how she'd taken control of the negotiation. What had happened tonight had obviously sent her back to her comfort zone of calling the shots. He let it slide. For now.

She gathered all the veggies in a bowl and brought them over to the stove where she heated a pan and drizzled some olive oil in it. "So let's get to the important stuff. Do I need a fake name?

Like are people going to expect me to have some recognizable well-to-do family name?"

He frowned. "Not an awful idea. We have to use your real passport, but no one at the retreat should have to see that. How about we use Kelsey Adams? It's common enough to blend in and easy to remember."

"All right. I can work with that. So how did we meet?"

"Through mutual friends." He watched her there, looking so at home by the stove, her movements efficient, second nature, and came up with an off-the-cuff backstory. "You were looking for an investor for a restaurant you want to open."

She peeked over her shoulder. "Why would I have come to you for that?"

"I do some venture capitalist stuff on the side, invest in local startups on occasion. Or help businesses expand like I did with Jace's store. I'm a silent partner in that now."

"Wow, that must be fun to do."

"What do you mean?"

"Giving someone money to help their dream business get up and running. It's got to feel like being a fairy godmother or something."

He smirked, amused by the notion. "You make it sound quite romantic, but it's not an emotional decision. It's simply business. If I believe something will make money, it's a good use of my funds."

"I want a bakery."

"Hmm?" he said, dragging the cutting board to his side of the island and taking it upon himself to slice the French baguette she'd bought.

"Let's make the story that I wanted to open a bakery. If I get to create a faux life, I may as well use my real pie-in-the-sky goals to fill it."

"You want a bakery?"

She tossed some minced garlic into the sizzling oil. "I love to cook anything and everything, but my first love is pastry."

"Then a bakery you shall have," he said resolutely. "We can say that you've put those plans on hold for now since you want to refine your natural skills by going to culinary school."

She gave a quick nod of agreement. "How long have we been seeing each other?"

He sliced another piece of bread, failing in his effort to make each slice the same size. "Let's say two months. I was seen out at events with someone else before that, so that would make the most sense."

"Someone else?" Kelsey asked, adding the rest of the vegetables, all except the mushrooms. "A girlfriend?"

"A colleague."

She stirred the contents of the pan. "Who you were sleeping with."

"Yes," he said, not liking where this conversation was going.

"And why isn't she around anymore?"

He sent her a warning glance when she peeked his way again. "Is that so important to know?"

"I'm exceptionally nosy. You should know that about me." She flashed him an unapologetic smile. "My sister always joked that I should've become a therapist like her since I'm so fascinated by other people's personal lives."

He shook his head. Usually he was as private and tight-lipped about his life as anyone could be, even his brother had to drag things out of him. But Wyatt was having trouble mustering up the will to dodge Kelsey's questioning. "She knew what she was getting into when we started seeing each other. Her feelings changed over time, and she wanted more. I didn't."

She added the mushrooms, then poured cream into the mix and added a few pats of butter. "Sounds complicated."

"It wasn't. At least not on my end."

She seemed to consider that for a moment, her back to him. Then she dipped a spoon into the simmering sauce and turned around, blowing gently across the steaming sauce she'd captured. "Are all the things in your life always that cut and dried? That neat?"

He looked down at the uneven slices of bread, the imperfection annoying him more than it should. "I try to keep it that way. Yes."

"Mmm," she said, some indiscernible judgment underlying the innocuous sound. She held out the spoon for him to taste. "And then you invite a waitress, who has a gang after her, on a business trip. Are you sure you're not the practical Wyatt Austin's reckless twin brother? This is anything but neat."

He opened his mouth to answer but she guided the spoon forward. The delicate cream sauce hit his tongue, the buttery decadence balanced perfectly with the fresh herbs she'd added to it. "That's delicious."

She sniffed. "Of course it is. Told you I can cook."

"And no, I'm not my evil twin brother. But being around you does tend to tempt me away from my best laid plans. I was supposed to take things slow tonight."

She reached for his hand and gave it a squeeze. "To be honest, I'm kind of glad you didn't. I was getting really nervous to come over here tonight. After a week apart, I thought it might be awkward. Plus, despite what happened at The Ranch, it's still hard to wrap my head around all this. It feels a little surreal."

He curled his fingers around hers, rubbing a thumb over her wrist. "Surreal?"

"A few weeks ago, I was serving you eggs and now I'm—"

"Serving me, period," he said softly.

Her lashes dipped. "Yes."

He lifted her hand to his mouth and kissed the center of her palm. "It's just as surreal for me, love. Maybe best laid plans aren't all they're cracked up to be."

He could see her throat work as she swallowed hard. "You ready for dinner?"

"I'm ready for it all."

ELEVEN

Kelsey finished wiping down the table in the kitchen and loaded their dishes into the dishwasher while the storm still hammered the house. Wyatt had told her not to worry about any of the cleanup. He had a housekeeper who would be there the next day. But she wouldn't have been able to sleep knowing that dirty dishes were in the sink. Her sister, Brynn, had ingrained in her that no food was to ever be left out. They'd waged a constant battle with roaches in the crappy little rental they'd lived in growing up, and the habit of making sure everything was spotless had never gone away. In her days of addiction, she'd lost sight of that, but it'd been the first thing she'd gotten back on track with once she'd sobered up. Clean house meant clean Kelsey.

She washed and dried her hands, then took a deep breath. Time to get back to Wyatt. She didn't know what else he had planned for tonight, but she wasn't sure she could survive another round with him. The experience in the shower had flayed her. Her emotions felt raw and exposed, like shredded power lines writhing and sparking with danger. She'd managed to keep things relaxed and light during dinner, but beneath her smiles and jokes, she'd been trying to piece herself back together, slapping duct tape on broken shit and hoping it held together.

She needed to figure out how to hold on to some shred of control in all of this. Otherwise, she wouldn't survive him. She knew how she could be. In the past, she'd fallen too hard and too fast. And always for the wrong men. Her heart was entirely untrustworthy. She needed to keep that part of her out of this. Sex she could do. To endure those three days with Davis, she'd figured out how to shut off her emotions and just exist as something to be used. She didn't need to go that far with Wyatt, but if she'd learned anything over the years, it was how men wouldn't look too far past that physical stuff. She could play the vixen, the seductress, and that was enough for a guy. And someone like Wyatt, a man who treated his interactions with women like neat business arrangements, would probably be more than happy to keep it at that level, too. She could let the other stuff stay tucked away out of sight.

She turned off the light in the kitchen. Wyatt had told her he had a few phone calls to make, but when she walked into the living room, she found him frowning at the flatscreen TV that was perched above the massive stone fireplace. The weather radar filled the screen, complete with a lot of green blotches and an ominous swath of red. The television was on mute, but words ran across the bottom of the screen at a rapid pace.

"Everything okay?" she asked, stopping behind the cream-toned leather couch.

He glanced her way, then back to the screen. "They've just issued a tornado warning. A wall cloud was spotted a few miles west of here. You see that little dot of blue over there." He pointed. "That's the lake not far from here."

"Well, shit."

As if on cue, the slow-building whine of the county tornado

sirens started up outside—faint at first and then blaring as the siren rotated in their direction. Kelsey hugged her elbows, the sound familiar but no less eerie every time. She'd lived in Texas all her life and had gone through this ritual many a time, but those sirens never failed to ratchet fear right through her. "Where's the best closet to hide in?"

Wyatt got to his feet and held out a hand to her. "Come on. I've got a better place."

The rain turned from a pattering to the plink of tiny hail stones against the windows as Wyatt led her down an interior hallway and past a number of doors. At the final door on the left, he stopped and turned the knob. "Watch your step. The stairs are a little narrow."

"You have a basement?" she asked in disbelief. That was about as rare as having a snow blower in this part of the world.

"Sort of," he said, leading her down the narrow staircase and shutting the door behind them. The steps were carpeted and as they went lower, the sounds from above faded, leaving a thick silence behind.

When they reached the bottom, he turned a knob on a panel of controls on the right side wall, bringing the dark room into view. Recessed lights slowly came to full strength from above and illuminated the posh leather couch and chairs in the center of the room. On the far left, there was a wall of dark wood shelving packed from floor to ceiling. But what drew her attention was the large screen gracing the main wall. It was a movie lover's dream come true. "Wow."

He let go of her hand, shifting his stance and looking a little uncomfortable all of a sudden. "We're below ground level in here. So we should be fine if anything comes through."

"This is some personal theater," she said, crossing the thick red carpet and walking over to the wall of shelves. Rows and rows of DVDs filled the spaces. More than she'd ever seen in one place before. She scanned some of the titles, running her finger along the spines. "Wow. Did you buy out Blockbuster?"

He cleared his throat. "I have a bit of a thing for film."

She peeked over her shoulder, amused at the faint edge of embarrassment in his tone. Wyatt Austin could be sheepish about something? Who knew? She'd never seen even a chink in his collected facade, but she found the little glimpse more than a bit endearing. "I would say so."

She went back to scanning. There was obviously some prescribed order to the collection, but it definitely wasn't alphabetical. Her finger ran over a group of foreign films, then what looked to be Academy Award winners, and the last of the row was a group of eighties teen movies: *Back to the Future, The Breakfast Club, Ferris Bueller's Day Off, Dirty Dancing.*

She grabbed the last one and spun around, smiling. "*Dirty Dancing*? Tell the truth. You only have this one to woo women when they come over, right? No straight man voluntarily owns this movie."

He rubbed a hand over the back of his head. "For the record, I've never taken a date down here. But truth be told, I got that one for when my sister, Leila, comes over. It's her favorite movie."

She grinned. "She and my sister would probably get along. Brynn used to be obsessed with this movie when we were growing up. Always the hopeless romantic."

"And you're not?" He sat down on the couch, propping an elbow on the back cushion.

Not anymore. Life had beaten that ridiculous notion out of her.

"Hardly." She turned and slid the movie back in its place. "My favorite movie growing up was *Terminator 2*."

"Good choice. Amazing effects. Four Oscars."

"Plus Sarah Connor was badass. I like movies that make me laugh or scare the crap out of me. That one did a little of both."

She lifted her head to peek at the row above her. Documentaries. Horror. Sci-Fi. And enough Hitchcock to require its own section. "You've got so many. Have you actually seen all of these?"

"Every one of them. Many more than once." He shifted on the couch to fully face her. "I got kind of obsessed with movies when I was a kid."

She walked over and sat on the opposite side of the couch, pulling her knees to her chest. "How come?"

His shrug was near imperceptible. "The whole genius IQ thing has its perks now, but wasn't so much fun when I was young. Academic stuff made sense to me, but I was a disaster on the social front. I couldn't read other people at all. It was like they were using a different language—saying one thing but really meaning another. And my father had no tolerance for that deficit, so he was always pushing me into social situations."

She sat her chin on her knees and wrapped her arms around her legs. She'd already figured Wyatt's father wasn't dad of the year based on how he'd disowned Jace. But the guy sounded like an unsympathetic asshole. "That must've been a nightmare."

"Looking back, I'm glad he didn't let me get away with hiding from it. This world isn't built for introverts. But it felt like sink or swim back then. So, I started to watch movies and TV shows as a way to study people, to teach myself to read expressions and subtext and subtle shifts in body language. Actors are more deliberate about it than everyday people. I had to learn that when someone's lip curled, they were usually being sarcastic. Or that laughter didn't always signal something was funny. Picking up those cues didn't come naturally to me."

"And like everything else, you became the master at it," she guessed.

"I was determined to. I also became a fount of useless movie trivia."

"So why don't you ever bring girls down to your secret movie lair? It's pretty cozy down here." And probably soundproof. For someone who hadn't practiced BDSM in a long time, Wyatt had a near perfect setup for a private dungeon. Maybe he wasn't telling the whole truth about his supposed hiatus.

He lifted an eyebrow. "You don't believe me?"

She blinked, disconcerted by his spot-on assessment. "What?"

"Doubt just crossed your face," he said, laying his arm across the back of the couch. "I assure you, you're the first woman I've brought down here who's not family. I don't make a habit of exposing my geeky pastimes to others."

She smiled. "It's not *that* geeky. And I actually had a little bit of weird TV thing myself as a kid. I was obsessed with all those old shows from the fifties and sixties. *Donna Reed*, *The Patty Duke Show*, *Dennis the Menace*. Other kids were into cartoons and I just wanted to watch black-and-white sitcoms on Nick at Nite and dress like I belonged in *Grease*."

"Huh," he said, tilting his head as if intrigued by her revelation. "Why do you think you were so drawn to that?"

She shrugged. "My childhood wasn't exactly conventional, so I guess I was fascinated by these families where dads came home every day and moms cooked casseroles and everybody seemed so damned happy. Looking back, that's probably what drew me to cooking in the first place. A home-cooked meal represented some piece of that fantasy world. So when my sister started college, I bought this stack of old Betty Crocker cookbooks at a garage sale and started trying the recipes. Brynn probably never wants to eat anything made with Cream of Mushroom soup again."

He smiled, but it didn't touch his eyes; compassion rested there instead. "Why didn't you go to culinary school after high school?"

She combed her fingers through her hair, not wanting to have this conversation. "I wasn't in a good place back then. Partying and my boyfriend became much bigger priorities than casseroles."

"Ah," he said, those watchful eyes still on her.

"So were you into TV as much as movies?" she asked, desperate to get the topic back to something safe.

"Not as much, but I can recite entire episodes of *Family Ties* and *The Cosby Show*. Not pretty."

"I never saw either of those."

A brief look of horror crossed his face, then he shook his head. "Man, I keep forgetting how young you are. I think I'm in denial."

She smirked and stretched her legs out, pressing her feet against his thigh. "I'm old enough in the ways that count. And truth be told, there are days I feel like I've lived three lifetimes already."

He slipped a hand around her ankle, rubbing a thumb along the delicate bones as he watched her. "An old soul."

A wounded one at least. But she didn't say that part out loud. They weren't here to dig into her ugly, good-girl-gone-bad life. That was off limits. She allowed her other foot to slide up and over his thigh, her toes tracking closer to his crotch. Maybe if she could get the focus redirected back to the reason they were here, he'd stop looking at her like he wanted to scoop all her secrets out of her.

He locked his other hand around the ankle of her roaming foot, his grip firm. "I don't remember giving you permission to touch me there, love."

She wet her lips and lowered her lashes, going into her safe zone—temptress mode. "Are you complaining? We've got nothing better to do while we wait out the storm."

His gaze narrowed as he held both her ankles and moved them away from his lap. "That's not going to work on me, Kelsey."

She frowned, her spine stiffening. "What are you talking about?"

"I know you're used to controlling the situation. And not many men could resist that come-hither look you just threw my way. But you need to know, it's not a wise tactic to take with me. Topping from the bottom won't be acceptable."

"I wasn't—"

He let go of her ankles. "Stand up."

She bit the inside of her cheek to keep from talking back again and got to her feet. He was right. She'd known exactly what she'd been doing. And if the roles had been reversed and a submissive had tried that with her, she wouldn't have let it slide either. But she hadn't expected Wyatt to take this so seriously. They liked each other, had good chemistry. Wasn't having a little sexy fun what this was about?

But clearly she'd underestimated Wyatt in this arena. She'd expected him to throw some power around in the bedroom, act the part. But as he followed her movements with a hard gaze and a locked jaw, she realized he wasn't putting on a show at all. He may be out of practice, but this was no role. This was who he was—the real man beneath the urbane surface.

She swallowed hard, honest fear entering the equation for the first time. Wyatt was expecting her to truly submit. For this to be real. He wanted her surrender. Her palms went damp.

And so did her panties.

She blinked, surprised at her body's almost instant response. "I'm sorry, sir."

He pointed at a spot on the floor. "In front of me. Now."

She lowered her head and stepped to where he'd indicated, standing between his spread knees. She couldn't miss the twitch in his pajama pants, his own arousal stirring. She had the ridiculous urge to fall to her knees and beg his forgiveness, to take him in her hand, her mouth, to replace that look of disappointment with one of pleasure.

What. The. Fuck?

She clenched her fists. This wasn't how she responded to men. She had the utmost respect for both sides of the D/s dynamic, but she was *not* on the *s* side. Why was her mind trying to sink?

"Stop fighting your natural response or you're going to earn more punishment," he said, his tone cool but his gaze hot.

"I'm not fighting anything."

He sighed and reached out to unfurl her clenched fists. "I hope you realize the more you try to scramble for a ledge to grab, the harder I'm going to tug."

She shifted her weight from one foot to the other, his quiet threat making it hard to be still. "This is only supposed to be training, sir. It's not required for me to go into total surrender mode. I can't. It's not how I'm wired."

His smile was slow, ominous. And she realized that instead of warning him off, she'd set a challenge in front of a man who fed on winning. *Shit.*

"Strip, Kelsey."

"Sir—"

"Ten seconds to get out of those clothes or I'm yanking them off you."

Her limbs reacted before her brain caught up, her hands grappling for the hem of her shirt. She hustled out of her garments, sparing any grace. He couldn't make her surrender if she didn't want to let him. Her mind was her own. But she had agreed to this training, and she wasn't going to continue being a brat about it. Physically, she could handle whatever he wanted to mete out. And if she was honest, she was looking forward to that part. Having his hands on her earlier had been one of the most thrilling moments she could ever remember having with any man. But if he expected her to succumb to the mindfuck part of the program, he was going to be sorely disappointed. She was just getting her mind put back together. He wasn't allowed in there.

Hopefully, her body would be enough. It always had been in her past relationships.

She bent forward and slipped out of her underwear, then straightened, standing bare before him. His eyes tracked over her from crown to foot, his perusal like hot coals rolling over her skin. She shivered, her nipples tightening and her heartbeat picking up speed. He had a way of looking at her that made everything else around her seem to fade and blur, like the only thing that existed in the world was him and his desire to have her.

His tongue swept over his bottom lip, a little tell. Like he was working hard to keep his composure and not pounce on her. She almost wished he would. That would prove she was really in control after all. But he didn't move. "Over my knees, love."

She closed her eyes for a second, shoring up her nerve. She could do this. Pain wasn't her concern. She'd handled outright brutality and survived. But the spark of lightning that had gone through her at the mere suggestion of his hand on her backside had her more than a little panicked. She wasn't supposed to like this part. "Yes, sir."

She circled to the side of his legs, then lowered herself downward, draping herself across his lap. Before she could press her fingertips to the floor to balance herself, he captured each of her wrists and drew them behind her back, holding her in place and rendering her completely dependent on his hold not to fall. She swallowed back the anxiety that was tightening her throat.

A soft expelled breath coasted over her tailbone as Wyatt took in the view. "I could be polite and say that I won't enjoy punishing you." His hand caressed the curve of her ass, softly, reverently. "But you look so fucking sexy like this, I find myself hoping you'll try to get defiant with me again."

"I didn't mean to be defiant, sir," she whispered, her body beginning to thrum with anticipation. Each caress he gave her was like a dump of electricity into her bloodstream, sending every bit of her into a vibrating, needy state. Her skin began to warm beneath his hand. She found her lips moving in silent pleas. Pleading for more, for the sting of his palm. She didn't know what to do with that foreign desire, but she was beyond the point of being able to tap it down or analyze it too deeply.

His knuckle traced her slit, the telltale moisture sliding along his skin. A soft whimper passed her lips. "Very nice, love. Now, five swats for trying to top, and ten more for talking back to me twice. Do you understand?"

"Yes, sir."

"And no coming."

"How would I come from—"

His hand came down on her with a breath-stealing blow. Her body rocked forward, the hot sting rippling over her backside and the flannel of his pants brushing her clit with wicked accuracy.

Sensation rumbled through her. And before she could suck in a breath, he spanked her again—once, twice, three times. *Smack! Smack! Smack!* Each time brushing her sensitive bits more roughly against his legs. *Fuuuuuck.* The pain and edgy pleasure twined together, and she let out a woeful, desperate moan.

"That's right, love. Feel it all."

His hand came down again, and her brain began to buzz. This was different. So different than what she'd experienced before. Pure. Sweet. *Good.* Without conscious effort, her toes pushed into the floor, lifting her ass higher for his hands. He smacked her again, right at her center. Hard. Thoughts evaporated. Like the string of a balloon slipping from a child's fingertips, she grabbed for that last ribbon of control. But it was too late.

It was already gone.

She was already gone.

TWELVE

Wyatt recognized the exact moment Kelsey slid under. Her body softened against his legs, the tension in her muscles melting into liquid warmth. His. Completely. The sight knocked him right off his rhythm. His cock throbbed against the fly of his pants as he lifted his hand and brought it down on the lower curve of Kelsey's ass. Her smooth, golden skin had gone the prettiest shade of fiery pink. He had the urge to lean down and lick the stinging marks he was leaving, to feel the heat of her against his tongue. And God, her scent. Sexy and spicy and sweet.

He nudged her thighs open a bit wider, exposing the swollen lips of her pussy and the shiny moisture glistening there. Despite her resistance to get to this point, her body was obviously on board. And his was about to explode from the vision of her gorgeous surrender. He pushed the hand he had holding her wrists more firmly against her back and then slid two fingers from his free hand inside her, stroking her in a spot he knew would test her ability to hold off orgasm.

She jolted in his hold, the hot, wet clasp of her sex clamping down around him and nearly making him groan aloud. He wanted to be inside her so badly, to feel her around his cock again. But he didn't keep condoms down here, and there was no way he was walking away from her for even a second. Not when he'd managed to push her into the yielding state she'd made clear she had no intention of getting to.

He stroked her inner wall again, slow and steady, determined to drag her even deeper into her body, her responses. No escape. No separating her psyche from the fact that *he* was the one making her feel this way. She huffed breaths as she fought her way through the need to come. "Wyatt, please . . ."

"Shh," he said, the soft begging making him even harder. He loved that he could bring her to this desperate point, to make such a strong woman plead, that she trusted him enough—whether consciously or unconsciously—to let him see her this way. "You have five more swats left, love."

He slipped his fingers from inside her, earning him another soft whimper, then took his time delivering the rest of the blows. A nicer man would've made quick work of it, would've let her off the hook. But he was enjoying her too much. Even when he'd been deep in the scene in college, spanking hadn't been a particular fetish of his, but he could see it quickly becoming one with Kelsey. He could imagine himself spending hours bringing Kelsey to the brink and back, reveling in those sounds and quivers she made.

He put his strength into the last blow, the power of it rocking her roughly against his lap. Kelsey cried out but it was all gritty desperation now, not pain. She was way past that point, writhing against his legs, seeking the last little bit of stimulation that would send her over. But this was punishment after all, and he wasn't going to grant her what she wanted quite yet.

He released her arms, being sure to keep her steady, and eased her to her knees on the floor in front of him. She let out a soft mewl of protest but kept her gaze downward, her blonde hair damp and framing her flushed cheeks. Beautiful. Perfect.

"Look at me, Kelsey."

She raised her face to him, those blue eyes soft and yielding. Eager.

He tucked his hand inside his pajama pants, taking his now-aching cock in his palm. "You see what you do to me. How much I love having you under my hand?"

"Yes, sir," she whispered as she watched his hand with rapt attention. He pulled his cock free of his pants and stroked upward. The tip of her tongue touched her lips.

"I was going to fuck you again tonight. Was going to bring you to my bed, take my time, and taste every sweet bit of you."

A pained look crossed her face.

"But you tried to push the issue. To control how things went down. And so now instead of tonight being about me pleasuring you, you will please me instead."

She nodded. "I understand. I want to please you, sir."

He rubbed the bead of moisture along the crest of his dick, watching her watch him. She wanted this. Either the submissive in her had kicked into full stride, and the thought of pleasuring him would please her. Or the defiant part of her knew that the best way to get the upper hand on a male dominant was to bring him past the brink of his self-control—and her mouth around his cock would be a surefire way to get there.

Either way, he was one step ahead of her. She just didn't know it yet.

He spread his thighs wide, clasping his fingers around the base of his cock. "Take me in your mouth, love. Show me how much you yearn to please."

Kelsey's lips twitched at the corners, a secret smile. Oh, yeah, the effect of the spanking was fading and she was looking for a way to grab the wheel again. She scooted forward on her knees and with the litheness of a cat, lowered herself to his lap, wrapping her lips around the head of his cock and sliding down, down, *down*. Slow. Past the point where most women stopped. He felt the tip of him tap the back of her throat.

He didn't hold back the strangled groan that welled up in him. "Fuck, that's good."

She lifted her gaze, locking with his, as she slowly dragged her lips and tongue upward, caressing him in the hottest, wettest, sensual slide. His feet arched—actually fucking arched—with the sensation of it all. He laced a hand in her hair, gripping the side of her skull as she continued her expertly crafted assault. And that's what it was, a full frontal assault on his willpower.

As if sensing the tug-o-war shifting in her favor, she let his cock slip from her mouth, then dipped lower, gliding her tongue along the base and laving at his sac. Like she loved it. Like she craved a taste of every part of him. And regardless of skill or experience, nothing was hotter than a woman who sincerely enjoyed giving pleasure—not marking time until it was her turn but truly relishing every moment her mouth was on him. Unable to stop himself, he grabbed his cock with his free hand to stroke as she took one of his balls in her mouth.

Fuck. Me. His eyes felt dangerously close to rolling into the back of his head.

Then, as if to prove she wasn't going to let up until he completely lost it, her spit-slicked fingers teased lower, along his perineum and ringing the sensitive rim of his ass. His hips lifted off the couch, his body going taut with the onslaught of responses firing in his body. His balls drew up tight, his whole system on the verge of meltdown. He thought he'd been prepared for the feel of her, had a plan, but goddammit, she was throwing grenades at him left and right. This woman knew exactly how to bring a man to his knees.

With the last shred of control he possessed, he gripped her

hair and tugged her away. Ragged words scraped across his vocal cords. "Enough, love."

She blinked up at him in confusion with big doe eyes that nearly made him lose his resolve. "Did I do something wrong?"

"No, you're doing everything too fucking right. Believe me." He released her hair. "Turn around, face down, let me see my marks on your pretty skin."

Though she seemed taken aback by the shift, she followed his instruction, turning and lowering herself into a graceful pose, arms stretched out in front of her, the long line of her back and the curve of her ass exposed to him, knees parted. The pink welts on her flesh only served to make his cock throb harder in his hand.

He leaned forward on the couch, reaching down, and dipped his fingers into her pussy. Christ, she was soaked, the evidence of her arousal now coating part of her inner thighs. He couldn't remember ever seeing someone so fucking sexy. He drew her moisture onto his fingers, then pulled out and brought them back up to his cock, coating himself with her juices and mixing it with the slickness she'd left behind from her mouth. Her scent wafted up as it hit his hot skin, wrapping around him as he pumped his cock with his fist.

It was no substitute for her mouth or the feel of her body around him, but the sacrifice was vital to reiterate who was in control. He needed her to see that he wasn't going to let her down in this training by being easily manipulated. Every response she'd given him showed how much her body and mind craved this kind of surrender. She might not be ready to accept it yet, but he was more than ready to show her how much he wanted to be the one to bring her there.

"Touch yourself for me, love. You have permission to come when I do."

He stroked his fist along his cock with measured speed, drawing out the inevitable, savoring the sight of Kelsey bowed and spread before him. She braced herself on one arm and reached between her thighs, those slender fingers parting her folds and rubbing her clit. No hesitation. No shame.

He loved that unapologetic sexuality of hers. In front of the world, she came across as that sweet girl next door with the secret smile. But behind the scenes, she was vixen personified, a woman who didn't worry about how "nice" girls were supposed to act. And after living his life in circles where "proper" behavior was like religion, the sight of Kelsey taking her own pleasure was enough to make his blood feel like it was going to burst out of his veins.

"That's right. Show me how you like to be touched."

She tilted her head back, her spine arching, and slid two fingers inside with a breathy moan. Her hips rocked against her hand as she alternated fucking herself and stimulating her clit. Wyatt found himself mesmerized and unconsciously matched her rhythm, as if it was his cock pumping inside her instead of her fingers. He gripped himself hard as he stroked, thrusting into his fist as Kelsey's speed increased.

Acting on pure instinct now, he reached out and smacked her still-pink ass as he charged closer to release.

"Ah, God." Her back bowed again and she let out the cry, her fingers moving even faster. "Please . . ."

Seeing her react so well to the pain only dialed up his need more. He hit her again, his balls tightening and the pressure building inside him. "Come with me, love."

Kelsey's hair touched her back as she arched with the first wave of her orgasm, and pleasure exploded through Wyatt, racing down his nerve endings and outward. He moaned as his release slammed into him, his cock pulsing and fluid jetting forward, splashing against Kelsey's bare back.

Kelsey let out a few more gasps, her orgasm quick and intense, then she sank onto her elbows, head to the floor, panting. She looked spent and a mess, in the best possible way—her skin pink with his handprints and her back covered with his semen.

Marked. By him.

A dangerous warmth stirred in his chest at the sight. *No, don't go there.*

Wyatt tugged off his T-shirt and wiped his hands, then gently cleaned the remnants of his release from her skin. "Kneel up, love."

With languid movements, she pushed herself upward, and he wrapped the throw blanket he'd grabbed from a nearby chair around her. She didn't fight him when he kissed her gently, picked her up, and brought her onto the couch with him. He arranged her across the cushions and then tucked himself beneath her, letting her rest her head in his lap. Not wanting to break the moment with a lot of talk, he turned on the television, keeping it on mute, to check on the storm.

"I'm sorry I talked back," she said, nuzzling into position like a cat. "I know better than that."

"Shh." He combed his fingers through her hair, stroking any remaining tension from her and enjoying having her there at his fingertips. "Was the punishment so bad?"

She smiled a bit, but kept her eyes closed. "Nah, but I may have trouble sitting on the plane tomorrow."

He chuckled. "Will it be wrong if I find you squirming in your seat particularly arousing?"

"Sadist," she said with a real smile now.

"Only a little."

She got quiet for a while, and he thought she'd dozed off, but then she shifted against his lap. "Thank you for that. I've never . . . men have hit me before . . . but I've never enjoyed it or felt safe while it was happening."

He continued to stroke her hair even though her words made

his other hand ball into a fist. She'd said it as if she'd just tried a little pain play before and it hadn't worked. But he heard the hesitation in her voice, the part she wasn't saying. Men had hit her without her consent. The thought of anyone hurting her had murderous notions forming in his head. And he couldn't stop the under-the-breath question from slipping out. "What happened to you, love?"

Her breathing stopped for a moment, like an animal caught in the beam of a flashlight.

"It's okay if you don't want to talk about it," he said softly. "But the more I know, the better this will work for both of us. I don't want to do something that's going to inadvertently hurt you."

She lay there for a long time, her hand idly tracing over his knee, and he thought she'd decided not to share, but finally she seemed to deflate, releasing all her breath. "Did Jace tell you what happened last year when Reid was shot?"

His stroking paused. "Jace and I weren't really talking a lot then, but I saw the news story. Reid and your sister tracked down your mom's murderer."

Kelsey wet her lips, her focus fixed on the TV screen but a far-off look in her eyes. "No other names were ever released because of the nature of the crimes. But Brynn didn't track him down randomly. She was chasing after him because Davis had kidnapped me. I had incriminating evidence he wanted. He held me against my will for three days—beating me mostly, raping me twice."

"Sweet Jesus." His blood turned to ice and a sick, clammy feeling washed over him.

She closed her eyes, the muscle in her jaw twitching. "I'm not telling you to get sympathy. I don't want that. But you probably should know . . . in case I freak out over something. I don't get panic attacks or anything, and I've worked through a lot of it with a therapist, but occasionally there are nightmares. And relinquishing control will probably always be a little scary for me."

Wyatt could barely breathe he was so horrified on her behalf. God, how had she gone through so much brutal trauma and still come out on the other side with such a bright light still burning in her? The strength of will that had to have required awed him. If he'd gone through something like that, he didn't know if he'd ever be able to face life with anything but hate and why-me bitterness. "Baby, I can't even—"

She turned her head to look at him, her blue eyes pleading.

"Please, don't," she said softly. "I was scared to tell you because I didn't want that look. I was a victim of a crime. But I'm not a victim now, and I don't want you to treat me like one. Or change what we're doing because of it. I can't bear it. I need you to treat me like the Kelsey you met at the Sugarcane. That's who I want to be. It's who I am underneath all the other crap."

He brushed hair off her face, a knot of tears in his throat. "That's the only girl I see, love."

She gave a little nod, her eyes shiny. "Thank you."

She rose up to brush a kiss across his lips, then snuggled back down on his lap. She didn't say anything else after that, and after a while her breathing became deep and regular, her body limp against him. He moved a few strands of hair away from her face, watching her sleep. She looked even younger and more fragile in slumber, the wounds in her eyes hidden. His instinct to protect and shelter welled up in him in an overwhelming rush. This woman deserved a champion, a warrior to shield her from any future hurt. But he couldn't stop his mind from drifting backward in time, to when someone else had put herself in his hands.

He'd thought back then that he could handle it, that he could slay dragons and save the girl he loved both from outside forces and from herself by taking the reins. But he'd been a prideful idiot to think he could handle that kind of responsibility. That kind of relationship couldn't be maintained long-term, at least not with him. He didn't have the time or the self-control to be somebody's everything.

But right now, he wasn't going to question the universe's unexpected gift of Kelsey LeBreck. His life wasn't set up for a forever arrangement, but right now he had seven precious days to savor this beautiful, amazing woman. And he wasn't going to waste a second of it. He couldn't erase her past and he couldn't be her future, but he could give her exactly what she wanted and needed right now—a few days to be the fun, carefree girl she hoped to one day become.

Trying not to jostle her too much, Wyatt pulled Kelsey into his arms, arranged the blanket around her, then stood. The radar showed the storm had moved past them and there were no reports of tornado touchdowns, so they were in the clear. He carried her up the basement stairs and through the hallway, then found his way to the other set of stairs leading up to the bedrooms.

Originally, he'd planned for Kelsey to stay in the guest room tonight. He'd wanted to give them both some breathing room before the trip. Plus, he never had women stay overnight with him. But the thought of her sleeping down the hallway didn't sit well now. What if she woke up in the night and needed to know where something was? He knew how disorienting a new place could be, especially in the dark.

If he gave her a choice, she'd probably take the guest room. Alone time would give her a chance to gather herself in the morning, to rebuild her defenses before she saw him again. If he were in her position, that's what he'd try to do, too. But since they'd agreed to this arrangement, the decision should be based on what he wanted and thought was best, not on what she'd prefer.

And what he wanted was for her soft, warm body to be next to his all night. He didn't want her retreating behind her fortress again. He needed her bare and exposed. Open to him. Both physically and mentally. So that she could see without a doubt that he would be good to her and never, ever do anything to hurt or exploit her.

Kelsey stirred in his arms, curling into his hold. "Where are we going?"

"To bed, love."

"'Kay," she said, her voice sleep-softened and content.

He smiled and kissed the top of her head as he nudged his bedroom door open. The sheets were already turned back, so he gently laid her down on the right side, removed the blanket he'd wrapped around her, and then brought the bedcovers over her.

Without a sound, he went to his side and stripped off his pants, then slid beneath the cool sheets. Already, her sweet scent was invading his space, stamping her presence there. And he liked it. He liked it a lot.

And though he hadn't had someone sleep next to him in more than a decade, his body seemed to know exactly what it sought. He curled around her backside, her silky skin pressing into his chest and the curve of her fitting against him perfectly. Everything in him seemed to relax in sated contentment.

The feeling was as loud a warning as he could get.

Be careful with this one, Austin. Be real careful.

You can't keep her.

THIRTEEN

"Am I out of my ever-loving mind?" Kelsey asked, balancing her cell phone between her shoulder and ear while reclining in the window seat in Wyatt's kitchen and trying to keep her voice from echoing through the cavernous space.

"It's five thirty in the morning, Kels," Brynn said with a groan. "I thought you had an emergency or something."

"This *is* an emergency." She glanced at the entryway, verifying she was still alone. "I'm going to be leaving in a few hours for this trip, and I think I'm losing it. How in the hell is anyone going to believe I'm really some rich chick? Or that I'm actually dating someone like Wyatt?"

"Why wouldn't you date someone like Wyatt? From everything I've heard from Reid and Jace, Wyatt's a good guy. Smart and level-headed."

She blew a wisp of hair off her forehead. "Exactly. The kind of guy who never dates girls like me. I just know I'm going to slip up and do or say something that waves a big white trash flag."

"Oh, honey."

"I'm serious." Kelsey leaned her head back against the windowsill. "I'm going to fuck this up."

"You are not—hold on." There was a rustling of what Kelsey assumed were bedsheets on the other end and then a grumbled *Where you going so early, sugar?* from her sister's fiancé, Reid. After a quick, muffled exchange, Brynn came back on the line. "Okay, I'm awake now. I think. And I don't want to hear you calling yourself trash. Where we came from is not who we are now. You know that. And money is just that—money. It doesn't make the crowd you're going to be with any better than you. All you need to do is stay by Wyatt's side. People will believe you're together if you act like you're into him."

Kelsey sighed and barely resisted tapping her head against the wall. "I don't have to act that part. I am into him. I slept with him. *Am* sleeping with him."

"You're what?" Brynn asked in hushed surprise.

Kelsey watched a squirrel scamper through the wet grass outside, knowing she probably shouldn't say anything but not wanting to keep something from her sister. She'd told Brynn enough lies in her lifetime already. "I didn't tell you all of the agreement."

"Uh-oh. Lay it on me."

Kelsey explained quickly what she'd signed up for. Brynn, a submissive herself, wouldn't need many details to know exactly how big of a deal this was for Kelsey.

The line was silent for a few long moments, and Kelsey wondered if the call had dropped, but then her sister cleared her throat. "Kels, you know I'll never be one to judge anyone in this arena. Heaven knows I'm in a glass house in that respect. But are you sure you're ready for such an intense experience? I don't want you—did you talk to Melody about this?"

"Yes. Of course, she wasn't a hundred percent behind the idea, but said it was my call if I felt strong enough to handle it." Kelsey had been seeing Melody, a therapist at the women's crisis center where Brynn worked, once a week for the last year. "She wants me to keep a daily journal of my moods and wants me to call her and check in every few days. And if anything triggers me, she wants me to call her immediately."

Brynn released a long breath. "This is risky, Kels."

"You think this is going to make me slip up, don't you?" she asked, voicing her own fears. After last night, she felt more off balance than she had in months—like walking down a long pier with broken boards, never knowing when one was going to snap. The disorienting state of surrendering under Wyatt's dominance had a constant hum of panic vibrating through her. Every time she'd tried to hold on to to some safety rope of control last night, he'd ripped it right out of her hands and sent her into free fall. And though she'd sworn she wouldn't ever breathe a word of it, she'd found herself trusting him with the ugliest piece of her past. God, how had that come tumbling out?

"Of course not, honey," Brynn answered, her voice all empathy and big-sisterness. "You're stronger than you think. But I also know what it can be like to be emotionally stripped down by a skilled dom. The first time I was with Reid after I got back together with him, it triggered a monster of a panic attack. I know you don't get those like I used to, but you never know when a scene might bring scary shit back to the surface. And beyond stirring up the trauma, it can also create a false sense of intimacy and security with the dom, make them look like a savior."

"Is that your therapist way of telling me not to mistake good sex for love?"

"It can be an easy trap to stumble into," she said gently. "And D/s only makes that trapdoor harder to see."

And it'd been a mistake Kelsey had made before—not with D/s but with every relationship she'd ever been in. Her history of falling too fast and for the wrong guys stretched out behind her like streamers of regrets flapping in the wind. "Wyatt's not look-ing for a relationship and neither am I. We both know when this thing will end."

Kelsey could almost hear her sister's frown over the phone. "Just take care of yourself, Kels. If at any point you feel like it's too much or you find yourself wanting to slip back into old hab-its, you call me. I don't care what time. I'll get on a plane and come and get you. Nothing and no one is worth going backward over. You've come too far."

She nodded, though it was to an empty room. "Okay."

In that moment, she hated how fragile she felt, how on the brink her life always seemed. She shouldn't even have to worry about this. Most people were tough enough to deal with what life gave them. Brynn had been one of Davis's victims as a teenager and had lived the same childhood Kelsey had—maybe worse because she'd been the oldest and responsible for herself, their alcoholic mother, *and* Kelsey—and look how Brynn had turned out. A great career. A loving relationship. No addictions. No fear that any wrong move would land her on junkie row.

Kelsey was tired of living her life on an electrified high wire. She wanted to be able to try new things and take risks without the worry that she'd fall victim to her past or her weaknesses again. Maybe if nothing else, this trip with Wyatt could help her prove to herself that she was capable of dealing, that she wasn't a slave to her history.

The only terrifying part was . . . what if she was wrong? What if the craving to get numb came back? She wasn't sure she could climb out of that pit again if she fell back in.

Brynn yawned, breaking Kelsey from her whirling thoughts, then quickly apologized.

"No, it's fine. I'm sorry about waking you, B. I shouldn't have done that. But I've been up since four, have tried to write my journal entry three different times, have had to reapply deodorant twice, and am making desperation muffins as a calm-your-ass-down plan. You were my last hope."

Brynn laughed lightly. "It's okay. You know you can call me anytime. Sometimes talking it out is the only thing that works. And for the record, I think you're going to do great on the trip. You're naturally good with meeting new people."

Right. Except usually those people wanted waffles from her, not her opinion on politics or the stock market. She checked the timer on the oven. Two more minutes until the muffins were done. "I figured at worst, I can talk about food. That's like the weather, right? Everyone loves food."

"It'll be fine," her sister said, using that talk-you-off-the-ledge therapist tone of hers. "You be yourself as much as you can and follow Wyatt's lead. He's not going to expect you to know it all."

"I know. And believe me, so far, I've been good at doing what he tells me to do." She bit her lip, peeking at the doorway again.

"Oh, really," Brynn said, her voice taking on a don't-mind-me lilt. "So Jace isn't the only Austin who knows what he's doing in that department?"

Kelsey's cheeks burned at the question, but before she could respond, another thought hit her. "Wait a minute, how exactly would *you* know anything about Jace in the bedroom, Ms. Engaged-to-Reid?"

Brynn coughed. "Don't turn the question around me."

"Oh, nun-uh. You're not backing out of this one. Spill."

Brynn sighed. "Reid and Jace are best friends, so . . . you know. It was only a one-time thing, though. Turns out sharing isn't really Reid's thing."

"You trashy whore," Kelsey teased. Up until last year when Brynn had admitted to her that she was in a D/s relationship with Reid, Kelsey had always thought of her sister as the ultimate vanilla good girl. But more and more she was realizing she and Brynn weren't *so* different. Somehow Kelsey found that comforting.

"I have my moments," Brynn said breezily. "So now it's your turn. Dish."

Kelsey slid off the window seat and headed toward the oven to pull out the muffins. "Well, I'm not one to kiss and tell like you are. I have some class and all."

Her sister sniffed.

"But I will say the Austin gene pool is *strong.*"

Brynn laughed. And Kelsey realized how good it was just to girl talk with her sister for a change. For so many years, it was always Brynn playing parent/protector/therapist to Kelsey, taking care of her because she sucked at taking care of herself. But now they were finally getting a chance to develop a friendship. It was . . . nice, normal. Bizarre.

"Well, good for you, Kels. I hope you let yourself enjoy this then. A sexy trip with a nice guy may be just what you need. As long as you—"

"I know." Kelsey slipped on an oven mitt and pulled out the tray of orange macadamia muffins, nearly dropping her phone in the process. "I'll be careful. If he tries to push me too far, I'll channel my alter ego."

"That's right. That'll straighten him out. No one puts Lady K in a corner . . . or something."

Kelsey groaned. "Lame."

"Sorry, I need caffeine. Are you still going to be back in time to do the last-minute wedding stuff with me? I mean, if everything is cleared up with that jackass Howie Miller by then?"

Damn, was it that time already? All this drama had sprung up so fast, she'd lost all sight of what had been going on before that day in the alley. She hadn't even broken the news to her sister that she planned to move after all this was over. Some maid of honor she was going to make. "Sure, you bet."

"All right, well, take a deep breath, bake your muffins, and walk into that retreat like you belong there."

"Will do."

But she knew the words were still a good percentage bravado. She was skilled at playing roles, at being whoever she needed to be when the situation called for it, but she knew if anyone looked too hard, they'd see the frayed edges, would see that she didn't belong.

She just had to hope to God no one would take the time to really see her.

The guy sleeping upstairs had already seen far too much. She prayed he'd keep his promise and not treat her any differently now that he knew. She didn't want to be Fragile Girl on this trip. She wanted to be his sub. A little fun. A little training. A lot of sex.

Which is exactly why she'd hopped out of bed so quickly this morning when she'd woken up and realized they'd slept next to each other all night, spooning. Waking up in his arms had felt too damn good, the urge to turn over and cuddle too strong. This was not supposed to be about lazy mornings in bed.

She set her phone down and slid the muffin tray onto the stove to cool. She couldn't put the drizzle of white chocolate on them yet or it'd melt off. So she went to her purse to pull out the little notebook she'd bought on Melody's suggestion. She turned to the first page and began to write.

She was still scribbling a few minutes later when Wyatt strolled into the kitchen, all tousled hair and wrinkled pajama bottoms. "And I thought I was an early riser."

She stared at him for a moment, the contrast to his normally super-polished look hitting her like a punch to the gut. Man, how could this version of him be even more knee-weakening? It wasn't fair. How was she supposed to keep things cool and casual when her body had some sort of pre-wired, lose-your-shit response to him?

"I woke up and couldn't go back to sleep." *And felt you curled around me naked and warm and too damn tempting.* "So I figured I'd make us some breakfast."

"I'm not sure I've ever woken up to such a delicious scent." He walked over to her, dimples showing, and pulled her to a stand, making her wonder if he was referring to the muffins or her. Lord knows she'd buried her nose in his pillows absorbing *his* morning scent—soap, fabric softener, and that spicy undercurrent of man—before climbing out of bed. She'd only slipped on one of his dress shirts and a pair of panties this morning, but the look on his face said he appreciated the outfit. He tugged her by the front of her shirt and hauled her against him. "But I was looking forward to having *you* for breakfast, Ms. LeBreck. Imagine my disappointment when I rolled over to a cold bed."

Her heart lifted at the fact that he wasn't all puppy eyes and *Are you okay?* after her revelation last night. His tone and expression were pure sex, served up hot. She slid her hands up his bare chest, her body quaking with awareness at his nearness, his warmth. "I'm sorry. I figured you'd want to sleep in, and I didn't want to risk waking you."

"Mmm, thoughtful. But unnecessary." He nodded at the notebook sitting on the table. "What are you up to?"

"Just making a few notes for the trip," she said, the lie rolling off her tongue like an automatic reflex.

"How diligent of you. But that furrowed brow you had is way too serious for so early in the morning." His hands drifted down over the curve of her ass, causing her to wince ever so slightly. "Are you sore?"

"A little, but not in a bad way." Her rear had been tender when she'd first sat up this morning, but the effect had been anything but unpleasant. To her own surprise, she'd gone hot and bothered in an instant at the sensation, at the memory of his hands on her.

"I have to say, when I woke up without you next to me, I was a little worried I'd scared you off." His warm palms spanned her waist beneath the shirt. "I know you revealed more about yourself than you planned to last night. And I was harder on you than I'd originally anticipated being for our first time together."

She looked up at him, finding his expression a little guarded, tentative. Like he was half-expecting her to scamper right out the door. "I'm not going anywhere, Wyatt. Last night was good, really good. Yes, you surprised me. I didn't think you'd be so . . ."

His gaze was heavy on hers. "So what?"

"So all in," she said, searching for the right words. "When you said you didn't do this anymore, that you could put it aside, I figured you had just done it as kinky fun in the past. You know, played around with it. I didn't expect—"

"Yeah," he said, releasing a breath and reaching up to touch her face. "I didn't know how it would go either. But it seems the door is either wide open for me or locked tight when it comes to this. And being around you busts that door right down. I need to know you're okay with that."

She licked her lips. A few days ago, that probably would've scared her off. Part of her had anticipated being able to hold on to a little control, to manipulate him a bit. But when he'd turned down her offer to finish the blow job, she'd realized how seriously he was taking the training. He'd wanted her to finish him off, and she could see the need painted all over his face. But she'd earned a punishment, and he wasn't going to let her take control by using his own pleasure against him. So, he'd set aside his needs and had taken the less pleasurable route to remind her of her mistake and her role. It was the move of a seasoned dominant. It had scared the hell out of her. And had also soothed her in some undefinable way.

He'd put her first. No guy had ever put her first.

"You're very good at it," she said, being honest but dodging his question about how she was feeling.

He pushed her hair behind her ears, his gaze tender. "And I

thought you were beautiful already, but you're breathtaking in submission, Kelsey. Like punch-me-in-the-gut gorgeous."

She glanced down, her cheeks warming at the compliment. She was used to guys telling her she was pretty or sexy or whatever. She'd heard every version of male bullshit imaginable while working at the strip club. But somehow, the way Wyatt said it made her believe he wasn't simply talking about her ample rack or how she looked naked. "Thank you."

"So I didn't scare you, huh?" he asked, lifting her chin upward.

Yes. But not in the way he feared. And even if her mind was yelling at her to run, to hide from this man who seemed to get under her armor so easily, she couldn't bring herself to do it. Even now, all she wanted to do was touch him, be touched, have him command her body in a way no one else ever had. "I want to be here, Wyatt."

His mouth curled upward, pure pleasure in his eyes. "Glad to hear it."

He leaned past her and set her closed notebook down on the chair, then shoved the bowl of pears on the kitchen table over to the edge, almost sending it crashing to the floor.

He grabbed her waist and guided her toward the tabletop. "Lay down, love."

She glanced back at the long wooden table. Her lips parted to question him, but the singular look in his eyes didn't leave much room for interpretation. "Yes, sir."

She scooted onto the table and lay down, leaving her calves hanging over the edge. Without a word, he tugged her underwear off, then came around to the other side and helped her pull the borrowed shirt off, leaving her bare in the daybreak sunlight filtering through the windows.

When he made his way back to her lower half, he guided her ankle to the corner of the table and wrapped soft material around it. She pulled in a breath.

"I should be more prepared," he said almost to himself as he secured her ankle to the post. "But I don't have any cuffs that will work with the legs of this table. So this shirt and a kitchen towel are going to have to do. Does that feel too tight?"

"No, sir," she said, her voice catching in her throat.

"Good, girl. Now reach out and grab the edges of the table. If you let go, I'll find something to tie your hands as well." She did as she was told, her temperature climbing from simmer to steady burn as she lay there for him. She hadn't been bound by anyone since Davis. If anything should trigger her fear, this should. But none came. This was on a different planet from being tied against her will with those painful zip ties, and her body registered that fact immediately. This was sexy and fun and so . . . fucking . . . hot. Wyatt bound her other ankle, leaving her spread wide and exposed for whatever he planned to do with her. Once he rose to his full height again, his hot gaze swept over her naked form, and amusement tugged at the corners of his mouth. "Now this is a beautiful breakfast."

He gave her knee a quick squeeze and then headed back toward the stove. She'd made a pot of coffee already, and he turned his back to her for a moment, fixing himself a cup like he had all the time in the world.

"Uh, sir?"

He peeked back at her, a naughty boy smile. "Yes, love?"

"Did I do something wrong?" Was this her punishment for getting out of bed without asking him if that was okay?

"Of course not." He poured a dash of skim milk into his cup. "But I spend every day of my life with a packed-to-the-gills schedule. This morning is about indulging. And right now, I want to take my time indulging in you."

She swallowed past the sudden dryness in her throat. "Oh."

He took a long sip of his coffee, keeping his eyes on her. "So tell me about these muffins."

A quick laugh bubbled out. It was the question he asked her each morning in the restaurant. Only she'd never had to answer him while naked, flat on her back, and about as turned on as a person could be. She cleared her throat, preparing her specials-of-the-day voice. "They're orange macadamia nut with a white chocolate drizzle. Well, they will be once I get around to drizzling them."

"Sounds delicious. Your baking is going to be hell on my strict eating regime, Ms. LeBreck. All this temptation. I'm not usually one to indulge, but I find it hard to resist when you're around." He picked up the little bowl of melted white chocolate she'd set on top of a hot mug of water to keep it warm. "Is this the drizzle?"

"Yes, sir."

He set down his coffee and dipped a finger in the chocolate, then brought it to his mouth, tasting. "Mmm, that's amazing. What'd you add to it?"

"Orange zest. It's even better on top of the muffins."

He raised an eyebrow and grabbed a whisk from the carafe of utensils next to the stove. "Is that right?"

She couldn't answer as she watched him stir the mixture slowly, then draw the whisk above the bowl so that little ribbons of the chocolate ran off the whisk and back into the bowl. The wicked quirk of his mouth told her everything she needed to know.

He strolled her way again, the front of his pajama bottoms showing signs of his growing interest in *breakfast*, and set the bowl next to her. His hand caressed her hip, sending hot goose bumps marching across her skin. "Last night was going to be about your pleasure. About me discovering how you liked to be touched. But you tried to steer the ship instead."

Her tongue darted out, swiping across her bottom lip. "I'm sorry, sir."

"Shh." He pressed his finger to her mouth, the remnants of the chocolate sweet against her lips. "You accepted your punishment beautifully last night, so no need to apologize again. But now, it's my turn to get what I wanted in the first place."

He lifted the whisk from the bowl and held it over her chest. Warm ribbons of chocolate drizzled down, coating her nipples and sliding down over her breasts. Her neck arched, the sinful sensation racing straight downward, heating everything in its path, and settling between her thighs. The scent of orange hit her nose. Wyatt smiled and drew the whisk over her belly, leaving a swirling splatter pattern of glossy white chocolate in his wake.

"Too warm?" he asked.

"God, no," she breathed. "It's . . ."

Then his mouth was on her, stealing her words. His tongue glided over the side of her breast, following the trail of chocolate until his lips locked around a nipple. The softness of his mouth mixing with the abrasive grit of sugar in the chocolate was almost too much to take at once. She moaned into the touch, and he sucked hard, bringing her nipple to an aching point. Her clit throbbed in time with each suck, her ankles tugging at the bindings as her thighs automatically tried to close and provide pressure for the insistent need there.

Wyatt eased back a bit, flicking her once more with the tip of his tongue. "So the question is, love, do you respond to the soft and sensual approach . . ." He reached out and circled her nipple oh so gently. "Or do you prefer a little bite?"

His thumb and forefinger clamped onto her, pinching. Her back arched off the table, a hot boom of need rippling outward from his touch. "Fuck."

He chuckled, a darkly pleasant sound. "Well, that answers that. Guess it's a good thing Jace talked me into buying some brutal little clamps for our trip."

She shivered, and Wyatt cupped her other breast, bringing his mouth down again—sucking and laving, cleaning every drop of confection off her. The warm chocolate he'd painted on her belly dripped down her sides, making it feel like she had more than one hot tongue licking at her. Even the sticky, wet sounds of chocolate-covered lips against skin were driving her to the brink of desperation. She wriggled beneath him, the need coiling and pulsing in her, energy demanding to be let out.

He gave her thigh a sharp little smack while grazing her nipple with his teeth. *Stay still*. He didn't have to say it; she got the message. Her fingers gripped the table harder, and moisture coated her sex, her own scent drifting up to her nose and mixing with the orange from the chocolate.

The house phone rang, startling her for a moment, but Wyatt lifted his head, looking down at her. "Ignore it. All your focus on me and what you're feeling."

"Yes, sir."

The phone continued to ring as he straightened and grabbed the bowl again. Before she knew it, he was in between her spread thighs, looking down at her with unabashed hunger. He lifted the whisk and drizzled the chocolate over her inner thighs and over her freshly waxed mound. The warmth alone reminded her of how it'd felt to have him come on her last night, his semen sliding down and over her back. It'd been one of the sexiest things she'd ever experienced.

He touched the lips of her sex, a gentle caress. "You're so pink and swollen, love. I can't wait to taste every inch of you. Would you like that?"

"Yes, sir," she gasped. "Please."

He grabbed her leg and drew his tongue up her thigh, licking off the chocolate and making her quiver. "I will. As soon as I get you all cleaned off. As much as I love your cooking, when I eat this pretty pussy of yours, I don't want to taste anything but you."

She whimpered at that, the pulsing in her clit becoming like a bass drum reverberating through her body.

Then he was doing exactly what he promised, tasting and dragging his tongue along every inch of her inner thighs, laving it off her mound, taking his time and driving her to a panting, begging mess. Unable to keep ahold of the table, her hand balled and pounded in a steady rhythm against the table, the energy having to go somewhere.

Wyatt paused in his tortuous treatment, his voice gritty with his own restraint. His thumb grazed over her clit, a gentle stroke, but it sent sparks through her nonetheless. "Touch your tits for me, Kelsey. And don't be shy. Let me see just what you like."

She raised her head to meet his gaze. His eyes were dark with intention as he hovered there between her thighs, looking up the length of her body. She held his eye contact and brought her hands to her breasts, cupping and sliding her hands over her wet, sticky skin. She knew how to do this for effect, to put on the dancer show, but she had no desire to fake it with Wyatt. So instead she touched where she needed and how she wanted, pinching and plucking at her nipples until they were pulsing in time with her clit. Then, lifting her head higher and arching her back, she grabbed her breast and did something she'd only ever tried in private. She dragged the tip of her tongue over her own nipple, tasting the chocolaty remnants. Wyatt's groan echoed off the high ceilings of the kitchen.

"You are the sexiest fucking thing I've ever seen." He held her thighs wide, his grip tight and his voice lowering. "You keep this up, and I'm not going to want to let you go at the end of this trip. I'll be cuffing you to my bed so I can keep you."

Her eyes squeezed shut and her hand fell away from her breast as startled alarm went through her. *No.* He wasn't supposed to say things like that. He wasn't supposed to make this more than it was. But before she could react further or respond to Wyatt's declaration, he lowered his head and buried his face between her legs, his lips and tongue hitting her exactly where she needed.

She bucked against him, moaning, as he lit up her nervous system with his tongue. Thoughts emptied out of her head. All that was left was the mind-bending ecstasy he was giving her with his relentless, sensual ministrations. Breaking the rules, she reached down and threaded her fingers in his silky dark hair, her hips now rocking in rhythm with him, riding the pleasure. His nose nuzzled her clit as his tongue delved inside her fully, in and out in an erotic slide. Fucking her with his mouth.

She couldn't hold it back or stop the pressure from building. And when he returned his full attention to her clit and buried his fingers inside her, everything burst through her like a flash of light. The table rattled beneath her as a shout tore from her throat and her body rode the waves of her orgasm.

He held her against his mouth, not letting up until her first peak had passed and another was building on its heels. Then when she was about to go over again, he rose up, grabbing at her thighs and yanking her ass to the edge of the table. Before she could take another breath, he slipped on the condom and pushed inside her, his cock thick and hot, stretching her without mercy.

"Again," he demanded, thrusting into her with delicious brutality. "Come for me again. I want to feel you."

She didn't need the order. Her body was already charging up the next mountain. She wasn't even sure the first orgasm had ever stopped. Her nails cut crescents into her palms and she cried out again, pleasure pulsing through her and her sex clasping around Wyatt.

He came along with her, and the world felt like it was spinning off course beneath her as he held on to her tight.

He'd said he might not want her to leave.

He wasn't supposed to say things like that.

He wasn't supposed to make her feel this way.

No, no, no . . .

FOURTEEN

Wyatt scanned through a report on his laptop and tried to make sense of the week's numbers, something under normal circumstances he could do in his sleep. But this was the third time he'd been through the same report since the company jet had taken off, and he still hadn't processed any of the information. His attention kept straying to the woman playing possum in the seat across the aisle from him. Kelsey had reclined her chair fully and had turned her face away, claiming she was tired from getting up so early.

But no one slept with a white-knuckled grip and breathing that shallow.

She'd admitted to him before getting on the plane that she'd never flown before and that she was nervous. He'd offered her a glass of wine to help her relax, but she'd quickly declined it. Now she was clearly going the try-to-tough-it-out-in-silence mode.

God, he was a mindless idiot. This morning in the kitchen he'd made the egregious error of speaking before thinking, which was something he thought he'd trained out of himself. But apparently when he was in the midst of fucking a beautiful woman on his kitchen table, his filter went to shit. He'd voiced his in-the-heat-of-the-moment desire to cuff her to his bed and keep her.

Fucking brilliant.

File that under Things You Should Never *Ever* Say To a Woman Whose Been Held Fucking Captive. He'd wanted to beat his head against the wall when he'd realized what he said. *Stupid, stupid, stupid.*

And it'd sent Kelsey into retreat mode as soon as she'd floated down from her orgasm. He'd tried to apologize, but she'd waved him off as if it hadn't mattered. *Sure.*

Now, instead of allowing him to help her through her fear of flying, she'd shut him out with faux sleeping. He needed to fix this fast. Otherwise, they'd never pull off this sham. He needed her fully into this and feeling safe with him if they had any chance at this working. And beyond that, he hated feeling like he'd scared her in some way.

He tapped a few keys on his keyboard and kept his eyes on the screen. "I know you're awake over there, so I'm going to talk and you're going to listen."

She didn't move.

"What I said in the kitchen was so out of line I can't even begin to apologize. It was off the cuff, and I didn't mean to frighten you."

She remained still for a long moment, and he wondered if she was going to keep up the act. But finally she shifted infinitesimally, keeping her eyes closed, but letting him know she'd heard him. "It didn't scare me like you think. Davis never said anything like that to me. He kidnapped me because he wanted the information I had. His obsession was with my sister. When he raped me, he told me how repulsed he was by me and blamed me for tempting him with my whorish body. He wouldn't even touch me without wearing surgical gloves because I was so *dirty*. The silver lining is that it meant he wore condoms."

Wyatt sucked in such a harsh breath, it felt as if his ribs would crack. *Christ*. The things she'd gone through . . .

She turned her head toward him, her expression tired. "He didn't want to keep me, he wanted to hurt me, kill me. I know you're not like him. You're the opposite. When you dominate me, you . . . cherish."

He did. Because he knew she was the most beautiful, precious thing he'd ever had the privilege of touching, but he didn't say that aloud. In his gut he knew that wouldn't be well received right now. Any attempt at tenderness or sympathy in this moment and she'd shut down. "Then what was it that upset you this morning?"

She shook her head, a sadness there. "Because we agreed this is temporary. What you said . . ."

Ah. He met her eyes. Was it possible she was more commitment phobic than him? He didn't think that could ever be the case with a woman. But after what Kelsey had been through, how could she possibly trust anyone with her emotions? She was a survivor, and survivors learned how to protect their vulnerabilities at all costs. His heart broke for her. Being so jaded and world weary at twenty-five was its own tragedy. But at least this was territory he could handle. "I like you, Kelsey. I enjoy being around you."

She flinched like he'd pinched her. And it confirmed exactly how averse she was to the idea of this turning into something emotionally driven. He had to make it clear that he wasn't there to sell her that bill of goods—even if it risked him sounding harsh. She'd appreciate that more than coddling.

"But this arrangement we have is about two things for me: my business and a little fun. In that order. This is not me trying to manipulate you into a relationship, and it's not me trying to convince you into some master/slave setup beyond our training. I told you I don't have room in my life for either."

Her expression remained wary.

"We made this agreement because I need your help and you need mine. A very nice side benefit is that I get to have you in my bed and under my tutelage for a little while. I consider that a great privilege and don't take that lightly." He closed his laptop screen and turned toward her. "But that's all it is. Anything I say in the heat of the moment is simply dirty talk and errant thoughts." He reached out and took her hand, squeezing it. "You don't have to run from me, love. I'm not trying to catch you."

She closed her eyes and nodded, her shoulders sagging with what looked to be relief. "I'm sorry. I'm not trying to lay all my shit out there. I just don't know how to do this."

"Do what, love?" he asked, rubbing his thumb along the top of her hand.

She watched him for a moment, some battle going on in her eyes, and then she let out a breath and slipped her hand from his. "I realized as I was lying here that I haven't had this kind of sexual relationship since I was seventeen."

"What kind?"

She looked down at the blanket she had pulled over her lap for her nap, pinching the fabric between her fingers. "A sober one. One where I wasn't numb."

He took a breath. "Oh." *Oh.*

She glanced over at him quickly, gauging his reaction, which he hopefully masked well enough, then went back to fiddling with the blanket. "I've lived a fucked-up life, Wyatt. Partially because of the hand I was dealt, but mostly because of me and a string of bad decisions after I turned sixteen and started dating a guy who wouldn't take me to prom but was happy to take me on my first bender. Yes, I know the assault wasn't my fault. But even before that, I wasn't a stable person. If you knew even half of what I've done, what I've allowed to be done to me . . . well, you probably wouldn't want to talk to me much less touch me."

He shook his head. The words sounded eerily similar to the ones she'd said her captor had tortured her with. *You're dirty. Worthless. Untouchable.* "Kelsey—"

"But sex to me has always been like another drug thrown into the mix—a way to not feel, to get lost, a way to manipulate. An easy escape."

He wanted to reach out and brush her hair away from her face, to take some of that shame from her expression, to comfort her, but he sensed she'd only slam the door in his face.

"So I don't know how to handle this . . . or you. I've been clean for a year and celibate during that time until last night. And I thought I could add sex back in without an issue. Obviously, I'm not going to live without it for the rest of my life. But I didn't realize how different doing this sober would be. Submitting to you rips me open. That's why all those things bubbled up last night. I don't know how to deal with all that *feeling*." She turned toward him. "I thought I was handling it, but when you said what you did this morning, it gave me this rush of confusing emotions. I don't want to feel things for you, Wyatt. It scares the fuck out of me. It makes me want to run."

He reached out this time, cupping the side of her face, trying to offer her comfort even though a clammy feeling had locked around his gut. He was happy Kelsey was opening up to him about her past. That showed that even their brief encounters had built some layer of trust there, had peeled back that veneer that shouldn't be present between dominant and submissive. But what she was revealing was so trauma-laden, so rife with open wounds. And it began to feel far too familiar. He could sense his own psyche going into duck-and-cover mode. He couldn't let her get attached to him—even unintentionally.

He'd made Kelsey promise when they came to this agreement that she wouldn't let him hurt her. It'd been his only condition. And whether she knew it or not, this was her keeping her promise, ringing the warning bells. Maybe nothing had changed with him over the years. Maybe staying away from this side of himself had been a necessary move. Because in under twenty-four hours, he was already putting another woman at risk.

For the last week, he'd allowed himself to entertain the notion that maybe his situation with Mia had been an anomaly, maybe his dominance hadn't pushed her off the ledge. But here he was again, tearing things open and leaving a woman vulnerable to her own dangerous demons.

"Thank you for being open with me," he said, forcing the words to come out steady and not like they were splitting him in two. He lowered his hand to his side. "And I refuse to put you at risk any longer."

Her gaze snapped upward to meet his, but he was already turning away and grabbing his briefcase from under the seat. He set his laptop aside and pulled what he needed from his bag, then started to write.

"What are you doing?" Kelsey asked, concern lacing her voice.

He didn't look up, just continued scribbling, doing what he should have done in the first place even though it was digging out a huge hole in his chest. When he was done, he tore the little rectangle of paper from the book, sealed it in an envelope, and handed it to Kelsey. "This is my last command for you, love. I don't want you selling yourself in order to go to school and start the life you deserve. If you want to be a dominant or a trainer, do that. But do it on your own terms, not for a paycheck. And I don't want you submitting to me when it's only hurting you."

Her eyes went round. "Wyatt—"

"That check will give you what you need with no strings attached. It's not payment for being here; it's not money for what we've already done. It's a gift."

She looked down at the envelope, not opening it, but knowing very well a check lay inside. "Wyatt, I can't . . . No . . ."

He straightened his suit jacket, trying to shake off the hollow feeling letting her go was giving him. "I've spent far more money on far less important things. I want to give you your freedom. Without obligation, without rules, without ramifications."

"I should've never told you about my past." Her eyes went glassy as she gripped the envelope in her hand. And he knew she was fighting with herself. Kelsey was nothing if not prideful, and handouts weren't her style. But she also wasn't stupid.

They both knew that check meant she'd never have to get on her knees for anyone—literally or figuratively.

"Now that you know, you don't want to touch me either," she whispered.

He looked up sharply, the words like razors burrowing into his chest. "You listen to me," he said, his words angry, measured. "I've *never* wanted to touch anyone so much in my life, Kelsey. Don't take that sick fuck's words and put them in my mouth. That's not fair to me or you. But regardless of how much I want you, I refuse to risk your well-being."

"I can't take the money," she murmured, her fingers tight around the envelope.

"You will. And if you try to hand that check back to me, I'll find out your account number and deposit it anyway. So don't try it."

She shook her head, some mixture of stunned awareness and heartbreak on her face. "I don't understand why you're doing this. I wasn't trying to get out of our agreement. I only wanted to explain why I was such a head case this morning."

He leaned back in his seat and shut his eyes, rubbing the bridge of his nose beneath his glasses. "I don't want to be the person to make you feel that way. No matter how much I've enjoyed being with you, dominating you, your emotional health and stability aren't things I'm willing to put in jeopardy. When we land on the island, I'll send you back to Dallas on the jet."

"The hell you will," she said in a choked retort.

He opened his eyes to find her glaring at him—the wounded girl replaced by the determined woman. "If you think I'm going to bail on my promise to help you just because I got a little freaked out, you don't know me very well."

"Kelsey."

"No, you need to listen to me now. You're trying to help me, so let me help you, Wyatt. I *want* to be here. Not because you're throwing life-changing money at me or helping me out of a bind, but because I like you and because this trip is important to you. All of the shit in my past was there yesterday just like it is today. It'll still be there tomorrow. Nothing has changed except that now you know." She pointed a finger at him. "And I'm staying because I memorized every damn one of those index cards you gave me on the other guests, and I can't get those hours of my life back."

He blinked at her, taken aback by her outburst, but then couldn't stop his smile. "Tell me you didn't memorize every one of those cards."

She cocked her head to the side. "Care to test me? I was up very early."

He raised a palm. "No, no, I trust you. But I don't want you to feel obligated to do this with me."

She sighed and slipped the envelope in her purse. A small victory for him. "You said yourself that this money is to buy my freedom, right?"

"Yes."

"Then let me make my own decisions. I'm staying with you this week and will play the role to the best of my ability because I want to." She wet her lips. "And the training *is* off."

He gave a curt nod. "Agreed."

She glanced up the aisle of the empty cabin, then unhooked her seatbelt and came over to him, bracing her hands on his armrest and leaning down, giving him an unimpeded view down her blouse as she bent close to his ear. "So now you know that when I get on my knees for you, it has nothing to do with training for a job."

"Kelsey." The word came out as a strangled whisper.

She surreptitiously glanced toward the front of the cabin, making sure the flight attendant hadn't stepped through the curtain, then lowered herself to a kneel next to his seat. "Your dominance strips me, Wyatt, flays me open and leaves me bleeding. But it's a good bloodletting. If I'm really going to start a new life, I want it to be without fearing that I'm going to tumble backward at the first hiccup. I need to know I'm strong enough to face the fire and walk through it. I need to bury the girl I used to be."

She was looking up at him, determination in the tilt of her chin but anxiety still lingering in her eyes. He stared down at her, almost afraid to touch her, knowing the minute he did he'd lose the resolve to do the right thing. "But what if I take you too far, Kelsey? What if those fires are too hot?"

"Then I don't deserve that money or a fresh start because I wouldn't be ready for it."

He took a deep breath and set his hands on her shoulders. "I promise you there's nothing I want more than to spend this week with you in my bed and under my command. But thinking this can be some kind of therapeutic experience is a dangerous fucking path to travel. Sure, maybe you'll walk away from it feeling stronger. But it's just as possible that you'll walk away ripped to shreds and decimated. I've seen what can happen."

The corners of her mouth dipped. "Is that what happened the last time you did this?"

He grabbed his briefcase and shoved it beneath the seat, needing something to do with his hands. "Yes. I ruined someone, Kelsey. Fucking *ruined* her."

He caught her wince in his peripheral vision. "What happened to her?"

He gave her a hard look, trying to stave off the barrage of breath-stealing pain that came along with the memory. "I loved her. But in the end, I loved my job more. I told her I needed space. She took a fistful of pills and never woke up. She gave me all the space I could ever need."

"My God." She sat back on her calves, as if the revelation had physically shoved her backward. "I'm so sor—"

The speaker dinged overhead and a little red light came on. The flight attendant gave her warnings.

"We're beginning our descent," he said gruffly. "You need to get in your seat and fasten your seatbelt."

"Wyatt—"

He turned away from her, unable to bear the naked sympathy in those blue eyes. Sympathy he damn well didn't deserve. Mia may have put those pills in her mouth, but he'd been the one to break his promise to her. She'd given him all of herself, and he'd left her with nothing.

"I won't risk it, Kelsey."

I won't risk you.

FIFTEEN

Kelsey didn't know if her stomach was upside down from the plane landing or from the conversation leading up to it. But either way, she was happy to get her feet on solid ground again as she walked side by side with Wyatt into the small airport.

He had his hand on the small of her back and had smiled politely as people had helped them off the plane, took care of their customs paperwork, and welcomed them, but Wyatt hadn't said another word to Kelsey after he'd revealed why he didn't do D/s anymore. So while they rode in the limo that would take them to a chartered boat, she'd watched silently as the man who'd seemed so warm and open over the last day and night disappeared back into the armor of an unruffled business man. She thought she was the pro at slamming the doors and shutting people out, but apparently she'd met her match.

And though her chest ached over the tragedy he'd been through, and she respected his reasons for backing away, another part of her burned with the desire to not let this go, to not take the easy way out. Submitting to Wyatt frightened her, made her feel things. The way he looked at her, spoke to her—like she was something to be revered and protected—was unlike everything she'd ever experienced. Her mind didn't know how to digest all of that without panicking a bit. Getting used to that kind of affection could hurt her when she walked away from him. She knew that risk. And obviously that terrified the hell out of him, too. But his doubt about her being able to handle this, his worries about her fragility, only made her want to prove him wrong.

Was she really at the point in her life where some man could *crush* her? Even if she did something idiotic like develop feelings for Wyatt, would she freaking fall apart when their time was up?

No.

Fuck. That.

She wasn't that person anymore. She didn't pin fairy tale expectations on reality. Like she'd told him, she wasn't looking for a prince to save her. She'd been living on her own for a year—had been happy even, until Howie had showed up. If a knife to her throat and knowing a gang wanted her dead hadn't sent her to pick up a drink or get high, then what would? She was tired of feeling weak, of worrying about slipping up.

This trip was supposed to be fun. She liked Wyatt. The man, the sex, *and* his dominance. And there was no reason the two of them should spend the rest of the week dancing around each other. But now she had to convince him of that.

"The boat ride isn't supposed to be too long," Wyatt said absently, his eyes focused on his phone, his thumb scrolling through emails. "They don't have an airstrip on Devil Cay."

She nodded, fiddling with the hem of her cotton skirt, trying to find the right words to kill the awkwardness between them. "I've never heard of Devil Cay."

He glanced up, a quick flick of a look, then he was back to his phone. "You wouldn't have. It's a private island and resort owned by the guy throwing this shindig. Well, this year, it's his son's deal actually. Edward Carmichael usually hosts this retreat at his resort in Tahoe since it's ski season, but he's having health problems and handed the duties over to his son. This place is his son Andrew's newest acquisition. My guess is the prick wants to show off."

Kelsey's eyebrows lifted. She'd never heard such a bitter tone from Mr. Stoic. "Not a fan of Andrew's?"

"I went to school with him. He's an arrogant dipshit with too much money and just enough brains to be dangerous. And we hated each other." He smirked. "He's also the client my father most wants me to land this week."

"Fun."

"Getting his business alone would be worth all the other clients I could gather here put together," Wyatt said, sounding tired and finally putting his phone to the side. "But I don't think I'm physically capable of acting like I'm interested in what he has to say."

"I don't remember seeing his name on an index card. What's he into?"

Wyatt sniffed. "Up until a few years ago, he was just another playboy rich kid, spending his time jet-setting, gambling, getting high, and getting laid. Supposedly, he's taking over the reins of his family's empire these days with a focus on the luxury hotel division. But my guess is he hasn't changed that much. He was always more interested in the flash than the work."

Kelsey crossed her legs and smiled. "Then you're in luck."

Wyatt frowned. "What are you talking about?"

"Those types are my specialty. They're the easiest customers to manipulate. You bat your eyelashes and feed their ego, and they'll buy whatever you're selling. Let me help you with him."

A cloud crossed over Wyatt's face. "When exactly have you come across rich playboys in that little diner?"

"Besides you?" she teased.

"I'm serious, Kelsey."

She sighed. He knew all her other shit now, so she might as well tell him. "After high school, I danced at a high-end strip club . . . and eventually a few not-so-high-end ones. The only way I made any money was learning how to play my customers just right. I was good at it. If I hadn't dumped all that cash into my habit, I would've been making a pretty nice living."

"Christ, Kelsey." Lines creased around his eyes, as if the revelation had physically hurt him. "Did no one protect you?"

"My sister tried, but she didn't have a shot. I thought I knew it all." She glanced down and shrugged. "Told you I wasn't that sweet."

"Don't," he warned. "Don't do that."

"What?"

"Look ashamed," he said, his tone firm. "I won't sit here and allow you to do that."

She pressed her lips together and looked at him from beneath her lashes, taking a risk. "Or what? You're going to spank me?"

He scowled, but she didn't miss the need that crossed his features before the cool mask slid back in place. "We've already discussed that."

"And I'm not sure I agree." She uncrossed her legs and leaned forward, the seat bumping beneath her as they went over an uneven road. "I don't love you, Wyatt."

His eyebrows drew together. "What?"

"And you don't love me," she continued, her voice matter-of-fact. "Correct?"

He held his hands out to his sides, clearly confused by her line of questioning. "What does that have to do with anything?"

"It has *everything* to do with it. Don't you see? You're scared of harming me, of repeating the past, right?"

His lips pressed into a line.

"I can't begin to tell you how sorry I am about what you've been through, but you had a relationship with that woman. Love.

That can tear you apart. Can devastate you. But what we're doing isn't that. This is a week. It's fun, sex, and kink. I'm not pledging my lifelong allegiance to you. You don't need to be responsible for me. I just want to have this experience with you and enjoy it."

A battle warred in his solemn stare. "But what you said earlier scares me. When feelings get involved, things get messy and dangerous."

She reached across to slide her hands over his knees, feeling stronger than she had in a long time. "Maybe it's okay if I feel some things. I've lived most of my adult life completely numb. Of course something as intense as D/s is going to stir up those unused emotions, but that doesn't mean they need to be attached to anything significant."

"But—"

She smiled. "You make heat-of-the-moment declarations. I have heat-of-the-moment feelings. Doesn't make them real. But when I'm in a scene with you, when you're pushing me, I feel more free than I have in as long as I can remember. I want to be able to let go and have a good time with you. Being with you makes me feel like I don't have a past for a little while." *Like all the dirt is washed away.*

He watched her, his jaw twitching and his hands braced on the seat.

"And maybe you need that, too," she said, her determination building and her voice lowering as she slid her hands up his thighs. "You're fucking gorgeous when you take the reins, Wyatt. My skin goes hot just thinking about you standing over me. You shouldn't have to deny that part of yourself. And you shouldn't deny me."

His gaze darkened as it slowly tracked down the length of her throat and the vee of her blouse, then back up to meet her eyes again. "You must be a goddamned force in the dungeon, love.

You're sweet temptation wrapped in the armor of a seductress. Men must go stupid at your feet."

She smiled. "I could always tie you up instead. You could see how you like it at the bottom."

He growled and then he was pitching forward, grabbing her wrists and pinning her back against her seat. "Not a fucking chance, love. And *you* don't want me that way. That won't make your body go soft and wet like you did for me this morning."

Her heart was thumping in her ears, the sudden shift in Wyatt welcome but overwhelming her senses. His scent, the soft scrape of his dress shirt against her inner arms, the powerful hold—it all coalesced into instant, throbbing need. She pressed her forehead into his shoulder. "I don't want to spend the week not touching you. So we're both a little fucked up. Can't we be fucked up together?"

"I won't survive not touching you either," he said, defeat in his breathless voice. "I can barely share a damn car with you without wanting to pounce."

"So stop fighting it," she said softly.

He let out a long, weary breath against the back of her neck. "If we do this, you have to swear not to run from me each time. Treat me as your dom. You have a problem or issue, you come to me. Shut me out and this ends. You scare me when you go quiet."

The prospect of being that open to any man was daunting. But she knew it was the only way he'd feel safe with her. If she shut down after a scene, he was going to worry she was spiraling to some dark place. "I promise. Sir."

He lifted her face to him, his eyes flaring blue flame. "I'll never tire of hearing you call me that."

"Touch me, sir. Please." She needed him against her, swiping away all the memories they'd kicked up, all the ugly ghosts.

One hand lowered, cupping her breast and teasing her nipple through the soft cotton of her blouse. She arched into his gentle touch, hoping he was about to take her right there in the back-seat. But in her haze of having him over her, she hadn't realized the limo had stopped.

There was a quick rap on the door and then the sound of the handle being pulled. She froze. Wyatt grinned and gave a sharp pinch to her nipple, making her groan. "Guess I should've told him to take the long way."

The driver cleared his throat, obviously noticing what he'd interrupted. "We're here, Mr. Austin."

Wyatt looked over his shoulder as the warm, salty breeze filtered into the car, clearly not at all concerned about being seen in a compromising position. "Thank you. We'll be right out."

He pushed himself back onto his seat and straightened her blouse for her. She brushed her hair off her face, trying to cool her flushed skin. "Some proper debutante I am."

He reached out to take her hand and guide her toward the door, his smile rakish. "Whoever said I wanted proper?"

The driver took her hand from Wyatt's and guided her out of the car. "Watch your step, Miss. The gravel isn't even."

"Thank you," she said, trying to get her footing in the wedge sandals she'd chosen for today. The breeze whipped through her hair, filling her nose with the scent of ocean, and she had to grab for her skirt before it attempted a Marilyn Monroe moment.

The driver gave her an amused smile and tipped his hat at her before turning his attention to Wyatt. Wyatt climbed out of the limo, his open collar flapping in the breeze, and paid the driver. Even in the casual chinos and an untucked shirt, the man reeked of power and money. How the hell was she going to pull off that same kind of image for this trip?

The driver pulled their bags from the trunk and set them on the ground. "Would you like me to get these to the boat for you, sir?"

"I've got this one." Wyatt grabbed a small duffel bag from the pile. "But yes, please take the rest."

He tipped the driver and turned to her, pulling a pair of aviators from the outside pocket of his bag and replacing his eyeglasses. The arch of his eyebrow was pure sexual promise. He set his bag down, and his arm snaked around her waist, tugging her against him. "It's fucking cruel that we're going to have to share this island with other people this week. We should just get a hotel room here and not leave the bed until next Saturday. Why waste time kissing their asses when I could be kissing much more tasty things?"

He pressed his mouth to the curve of her shoulder, sending ripples of hot sensation straight south. And she was tempted to say, *Yes! Let's do that.* But before she could respond, another voice cut in from behind her.

"*Wyatt?*"

Wyatt's forearms stiffened against her back, and he lifted his head, looking in the direction of the woman's voice. An *oh-fuck* glimmer went across his features, but he quickly covered it with the implacable mask of politeness. He released Kelsey and stepped back. "Hello, Gwen."

Kelsey turned around, the tension from Wyatt leaking into her system as she took in the pretty brunette. Her brown eyes flicked over Kelsey's way, annoyance in her gaze despite the prim smile. The woman looked back to Wyatt. "I didn't expect to see you here."

Wyatt cleared his throat and pressed a hand to the small of Kelsey's back, a statement. "My dad couldn't make it, so I'm here in his place. You never mentioned you attend this event."

"I'm accompanying Mr. Weller since his wife had other obligations. He thought the trip would be a nice reward for my performance this quarter."

"Hmm," Wyatt said in a bland tone, one that could've been read as complete and total disinterest or complete and total judgment.

Gwen's spine starched, so Kelsey guessed the woman didn't

like either option, but she maintained a tight little smile that cooled further as she turned to Kelsey. "And who is this?"

Wyatt's thumb caressed the base of Kelsey's spine. "This is Kelsey Adams. Kelsey, Gwen Harrison. She's an attorney in the building next to mine."

And had some kind of history with Wyatt. Whether that was in the bedroom or in the boardroom, Kelsey couldn't quite tell. She stuck out her hand. "Nice to meet you, Gwen."

"Charmed." The handshake was about as warm as her tone. "And what do you do, Kelsey?"

Her inner bitch wanted to say, *Him.* Just to see the look on this woman's face. But she held her tongue and retracted her claws. It's not like Wyatt was really hers anyway.

"Kelsey's planning to open up her own bakery," Wyatt said smoothly, a tinge of pride in his voice.

"How lovely for you," Gwen said, the condescension not quite fully masked. "Are you one of Wyatt's pet projects, then?"

Kelsey coughed. "Excuse me?"

"You know, those silly little investments he likes to entertain himself with." She slid her sunglasses from atop her head down to her eyes.

"Gwen," Wyatt said, the word holding warning.

She laughed and laid a hand on Wyatt's chest. "Oh, don't get all grumpy. I'm just teasing you. You can do what you like with your money. I'm sure you're very . . . talented, Kelsey."

Kelsey's eyes narrowed. Fuck claws, she was about to sprout talons and fangs. But Wyatt was already two steps ahead. "Gwen, I suggest you don't try this tactic with me. Feel free to throw your ire my way, but you won't insult my girlfriend."

This time it was Gwen's turn to choke. *"Girlfriend?"*

"Babe, I think the boat is waiting for us," Kelsey said, ignoring Gwen's bugging eyes and turning toward Wyatt to lay a hand on his forearm. She didn't know where the words had come from or how'd she'd said them with such a casual air, but there they were. "We probably should head over."

Wyatt smiled down at her and pressed a quick peck to her mouth. "You're right, love. Let's get going. I'm ready to relax in our room before the festivities start tonight." He looked over her shoulder and nodded. "Enjoy your trip, Gwen."

Then he was wrapping his arm around Kelsey, picking up his bag, and leading her toward the dock without peering back. Kelsey didn't let out the breath she was holding until they were a good thirty strides away.

"I'm sorry about that," Wyatt said, regret heavy in his voice.

She peeked up at him as they walked. "Let me guess. The former colleague with benefits?"

"That obvious, huh? I thought we ended things on friendly enough terms, but apparently not."

She shrugged, trying to shake off the little whip of jealousy that hit her at the thought of Gwen and Wyatt together. Had he fucked Gwen in the bed Kelsey had slept in last night? She tried to shove the image from her brain. *He's not yours. Not then. Not now.* "It's never easy to see someone you've slept with kissing someone else, especially if you had feelings for them."

He sighed as their shoes thudded along the weathered wood planks that led down to the boats. "I would've never taunted her on purpose. But hell if I'm going to be polite while she insults you. She can be a bitch to me if she wants, but she has no right to shoot arrows your way."

"It's okay. I have a badass bitch in me, too, if I need it. I can defend myself," she said, leaning into him and giving his side a poke to lighten the mood. "And that chick was already drawing out my street side."

"Oh, really," he said, looking down at her and smiling. "You have a possessive streak, Ms. LeBreck?"

She lifted a shoulder. "There's a reason no one else ever served you at the diner. I would've cut a bitch who tried. That includes Nathan."

He chuckled and spun her against him. "Is that right? Lucky for you, Nathan's not my type."

"Yeah, what is your type then, Mr. Austin?"

"Hmm, let's see. Sexy, nice ass, gives good head."

She punched his chest. "Jerk! And by the way, that means Nathan *is* your type."

He laughed, mirth dancing in those blue eyes. "Okay, how about all those things plus funny, gorgeous, strong, ambitious, submissive, possessive, and knows how to bake a muffin that will make you weep?"

"Better."

Wyatt eyed the end of the dock where a group of people were gathering near what Kelsey assumed was the yacht that was going to take them over to Devil Cay. *Yay, more time to hang with the oh so sweet Gwen. Fun times.* Wyatt brought his attention back to her. "Looks like it's time to board."

"So it seems."

"But first, I have a little confession," he said, touching his forehead to hers.

"Yeah?"

"Yeah. Truth is, I'm wildly possessive, too. And I'm not quite ready to share you yet." He stepped back and tugged her hand, guiding her down another stretch of the pier and toward a separate row of smaller boats that bobbed and dipped in the water. Though, smaller was a relative term since they were all bigger and fancier looking than any boats she'd ever seen.

"Where are you going?"

"Fuck the communal yacht. We're getting our own ride."

"But—"

He stopped and pressed a finger to her lips, his hot gaze singeing right through her protest. "Not asking you. We got interrupted in the car. I'm not going to let it happen again. Plus, I can't very well fuck you with thirty people watching, now can I?"

She arched an eyebrow.

His dimples flashed. "Dirty, dirty girl."

Oh, he had no idea. With the way he was looking at her right now, she'd probably let him take her right there on the dock.

She took a deep breath. No looking back now.

"I'm all yours, sir."

SIXTEEN

Wyatt spoke in low tones to the young guy he'd commandeered to take them over to the island. He didn't want Kelsey hearing his instructions. He was enjoying that curious look she was giving him from her perch on the large cushions on the back deck of the small yacht.

"You sure you know how to handle this thing?" Wyatt asked. The kid couldn't have been more than twenty-two or twenty-three.

"No problem, sir." Johan slid his sunglasses to the top of his head. "I've been helping my father captain the boats since I was sixteen. You're in good hands."

"Excellent." The boat rocked beneath them with the wake from the large luxury liner the other guests had boarded. Wyatt reached out for a railing, watching with satisfaction as the other ship pulled away without them. "You see that boat, my friend. Stay a good distance from that one. I'm paying you for privacy."

"Yes, sir. I understand completely," Johan said, a shy but sly smile breaking through all that suntanned skin, his cheeks coloring a bit. His gaze strayed to Kelsey for a moment, and there was no missing the flare of appreciation.

Wyatt couldn't blame the kid. Hell, he probably shouldn't even think of him as a kid, as he was no doubt closer to Kelsey's age than Wyatt was. He laid a hand on Johan's shoulder. "You can look all you want, but touch her and I'll throw you off the side of the boat."

Johan gave an uneasy laugh. "May be worth it, sir. I'm a good swimmer. But I promise to keep my hands on the wheel."

Wyatt smiled and headed back down toward Kelsey. She held her hand over her eyes, shielding the sunlight and watching him walk toward her. Lord, she was beautiful, all sun-kissed and wind-blown. Her grin was a bright ray of light even amongst all the tropical beauty surrounding them. To think she'd been through so much darkness in her life, so much hurt . . . The knowledge was like a lead weight pressing against his chest. It didn't seem fair that he'd been gifted with so much in his life when someone like Kelsey had been given so little.

Yet, here she was, a survivor, a fighter. And even though he knew she had mixed feelings about him giving her money, and would probably lose her shit when she actually opened the envelope and saw how much, the move had been pure selfishness on his part. He couldn't give her what she deserved—love, a relationship, a soft place to fall. But he could make sure she never had to ask anyone for anything again.

It wasn't money for her time here. But it *was* a thank you. Because even though this was going to be brief, he knew already that this week was going to be one of the best of his life. The old fears would still rumble in the back of his brain, but he wasn't going to waste another minute ruminating. Not when he had something so precious waiting for him.

"Does Abercrombie know what he's doing?" Kelsey asked as Wyatt lowered himself to the deck cushions.

"Abercrombie?"

She smirked. "Never mind. I'm guessing you don't get that catalog."

He glanced over at Johan. "You're telling me you think our young captain looks like a catalog model. Should I be jealous? He *is* closer to your age, after all."

She shoved his thigh with her bare foot. "First off, why go for cute, when I have six feet of gorgeous man right in front of me? And, second of all, that kid wouldn't know what to do with me."

"Mmm," he said, sliding his fingers around her ankle and gripping, enjoying the little catch of her breath it caused. "Too much for him, huh?"

She leaned back on her elbows, her gaze leaving heat trails over his skin in its wake. "Yes, sir."

The simple reply pushed that button inside of him, had everything he'd kept banked all morning leaking through. "Tell me, Kelsey. Is he the type of guy you'd pick to be under your boot heel at The Ranch? Grant told me you prefer the more innocent ones."

Her focus slid away from his face and to the horizon, a curtain falling. "Do you really want to know about that part of me, Wyatt?"

His hand slid up her calf, but he continued to watch her. The thought of her having to dominate someone for cash pissed him off. But the idea that she had that side to her was more than a little intriguing. Submitting held no appeal for him personally, but he couldn't pretend that the image of her making other men grovel at her feet didn't turn him on just a little—as long as those men never touched her. In those fantasies he'd weaved since finding out about her dominance, she was *his*. Her submissives could be lashed by her, made to beg, touch themselves, but only *he* had the privilege of bringing her pleasure. Maybe right in front of those very men, showing them what they could never give her.

Yes, he knew it was a caveman urge, but fuck it. His fantasies. His rules.

"I want to know about all sides of you, love," he said evenly as the ship's engine rumbled to life beneath them.

She continued to stare toward the open sea but relented. "I do like the gentler souls, the ones who come to me because they crave the experience and are appreciative of it. Those who aren't just saying the right things and playing some game because they want to see a chick in thigh-high boots and a corset. Or worse, the ones who think I'm going to break my rules and let them fuck me."

"You've never slept with any of your subs?" he asked, honestly curious.

She shook her head. "There are some I'm fond of and care about. And there are times I get turned on in a session. But the pleasure for me is in the power exchange and seeing how my sub responds to it. Knowing I can provide them with something they so desperately ache for makes me feel . . . valued. But there's not this burning desire to sleep with my submissives."

He cupped the backside of her knee, bending it and tugging her closer to him. "I can't say I feel the same way about my submissive."

Her lips curved as the boat pulled out of the harbor. "Or I about my dominant."

"Hmm, good to know." He dragged her onto his lap, loving how she offered absolutely no resistance, and then tucked her between his knees, letting her lean back onto his chest. He brushed his fingers along her bare arms. "I told Johan to take the slow route, so the trip will be about an hour."

"The slow route?" she asked, her voice going soft and pliant, like she was already sinking under his command. His blood heated at the thought.

"Yes. I have plans for you. But for now, love, enjoy the pretty view." He brought his fingers to the curve of her neck, caressing. "And I'll enjoy touching you."

And maybe, just maybe, young Johan would get more of a show than he anticipated.

Kelsey stared out over the expanse of sapphire water, watching the ripple of white-tipped waves the boat was causing in the rolling surface. "I've never seen water this color. The only beach I've ever been on is Galveston Island."

Wyatt sat his chin atop her head, his arms still wrapped around her from behind. "Yeah, this is no Gulf of Mexico, that's for sure."

The sky was turning shades of pink and orange as the sun tracked its way lower toward the horizon, making the island they'd left in the distance look like it was gilded with fire and diamonds. Everything was so bright here, so clean and vibrant, like slashes of paint had been thrown everywhere. She could almost feel all that color seeping into her skin and bleeding into the dark corners that lurked inside her, chasing out the grays. It was hard to believe that some people got to see all this beauty every day.

But even with the stunning view, she was having a hard time concentrating on anything but the man behind her. Wyatt's fingers were drifting over her skin, absently caressing her arms, her neck, the tops of her thighs. The touches were simple, but each one was stoking the embers that had been burning in her since the car ride. His promise he'd made on the dock hung heavy between them. He had plans, illicit plans, and all she could do was wait to see what those were.

She knew there was a cabin on the other side of the wooden doors at the base of the steps behind them. And undoubtedly Wyatt had paid for full use of all the boat's amenities. She'd seen the wad of cash that had passed hands. But Wyatt didn't seem to be in any hurry to get up and go down there.

His touch traced along the collar of her blouse, teasing at the top button, then plucking it open. Without concern for the guy steering the boat a few feet behind them, Wyatt dipped his hand inside and fondled her with a teasing touch. "You have far too many clothes on, love."

"Maybe you should take me inside, then, sir," she said, leaning her head back against his shoulder and relishing the little threads of anticipation that drew her nipple tight against his palm.

"And miss the breathtaking view? Not a chance." His lips pressed against the shell of her ear. "Take your shirt and panties off, Kelsey."

A spark of disbelief shot through her, a knee-jerk response, but an achy *oh hell yes* was fast on its heels. "Right here?"

"Are you questioning me, love?" he asked, that smooth, dark edge of dominance lacing his deep voice.

She dragged her teeth over her lip. "No, sir."

"Then get to it."

Her heartbeat climbed up into her throat, but she went to work on her remaining buttons. It wasn't like she hadn't been naked in front of strangers before. God knows it should be second nature to her by now. But knowing that Wyatt was commanding it, that he wanted her exposed for him regardless of who was nearby, sent hot, hungry desire pulsing through her. He'd promised her he wouldn't share her, so she trusted he didn't have that in mind, but he'd never promised not to share the sight of her.

She spread the blouse open and off her shoulders, leaving her in her demi-cup lace bra. Then she slipped her hands beneath her flouncy knee-length skirt, hooking her fingers in the sides of her panties and tugging them down. She had to get to her feet to work them fully off and when she stepped out of them, the warm ocean breeze swept beneath her skirt, kissing and caressing all the warm, wet parts of her. Shivers tracked across her skin. She turned toward Wyatt and caught sight of Johan sneaking a peek over his shoulder.

When he realized she'd seen him, she gave him a pointed look and he lowered his gaze and turned back toward the wheel. *That's right*, she thought with satisfaction, her own dominance simmering at the surface. *You haven't earned that look yet, pretty boy.*

Wyatt gave a chuckle there at her feet, his eyes crinkling at the corners as he took her hand and guided her back down to him. "I have to say, love. Dominance looks hella sexy on you. After a look like that, that poor kid's either terrified or hard as a rock, depending on his persuasion."

She settled down on Wyatt, straddling his legs and examining his expression, surprised by what she saw there. "Well, look at you. You like the idea that he might be turned on, don't you?"

He drew his big hands up along her waist, skating them up her sides until he was cradling the lace cups of her bra. "I may have a bit of an exhibitionist streak, truth be told." His thumbs circled her nipples, teasing them. "But I have a feeling you share that inclination."

She curved her back, pressing into his touch, her bared sex rocking against his soft linen pants. "Would've never survived dancing if I didn't, but I wouldn't have suspected it of you. You're so private."

He slipped his hand behind her bra, unhooking it with a quick flick of his fingers. Her bra fell away, and he scraped his stubble over her tender pink points. "I've lived my life always being aware of my family's position, of who was watching, who would gossip. I don't have the luxury of being indiscreet. But if it wasn't for that, I'd have no problem spreading you across my conference table and fucking you right in the middle of a board meeting."

She rubbed her lips together, the image both filthy and enticing. Who would've ever thought that the quiet businessman could shock her? "Wyatt Austin, how did I ever miss seeing this side of you? You are one down and dirty pervert."

He laughed and nipped at the soft underside of her arm. "Guilty as charged. You probably don't want to see inside this head."

"Oh, I think I do," she said, grabbing for his hair as he lowered his head and took her nipple fully in the hot cavern of his mouth, sucking hard. "I really, really do."

He pulled off with a soft popping sound and sent her a smile dripping with sin. "Let's see about that." He tilted his head, looking back over his shoulder. "Johan."

"Yes, sir." Johan swiveled in an instant, his pale green eyes going wide as he took in the spectacle. His tongue swept over his bottom lip, nervous . . . interested.

"You think we can stop and drop anchor here for a few minutes?" Wyatt asked, turning back to Kelsey, wicked smirk still in place. "I don't want you crashing into the rocks, trying to see behind you."

Johan's gaze darted to Kelsey's, then downward, his tawny cheeks darkening as he took in her near nudity. "I, uh, yes, sir. Whatever you need."

Kelsey smiled, Johan's bashful reaction reminding her of Hawk's first time in her dungeon. He'd been so halting, respectful in the way only Southern men could be, but there had also been a keen desire underlying that layer of shyness. A hungry space to be filled.

"You don't have to watch anything if it makes you uncomfortable, Johan," she said gently, drawing her hair forward to cover her breasts. "We don't mind you looking, but it's your decision."

If Wyatt thought she was overstepping her bounds by taking control of the situation with Johan, he didn't say anything. His hands just stroked the small of her back, his cock growing hard against her spread legs.

Johan turned fully around, his board shorts looking a little tighter in the front and his fingers fiddling with the braided leather bracelet on his wrist. "I think I'd do just about anything to watch. As long as it's okay with you."

Wyatt lifted an eyebrow at Kelsey, a question mark. "Your call, love. I won't command you on this one."

"Drop anchor, Johan," she said without tearing her gaze away from Wyatt.

Wyatt's full lips curved. "Get on your knees, love, and face the side railing. Time for me to fuck you."

"Yes, sir," she said, feeling that rush that came when he used *that* tone.

She climbed off Wyatt and crawled on her hands and knees to the side railing, the Caribbean stretching out in front of her, an endless blue horizon. Johan scrambled around, hitting buttons and causing a loud grinding beneath them as the anchor dropped. But Kelsey was no longer paying attention to him. Not when Wyatt sidled up behind her and stroked her waist.

"Put your hands on the bottom rail," he breathed against her ear.

She did so without hesitation, her blood quickening in her veins. He pulled cuffs from the duffel bag he'd brought with him, ones with soft, supple leather and a little chain between them. With deft movements that belied his I-haven't-done-this-in-a-while experience, he locked her to the railing, leaving her chained and resting on her forearms, her nipples brushing the canvas of the cushion she was perched on and her ass in the air. The wanton position probably should've made her self-conscious, but instead a surprising stillness bloomed inside her, intense calm.

Wyatt stroked the back of his hand down her spine, sending tingling sparks outward and all the way to her toes, and then he pushed her skirt upward, exposing her fully. His palms skated over her curves, warming, worshiping, lulling her into an even deeper state of focus. The man knew exactly how to wake up her senses, how to make her aware of every part of herself. No hiding. No separating her mind from the things stirring her body.

Stay here with me, love. Your responses are mine. She could almost hear the whisper of that command in his deliberate movements.

Then, right as she thought she'd memorized his rhythm, his next move, a sharp smack landed on her ass cheek, the force of it making air whoosh past her lips. Wyatt pressed his palm to the stinging spot, soothing again. "So very pretty, love. You should see how your pussy has already gone dark and pink for me."

He spanked her opposite cheek just as hard, the sound echoing in the air around them. She whimpered softly, the fierceness of his blows sending a flood of moisture between her thighs, the burning sting only making her squirm for more of his touch. Fiery need engulfed her.

He gusted a gentle breath over her soaked sex. "And your scent, I could just bury myself in it, eat this sexy cunt until they heard your screams all the way back on the main island."

"Fuuuuck."

Kelsey thought at first that she had been the one to breathe that word; it had been what she was thinking. But the low, male voice was not her own. She turned her head to the side to find Johan sitting a few feet away, his gaze burning, his lips parted, and the front of his shorts tenting with a rather impressive erection.

"You like him watching you, Kelsey?" Wyatt asked before slowly drawing the tip of his tongue over her slit. "Like knowing that he wishes it was him about to fuck you instead of me?"

She squeezed her eyes shut, the dirty words and touch of his tongue vibrating through her and lighting up all those needy deviant parts of herself. "Yes, sir."

"If you want to please her, Johan, take off that shirt of yours and give her something to look at. My pretty girl thinks you look like an Abercrombie model," Wyatt said with playful sarcasm.

There was a scrambling sound of quick movement.

Wyatt's fingers dipped inside her, curling and stroking, and she moaned, her eyes fluttering open. In her peripheral vision, she saw Johan yanking his T-shirt off like it was on fire, and he exposed the tan, fit physique of a guy who spent his days swimming against the waves. Lovely and lean. Not in the honed, broad-shouldered way Wyatt was, but easy on the eyes nonetheless. Johan gave her a small, abashed smile when he noticed her looking.

But the sight of Johan didn't affect her nearly as much as what his presence represented. The fact that Wyatt was behind her, indulging her with a good-looking college guy to play with, imposing no shreds of jealousy or insecure male posturing, was about the hottest thing she could imagine. That supreme confidence of not thinking but *knowing* that no one could compete with him for her attention made her ache all the more. She was all his, and he knew it.

But Kelsey couldn't focus on their one-man audience for long because Wyatt's mouth was on her again, his thumbs spreading her open and giving him full access to every sensitive spot. Her head lolled forward, her eyes closing again, as tight, winding sensation worked through her. He took the slow and sensual approach, like he didn't care if they sat here in the middle of the water until the sky went black. Long and languid strokes that made her legs quiver; soft, sucking kisses to her clit; and light teasing brushes over her back opening all coalesced and transformed her into a mewling, panting mess. The cuff chain rattled against the metal railing as she fought to hold herself still, and the blue horizon swam in her vision.

This man didn't simply use his mouth as a step to get to the main course, he feasted and savored her like this was the five-star meal. "Wyatt, please, I'm going to come."

A hand swatted her thigh, swift and biting, making her choke on her moan. Wyatt shifted behind her. "You won't. Not until I tell you."

She lifted her head, trying to catch her breath and push back the climbing urge before it moved past the point of her own control. Her sight snagged on Johan. The laces were now undone on the front of his board shorts and his hand was tucked inside. His eyelids had gone half-mast, but his focus was still locked on the two of them. She glanced back over her shoulder at Wyatt, who was sitting back on his knees, his fingers stroking her again. "He doesn't get to come until I do either."

A soft, strangled gasp escaped Johan.

Wyatt smiled, dark appreciation in his eyes. "He's not yours to command, love."

"I'll do it," Johan cut in, the words rushed and eager. "I'll wait for her."

Wyatt's gaze seared her, his own desire like a physical blow to her body. "Lucky, lucky me. Now I have two of you at my mercy." The back of his hand brushed her slick folds. "There's lube in my bag, kid, if you need it. I like to take my time with her."

Johan cursed softly.

"Open for me, Kelsey."

She spread her knees wide and tilted her hips upward, all of her tender parts now pulsing with the blood pumping fire through her. Her fingers curled around the railing.

"Tell me what you want, love," Wyatt said, the sound of his zipper like thunder compared to the quiet sounds of water lapping, her own breath, and the slick slide of Johan's pumping fist. Wyatt rolled on a condom and positioned himself behind her, tracing the tip of his cock along her folds in an agonizing tease. She rocked her hips backward, trying to take him in, to force things, but he wasn't going to let her control that. He pinched the back of her thigh with evil intensity. "Tell me or you won't get any of it."

She cried out at the pinch, the sharp pain shooting upward and somehow making her nipples ache for the same. "I want you, sir. Your hands, your cock. I want you to fuck me until I scream and Johan comes all over himself."

"Fucking hell," Johan groaned, his voice sounding desperate and distant to Kelsey's buzzing brain.

Wyatt gripped her hips and shoved forward, stretching her hard and fast, and stealing all her oxygen. She arched upward, the sudden sensation of being so full an intense one. "Oh, God."

Her teeth sunk into her lip as he reared back and plunged forward again. No sweetness or gentleness there, just determined dominance. His fingers bit into her hips with bruising force, and the pain was like sweet, sweet fire racing over her nerve endings. "That's right, love. Take it hard. Show me how much you like to be fucked."

She sagged fully onto her forearms as he thrust over her slick tissues, holding her at the perfect angle to grind right over her hot spot. Her mind began to fuzz from the pleasure, the pain, the perfect cocktail of both.

His hand locked in her hair, pulling tight against her scalp, and he turned her head. "Look at him, love. Look what your sexy moans are doing to him. Feel what they're doing to me."

She pried her eyes open, even though she was drifting into that near-narcotic headspace Wyatt seemed to bring her to, and saw that Johan had shoved his shorts down his thighs and was reclined against the other railing, his jutting cock ruddy and thick in his glistening fist and his other hand cupping and squeezing his balls. Clearly he had his own appreciation for a little pain. All shyness had disappeared in the blinding haze of lust and desire. His gaze latched onto hers. He looked on the brink, desperate, but determined not to break before she did.

Wyatt released her hair, but she understood he wanted her to keep watching. Johan was a gift to her. And Wyatt seemed to be enjoying her teasing another. His arm wrapped around her, finding her swollen clit and pinching. She groaned, a wholly unfeminine sound, and spots appeared in her vision. "Please, Wyatt, please, I can't—"

"You can come, love. Come all over my cock and watch your boy lose it."

He thrust into her, the tops of his thighs smacking the back of hers and his fingers worked her clit with the skill of a man who knew exactly what she needed. Johan's eyes went foggy and she knew hers had to look the same. She watched his tan fist slide along his erection, a beautifully carnal site, but it only made her imagine what Wyatt's thick cock looked like right now, wet and shiny with her juices, plunging and disappearing inside her as he claimed her, her body open and desperate for him. Pleasure sizzled through her like sharp, electric shocks.

"Fuck, I can feel you squeezing me. You're so goddamned hot around me, love." Wyatt's fingers branded her hipbone as his opposite hand rubbed along the sides of her clit, lighting her up and obliterating any remaining control. She exploded with a sharp cry that carried over the water and pushed her over the edge. Her wrists yanked at the chains as the waves of orgasm slammed into her, making her body writhe against Wyatt's tight hold on her.

Then dual male groans overtook her noises, both Wyatt and Johan going over at the same time. Wyatt's cock swelled and pumped inside her, his body going tense against her, as she watched Johan's eyes roll back and thick spurts of his release shoot over his belly and chest.

Ahhhh, God. That's all she could think as another wave of her orgasm crashed over her.

Everything was so hot, so electric, so *alive*.

She was no angel or wide-eyed innocent. But somehow no

matter how many wild, debauched nights she'd had in her life or how many drug highs she'd ridden, nothing compared to the pure, unencumbered pleasure she experienced being topped by this man.

He was better than heroin.

And more dangerous.

But right now she couldn't find it in herself to care.

SEVENTEEN

Wyatt leaned against the railing of the dock, waiting to help Kelsey down from the boat and watching with warm amusement as she said her say good-bye to Johan. The kid was in full *aw, shucks* mode, his hair falling forward as he ducked his head and smiled at Kelsey's murmured words.

Wyatt crossed his arms over his chest, a little surprised by his own reaction. When he'd been with Mia, he'd been ready to tear apart any guy who came near her like some junkyard dog protecting his territory. And she'd known that it was his weak spot. When she'd wanted him to take her further, push the punishment and the pain past where he thought safe for her, she'd taunted him with other men to draw that meanness out of him. He'd taken the bait more often than he'd care to admit.

But with Kelsey that feeling of possessiveness was different. When she'd mentioned that she'd help out with Carmichael, he'd had a surge of *fuck no*. He didn't want her anywhere near that prick, but only because he felt the urge to shield her from any and all ugliness. She'd seen enough of that in her life already.

Otherwise, he felt this odd sense of calm trust in her. The way she looked at him when he commanded her made him feel like a giant, like as long as he was there, she wouldn't really see any other guy around. That rush was something he'd never experienced before. And seeing her weave her spell around Johan, knowing that Kelsey was strong enough both to submit to Wyatt yet trust him to see her other side, had gotten him so turned on, he'd damn near impaled Kelsey when he'd finally gotten behind her.

And she hadn't been putting on a show for his benefit or Johan's. Her responses had been genuine, her kinky side blooming right there in front of him like a hothouse flower. No fear or hesitation. His sweet waitress was dirty in the best way possible.

Kelsey laid a hand on Johan's forearm and pressed a quick kiss to his cheek, then she glanced down toward the dock, finding Wyatt's gaze and sending him a smile that hit him right in the sternum. "Gonna help me down, Mr. Austin?"

He pushed off the railing and stepped forward, offering his hand. "I'm here to serve you, love."

"Liar."

He helped her down to the pier, and Johan went to work getting their bag unloaded. Wyatt curled her against his side and pressed a kiss to her temple. "We need to find our ride. This private charter was well worth it, but I think we only have a little over an hour to get to tonight's cocktail party now."

She leaned into him. "I probably should be nervous, but I feel like I've had a couple of shots of tequila."

He chuckled. "You had a couple of shots of something."

She poked his ribs, but then turned into him, pushing up on her toes and kissing him like they'd been lovers forever. Her blue eyes were soft when she pulled away. "Thank you for that."

"For what, love?" he asked, sensing she wasn't simply thanking him for the sex.

She moved her hair all to one side, gathering it over her shoulder. "For not treating me with kid gloves after everything we talked about. For pushing me anyhow."

He touched her jaw. "I can't seem to help myself with you. You break down my good sense."

She smirked and grabbed his hand to tug him toward shore. "Good. I like when you lose a little bit of your polish."

He laughed. "I'm not all that shiny, love."

"Well, time to put your armor back on then because we have some client fishing to do."

Kelsey adjusted the neckline of her strapless maxi dress, trying to make sure she was still in the classic sexy zone and not the trashy hooker one. The line was kind of blurred in her mind these days. "You sure this looks appropriate? There's not much else I can do with the girls to hide them."

Wyatt's attention slid over to her as they made their way along the sandy path that led down to the beach, his gaze tracing along her throat and cleavage. "First of all, hiding them would be a crime against mankind, so I'm against anything that would do so. And second, you look beautiful. You have a glow to your skin like you've been lying in the sun. *Or* have recently had a screaming orgasm in the middle of the Caribbean."

"That is good for a girl's coloring," she mused, squeezing his hand.

He dipped his head next to her ear as they approached the decked-out beach party. "Here we go. Lights. Camera. Ass-kissing."

Kelsey pasted on a smile, but her stomach felt like marbles were rolling around inside her and knocking together. The party had commandeered a big portion of the beach, more than necessary based on the number of partygoers. Though Kelsey guessed if you owned the whole island, you could have as much space as you wanted. People were spread out in small groupings, the flames of tiki torches swaying and dancing around them in the salty breeze, mixing with the smells of roasted meat. Off to the far side there seemed to be a makeshift dance floor on a spot where the sand was harder packed. A three-man steel drum band was playing a beat that mixed in with the crashing of the waves.

The whole setting was idyllic. Built for the carefree. Too bad she was about as far from carefree as she could be at the moment. And her date didn't seem much better. The set of his jaw looked like he was preparing to go into a battle with no weapons.

"Where's the keg?" Kelsey whispered as they slipped off their sandals and stepped into the silky sand, hoping humor would take the bite out of her nerves.

Wyatt hip checked her lightly, a playful tease, but his face remained stoic and smooth as a waiter approached with a tray. "Miss, can I offer you a refreshment? Champagne? Rum punch?"

She eyed the bubbly and fruity-looking drinks, the ghost of her old self automatically calculating how many of those it would take to get a buzz. She pushed back the thought, disgusted her mind still went there. "Do you have anything non-alcoholic?"

"We have fresh-pressed mango-pineapple juice at the bar. Would you care for that?"

"We'll take two of those," Wyatt said evenly.

"Right away, sir." The waiter gave a little nod and strode off to get them their special order.

"You don't have to abstain on my behalf. I'm used to being around alcohol," Kelsey said, absently adjusting her top again. Apparently that was going to be her nervous tic tonight. "It doesn't bother me if others drink."

He stared out across the crowd as if scanning for the best point of attack. "I didn't do it for that reason. I'm not a big drinker to begin with, but I like to stay sharp at something like this. Let other people get tipsy around me and start spilling their personal business, and I'll be sober enough to remember it."

She shook her head, smirking. "So you can use it against them?"

He looked down at her, that blue gaze a bit wounded. "So I can use it *for* them, love. I want to make them money, not swindle them."

The waiter returned with their drinks, and both she and Wyatt ventured farther into the mix of people. Her heartbeat picked up speed as she took in the other guests and the snippets of conversation. If wealth had a sound it was this—lofty laughter, clinking glasses, claps on the back. She took a long sip of her drink, trying to still her shaking hands. She reminded herself that these were just people like the ones she chatted with every morning at the diner. And it wasn't like she wasn't around the filthy rich at The Ranch. But in that environment different rules applied. It didn't matter who had the biggest bank account or fanciest pedigree— her domme status granted her instant respect.

Wyatt put a hand on the small of her back. "Let's head closer to the water. I think I see an acquaint—"

"Wyatt Austin?" A very shrill, *very* southern voice came from their left, cutting off Wyatt. "As I live and breathe, is that you?"

Both Kelsey and Wyatt turned to find the owner of the outburst coming toward them with a halo of teased red hair. Her smile was so wide and her approach so urgent that Kelsey feared for a moment that the older woman was going to tackle Wyatt like a linebacker.

"Brace yourself," Wyatt said under his breath, but he wore an amused smile as the hurricane of a woman got near. A younger ginger-headed guy hurried after her like an owner who'd realized his puppy had broken off the leash. "Hello, Mrs. Pritchard."

The lady pulled up short in front of them, hands on her hips, her shrewd brown eyes taking in Wyatt from head to foot. "Well, my word. It *is* you. And look how good looking you turned out." She turned and smacked the arm of the younger guy who'd followed her over. "See, son, I told you that was him."

The guy, who looked to be in his thirties, gave her a bemused smile. "I know, I should never doubt you, Mother." He stepped forward and shook Wyatt's hand. "Good to see you, man."

"Same here, Ferris. It's been years." Wyatt released the handshake and slipped a palm onto Kelsey's back. "This is my girlfriend, Kelsey. Kelsey, this is Mrs. Regina Pritchard, a former neighbor of mine. And her son, Ferris. He was a few years behind me in school. I used to tutor him in math."

Mrs. Pritchard gave her an enthusiastic hand squeeze and a beaming smile. "So nice to meet you, Kelsey. And what a pretty dress. I love that print."

The tension in Kelsey eased as she returned the woman's greeting. Mrs. Pritchard reminded her of a home ec teacher she'd had in middle school—a force of nature but a benign one. "Thank you."

Mrs. Pritchard swept a hand, indicating her own bright purple dress and generous curves, then lowered her voice. "I had to give up the prints a long time ago. Ferris told me there really *can* be too much of a good thing. And I'm not going to go against the opinion of a gay fashion designer."

Kelsey pressed her lips together, not sure how to react to that.

But Ferris didn't miss a beat. He shook Kelsey's hand. "And I'm the gay fashion designer. Nice to meet you."

She laughed. "I'm the straight baker."

And that felt good to say. Even though it was a vast expansion on the truth. *This* is what it would feel like to be proud of a job.

"Excellent," he said, his warmth as genuine as his mother's.

Wyatt cleared his throat, clearly searching for small talk, and eventually landed on what was comfortable for him—facts. "Mrs. Pritchard owns the Belle Bridal Boutique chain and the

Belle of the Ball wedding planning service. She handles a lot of celebrity weddings."

"Oh, wow," Kelsey said, genuinely impressed. Even she knew those wedding boutiques were the best of best. And she could definitely picture the boisterous Mrs. Pritchard directing an army to put together an event. "What an exciting job that must be."

She patted Kelsey's arm and leaned forward as if telling her a secret. "To tell the truth, the celebrity ones exhaust me. Nothing like having paparazzi trampling all over the place like raccoons digging through the trash. I much prefer the more private affairs or smaller destination weddings." She sent Wyatt a pointed look. "So when this one pops the question on you, you give me a call, sweetie, and I'll give you a fairy tale."

Kelsey nearly choked at the preposterous thought, though it didn't stop the little girl thrill of thinking about a fairy-tale wedding from zipping through her. God, where had *that* come from? "Oh, we're just dating, ma'am."

Mrs. Pritchard looked between the two of them, her bright pink lips curling into a conspiratorial smile. "I've been doing this for a few decades. I can recognize the lasting couples from the temporary ones."

Kelsey glanced at Wyatt, expecting to find that panicked look men get when anyone mentions marriage, but he looked more thoughtful than anything. Kelsey needed to think quick. She remembered Mrs. Pritchard being on the index cards. Surely a woman in charge of such a wedding empire could be a great potential client, especially when she seemed to have genuine warmth toward Wyatt. This was her chance to take some action and help.

She reached out a hand to Ferris. "Would you care to dance? I'd love to hear about your designs."

"Sure."

Wyatt did send her a panicked expression now, and she slid her gaze toward Mrs. Pritchard, hoping he got the message. He did. They had a brief, silent argument. She won. His polite smile reappeared. "Mrs. Pritchard, would you do me the same honor?"

The older woman pressed a hand to her chest like she was having a slight palpitation. "Of course. Who am I to turn down an offer from such a handsome gentleman? Though, Ferris may be jealous." She leaned closer to Wyatt, but didn't lower her voice. "He had such a schoolboy crush on you back then. I've never seen him study so hard."

Ferris tilted his face toward the stars as if praying for patience. "I think my next design needs to be a customized muzzle."

Kelsey bit her lip to hide her smile and Wyatt chuckled, unfazed by the revelation. "Hopefully, your taste has improved since then."

Ferris gave Wyatt a good-natured smile. "I do try to avoid going after the straight guys these days. But hey, at least now I'm good at math."

Mrs. Pritchard winked at her son, her pride and affection toward him obvious. "So, Wyatt, are you going to dance with a broad or what?"

"I'm all yours, ma'am." Wyatt offered her his arm, the set of his shoulders softer than a few moments before. This woman was impossible to remain uptight around. "Maybe you can teach me a few moves."

Kelsey watched them walk toward the dance area as she and Ferris trailed behind, and she barely resisted the urge to spin around in a victory dance. She didn't know if Wyatt could keep up with Mrs. Pritchard on the dance floor, but she knew one thing for sure—she'd just helped him go the extra step to get a potential new client. Maybe she really could be useful for him here.

Kelsey danced with Ferris, who was just as charming as his mother, then circulated the party with Wyatt for another half hour. Wyatt hadn't been kidding about his hatred for small talk, but she'd let him play the strong and silent type while she filled in the gaps. Luckily, when Wyatt did have something to say, people seemed to want to listen. He already had two meetings set up for when they got back to Texas. And that fact seemed to lift his mood considerably as the night pressed on.

Kelsey was pleased to know she was actually contributing as well. She'd even suffered through a dance with Wyatt's rival, Tony Merrill, in order to give Wyatt a chance to chat with someone Tony had been monopolizing. She'd been skeptical that she could offer any value for Wyatt, but she should've never doubted herself. Wyatt wouldn't have taken her along if he didn't think she could help. He was nothing if not intensely practical. And it wasn't like he needed to come up with some tropical vacation scheme to get her into his bed. When it came to him, she was an easy sale.

After another chat with one of the people on Wyatt's list, Wyatt grabbed Kelsey's free hand and brought it to his chest, dragging her against him. "Getting tired, love?"

"Maybe a little."

He lifted her hand to his mouth and kissed it. "Go sit and relax. I'll grab us something to eat."

"Yes, sir," she said low enough that no one else would hear.

The corner of his mouth lifted. "Keep saying that, and I'll make sure we retire to our room early."

She returned his saucy smile and, after a quick kiss, he sauntered off toward the buffet table. She made her way to the edge of the crowd and sat on one of the deck chairs that had been spread around the perimeter of the party. She buried her toes in the sand and took a deep pull of the sea air. *Ahh.* It had definitely been a long day, but this sure beat hanging out in her little apartment with only the Food Network to keep her company. She drew patterns in the sand with her feet as she watched Wyatt stroll her way with a fresh drink and a plate of the biggest shrimp she'd ever seen. The flames of the tiki torches flickered over his dark features and smiling eyes, which were half-hidden by hair mussed from the steady ocean breeze. The sight of him stole her breath. She'd thought him beautiful in his buttoned-up suit and that always serious gaze he wore behind his glasses, but seeing him like this—relaxed and open—churned up something warm and achy inside her chest.

In that moment, she wished this were all real. That she was his. And he, hers.

She shoved the thought away and the twist of pain it caused. *Rein it in, girl.* There was old Kelsey latching onto impossible hopes again. You'd think she would've learned by now and trained that instinct out of herself.

Another man put his hand on Wyatt's arm before he reached Kelsey, halting him and pulling him into conversation. Wyatt glanced over with an apologetic shrug, but she waved him off. She didn't need him to babysit her. In fact, a little quiet people watching sounded like a nice break. Plus, she needed to get her game face back on so Wyatt didn't catch her looking at him with hearts in her eyes.

But before she could even lean back in her chair to relax and take it all in, an unwelcome visitor settled herself in the chair next to her. "Is this seat taken?"

Kelsey's teeth pressed against one another, and she didn't even bother to look Gwen's way. "It will be when Wyatt makes his way back over."

Gwen sniffed. "I'll be sure to hand over the seat if he needs it. But if Piedmont got a hold of him, he'll probably be there for a while. That man likes the sound of his own voice."

Seemed like Gwen had something in common with Piedmont. Kelsey downed the last sip of her juice and nestled the glass in the sand. Maybe if she didn't respond to Gwen, she'd get bored and go the fuck away.

"Juice. Nice," Gwen said, eyeing Kelsey's empty glass. "Have a reason not to drink? Or just not old enough yet?"

Do not get in a fistfight at the fancy party. Do not get in a fistfight at the fancy party. "Baptist."

"Sure you are."

Kelsey looked at her finally, hoping her expression revealed how close she was to a throw down if Gwen didn't shut the hell up. "You have a point to being here?"

"So you're the Saturday night special now, huh?" she asked, primly sipping her own champagne. "I only thought I'd be friendly— you know, woman to woman—and warn you not to hang your hopes on him. I see how you look at him."

Kelsey opened her mouth to deny it, but who was she kidding? "It's not like that."

"Right." Gwen shook her head almost imperceptibly, a flash of pain tightening her features when she glanced in Wyatt's direction. For the first time, Kelsey felt a dash of sympathy for the woman. "All I'm saying is Wyatt will only ever love one thing— his job. Nothing will take over that space. Not a woman. Not a family." She pinned Kelsey with a cold look. "And certainly not a stripper with a record who's lying bald-faced to him."

Kelsey sucked in a breath.

Gwen's features dripped with smug satisfaction. "Next time you try to sneak into some wealthy guy's bed, do a better job of hiding your tracks and don't leave incriminating evidence in a bag that you don't keep with you."

She tossed Kelsey's passport onto her lap, and everything inside Kelsey went cold. This bitch had gone through her *luggage*?

"I can't believe he didn't run a background check on you and took you at your word. Apparently, blonde hair and big tits make him stupid."

Kelsey almost punched her then. Her fingernails bit into her palm.

"What the fuck did you just say to her?" Wyatt growled.

Kelsey's head jerked to the right, finding Wyatt standing a few feet away, his eyes on fire.

Gwen smiled, so pleased with herself. "Your little *girlfriend* is scamming you, Wyatt. You might want to check your credit card accounts to make sure she hasn't already stolen your numbers. She's no chef, she's just a garden variety whore."

Whore.

The word had been used so often around Kelsey. First directed at her mother, then at her. The single word could twist a blade right through her insides. Tears burned her throat, but hell if she was going to cry in front of this woman. No fucking way.

Wyatt charged forward, absently handing the drink and plate he'd been holding over to Kelsey. Gwen stood, leaving she and Wyatt toe to toe. His expression was a roar of rage, but his tone was pure ice water. "You know, the fact that you would stoop to digging through my girlfriend's things and using your contacts to pull information about her is fucking pathetic, Gwen. And calling her a whore? That's ripe considering you're here with your married boss."

"We're not—" But her protest sounded weak even to Kelsey.

Wyatt smirked, his eyes cold behind his glasses. "Sure you're not."

"I'm trying to help you!" she said, her voice a whisper version of a shout. "She's lying to you."

"No, she's not. I know exactly who she is. She's the most beautiful and honest woman I've ever met." He put out his hand to Kelsey. She set down the drink and food and took his hand, letting him pull her to her feet. "And if you dare say a word to her again or to anyone else here about her, I'll be sure your boss's wife gets an email from a concerned friend."

Her eyes narrowed. "You don't have any proof of anything."

Wyatt smiled and wrapped an arm around Kelsey's waist. If someone else looked their way, it could be mistaken for a pleasant conversation. "Gwen, you're a smart woman. So don't push me because you won't win."

She pressed her lips together until they disappeared into a thin white line.

"Come on, love. I have some other people I'd like you to meet," Wyatt said through clenched teeth.

Kelsey had the urge to say something sharp, to defend herself against the earlier comments. But despite the woman's hateful words and motives, Kelsey couldn't help but hear the truth in her warning: *I fell in love with him, and he walked away without a scratch.*

He will never be yours.

This will *never* be real.

EIGHTEEN

Wyatt guided Kelsey away from Gwen before he could let his ire get the best of him and make a scene. But his jaw hurt from locking his teeth together and not saying what he really wanted. Before all this, he'd had nothing but respect for Gwen, but obviously she'd never shown him what a hateful bitch she could be. The horrid things she'd said to Kelsey . . . Anger pulsed through him with a raucous beat, making his head pound. How Kelsey had kept her class about it all and not stooped to Gwen's level was a wonder. The girl must be made of iron.

Kelsey glanced up at him. "I'm so sorry I screwed up, Wyatt. I never thought to worry about the passport. When they took our bags to the main boat, I should've—"

"You should've done exactly what you did," he said firmly. "You couldn't have anticipated someone acting like a goddamned lunatic."

"You think she's going to say something to the others?"

"No, Gwen's not stupid. She knows I wasn't making an idle

threat about exposing her relationship with her boss." He leaned over and kissed the top of her head. "But I'm sorry you had to hear those hateful things she said. It's my fault. I never should have left you alone, knowing she was around."

Kelsey squeezed his hand as they began to walk again, though she looked much more somber than she had a few minutes ago, the mirth in her eyes gone. "I'm fine. Really. I've heard worse, and honestly, the whole thing just makes me feel sorry for her."

That pulled him up short. He turned toward her, leaving them at the perimeter of the party. "Sorry for *her*? She attacked you."

Kelsey shrugged. "She's got a broken heart and a bruised ego. That can turn even a decent woman into a piranha. She's gorgeous, smart, has a good job. For all intents and purposes, she's way more suited for you than I could ever be, and she thinks she's lost you to an air-headed floozy with a nice rack."

"She and I aren't suited at all," he bit out, then smirked. "And you're far from an airhead or a floozy."

She put a hand to her hip and quirked an eyebrow.

"What? I can't deny the nice rack thing. That's simply a verifiable fact."

She sniffed, but there was laughter in her eyes.

"And I don't know where she gets this big broken heart sob story. I was very clear from the beginning what our relationship could and couldn't be."

Kelsey's gaze drifted toward the water line and the crashing waves. "Sounds familiar."

He frowned at the implication. "Hey, that's not why I was saying that. This is a very different situation."

She turned back to him, a small smile in place, but cynicism in the lines around her mouth. "No, it's not. It's the same exact thing. Only you offered me money for it. And it's a shorter term of service."

"That's not what the mo—"

"It's okay, Wyatt," she said softly. "It's what I signed up for, too."

Before he could respond, a hand clapped him on the back. "There you are."

Wyatt swallowed the rest of his words and turned to the newcomer, Kade Vandergriff. Wyatt had run into him a few minutes ago and had wanted to introduce Kelsey to him. But that'd been before he'd seen Gwen perch next to Kelsey with that predatory look.

Wyatt exchanged a quick handshake with Kade and nodded at Kelsey. "Kade, I'd like you to meet my girlfriend, Kelsey. She's looking to start her own bakery. Kelsey, this is Kade Vandergriff. He owns—"

"A crap-ton of restaurants," Kelsey said, grinning.

A wide smile broke over Kade's face, and he swept Kelsey into an enthusiastic hug, taking Wyatt by surprise. "Hey, dollface, how the hell are you?"

"I'm good, I'm good," Kelsey said, embracing him back and laughing with the tight squeeze he gave her.

Wyatt cleared his throat, not exactly pleased that the big blond seemed so happy to see Kelsey. "You two know each other?"

Kade's grin remained in place, but a flicker of unease went through his eyes. "Uh, yeah, we have mutual friends."

Kelsey glanced at Kade and nodded, but didn't offer any further clarification. Wyatt's bullshit meter shot up like a thermometer in summer. How exactly would a waitress and a restaurant mogul have mutual friends? And that embrace hadn't been a *Hey, friend who I vaguely know through other friends*. It'd been comfortable, warm. An ugly crackle of jealousy went through Wyatt. Was Kade Vandergriff one of Kelsey's clients or maybe one of her customers from the strip club?

"Well, I thought I'd introduce you two since you have an industry in common, but I guess introductions weren't necessary," Wyatt said, feeling his stoic mask slip into place.

Kade tucked his hands in his pockets, the picture of casual ease. "Actually, I had no idea Kelsey was wanting to open a bakery. That's fantastic to hear."

That niggling feeling in Wyatt's gut grew even stronger at that statement. So he didn't know Kelsey through their shared interest in food.

Kelsey pushed her hair behind her ears, looking a little shy under Kade's gaze. "I'm still a long ways off. I want to go to culinary school first, become a pastry chef."

"That's terrific, Kels. Really great," Kade said, giving her shoulder a squeeze. "You should've told me that's the direction you were wanting to go. We do apprenticeships in a lot of my locations. If you ever need a job, you let me know. I know how hard of a worker you are."

Kelsey beamed. "Really?"

It was the kind of business connection for Kelsey that Wyatt had been hoping for by making the introduction, but now he just wanted to step in front of her and stomp his foot like a petulant child. *Mine!*

Ridiculous. What the fuck right did he have to do anything of the sort? Sure, she was his right now, on loan for a few days. But after their time was up, she could date any guy she wanted to. Hell, he wasn't close with Kade Vandergriff, but he knew enough to know that he was probably a settle down and have a family kind of a guy. And he sure as shit had enough money to take care of a woman and make sure she never wanted for anything. Kade could give Kelsey everything she needed *and* what she deserved.

Wyatt knew he was reading too much into it, fast-forwarding Kade and Kelsey's life like some epilogue in a romantic comedy, but he couldn't help it. *Oh, remember how me met, sweetie? We were at that island party and I was with . . . what was his name?*

That guy with the glasses who paid me to pose as his girlfriend? I wonder what ever happened to him.

Wyatt moved closer to Kelsey and grasped her hand, while she and Kade talked about how impressive the appetizer spread was tonight. But he barely heard the conversation, his heart thumping loud enough to drown out the words and the steel drums in the background. Wyatt had no idea what was going on with him. Never before had he ever had an issue keeping things business-like and casual with a woman. Jealousy wasn't an emotion he entertained. Not since Mia. And even with her, it'd been a fleeting state. He hadn't fought for her when she'd used those other men to get his attention. He'd simply cut her off, removed the unproductive emotion. She'd wanted him to fight and challenge, and instead, he'd walked away and left a vulnerable woman feeling worthless.

Regardless, right now he had an overwhelming urge to stake his claim on Kelsey, to be the kind of guy who was offering her so much that no other man could possibly compete. But he had no idea if he was even capable of *being* that guy. Sure, in fantasy-land he could picture coming home to find her humming to herself in his kitchen while she created some new dish for them to eat. He could imagine her curled up on the couch in the media room while he introduced her to movies she'd never seen. Waking up next to her in the mornings. The images dug deep, cavernous holes in his chest.

But he hadn't been lying to her when he'd told her he didn't have room in his life for a relationship. The business took so many hours, so much energy. Kelsey would wither from neglect. And that would kill him . . .

Kelsey nudged him, cutting off her conversation with Kade mid-sentence. "Hey, is that the guy throwing this whole clam-bake?"

"Huh?" Wyatt asked, taking a second to shake off the morose

reel of thoughts in his head, then looked in the direction Kelsey was nodding toward. A man had entered the party and already had a cluster of people gathering around him. *Ah, fucking perfect.* Just what he needed right now. "Yeah, that's Carmichael."

"You know him?" Kade asked.

"Yeah, don't you?"

"Nah, have never met him in person," Kade said, sipping his champagne. "I only got an invite because he's interested in putting a few of my restaurant concepts in one of his hotel chains."

"Nice," Kelsey said.

Kade shrugged. "We'll see. I've heard he can be a little difficult to work with."

"He's a prick," Wyatt said in too foul of a mood to fake it.

Kade laughed good-naturedly. "Yeah, but when it comes to business, aren't we all?"

Wyatt frowned, the statement hitting a little too close to the mark. "Being hard-nosed and being a dick are two different things."

Kade raised his glass. "True enough. But if you dislike the guy so much, why are you here?"

Wyatt started to answer. The truth was as simple as could be. The company needed accounts like Andrew Carmichael. His dad *wanted* accounts like those. For the bottom line, for bragging rights, for a big *fuck you* to their competitors. But watching all the other partygoers fawn all over Carmichael like he was the second coming made Wyatt want to spit. It was all so fake, bullshit piled on top of bullshit wrapped up in sugary compliments and ass-kissing. And he knew, right then, that this was going to be the first time in his life he wasn't going to follow his father's directive.

"You know what, Kade? That's a good fucking question."

Kelsey's head snapped his way, her eyebrows scrunched. "Wyatt."

"Excuse us, Kade," he said, tugging on Kelsey's hand. "I think it's time for a dance with my girl while everybody else verbally jerks off Carmichael."

Kade grinned and gave a little head tip. "Enjoy yourselves. I'm sure we'll see each other around this week."

Kelsey sent Wyatt a questioning look as they gave the knot of people around Carmichael wide berth and headed toward the now abandoned dance floor. Once they reached it, he pulled her against him, finding calm in the feel of her warmth and the sweet scent of her shampoo.

"What are you doing?" she asked as she easily fell into step with his lead. "Isn't that guy the main reason we're here? Ignoring him is going to look rude."

"Change of plans." He spun her out from him, then guided her back. The steel drum band played an up-tempo beat.

She blew out a breath, clearly exasperated. "Meaning?"

"I thought maybe I could get past my dislike for the guy to do what's best for the company, but I can't even look at him without wanting to punch that smarmy smile off his face. I don't want his money. He's a bad human being. I don't want to build more fortune for him."

"But your father—"

"Is going to fucking deal with it," Wyatt said, his words resolute. "And if he doesn't, let him fire me."

Kelsey's eyes went wide. "Shit. Can he *do* that?"

"Technically, yes. But he won't. He's smarter than that."

"Wyatt, I don't know . . ."

There was a hard tap on his shoulder. "Mind if I cut in?"

Jet fuel went through Wyatt at the mere sound of that voice. Kelsey halted her dance step. Wyatt looked over at Andrew Carmichael who, of course, was smiling broadly, way too pleased with himself. He narrowed his eyes and flicked his shoulder-length brown hair out of the way like he was some male runway model. "Well, look who it fucking is—Quiet Wyatt."

Wyatt's teeth gritted together at the old nickname, and Carmichael slapped him on the back with pointed force. "Carmichael," Wyatt replied with lethal calmness.

"I saw your name on the guest list but I had to see for myself. Didn't think you ever came out and mingled with the mortals. Couldn't resist the lure of my beautiful island, huh?"

"I'm here because my father couldn't make it."

Andrew's winning smile stayed in place, but there were daggers in his gaze. "Well, I'm glad you could make it. I've been wanting to discuss some things with your father. Now I can do it with you. I've talked to a few of his other clients, and I think A&A might be just the kind of firm I'm looking to work with."

Wyatt opened his mouth to tell the guy to take his money and fuck off, but Kelsey stepped forward, sticking out her hand and cutting him off. "Hi, Mr. Carmichael, I'm Kelsey. I wanted to thank you for inviting us. The resort and the island are breathtaking. Really. Prettiest place I've ever visited."

Andrew turned the full power of his charm toward Kelsey, taking her hand and bringing it to his mouth to kiss the top of it. It took everything Wyatt had not to yank the asshole backward by his Fabio hair. How dare that fucker touch *his* woman. "I'm so glad you like it. And really, the pleasure is all mine."

Kelsey smiled demurely at Andrew's laying-it-on-thick tone and was that . . . eyelash fluttering? Fuck. She was doing as she promised. Working him. But Wyatt didn't want that. Hadn't she heard a word he said about the change of plans?

"Would you care to dance, Kelsey?" Carmichael asked.

"We were just—" Wyatt began.

But Kelsey sent him a fierce look that said *I got this* before replacing it with her Southern belle act. "That would be lovely, Mr. Carmichael."

"Please. Call me Andrew."

Andrew turned and winked at Wyatt, then led Kelsey away.

Fucker. The guy had simultaneously hijacked Kelsey and put Wyatt in a position where he couldn't do something without looking like a possessive asshole. The music switched to a slower beat, and Andrew pulled Kelsey way too close. That almost sent Wyatt charging like a maniacal bull, but Kelsey met his gaze over Andrew's shoulder, warning him off.

Wyatt forced himself to take a few steps back off the make-shift dance area, but kept his focus glued on Andrew and Kelsey. One errant hand going somewhere it shouldn't and Wyatt was going to break off Andrew's fingers and feed them to the sharks.

"She can take care of herself, you know," Kade said, sidling up next to him again and offering him a glass of what looked to be scotch.

Wyatt accepted the drink and downed it. Fuck keeping his edge tonight. "The guy's a creep."

He nodded toward the couple on the dance floor. "And Kelsey's tough *and* loyal. Whatever she's doing out there is for your benefit."

Wyatt released a weary breath, a deep tiredness settling over him. "How do you really know her, Vandergriff?"

Kade was quiet for a long moment, the ice cubes in his drink clinking against the glass as he rolled it in his hands. "I can't really—"

"Are you one of her clients?"

Kade snorted.

"Well, are you?"

"Uh, no. Kelsey's a doll. But we play for the same team."

Fuck. So Kade was a dom. Perfect. Now that shitty romantic comedy Wyatt had been weaving in his head about Kelsey falling for Kade had an NC-17 element added to it.

"Don't we all." Wyatt glanced over at him, his tone wry.

Kade lifted his eyebrows as he sipped his drink. "So what are you doing with her then?"

Wyatt tilted his head back, looking to the stars above and sighing. "Losing my goddamned mind."

Kade chuckled. "Yeah, I could see that. That girl is one who can leave a mark."

Wyatt rolled his shoulders as the song came to an end and set his empty glass on a passing waiter's tray. "She already has."

Sure, Wyatt marked her physically, but Kelsey had left a brand on him that wasn't fading so quickly. And that scared the shit out of him. He didn't want to care. He didn't want to be jealous. And most of all, he didn't want to hurt her.

"You gonna do something about it?" Kade asked, his tone mild but an edge of protectiveness over Kelsey screaming in the subtext.

"Worst idea ever."

"Ah," Kade said with a knowing nod. "Which means you're going to do it anyway."

"Fucking A."

Kade huffed a laugh and lifted his glass in support. "May the force be with you, man."

"I'll need more than the force." Especially when he'd promised Kelsey he wanted nothing more than a little fun.

After exchanging a quick good-bye with Kade, Wyatt walked across the sand and reclaimed his woman from Carmichael. No other hands but his were going to touch her. Not tonight. And if he had anything to do with it, maybe not for a long time after that.

He hadn't lied to Kelsey when he'd said plans had changed.

Wyatt had a new goal for this trip.

And it had nothing to do with the bottom line.

NINETEEN

"Tell him I don't fucking care what his gut is telling him. He pays *me* to be his gut, and if he doesn't sell that shit off tomorrow, he's going to get crushed. All the indicators are there."

Kelsey blinked in the muted morning light, the living room couch creaking as she turned toward the sound of Wyatt's hushed but firm voice. He was at the small kitchen table with his back to her and his laptop open, hands-free earpiece looped over his right ear. She pushed the blanket off her legs, regretting that Wyatt had woken up before her. Yesterday morning, she'd pulled off the maneuver without a hitch. She'd hoped to manage it again—to sneak back to bed before he realized she'd slipped into the living room in the middle of the night, but she'd slept right past her normal waking hour.

Wyatt grunted at whatever the person on the other end of the phone said. "Yeah, I saw the preliminary numbers on that one, too. It'll look tempting to him, but he needs to sit on his hands. After it goes public and the fanfare dies down, the price is going to drop considerably. It's not as strong a company as the media is making it out to be. He'll be able to get in later if he wants it."

Kelsey sat up and wrapped her arms around her knees, watching Wyatt work. His hair was mussed and he hadn't bothered to put a shirt on, but the set of his shoulders and his tone were all business. She knew if she could see his face, she'd find that oh-so-serious intensity there. That intensity did things to her it shouldn't, warm and tingly things.

Before he could notice her, she tiptoed to the bathroom and took care of her necessities then dug through her bag to find one of the lacy confections she'd bought on her lingerie shopping trip—a near translucent camisole and a matching panty. She checked herself in the mirror and smiled. There. That should be distracting enough to get Mr. Workaholic away from his computer. Yes, it was Monday. But this was supposed to be his vacation after all. No stress allowed.

As she made her way back toward the living room, she could hear Wyatt still barking orders on the phone, his frustration growing. "No, that's not how I told you to do it. I needed those reports broken out separately."

Without looking his way, she strolled past him and into the kitchen.

"And I need you to drill down into that second—" His words cut off abruptly, the rest of whatever he had meant to say hanging in the air.

Kelsey peeked over her shoulder, smiled, and then went about digging through the cabinets to find the canister of coffee.

"Yeah, yeah, I'm still here," Wyatt said, a gruffness to his voice now. "That second report. I want a drill down."

Kelsey set up the coffee pot and got it brewing, but she was amused at how distracted Wyatt sounded as he continued his conversation. She bent over to pull the cream out of the fridge, giving him a clear view of her backside, and Wyatt let out a groan. His response fit into the conversation, but she knew who that groan was for. He snapped his fingers sharply. Startled, she set the cream down and turned his way.

His eyes were blazing with challenge. He crooked a finger at her and pointed to the spot next to his chair. Uh-oh. She chewed her lip and hurried to get over there. His hand jutted out and grasped her shoulder, pushing her down to her knees on the polished wood floor.

Her knees landed on the floor with a soft thud, and Wyatt turned his chair outward to face her.

"Yes, that's exactly what I want you to do," he said into the phone, but he had his hand on the fly of his pajama pants and his eyes on her. *Snap. Snap. Snap.* The buttons on his pants opened. A soft gasp passed her lips when he pulled his hard shaft free and stroked a hand over it. With his other hand, he captured the back of her neck and dragged her forward until she was settled between his spread knees. Then he clutched her jaw hard between his fingers, his look holding hot warning. *You broke the rules again*, it said. *You're trying to control the situation.*

A shiver worked over her at the sternness of his gaze and the unspoken threat. She dipped her head, hoping he heard her own silent response. *I'm sorry. Forgive me.*

"I don't need your apology," he said to the person on the other end of the line, while lacing his hand in Kelsey's hair, wrapping the long strands around his fist. "Just make sure I get what I need."

With an unforgiving grip, he brought Kelsey's head down to his lap and pushed his cock past her lips. She choked at the sudden fullness, but quickly relaxed her mouth and throat around him, closing her eyes and yielding. Wyatt's belly dipped inward, his silent intake of breath a sure sign that he wasn't as steely calm as he sounded. He guided her down his length and then back up, his hold on her hair making her scalp tingle. On instinct, she tried to control the pace, but he wasn't having any of that. When she attempted to pull back a little too far, he reached down and gave her nipple a hard pinch. She whimpered around his cock, the sharp pain catching her off guard and sending a hot moisture flooding her sex.

"No, Cary, everything's fine," Wyatt said smoothly. "Go ahead and give me the rest of the messages."

Wyatt nodded and listened to whatever his assistant was saying but never broke rhythm of thrusting into Kelsey's mouth and moving her head just where he wanted it. His eyes stayed firmly locked on hers. The business chatter faded in her ears, and all she became aware of was her own heartbeat, the wetness gathering between her thighs, and the feel of Wyatt against her tongue. There at his feet, a sense of rightness rose in her, filling her veins and flooding her senses.

She dragged her tongue along the thick vein on the bottom of his cock and pressed at the sensitive spot beneath the tip. Wyatt's eyelids dropped closed, and his bare chest began to rise and fall with quickened breaths. The control was slipping, the need taking over. The transition rolling through his beautiful body was breathtaking to watch. He ripped the phone piece from his ear and tossed it across the table with a growl.

"Fuck, you're good at this," he said with strain in his voice.

She smiled around his cock. *Yeah, she was.* And she could make it even better. She lifted her hand to his mouth. He groaned and sucked her fingers into his mouth, sliding his tongue between her knuckles and getting everything slick, knowing what she was proposing. Last time, he'd stopped her when she tried this, but she'd loved how instantly he had reacted to the normally forbidden touch. She wanted to give him that kind of pleasure again, push it further.

He released her hand and tugged her head back so he could

shove his pants farther down. Then he was guiding her back, his cock sliding over her tongue and stretching her lips. She cupped his balls with her wet hand, spreading the slickness along the bottom and dipping lower. His thighs tightened against her as she teased his perineum and relaxed her throat to take him deep.

"Christ." His hold on her hair shifted, a tremor going through his fingers. "Your mouth is going to be the death of me. I stopped you last time, love, but don't expect that to happen this time. You're going to finish what you started and take it all."

Yes, sir, her mind whispered. She'd never heard more welcome words. She was dissolving with need right there at his feet and wanted nothing more than to give him all the pleasure she was capable of giving. Never before had she gotten so much satisfaction from this act, from serving a man.

She eased a slick finger farther back, teasing his back entrance and then pressing against the tight ring of muscle there. His body initially resisted, but when a long, hard breath hissed passed Wyatt's lips, his muscles relaxed and her finger pushed inside of him. His hand flexed in her hair as if unsure how to handle the invasion, but his knees spread wider, and a low, sexy grunt filled her ears.

Taking that as a good sign, Kelsey swirled her tongue around his cock and pumped her finger inside him slowly, brushing against that secret place she knew could drive a man wild. His shaft seemed to grow harder in her mouth, his verbal responses coming out in short, quiet bursts of sound. His quickening abandon only drove her higher. The fact that he was willing to let her try this with him even though she suspected no one had ever touched him like this gave her a heady rush. Most straight men had hang-ups about being penetrated in any way, even if they suspected it would feel good. She loved that Wyatt could simply enjoy.

His cell phone rang out in the quiet, but he didn't even flinch at the interruption. He tilted his head back and increased the pace, guiding her mouth over him in just the way he wanted. She closed her eyes and let her neck muscles go soft, allowing him to use her fully without any resistance. Her finger eased back and forth inside him, her thumbnail gently scoring his balls. And as he pumped into her mouth, her own mind started to fuzz at the edges—only the clean scent of his sweat and the sounds of their connection filling her senses. She pressed her thighs together, trying to relieve the throbbing ache he was causing.

"You're so fucking beautiful," Wyatt growled, his hips thrusting hard now. "And dirty and sexy and fuck . . ."

His body went taut, his cock swelling in her mouth as a rumbling groan burst from deep in his chest. His release spilled against her tongue, the salty fluid causing Kelsey her own moan of satisfaction. She let her finger slide out of him and gripped his thighs as he rode the end of his orgasm.

When he finally softened his grip on her head and let her hair pass through his fingers, she released him and sat back on her calves, her breath coming in quick huffs, her neck damp with perspiration.

"Eyes down, love. Hands in your lap."

She lowered her head, focusing on the joints where the floorboards met with each other, and tried to calm herself. Every sensitive point in her throbbed and pulsed with want for his touch—her lips, her nipples, the little bud between her thighs. But no touch came. She listened to the brush of cotton as he pulled his pajama bottoms back on, the chair legs scooting along the floor, keys on a keyboard. Then he started talking.

And it wasn't to her.

She looked up in shock, finding Wyatt's profile inscrutable as he resumed talking business with someone. He turned his head quickly, catching her staring, and gave her a cool glare that dared her to argue. She brought her gaze back to the floor, realization settling over her. This was punishment. She'd given him an orgasm that had clearly been fantastic, and he was *punishing* her? Anger flared in her, fire of a different sort heating her blood.

She stayed there on her knees, fuming, and losing track of how much time was passing. The sunlight moved a few inches across the floorboards as Wyatt made a handful of phone calls, never once addressing her in between conversations. She should get up, should walk out, and tell him to go to hell. But something in her refused to let her move. She remained in place, arguing with herself. But in the end, determined pride won out. She would prove she could beat him at his game. This would not break her.

After another terse phone call, Wyatt rose and left the room. She followed his footsteps with her ears, listening as they receded into the back part of the cabana and then grew loud again. His bare feet appeared in the spot on the floor she was staring a hole into. He squatted down in front of her and put a knuckle beneath her chin. She hoped her gaze conveyed her contempt.

His smile was amused. "Watch that feistiness, love. You'll get me hard again, and I may demand a repeat performance before letting you have what you want."

She narrowed her eyes, and he chuckled.

He reached forward and fingered the strap of her camisole before bringing it down her shoulder. Goose bumps prickled her skin at the gentle touch. He repeated the process on the other side, drawing her top downward until her breasts were fully exposed. He pinched a nipple between his thumb and forefinger, earning a gasp from her, and affixed a metal clip. Sensation shot straight downward, more wetness gathering despite her utter annoyance with him. He gave the other breast the same wicked treatment, then gave each clip a flick with his finger.

"Oh!" Her face tilted toward the ceiling, the surprising bite of pain making her dizzy.

"Maybe this will help you learn that you are not in control

here. It's Monday and I need to get some work done. I hoped to fit it in before you even woke up so that I wouldn't have to use up any of our time, but no. Instead, you insisted on parading in here, looking like a fucking wet dream, and teasing me away from what I needed to do.

She gritted her teeth. "I'm sorry, sir. God forbid, I get on my fucking knees and suck you off first thing in the morning. Your plight is truly awful."

"Smart mouth. Sexy but disrespectful." He flicked her nipple again.

"Fuck!" she cried out. How could one little flick of a finger hurt so damn much? She tried to ignore the moisture beginning to leak down her thighs. "Bastard."

He inhaled deeply, closing his eyes for a moment before meeting her gaze again. "You know, love? Your insults would probably be more effective if your scent wasn't giving you away and telling me exactly how turned on you are right now."

Taunting? He was *taunting* her? She couldn't keep her mouth shut. "I was trying to *help* you this morning. You're on vacation, Wyatt. You're not supposed to be working. Jace told me to do whatever I could to make you relax and leave work behind. I was only trying—"

He grabbed her jaw, his tone going fierce. "So you're taking orders from Jace now?"

"No." She tried to shake her head, but his fingers held her firm. "I was trying to help."

"I don't need that kind of help, Kelsey," he said harshly, her point apparently hitting some spot he didn't want poked. He released her chin. "My job is—"

"Everything," she said, looking away. "I know. I didn't mean to interrupt. I just thought you could use a distraction, a break."

He sighed, a sound of resigned frustration more than anger. "Kelsey."

For some ridiculous reason she wanted to cry at the defeated way he said her name. Her temper slid away from her, replaced by the perplexing need to make it okay. "I'm sorry, sir. I tried to control things again. I'm sorry . . ."

Hands spanned the side of her head. "Shh, love. Please don't get upset."

She pressed her lips together, trying to fight back the knot developing in her throat.

His frown dipped deep, regret there in his eyes. "Yes, you did try to control things. That *is* unacceptable. But hell, I didn't need to be an asshole about it. Come 'ere."

She sagged into his grip and met his gaze. His eyes said everything he hadn't. *I'm sorry. It'll be okay. I need you.* His lips met hers in a soft press, his hands sliding down to her neck. The tension slowly unwound inside her belly as he sat on the floor and dragged her into his lap. Her clamped nipples brushed against his bare chest, sending snaps of now pleasure-edged pain through her. She breathed his name into their kiss.

His cock, growing hard again, pressed against the thin silk of her already soaked panties. Her body trembled, need firing anew. She'd been riding on the edge so long, any touch now ignited her. He broke away from the kiss with a panted breath and laid back on the warm wood floor, propped on bent elbows and spread out like a delicious buffet of man and muscle. "I want you, love. And since I've been a jerk, it's ladies' choice this time. Tell me how you want me to make you come."

She briefly considered crawling up his body and straddling his face. The man was a master with his mouth. But she knew nothing else was going to satisfy her at this point except having him inside her. "I need you to fuck me."

A feral look entered his gaze, and he reached beneath her thigh for his pocket. He pulled the condom out, and she lifted up on her knees to give him room to unbutton his pants and sheath himself.

Before he even moved his hand out of the way, she was lowering herself onto him, her folds slick and ready to accept him. She let out a long sigh of satisfaction as he filled every space inside, and she sat fully against his hips. God, each time felt like the first time with him, every nerve ending standing at attention.

His eyes were closed in his own wave of enjoyment, but his smile was unrepentant. "You're going to have to do all the work in this position, love. I'm not accustomed to being on the bottom."

She lifted her hips in a slow drag and then plunged down again, shivering at the look of ecstasy on his face. "I think I can handle it, sir."

By the time she screamed out his name, sending them both into oblivion, the floor was shiny with their sweat and the noon-day sun beamed through the windows.

But as she lay across his chest afterward, their heavy breaths intermingling, she was all too aware that being on top meant nothing. In those few hours of that Monday morning, she realized exactly who had surrendered.

TWENTY

Kelsey lay stretched out in the late-afternoon sun as content as a turtle on a log. The rays had heated her skin to the perfect warmth, and the sound of the crashing waves smoothed out the anxieties knocking around in her head. She gave a languid stretch and a yawn.

Kade shifted on the lounger next to her, turning onto his side and peering at her through his dark sunglasses. He'd joined her about a half hour ago, but both of them had been happy to keep each other silent company. He smirked as she lowered her arms from her stretch.

"What?" she asked, glancing down at her tankini bathing suit. The top had ridden up from her stretch, revealing a fresh expanse of skin.

He nodded at the faint finger-length bruises on her hip. "You're suddenly making me bereft that I decided to come on this vacation with my assistant and not a date."

She laughed and tugged the bottom of the tank down again to hide the marks. "Well, that's your own fault. I see the submissives falling all over themselves at The Ranch to get into your dungeon. I'm sure you would've had a harem of them to accompany you if you'd asked."

"Nah, no one's really captured my interest in months. Well, at least no one who was available. I seem to have a thing for wanting women who already have owners . . . or husbands." He sighed and rolled onto his back, his restlessness palpable. "Last girl I thought could be the answer turned out to be Wyatt and Jace's very married sister. Either of them would probably punch me in the throat if they knew I'd made a pass at her."

"Ouch."

"Yeah."

She turned to face him, propping her head on her hand. "Your problem is you have a hard-on for vanilla girls. You want an innocent who you can mold exactly how you like."

He peeked over at her, his forehead lined with thought. "That's what you think?"

She lifted her eyebrow in challenge. "I don't think. I know. I've heard the subs whining behind your back. Those beautiful, well-trained girls are willing to let you do anything to them, and you're not interested."

"Fuck," he said, turning his face toward the sky again. "You're right. And isn't that just a fucking fantastic kink to have? Because how the hell am I supposed to find that kind of woman? Date a bunch of vanilla girls and see who gets all soft-eyed when I get rough? Good way to get a restraining order."

She reached out and gave his hand a squeeze. "Maybe talk to Grant. He's the one who admits the newbies. Maybe he can connect you with a girl who's curious but not experienced."

He laced his fingers with hers and brought her hand to his mouth for a quick, friendly kiss. "Thanks, dollface. Maybe I will."

"Ahem."

Kade released her hand, and Kelsey sat up to find Wyatt standing behind their lounge chairs, jaw tight, eyes glaring in Kade's direction. Kelsey offered a bright smile. "Hey, you."

"Am I interrupting?" Wyatt asked, his tone cool.

Kade turned in his chair, sitting upright and planting his feet in the sand. "Nah, man. Your girl was just giving me sage advice about my piss poor dating life." He slapped the tops of this thighs and stood. "And now that I'm thoroughly depressed, I think I'm going to go find Carmichael and see what he has to say about the hotel deal."

Wyatt crossed his arms, nodding. "Good luck with that."

Kade sent Kelsey an *oops* look from behind Wyatt and then gave a little wave. "See y'all later."

Wyatt waited until Kade was a good distance away before sitting on the lounger Kade had vacated. He leveled a stare at her.

Oh, shit.

Wyatt was working damn hard to keep his expression placid. The wave of *Mine!* that had flooded his system at the sight of Kade kissing Kelsey's hand was strong enough to make his hands vibrate. Pure adrenaline.

"How'd the meeting go?" Kelsey asked, her tone higher-pitched than normal.

"I'm about ninety-five percent sure she and her husband will go with A&A."

Kelsey's smile lit her face. "That's fantastic."

"Enjoyed your afternoon?"

She wet her lips. "Kade and I are friends, Wyatt. That's it."

He leaned back in the chair. "Did I suggest anything different?"

She crossed her arms over her chest, and he almost smiled at the petulant child expression on her face. "No, but you might as well have drawn a circle around me in the sand and mounted a *Keep Out* sign with the way you looked at Kade."

He reached out and unfurled her arms, then brought both her hands to his mouth for a kiss. "Seeing any man touch you makes me jealous and protective. I can't help that. It doesn't mean I don't trust you or that I suspect anything is going on."

She blinked at him. "So you're not mad?"

"Of course not. Plus, I think I used up my daily allotment of being an asshole this morning."

She laughed and lay back down in her lounger, facing him, "I'll be on the lookout tomorrow then."

He let his eyes travel over her. Her curves were all glossy with sunscreen, and he could see the barest of bruises peeking out near the bottom of her bathing suit. The sight nearly had him climbing on top of her out here where anyone could see. But he had to get shit off his chest first.

"I'm sorry for snapping at you earlier," he said, peering over his shoulder to make sure no one else on the beach was in earshot. "You deserved to be left kneeling and wanting. That part I don't apologize for. I'm your dom and you tried to control the situation again. But what you said about work was right, and I shouldn't have gotten mean about it."

"It's all right," she said softly. "It wasn't my place to say anything. It's your business."

He raked a hand through his hair, her understanding making him feel like even more of a jackass. "It's just, I don't know how to turn it off. I've never not worked on a Monday. Even when I had my appendix out, I held a conference call from the hospital the next day."

She frowned. "Why? Is your job that unforgiving?"

He released a breath. "No, but my dad once told me that being successful is all about inertia, and I took it to heart."

"Inertia?"

He stared out toward the dark blue waves and recited the law. "Yes. 'A body moving forward will continue in the same direction at a constant speed unless disturbed by outside force.' It's a law in physics, but Dad applied it to life, meaning as long as I kept moving forward with the same routine and intensity and didn't let anything distract me off that path, I'd reach whatever goal I had set for myself."

"Oh."

"The only time I let something move me off that path was in college. Mia." He turned to meet Kelsey's eyes. "Suddenly, I was so far off course, I didn't even know where the path was anymore. I was okay with it at the time. It felt freeing—a rebellion in the face of that tight hold I'd always kept on myself. But falling in love with her and then losing her fucking destroyed me. The year afterward, I became someone I didn't even recognize. My grades slipped, my thesis went unfinished, and I didn't give a fuck about much of anything. I just wanted to be numb."

"Been there," Kelsey said quietly.

"And the only one who stepped in and snapped me out of it was my father. Jace couldn't do it. He was wrapped up in his own drama after Evan disappeared. So I leaned on my dad like I never had before. He didn't know why I was so fucked up all of a sudden and didn't ask. He just kicked my ass like a drill sergeant and put me back on the trajectory I was originally on, one that would lead to success, to me eventually taking over the company. He reestablished my inertia." He took a deep breath and shook his head, no longer able to look Kelsey's way. "And since then I'm terrified of anything that deviates from my routine, that distracts me. That question is always lingering in my head: What if this move is the force that shoves me off course again? If I don't take care of my Monday-morning things on Monday and let myself indulge in the beautiful woman sashaying around my kitchen, will everything fall apart?"

The question hung heavy between them, the space only filled with the roar of the ocean and the distant sound of voices down

the beach. He didn't dare look at her. He knew what he was saying sounded ridiculous and weak. Like a man living in fear. If she
rolled her eyes, he wouldn't be able to bear it.

"Prom," she said simply.

The word was so unexpected, he swung his head to look her
way. "What?"

She turned in her chair to sit up and dug her toes into the sand,
her gaze firmly on her feet. "That's the day I got knocked off my
path, when I lost my inertia."

He swallowed, wanting to ask questions, but giving her time
to say what she needed to say.

Her hands gripped the bottom of the lounger. "I lied to you in
your movie room. I used to be even more of a hopeless romantic
than Brynn. All those eighties movies she watched imprinted on
my brain like some sort of disease, giving me hopes for things I
didn't have, love I didn't understand, and experiences I always
wanted. I remember watching *Pretty in Pink* and thinking, *Hey,
that could be me*. Andie was poor, too, and she made her dress,
went to the dance, and landed her Prince Charming. She got to
fall in love despite all the crap she had to go through." She gave a
humorless laugh. "So ridiculous. I was hopeless *and* stupid."

"Kelsey," he said, his chest hurting for her.

But she didn't stop. "When I was sixteen, I fell in love for the
first time. Or at least I thought that's what it was. Brynn didn't
like the guy, and my mom told me he was no good, but I wasn't
hearing any of it. When prom rolled around, he promised he'd
take me even though he'd already declared that prom was 're-
tarded.' And I didn't have the skill to make my dress, but I found
a pretty black gown at the thrift store and made it my own. Brynn
did my hair and makeup, and I was so freaking excited I could
barely wait for the day.

"But when it rolled around, my boyfriend picked me up and
told me there'd been a change of plans. Instead of going to prom,

he was taking me directly to an after party. Only the party turned out to be at a dealer's house. I woke up that morning thinking I'd experience my first prom, but instead I got my first taste of cocaine and lost my virginity. I don't even remember having sex, I just woke up sore and bleeding."

"Jesus."

She raised her head, looking at him finally. "And no one could get me back on track after that. Maybe your dad's theory is true. Makes me wonder what my life would've looked like if that night hadn't changed everything. If I had told him to go to hell and had gone to the dance alone." She gave him a wan smile. "Maybe you're right to be scared of deviations. Maybe you shouldn't have taken me here at all."

"Baby," he whispered, the pressure in his throat blocking anything louder. He reached out for her hand, and she let him guide her onto his lounger with him. He lay on his side and tucked her against him, his hand drifting up and down her arm. Something hot and determined burned in his veins, and for once, it had nothing to do with her body nestled against his. He kissed the curve of her neck. "There's no one I want here with me more than you."

She sighed, sadness lining the soft sound.

"And I turned off my phone."

"Hmm?" she said, obviously still lost in those bad memories.

"Every vacation I've ever taken since I've been an adult has been centered around work. I've been on beautiful islands like this and never put a toe in the water because I was tied to my phone and computer. Even when I was a kid, my father filled vacations with lessons for us—skiing lessons, sailing lessons, you name it. I'm ready to change that. So I turned off my phone. No more work calls for the rest of the week. Now I'm all yours."

She turned in his arms to face him, her curious gaze meeting his. "What do you propose we do then?"

He kissed her nose. "Think you can teach me how to have fun, love?"

Her lips curved at that, some of the weight of their histories lifting and swirling away in the breeze. "Absolutely. I know just the thing to start with."

He smirked. "Should I have brought protection?"

She laughed and rolled off the lounger, grabbing his hand and tugging him upward. "No, horny boy." She bent over and grabbed two abandoned plastic cups. "Come on."

"Where are we going?"

But she was already moving toward the water, so he followed. When she reached the line where the wet sand transitioned to dry, she plopped down like a child and patted the spot next to him. "Sit."

Amused at her bossiness, he complied. "Yes, ma'am."

She pushed a cup his way and laid a quick kiss on his lips before settling back in her spot. "The key is mixing the right amount of water with the sand. With all your math skills, I suspect you'll be an excellent architect."

"Architect?"

She grinned and scooped a pile of damp sand into her cup, packing it down. "Wyatt Austin, we're going to build ourselves a sandcastle."

He stared at her for a moment, then laughed. She was serious. He grabbed his cup and filled it with sand. "Well, okay, then."

He plunked the packed sand down, creating the first tower.

Never before had he wanted to get something just right.

Because if anyone deserved the perfect fairy-tale castle, it was Kelsey.

TWENTY-ONE

Wyatt circled his arms around Kelsey's waist and set his chin on the top of her head, giving her puppy dog eyes in the bathroom mirror as she re-powdered her nose. "Can't we bail on this get-together and go lay out on the deck? Naked. We've got all kinds of privacy out there. And think how fun it'll be to lather up with sunscreen."

Kelsey gave him her best attempt at a stern look, though it was hard with his fingers creeping beneath the bottom edge of her top and stroking her belly. "No way, Mister. I danced with Mr. Fancy Pants the other night to get you this invite. You are going to go play nice and get his business."

"I told you, love. I don't want Carmichael's goddamned business." His palms slid upward, cupping her breasts through the thin lace of her bra. "I want *you*. Plus, I thought I'd teach you to drive a jet ski later."

She shivered beneath his touch, her body going hot at the mere suggestion of spending the rest of the day beneath him. But she had to remind herself that they were here for another reason besides wanton sex and island fun. For most of the week, she'd let Wyatt tempt her away from time with the other guests because one look and sexy suggestion from him usually had all her resolve melting and her clothes magically falling off. And luckily, during the few couple's activities they'd participated in, he'd made good contacts and had a few meetings set up, but the gold medal of clients hadn't been landed yet. So when it came to today's plan, she had to turn the tables on her dom and push the issue. He could punish her for it later.

She set her compact down and turned in his arms. He didn't back up, but simply pressed his hands to the edge of the sink, caging her in. "You brought me here to help you."

"And you have. More than you know." He leaned down and kissed her. "I don't need to go spend time with that jerk. You're much more interesting."

"So the guy's an asshole, so what?" she asked, doing her best not to get sucked into the vortex of temptation. "You don't have other assholes on your client list?"

His smile dipped.

"Exactly. And this guy can help your company. You wouldn't have gone through all this trouble to come out here if you didn't need this to happen." She put her hands on his chest. "So let me help you. Play their game. Which today is poker for you boys and mani/pedis for we delicate ones."

"Delicate, huh?"

She slid her hands upward and wrapped her arms around his neck. "For the record, I could kick all of your asses at Texas Hold 'Em. I play at The Ranch with some of the other employees. But apparently getting invited to Andrew's exclusive poker game is only for a chosen few . . . and those chosen few must have external genitalia. So I'll go hang with the girls and see if I can make any more friends for you. And you go land yourself a whale."

He sighed and touched his forehead to hers, but she could tell she'd already won. "I thought *you* were supposed to be taking orders from *me*, love."

Her lips curled. "Not in this arena. But later . . ."

He drew his hand up from her waist and gently collared her neck, his thumb tracing the delicate skin there. Her muscles automatically went pliant, her weight leaning onto the sink, as if that simple touch hit some liquefy button inside of her. "Yes. Later there will be no talking back, unless it's to beg."

She closed her eyes, her heart hopping like she'd turned up the dial on the treadmill. It took everything she had not to give in and let him take her to the bed right then. She wet her lips, trying to put together her thoughts. "For the poker game . . ."

"Mmm-hmm," he said absently as he wedged his thigh between her legs, giving pressure right where she needed it, and kissed behind her ear.

She swallowed against his hold on her throat, her head tilting back on its own volition. "Don't play too well. Play good enough so that they know you're smart and make wise decisions about when to take risks and when not to, but don't cut off their balls by beating them into the ground and winning all their chips. Let them think you're evenly matched. Let them win some big hands against you."

He leaned back, releasing his hold and smirking. "You're assuming I'm some poker whiz. Maybe they'll beat me fair and square."

She scoffed. "You have a genius mind for math and probabilities, and you have a poker face that would rival a dead man's. Are you telling me you don't know how to play cards?"

His smile was slow, lethal.

She smacked his chest. "You've never lost, have you?"

He grabbed her wrist and brought it to his mouth, kissing the inside of it. "I promise to lose—a little—today. God forbid I injure one of the monster-sized egos in the room."

"Watch that glass house, stud." She pushed up on her toes and kissed him again, then ducked out of his hold, giving him a pat on the ass as she moved past him. "I'll see you after the big game. Go team!"

"Sure you don't want to come by in a cheerleader outfit? Maybe with a big *W* on your T-shirt?" he asked, following her out of the bathroom and leaning against the doorjamb with a sex-on-the-rocks smile.

She cocked her head to the side and tapped a finger against her chin. "Hmm, I think I may still have one of those outfits at home in the *dancer* box. No *W* though."

"Fuck me," he said, carding a hand through his hair and looking like she'd told him she had the best tasting dessert ever but wasn't going to share. "You kept the outfits?"

She shrugged. Truth was, she liked role play. She only hoped she'd never have to do it on a stage again. "Perhaps."

"God, I hate that you had to do that job, but hell if you didn't just make my brain explode a little."

She laughed. "Maybe if you're nice, I'll let you see a few when we get back to town."

The words were out before she had evaluated them, and she barely resisted a face-palm when she realized what they implied. Wasn't she the one who'd called him out on the plane for alluding to future plans? Now she was doing the same. She opened her mouth to backpedal, but Wyatt didn't give her a chance.

"Then I think I'm going to try to be very, *very* nice, Ms. LeBreck." His gaze showed no fear or concern, only searing-hot purpose.

She smoothed her hair, the promise sending a streamer of anticipation through her. "I better get going."

He pushed off the doorjamb. "Good idea, because you're suddenly not doing a very good job of convincing me why I need to go spend the next two hours with a bunch of blowhards when I could be here doing unspeakable things to you."

She blew him a kiss and gave a little wave. "Good-bye, Mr. Austin. Don't get into too much trouble while I'm gone."

"No, I'll save that for you, love."

At that, she slipped out of their cabana and down the steps to the path, smiling so wide her face hurt. She touched her mouth with her fingers, almost surprised to find the grin there. When had she ever felt this . . . light?

She looked to the wide blue sky, half-expecting a bolt of lightning to take her out.

But for once, there wasn't a storm cloud in sight.

"All in." Scott Redmond, one of Wyatt's father's biggest clients, pushed the rest of his stack of poker chips toward the pot and sent a challenging look Carmichael's way.

Wyatt had already bowed out of this hand, though he'd had a pocket pair he would've normally played with. So, he sat back in his chair and sipped his drink as he observed the two men. Scott was bluffing. Even with his stone-cold stare, his thumb had rubbed the band of his wedding ring when he'd made the call, revealing his tell. But this was how Scott ran his business—posture and intimidate until the other side gave in.

Carmichael eyed Scott, turning and turning a poker chip between his fingers as he did, then flicked his cards toward the center of the table. "Fold."

The older man grinned and raked the pot his way. He pushed his own cards toward the dealer, but didn't flip them over, leaving Carmichael to wonder if he'd been had or not. "Smart move, son."

"Keep it up at this rate and you'll need to call Wyatt's daddy to get advice on where to invest your newest fortune," Andrew joked, tilting his head Wyatt's way.

"Or you could just give that big stack of chips to me. I'll make sure it gets to him," Wyatt said with a wry smile.

"Oh, no you don't," Scott replied with a wheeze of a laugh. "There's no one I trust more with my money than your father, but these winnings will go straight into a new boat I've had my eye on."

The dealer dealt the next hand, and Wyatt peeked at his two cards, lifting just the corners and cupping his hand around them—queen, king, suited. He tossed in a few chips. Wallace and Cam Berthelot had already busted out and left, so it was only the three of them now.

Carmichael pushed in enough chips to match Wyatt's bet and nodded his way. "Yeah, Scott here has been singing your father's praises lately. Seems your firm's making him a lot of money."

"Damn straight," Scott said, shoving his own chips in.

Wyatt swirled his drink, still not trusting Carmichael. The guy had been ridiculously cordial so far today. Not a Quiet Wyatt comment to be heard. But that didn't mean Wyatt was letting his guard down. And if Andrew expected him to start begging for his business, he was going to be greatly disappointed. "We're the best at what we do."

"Not what Tony Merrill says," Andrew replied, his eyes on the dealer as the older man turned the first card of the flop.

"Tony promises a lot of flash. If you want to be wined and dined and swept off on their annual Mediterranean cruise so that you feel important, you go with Merrill and Mead. If you want people who actually know the market and see what's around the next curve before you get there, then you go with us." Wyatt tossed more chips in.

"And what if I need someone who knows how to be discreet?" Andrew asked, his tone as casual as the god-awful tropical shirt he wore today. He pushed his cards in, folding.

The question was simple and not completely off the wall. People wanted ultimate privacy when it came to their finances, but the way Andrew had said it had raised Wyatt's creep sensors. "Meaning?"

Andrew shrugged and glanced over at their poker partner. "Scott has told me your father has always been good at keeping things clean. You know, even when they may not start out that way."

Wyatt's attention snapped toward Scott, who only offered a ghost of a smile as he peeked at his cards to decide what his next move was. *Keeping things clean? What the fuck?* "I see."

"Honestly," Carmichael continued, "I wasn't sure if you had the *cajones* to handle something like that. You've never been much of a . . . risk-taker. I mean, you didn't even fuck that pretty girlfriend you had in high school. Shocked the hell out of me when she told me she was a virgin."

Wyatt gripped his drink so hard, he was surprised it didn't shatter in his fist. But there was no way he was going to make a scene in front of Scott, one of his father's most important clients. Wyatt leveled a look at Carmichael, refusing to respond to the bait.

"But when I saw who you brought with you as a date for this week, I realized I must've misjudged you." Carmichael tossed back the rest of his whiskey. "I mean, the Quiet Wyatt I knew would've never had the gall to take a stripper to something like this."

"Don't fucking call her that," he growled.

Scott coughed.

Carmichael smiled, raising his palms. "Whoa, there. Sorry. *Exotic dancer.* Forgive me. Gwen used a much less complimentary term. But she was drunk and on the verge of an orgasm, so you know, what can you do? I got quite a chuckle out of it, though. Mr. Buttoned-up Genius with a girl like Kelsey. And hey, who could blame you? That girl is a looker. I mean, whenever your . . . contract with her is up, I might have to make a little investment myself."

Wyatt was out of his seat before the next breath. He hauled Carmichael up from his seat by the front of his shirt and slammed him against the bank of windows overlooking the beach. The glass rattled and Wyatt vaguely registered the dealer calling for security and Scott calling his name.

"One more word about Kelsey and I will fucking throw you through this window," he seethed, inches from Andrew's smarmy face.

"Ah, just like old times," Carmichael said, his tone bland. "You really should talk to someone about your anger problems."

Wyatt's grip tightened, and he pictured undoing all the plastic surgery Andrew had probably gotten done in the last ten years. But Scott was grabbing Wyatt's shoulder, his voice calm and cajoling. "Come on, Wyatt. Let him go. This isn't the place."

"Don't worry, Scott," Carmichael said with a confident sneer. "He's not going to hurt me. He needs my business, and he's too smart not to know how much my money could mean to his company. All we need to do is agree to get this bullshit bad blood out of the way, so we can move on."

The clopping feet of the two security guards jogging their way sounded in Wyatt's ears. He punched Carmichael in the gut, sending the guy into a gasping front fold, and released him. Firm hands landed on Wyatt's forearms, dragging him backward. "Arms behind you."

Carmichael braced a hand on the window, still half-bent, and looked up at Wyatt. "Feel better now?"

"It's a start," Wyatt spat out.

"Let him go," Andrew said, waving at the security guards. "We're just handling an old matter. Nothing to worry about."

The two hulking guards glanced at Wyatt, and the one on his right gave Andrew a perplexing look. "You sure, Mr. Carmichael? We could take him to the main island, you could press charges."

Andrew finally stood upright again, though Wyatt could see the move was strained. He straightened his shirt. "No need. Just guys being guys."

Reluctantly, the two men released their death grip on Wyatt. One stepped toward Andrew. "Do you want us to send the medic, sir?"

Wyatt barely resisted giving Andrew a real need for a medic, but he knew that would only end up with him in some dirty island prison overnight and Kelsey left on her own here. Not an option. *Kelsey.* Jesus. If Gwen had told Carmichael, who was to say she hadn't told others or that Carmichael hadn't spread the gossip. Now Kelsey was out with women who potentially knew her secret. He needed to get out of here and go to her.

Carmichael declined medical attention and dismissed both the guards and the poker dealer, then turned to Wyatt. "Let's call us even now, all right? You got a free shot at me, and I resisted letting them throw you in a jail cell."

Wyatt gritted his teeth. "I have no idea what you're trying to accomplish—"

"A partnership," Carmichael said with a snake-oil salesman smile. "Just like Scott has with your daddy. And I promise it will be more than beneficial to both of us. You don't need to like me to make money off me. Don't let your pride make you stupid."

"Fuck you and your money." Wyatt turned and headed toward the door.

Carmichael chuckled. "Go have a drink and cool off, old friend. Once you realize you're letting adolescent emotions get in the way of a good business decision, we'll talk."

TWENTY-TWO

Wyatt stormed into the cabana, slamming the door so hard behind him that the waterscape painting on the far wall tilted askew and almost fell off the nail. Kelsey froze at the side of the bed, her open suitcase lying in front of her.

"Un-fucking-believable! Goddamn it all. Why I fucking agreed to come to some party hosted by Satan himself—"

Kelsey shook her head, the tears she'd cried over the last half hour threatening to return. "I'm sorry, Wyatt. I'm so sorry . . ."

His gaze snapped toward her, pinning her like a butterfly to a board. "What the hell are you apologizing for?"

"Someone figured it out, didn't they? I didn't say the right things. I choked." She looked down at the bed. "I'm such a fucking disaster. I don't even know how to *appear* normal."

"Kelsey—"

"I'm so sorry that I've . . . embarrassed you. You should've just taken a normal girl here with you. I know how much your reputation—"

He was across the room in the span between blinks. She

looked down at her toes, still fighting tears, but he pushed his fingers beneath her chin, forcing her face upward. "Listen to me. You didn't do anything. Gwen told Carmichael. And a 'normal' girl? What the fuck does that even mean?"

"Normal. A girl who doesn't have so many skeletons waiting to pounce, one who can go to a spa day with other women and talk about things like high school and college and her job without having to make shit up."

"Stop it," he said firmly. "I would never, ever be embarrassed by you."

She closed her eyes, shaking her head. "You don't have to—hell, *I'd* be embarrassed by me, Wyatt. The way some of those women looked at me today when I stumbled over my answers."

Her stomach flipped over at the memory of it, settling down into the pedicure chair all smiles only to see that judgment in the others' eyes when they started throwing probing questions at her. That . . . dismissal. *You are no longer worthy of our regard.*

"No," he said, his tone as sharp as an ax through ice. "Do not give those women and their opinions that kind of power over you. *I'm* embarrassed that I even know people who would cast you aside because you come from a different background than they do. Fucking elitist bullshit."

She shook her head, another awful realization hitting her, and tears snuck by this time. Those women had acted like they were on a mission today, like they were playing some kind of game they were sure they'd win. Kelsey had thought she'd attracted that shrewd speculation because she'd struggled with some of her answers. But if Gwen had told Carmichael, what if . . . "Oh, God."

"What's wrong?"

All of it started to make too much sense. "What if they *know*, Wyatt? I thought I'd made a mistake somehow today, so they'd figured out I didn't come from money. But God, what if they weren't just being suspicious and nosy but already knew it all? What if Gwen told them *everything*?"

Wyatt's jaw clenched. "I'll make sure she rues the day if she did."

A sick dread washed through Kelsey. "They're all going to assume you paid me to be here, that I'm a hooker."

"Screw what they think. You and I know that's not the case." He looked from her, to the clothes clutched in her hands, to the open suitcase on the bed. "What are you doing?"

"What do you think? I'm packing. I already called and verified there's another boat to the main island in an hour. We need to get out of here."

He took the shirt she'd been holding in her hand and tossed it to the bed. "We're not going anywhere."

"*What?*" Her voice was shrill in the quiet room. "We can't stay. Especially now. Everyone—"

"Can go fuck themselves," he said, his eyes blazing. "Running away now makes us look ashamed, like we've been caught in some big scandal. We haven't. Neither of us have lied—you like to cook, you want to go to culinary school, and you want a bakery."

"We told them I was your girlfriend."

He circled his arms around her waist, his expression softening. "So let's make that the truth, too."

She blinked up at him. "What are you talking about? We said—"

"Don't freak out. I know we promised each other this was just for fun, that it would end when we get back home. But this week has been one of the best I can remember, and I'm not so ready to give this up yet. Are you?"

She averted her gaze, unable to handle the earnest look in his eyes. More time with Wyatt? It was about as alluring a prospect as she could imagine. But it was so risky. Anxiety curled in her belly, her heart waging a battle with her head, and her libido cheering for the wrong team. "Wyatt . . ."

"I'm not saying til death do us part or anything, love. But what does girlfriend/boyfriend have to mean beyond the fact that we're seeing each other and no one else for a little while?" He stroked the base of her spine, sending hot chills along the column. "And all these assholes can move onto some other gossip when they see that you didn't disappear the minute we got back to town."

"Is that what this is about? Making the ruse look more real?" she asked.

The corner of his mouth lifted and he kissed the tip of her nose, which was probably still bright red from crying. "No, this is complete and utter selfishness on my part. I want you, Kelsey. In my bed. At my side. And I want it for longer than two more days. The other is just a convenient side effect."

She pressed the top of her head to his chest, the weight of temptation crushing her. Wyatt had been the subject of her fantasies for so long and now she was living them. Being with him was fun and sexy and goddammit, it made her feel happy. It was so, so dangerous. Was it better to taste the best, most delicious chocolate in the world, knowing you'd only get a few bites? Or was it better to have never tasted it and live your life not knowing what you'd missed?

She'd already had far too many nibbles of the forbidden confection known as Wyatt Austin and now he was offering more—girlfriend, more time, a legitimate place in his life—at least for a little while. "Wyatt, this scares me."

He rubbed her bare arms and sighed. "It kind of scares me, too. But this doesn't change anything except the amount of time. Let's give ourselves a month. If you had decided to do all your training with me, you would've spent the full month with me anyway. Believe me, I never had any intention of letting you finish it up with the lumberjack."

She laughed against his chest.

"Plus, I just punched our illustrious host in the stomach in front of security so I'm feeling ballsy today."

She pulled back, her jaw going slack. "You did what?"

"He's lucky I didn't throw him through a damn window."

"What the hell happened?" He frowned, and she knew instantly. "He said something about me, didn't he?"

"I don't want you going anywhere near him for the rest of the trip," he said, leaning over to close her suitcase and pull it off the bed. "And I was right not to want his business. He's not above board."

"What do you mean?"

"He alluded to some things that have my warning bells going off." He set her suitcase back in the closet, a weariness settling over his features. "Honestly, I don't even want to think about some of the implications he made. I need to talk to my father, but he's still at that therapy thing with my mom. Until then, I'm done worrying about it. It's probably Carmichael blowing smoke anyway."

She sat on the bed, exhausted by the roller coaster of the last few hours. "So what now?"

He reached behind him and pulled off his T-shirt, distracting Kelsey with that lickable torso of his. "Right now, we're taking a lazy afternoon nap because you look wiped out and we're going to need our energy to deal with everyone tonight."

She lifted a brow. "That's all I'm going to need energy for?"

He slipped out of his shorts, leaving him blessedly naked, giving her a view of the kind of sheer male beauty that made every tender part of her tighten. "Guess you'll have to stick around and find out."

She started tugging off her own clothes. "Tease. How am I supposed to sleep with you lying next to me, looking like that?"

He grinned and slipped beneath the sheets, pulling them back on her side. "Come 'ere, love."

She climbed into the bed, and he dragged her against him, pressing his lips to hers and brushing his fingers along her backside. The kiss was languid, his tongue parting her lips and stroking against hers in a soft, sensual tangle. Her body went liquid, her muscles going lax in his hold as he deepened the kiss. If he thought *this* was going to lead to a nap, he was delusional. Sleep was suddenly the farthest thing from her mind.

He traced a blunt fingertip along the crack of her ass, a featherlight touch that had heat gathering low and fast. She moaned into his kiss when he teased at her back entrance. He broke away from the kiss. "I need to have you here, love."

She nipped at his bottom lip, damn near purring at the feel of his dexterous fingertips exploring her. "You can have me any way you want me, Wyatt."

The flash of wickedness in his eyes had her heartbeat stuttering mid-beat. He sat up and flipped her onto her belly as if she weighed nothing. Her face buried into the soft pile of pillows. "I wasn't asking. But I also want you to rest."

She turned her head. "I don't need—"

He popped her thigh with a stinging smack, stealing her protest. "Quiet. I will tell you what you need and don't. And what you need is some sleep. I kept you up too late last night."

The sound of the bedside drawer being pulled open had her dragging her bottom lip between her teeth. He wouldn't let her look in there, but she knew that's where he kept all his fun stuff.

"Lift your hips up, love." She did as she was told, and he tucked something small with soft nubbed latex against her clit. The small but powerful vibrator hummed to life against her. She let out a soft gasp, but Wyatt didn't stop in his ministrations. Straps wound around her hips and thighs, securing the vibe against her. "Maybe this will take the edge off and let you get some rest."

Slippery liquid and warm fingers moved against her back opening, making everything clench inside her. *Ah, God.* The thought of him inside her, taking her there, had her entire system quivering in anticipation. And with the tortuous slow-slow-fast pattern of the vibrator, she felt on the verge of losing it already.

Wyatt eased a finger inside her, and she had to fight not to writhe on the bed. "Please, Wyatt."

A low sound of pleasure from him. "Patience, love. Though I don't think I've ever seen anything sexier than you begging for my cock in your ass. Believe me, I'll have you before the night ends. But right now, I'm going to help you be ready for me."

She buried her head back in the pillows and let out a groan of frustration, which only earned her a dark chuckle from Wyatt. Then his finger was gone and something far bigger was sliding inside her. Her breath whooshed out of her, the edge of discomfort turning a dial inside her, translating all that stimulation from the vibrator into something wholly more intense, forbidden. Her moan was long and pitiful.

"Shh," Wyatt said, caressing her back with his free hand while continuing to ease the implement inside her. "Relax, beautiful. This plug isn't as big as I am. I need to know you can take this so that I won't hurt you later."

She breathed through the overwhelming need to come, trying to focus on relaxing the tension coiling in her body. He nudged the plug deeper and the wider end slipped past the ring of muscle, earning a little cry from her as her body fully accepted the plug. The flared based tucked against her opening, holding everything in place.

"That's it, love. Now just ride the sensation of it all," Wyatt said, his voice as soothing as a thousand massaging hands. He trailed his fingers down her spine and over the globes of her ass. "And let me enjoy you while you come."

Wyatt clasped her hips and lifted her upward until she was on her knees, her back sloping down to the bed. She couldn't even help him get herself into that position. Her nerve endings were starting to spark and flame with need and all she could do was . . . exist and accept it all.

Then, as if he was determined to strip any shred of conscious control she may have left, his tongue was teasing at her soaked pussy and kissing her. Her clit pulsed against the vibrator and, without willing it to happen, her hips rocked against his mouth. He responded by thrusting his tongue inside her, his nose nudging and jostling the base of the plug.

"Holy shit." She squeezed her eyes shut, the involuntary sounds she was making muffled in the thick pillows. Her skin felt as if she were wrapped in live wire, everything humming with energy, alive. This man was going to kill her.

Wyatt didn't let up. He fucked her with his tongue, his own sexy grunts and groans providing her with a soundtrack she wouldn't soon forget. This man didn't simply go down on her, he fucking annihilated her. Never had she been with a man who seemed to relish giving pleasure with his mouth as much as he enjoyed receiving it. He turned it into a goddamned art.

Her fists balled in the sheets, the pressure building to nuclear meltdown level, and Wyatt's fingers dug into her inner thighs, holding her in place, reminding her who was in control, who was unraveling her. The dam broke and a cry tore from her throat as everything went white behind her eyelids, pleasure crashing down around her.

Wyatt helped her ride the wave as long as possible, then flipped off the vibrator when her gasping cries softened. She sank forward in a boneless heap. After a quick trip to wash his hands,

Wyatt quietly removed the harness, kissing each spot of skin the strap had reddened, and gave her a little swat, right at the center of her ass, rocking the plug and sending a sharp aftershock through her.

He ran a hand over the curve of her ass. "Does the plug hurt, love?"

"No," she murmured, too tired to lift her head.

"Good. 'Cause it's staying in for the nap."

She mumbled some unintelligible string of syllables.

He sniffed. "Think you can nap now, love?"

"I'm already asleep."

He laughed and slipped beneath the sheets with her, rolling her to her side and tucking her backside against him. Even in her totally satiated state, her sensors perked at the hard ridge of his erection rubbing against the curve of her bottom. "Good."

"What about you?" she asked, reaching back and stroking the firm muscle in his thigh.

"Don't worry about me, love. I'm going to get more than my share later. Get some sleep."

She nestled into him, already feeling her thoughts drift and stretch toward sleep. "Thank you for getting my mind off what we have to face later."

"My pleasure. And don't give tonight another thought." He rubbed her arm with the backs of his knuckles. "I'm not. You are so goddamned gorgeous. And sexy. And strong. When I walk out there with you tonight, all I'm going to be thinking about is how fucking proud I am to be with you."

She kept her eyes tightly shut, the words pulling emotional strings she didn't want tugged, and forced her breathing into a deep, regular pattern. Maybe if Wyatt thought she'd fallen asleep she wouldn't have to face the very real fact that she was beginning to love this man.

TWENTY-THREE

Wyatt rolled over lazily, reaching across the bed and seeking Kelsey's warmth, but only ended up with a handful of empty sheets. Swallowing back a sigh, he grabbed his glasses off the bedside table and slipped them on, blinking in the bright afternoon light of the cabana. Even though he'd already confirmed she wasn't there, he looked to the vacant side of the bed again. A little pang of disappointment went through him. Even after these days together, Kelsey still couldn't seem to stay sleeping next to him—not even for a simple nap.

She'd either get up in the middle of the night or super early in the morning and slip out. Some mornings he'd found her outside on the deck writing in what he'd deciphered was a journal or he'd find her dozing on the couch in the living room. He hadn't called her out on her nightly escapes, knowing she'd go into combat mode if he questioned her. But he'd hoped that as she grew used to him, she would feel comfortable enough to truly share his bed.

He rolled back to stare up at the ceiling. Kelsey was still running. He'd told her on the plane that he wasn't trying to catch her, but maybe she'd sensed that it'd been a lie—even if he had believed it himself at the time. Whether he wanted to acknowledge it or not, he'd been hunting her for months. Every day he went into that cafe had been one more step in a chase he hadn't realized he was on. And now he had her right there in his grasp, but each time he thought he had a good handle on her, she'd dissipate like fog through his fingers.

You can only have this little piece of me for a while. Every subtle step she took backward repeated those words to him. And he'd thought that would be enough for him. He, of all people, shouldn't want to poke too deep into the psyche of the woman he was with, especially one who was waging war with so many old monsters. But the more and more time he spent with Kelsey, the more he knew in his gut that she was nothing like Mia.

Mia had been fragile from the moment he met her, emotions swinging from one end of the spectrum to the other at a rate impossible to predict. Wyatt had been young, and after not exactly walking into college with a ton of experience with women, she'd seemed like some exotic bird. Wild. Rebellious. Daring. Everything he wasn't supposed to date. The attraction had been too hard to resist. She'd pursued him, and he'd been a willing target. After just a few casual dates, she'd brought him to a play party at one of the professor's houses off campus. He'd had no idea what he was getting into or where that introduction would lead. But a year later, he'd found himself in a full-time D/s relationship with Mia.

It'd been both the best and worst time of his life. He'd experienced highs he'd never thought himself capable of reaching and then lows filled with all the anxiety that came along with having someone else's well-being in his hands. He'd been pompous enough to think he could help balance Mia, soften her destructive edges. But the more he gave her, the more she wanted. He went down the path willingly with her—the light stuff they started with eventually progressing into heavy pain play, long-lasting marks, humiliation. Some of it he'd been into, some of it he did simply because he knew it was what she craved. The darkness of it all had been both frightening and enticing.

But when he started to see Mia's moods dip to more dangerous depths, he'd told her he was backing off until she talked to someone. As her master, he'd commanded it. And she'd listened . . . for a while. But then right when it seemed like things were getting better with her mood, she began to make more demands on his time, to develop a neediness that had never been there before. He'd been in the thick of his graduate program at the time and couldn't afford to be with her every second. So she called him with emergencies all the time, pulling him out of class. When that stopped working, she went after the jealousy card.

The day before she took the pills, she'd called him in class again, telling him he'd regret it if he ignored her this time. He'd shown up at her apartment and the place had reeked of sex, booze, and cologne that wasn't his. Two guys he'd never seen before had been passed out in her bed, naked. She'd been wildly apologetic, of course, but he'd heard the threat she was trying to convey. *Leave me alone, and I'll make you pay for it.* Then she'd begged him to punish her for her transgressions—right there, with those two fucking guys sleeping in her bed.

In that moment, he'd realized he had become a pawn in some elaborate game he no longer wanted to play. He *knew* that something had tilted way off kilter within Mia and suspected that he had played a hand in it. He'd taken a fragile girl into a world of mindfucking, a world built only for the strong.

But he'd been so livid that night. He *loved* her and she'd fucked two strangers just to get attention. He couldn't handle it, and he'd put an end to it right there. She'd grabbed at him, begged him not to leave, had told him she'd take whatever punishment he wanted to give her.

He'd pried her off him and had given her the punishment he knew would hurt her the worst—space.

Two days later he'd gone back to her apartment, worried that she hadn't made any attempts to contact him. And he'd found her in bed, an empty pill bottle on the floor and a note tucked into it. *There is no space for me in this world anymore.*

Wyatt scrubbed his hands over his face as he lay in bed, the memory like a sack of rocks pressing on his chest. His brother was the only one who he'd ever told the whole story to. And Jace had told Wyatt that he wasn't to blame, that Mia clearly had some underlying mental issues that led her to suicide. Logically, Wyatt recognized that, but in his heart he knew exactly what had pushed her over the edge. That note left no doubt. He should've never walked out and left her alone when she was in such a frantic state. Even if he'd wanted to end the relationship, it was his responsibility to make sure she was safe.

And he'd never ever wanted to take on that kind of responsibility for someone again. But these last few days with Kelsey had lit up old, shadowed parts inside him, showing him a glimpse of how D/s could feel when shared with someone who could handle herself. Kelsey worried that she was weak and vulnerable to her old addictions. But Wyatt saw nothing but strength within her.

The girl had fought her way out of a life that few ever escaped, had been raped and tortured, hunted by gang members. Yet each time, she'd picked herself up and moved forward, always with a goal in mind. Alcohol had been abundant on this trip so far, and she'd barely spared it a glance. Even today, she'd probably faced one of the most embarrassing situations anyone could think of when she'd walked into that group of women, yet she wasn't curled in a ball crying about it. She'd simply moved forward again. Shake it off. Form a new plan. That seemed to be how she handled everything.

And that's what made being with her so damn fantastic and

different from anything he'd experienced before. She didn't *need* him to be her caretaker. That heavy weight that had been constantly present in his and Mia's relationship wasn't there. Kelsey's submission wasn't a desire to give over responsibility of her life. Instead it was a mutual exchange between them. They both fed off each other. Balanced.

She didn't need a hero to save her. She'd already saved herself. And maybe had even saved him. He hadn't felt this happy and carefree since . . . well, ever, really.

But it was clear that she didn't see that side of herself. She feared really feeling things. He could see it mar her afterglow every time they made love. The sex would open her up, and then the moment would cool and the guard rails would snap back in place. He'd let her get away with it because he'd promised he wouldn't hurt her, wouldn't give her the impression he could give her something he couldn't. But his resolve on that front was about as strong as tinfoil now.

When Wyatt had seen her with Kade Vandergriff that first night, he'd been jealous and hadn't liked the vision of his future without her in it. No, his life wasn't set up for a girlfriend, but who the fuck created that jam-packed schedule? He did. Would the company fold if he ended his day at six instead of ten? Would the world stop spinning if he took a Saturday off? Obviously, no mushroom cloud had appeared in the distance when he'd stopped calling work earlier in the week.

Plus, he hadn't felt this relaxed, this fucking *good* in longer than he could remember. And he knew that state had nothing to do with the beach vacation and everything to do with the blonde who'd snuck out of this bed a little while ago.

The girl who didn't want to be caught.

He couldn't bait Kelsey with a promise that if she let her walls down things would definitely work out, that this could actually become something. He didn't have a crystal ball. The life they'd return to after this trip was much more complicated than lazy island days. But maybe there was some way he could show her that being open to the possibility was an option.

But he'd learned the hard way that words scared her. Earlier, she'd agreed to another few weeks with him, and he'd wanted to tell her he didn't want a time limit on it, but he'd bit his tongue. His few slipups before now had sent her scampering. Words wouldn't do it. Action. That's what she couldn't help responding to. Lucky for her, action was exactly what he had in mind this afternoon.

He pushed the covers aside and climbed out of bed. After a quick trip to the bathroom to brush his teeth and wash his face, he pulled on a pair of shorts and went to search for Kelsey. Her key was still sitting on the dresser so he doubted she'd left the cabana. He headed toward the living room, expecting to find her napping on the couch, but the room was empty.

However, when he glanced toward the glass doors that led to their private deck and the view of the beach, he saw a flash of painted toenails peeking off the edge of one of the loungers. Smiling, he made his way across the living room and slid open the door. But what greeted him on the other side of the glass damn near knocked him back inside. Kelsey had her face tilted toward the sky, a pair of big sunglasses and a hat shielding her, and a paperback had been set on a side table. But the hat and sunglasses were all she wore. Laid out in the dappled sunlight that peeked through the surrounding palms, her breathing in the even tempo of sleep, Kelsey was blessedly naked, adorned only by tan lines.

Christ. A rattle of hard, pounding need went through him.

Her skin gleamed golden in the late-afternoon rays, her nipples were hard from the kiss of the breeze coming off the water, and her legs were parted just enough to let him see her pretty pink folds and the lavender base of the anal plug peeking out. He went hard as steel in the space between seconds.

His woman was naughty. So gut-wrenchingly sexy that he didn't even have words for it. She made him feel like he'd spent his life on some colorless planet, only existing in black and white until she'd stepped into his orbit. And now everything was in color—bright and full and passionate. Unpredictable. Real.

After drinking in the spectacular view for another long moment, he went back inside to grab a few things. When he came back out, she was still sleeping. He set the items he'd grabbed on the table with her book.

Nap time's officially over, Ms. LeBreck.

Something tickled Kelsey's hand, drawing her slowly into awareness. Awareness that she was deliciously warm, that she wasn't dreaming anymore, and finally that she couldn't roll over. Her eyelids fluttered open, the sunlight dazzling her for a second before the tall backlit shadow in front of her came into focus. Wyatt.

"You left me in bed alone again, love," he said, his voice as balmy as the sunshine beaming down on them.

She tried to shift but her arms had been tied above her and secured to the lounge chair. "I couldn't sleep." *Because I was freaking out. And I could have feelings for you and I needed to get the focus back on the safe side of the playground—on sex.* "So I thought I'd surprise you with your suggestion from this morning."

"Hmm," he said, his gaze sliding along every bare part of her. "I approve. Though I wish I'd been here for the sunblock application."

She smiled under his blatantly carnal perusal, feeling back on solid ground. No tenderness or sweetness there, just pure filthy lust. That look she could handle. "I'm probably due for a reapplication."

"One step ahead of you, love." He moved forward and grabbed her under her knees, spreading her until each foot planted on the deck beneath. Then he sat on the end of the lounger and reached for something on the table next to her. "I'm a little surprised you chose to put temptation for me out here, though."

She looked toward the beach beyond the railing. The part of the shore their room faced was too rocky to walk on, and the sides of their deck were shrouded in trees with no other cabanas near. "How come? It's private enough."

He smiled as he drew a palm up along her belly and cradled her breast in his hand. "Yes, visually private."

He leaned forward and sucked her nipple into his mouth, swirling his tongue around it and teasing it to a tight, pulsing point. She dragged her bottom lip between her teeth, watching his dark head bob against her, his tanned fingers pressing into her paler flesh. He always made her feel so . . . handled. Like she could give herself over completely and know that he'd give her exactly what she needed even if she didn't know exactly what that was. He sucked hard for a moment, the luscious snap of pain drawing a whimper from her. Then moved to offer the same treatment to the other side.

After taking his time with that one as well, he released her with a wet *pop* and met her gaze. Silver glinted in his opposite hand. "But the things I want to do you, love. They're going to make you want to be loud. And sound can carry out here."

"Shit," she whispered, finally realizing the predicament she'd gotten herself in.

He grinned and opened the tiny clamp he'd been holding and positioned it on her nipple. The harsh pinch of it made her hiss, and she tilted her head back as the sensation zipped through her body. This one was different than the one he'd used on her in the kitchen. This one had vicious little metal teeth. Before she could breathe through the pain of it, he clamped the other one as well, and let go of a chain linking the two together. The chain added weight to the clamps and her fists balled in the bindings.

She knew how these kind worked, in theory at least. She used them on her subs often. But son of a bitch that hur—*oh*. Before she could even complete her thought the pain went through that beautiful section of her brain that converted it to sweet, burning warmth. Every part of her body seemed to heat, and the plug that she'd only been marginally aware of for the last few minutes began to throb inside her, making her sex ache for the same feeling of fullness. She sighed into the rush of it all.

"There you go, gorgeous. Let your body do the magic." He grabbed a bottle and squeezed liquid into his palm. "And I think we have enough shade, so you're not going to burn. But you still owe me the chance to give you a rub down. I'd hate for this pretty skin to dry out with all this sun and sand."

He grabbed one of her ankles and lifted her leg, parking her foot against the hard wall of his chest, then started working warm oil into her calf. The position spread her wide, tightened the plug, and left her completely and utterly exposed to him. The breeze swirled over her already damp folds with a warm caress, drawing her scent into the charged air between them. Wyatt sent her a smile that said *You're all mine now,* and her belly flipped at the thought. *His.* For the whole month.

He massaged the oil along her leg, moving down to her inner thigh and working in slow, methodical circles, getting closer and closer to the part of her that ached so badly, but never touching it. An embarrassing amount of wetness gathered between her legs, and when his knuckles grazed that spot between her thigh and her sex, she let out a pitiful whimper.

His hooded gaze slid from her parted mouth downward to the spot that most throbbed, the blue of his irises going almost black. Hungry. She bit her lip, a full body blush rushing over her. Being naked in front of him wasn't new, but she'd never felt so physically open and vulnerable to where he could see exactly how desperate she was for him, how uncontrollable her need was.

His palm tracked down along the back of her thigh and slid the oil along the bottom curve of her ass, jostling the plug inside her and making her hips lift toward him. "Why are you turning red, love?"

The question was low and easy, the sensual syllables of that deep voice rolling over her as she tried to keep herself from moaning. "I—I feel so exposed."

He traced a gentle fingertip along her already slick labia, a butterfly wing of a touch. "And you look beautiful, love. So pink and swollen and slippery for me." He jiggled the base of the plug, sending a ripple of sweet sensation through her. "You've even gotten the plug all slick from your juices. I could come from looking at you."

"Please don't do that," she whispered. She would die right here on this chair if he didn't get inside her soon.

He caressed the inside of her other thigh, tender, reverent. "Don't worry, love. I plan to fill every empty space inside of you. If you let me."

Her eyes lifted at that, colliding with a gaze that suddenly held more than lust in it. It held promise, hope. It held . . . She squeezed her eyes shut. No. He's just talking about fucking. That's all this is. "Please, Wyatt."

She didn't know what she was pleading for exactly—for him to stop saying things like that, for him to touch her where she most needed, for him to take away the fear that was creeping in.

He tugged on the chain between her breasts, sending a sharp bolt of awareness through her and knocking her worried thoughts right out of her head. "Stop thinking, Kelsey. Feel. That's all you need to do right now. You understand?"

"Yes, sir." She nodded quickly, thankful for the shift, for him yanking her back from the scary stuff.

He climbed off the lounger, wiping the oil from his hands on a towel, then tugged off the khaki shorts he'd been wearing. His cock was heavy and thick, jutting out proudly from between those muscular thighs. Wyatt took himself in his hand as he kept his eyes on her, stroking the bead of moisture at the tip and spreading it over the head. His mouth curved upward. "Keep sucking your bottom lip into your mouth like that, and I'll be forced to shove something in there."

She pressed her lips together, unaware that she'd been doing such a thing. But her mouth was watering at the thought of tasting him again, of having her lips stretched wide around that glorious cock of his. "That wouldn't exactly be a punishment, sir."

"You like sucking cock, love?" he asked, his voice going gritty with his own banked desire.

"I like sucking yours."

His smirk was pure sex. "Good answer. But I've got other plans for you right now."

He moved around the edge of the chair to the table and grabbed what looked to be one of the hotel hand towels. He rolled it lengthwise and then brought it to her mouth. She lifted her brows.

"Bite down, love. It will help you keep quiet."

She licked her lips, eyeing the towel with trepidation. "I can keep quiet."

He bent down and kissed her on the nose. "Not if I have anything to do with it. Will you trust me on this or are you saying it's a limit for you?"

The question held no accusatory tone, it was an honest one. If she didn't want to, he would never make her. When she'd been kidnapped, Davis had shoved his sock in her mouth and she'd almost choked on her own vomit. The memory was an ugly one—one that flared up on occasion when she'd gag on something. And she hated that it was there.

She would not let it ruin this moment. And maybe, just maybe, doing this with Wyatt could replace the ugly memory with a sexy one. She nodded. "I trust you."

The pleasure that broke over his expression at her trust was reward enough. He held the towel in front of her mouth and she bit down on it. "Good girl. Can you breathe?"

She nodded.

"Practice spitting it out."

She opened her mouth, shoved the terrycloth out with her tongue.

He grabbed it, re-rolled it, and put it back in, then let his hand drift down to one of her clamps, circling the sensitive area around it. She rocked into the touch with a muffled moan. "There you go. You can get rid of the gag if you need to. But this way, when I fuck those screams out of you—because, believe me, that's what I intend to do—you won't alert the whole island."

He bent down and followed the path his finger had traced with the tip of his tongue, nearly making her eyes roll back in her head. Then he was on the move again, leaving her bereft without his heat, his touch.

"Don't get that forlorn look in your eyes, love. I'm not going anywhere." He snagged a condom off the table and sheathed himself, then lowered his body between her thighs. His focus never left her face as he put his hands behind her knees and pushed her legs toward her chest. "I plan on being here a very long time."

His cock nudged at her soaked entrance, her body not opening as easily with the plug taking up real estate. But he simply pushed her legs wider and worked his way into the impossibly tight space. He groaned as she quivered around him, the feeling of fullness nearly sending her into orgasm instantly. She was so wound up already—bound, gagged, slick with oil and her own arousal that even the hint of him brushing against her G-spot had her nervous system short-circuiting. It was all so much. *He* was so much.

"I can feel you clenching around me," Wyatt groaned as he pumped slowly back and forth inside her. "You're fighting it already, aren't you, sweetheart?"

She made a miserable whimpering sound into the towel.

He let go of one of her legs and reached beneath himself, grasping the base of the plug and turning it easily, the lubricant still keeping things slippery inside her back passage. "Go ahead and take this first one, love. You've earned it. Come for me."

He kept his steady rhythm, fucking her with long, deep strokes, but as he did it he pulled the plug halfway out, lighting up the nerves at the sensitive rim and plunged it back in, fucking her with the toy in the same cadence as the grind of his cock over her G-spot. The dual sensations twined up her spine, radiating out like satellite signals to every molecule in her system.

"That's it," he said, his voice hot against her. "You feel so good. Come all over me. Show me how much you like me fucking that pretty cunt, that tight little ass. Show me how shameless you are. Take it, Kelsey. Take what you want."

At that, she couldn't stop the charging stampede of sensation. It knocked her back against the lounge chair and she groaned into the towel, her teeth gripping it hard as her body rode Wyatt's thrusting cock and his toy. Sweat broke out across her skin and she closed her eyes, drowning.

But before she could even catch her breath, Wyatt was sliding the toy out of her and pulling his cock free. Panic shot through her and she went to reach for him, but her hands were still locked to the chair. He placed a hand on her thigh, giving it a quick squeeze. "Shh, I'm right here."

There was the sound of something slick and then Wyatt was there against her again. Only not at her still-spasming pussy, but at her back entrance. The fat head of his cock pressed against the tight ring, and she shuddered hard, her body still tweaking from the orgasm.

"Try to relax, love," he said, an edge of strain in his voice. "I don't want to hurt you."

She made a frustrated moan. *You won't hurt me. Take me. Please, God, take me.* But the words were only in her head, the towel still gripped tight in her mouth. As if he'd heard her unspoken thoughts anyway, he spread her ass cheeks with his hands and nudged forward, pushing against the pucker of muscle until her body gave in and opened to him. The first full thrust was one of the most intense moments of physical sensation she'd ever had.

The combination of pain and sheer bliss rocked through her like an earthquake, sending fissures and cracks through every semblance of sanity she was clinging to. His fingers found her throbbing clit, converting any remaining threads of discomfort into pure ecstasy, and he began to move inside her, his sexy words falling over her like fiery rain. Words like *beautiful* and *amazing* and *sexy* and that nickname that made her bones melt, *love*.

"Look at me, love," he said in a near strangled whisper.

She forced her eyes open, her brain fuzzy, but her vision of him stunningly clear. His skin glistened with sweat, the muscles of his chest and shoulders flexing and tightening with each steady slide inside her tight passage—a beautiful male beast on a mission to claim. But what transfixed her was the way he was looking at her. Like no other woman had ever existed in the world before this moment and like no other ever would. The sheer power of that gaze ripped right through her, tearing through any distance she was trying to keep between them. Her eyes clamped shut.

"No, Kelsey," he said harshly. "I need your eyes. Look at me. *See* me. See me seeing you."

The words jumbled in her head, mixing in with the overwhelming feeling of her body tightening, revving. But she got the message. *This isn't a random fuck. You mean something. You mean something to me.*

Water filled her bottom lids but she held on to his eye contact, ensnared in it. And only then did he slide his fingers and angle his body in just the right way to take her over the edge. Pleasure shot through her like a thousand pinpricks of light flashing through her and bursting out of her skin. She screamed around the towel, a wretched grit-filled sound that hurt her throat. But she couldn't stop. The crazed noise just kept going and going, on loop. During the height of it, he took the nipple clamps off her, sending a shocking wave of pain through her that only seemed to make her come harder. Her eyes finally fluttered closed, an involuntary response she couldn't fight, and tears slid down her cheeks as the oblivion took her under.

Wyatt's own release was silent, but she felt the unspoken shout in his brutal grip on her thigh, in the shudder of his body. His cock swelled inside her, pulsing and pulsing as if he was determined to give her everything, every damn ounce of his being. Then, finally, he slipped out of her, letting her legs ease back to the cushions, and he bowed forward, laying his cheek to the space between her breasts and panting.

She laid her head back to stare at the sky, her jaw going slack and releasing the towel.

This time she didn't have the energy to run.

TWENTY-FOUR

"Welcome, Ms. Adams and Mr. Austin."

Kelsey forced her mouth to form some facsimile of a smile as a pretty dark-skinned woman handed her and Wyatt each a little white rectangle as they stepped into the main resort's ballroom.

"What's this?" Wyatt asked as he flipped the card over to peer at the numbers on the back.

"Mr. Carmichael is giving away fifty thousand dollars tonight. If you win, you get to pick which charity it goes to."

"How generous of him," Wyatt said, and though his tone was as smooth as glass, Kelsey could feel his grip tighten on her waist, as if saying anything complimentary about Andrew Carmichael costs him a little piece of his soul. "Are the tables assigned tonight?"

The woman smiled. "No, sir, sit wherever you'd like. Dinner will be served after the performance."

"Thank you. Come on, love."

Kelsey took a deep breath, letting him lead her forward. Some of the group had already arrived and tables were beginning to fill up. She kept her gaze forward but could almost feel eyes pressing on her. She didn't know for sure if anyone besides Gwen and Andrew had discovered her most damaging secrets. But based on how those women had treated her at the spa, she wasn't feeling very confident that the information hadn't traveled.

"I feel like everyone is watching us," she said under her breath.

"That's because you look so beautiful, love." Wyatt rubbed circles against the small of her back with his thumb. The dark green dress he'd chosen for her tonight was backless. She'd protested the gorgeous gown, worried that it was too sexy when they were trying to blend in. But he'd insisted, and already she was happy he had. His skin against hers was instant comfort, a soothing salve for the nerves strumming through her.

Wyatt found an empty table and pulled her chair out for her. She sat and heaved a sigh of relief that he hadn't attempted to sit with anyone. She needed a minute to put her game face back on. "I feel like I'm on the verge of a nervous breakdown or something."

"Shh," he said, reaching out and grabbing her knee beneath the table. "It's going to be okay. Just breathe, love."

But as the minutes ticked by, she watched couple after couple enter the ballroom and choose their dinner companions. The tables filled up around them, and a sinking feeling settled over her, like a sack of sand in the pit of her stomach. They were at the only table holding one couple now. She didn't believe in coincidences. And she didn't miss the surreptitious glances, the whispered words at nearby tables. People knew.

"Wyatt," she said, keeping her voice low.

"I know, love." A muscle ticked in his jaw, but he didn't get up and haul her out of there. He simply laid his arm over the back of her chair, exuding that pure I-dare-anyone-to-fuck-with-me confidence that seemed to come so easy to him. "And I'm giving you one order for tonight. You are not allowed to act embarrassed, ashamed, or apologetic."

"But, Wyatt," she protested, her stomach doing flips at the thought of all these people *knowing*, judging.

He turned to look at her. "The only opinions in this room that should matter to you are mine and your own. And *I* am nothing but proud of you. If you show shame, it shames me."

She closed her eyes, unable to meet the ferocity of his gaze and conviction behind his words. "I can take a lot. But don't lie to me. You have to be embarrassed by me. You wouldn't have come up with a fake backstory and last name for me if it didn't matter to you."

A hand touched her cheek. "Love, I came up with the ruse to protect *you*. Not me. Your past is your business, and I didn't want anyone prodding you."

She opened her eyes at that and couldn't help the sharp laugh. "Sure. You would've taken a former drug addict stripper to a business retreat as your real date. Right."

But his gaze didn't waver, his lip only lifted at the corner. "In case you haven't noticed, part of the reason I'm not so good with the social stuff is that I don't give a flying fuck what people like this think of me. If my father could've beat that trait out of me, he would've, but it's not going anywhere. My family, my friends, the girl I . . . care about, that's whose opinions matter. Not some hoity-toity assholes who like to jerk off to gossip." He glanced over his shoulder at the other tables. "I would happily stand up right now and tell everyone in here that I'm dating you—a girl who has kicked and scraped her way through a life that would've crushed most of the people in here. And that she's the most beautiful, kind-hearted, and tough-ass woman I've ever met. I'm humbled to be with her."

Kelsey stared at Wyatt, her throat burning as he made his way through his fervent declaration. No one had ever said anything to her like that before, and she didn't even know how to process it. "Wyatt . . . ," she whispered.

"Shh," he said taking her hand and bringing it to his mouth to kiss her palm. "You don't have to say anything. I just needed you to hear what I think when I see you. And I want you to be proud of that girl because that's who you are now. You're not a fuckup, you're a survivor."

"Are these seats taken?"

Kelsey turned toward the familiar voice, the interruption thankfully cutting off the tears that had been threatening to flow. Kade Vandergriff, looking dapper in his three-piece suit, smiled down at her. A pretty dark-haired Asian woman stood at his side. Kelsey shook her head and Wyatt let go of her hand. "No, please, sit."

"Great." He pulled out the chair for his companion. "This is Maile, my assistant."

They all exchanged introductions, and Kade sat in between Kelsey and Maile.

"I didn't realize you'd brought anyone along," Wyatt said, smiling so deeply his dimples peeked out.

"I was told showing up to this thing solo was frowned upon, so Maile graciously volunteered to come with me even though she barely tolerates me most days."

Maile laughed. "A private island and a free vacation make you a bit more tolerable. Though, if I never have to share a room with you again, it will be too soon."

"What?" Kade asked, all innocent eyes. "I've been good. I've even managed to keep myself covered at all times."

"Thank God. I wouldn't want to have to gouge my eyes out on top of everything else I've been through this week."

Kelsey lifted her eyebrows. So Maile wasn't here *with* Kade. Wyatt's smile faded as if this was disappointing news.

Kade shrugged. "Maile's girlfriend apparently keeps things neater at home and doesn't snore. Though, honestly, I think she's making the snoring thing up. She can't possibly hear that all the way on the other side of the suite."

"Believe me, when you're up sick all night with food poisoning, you hear everything," Maile said then sipped her water.

"Maile had the unfortunate luck of eating at the wrong restaurant on the main island before we got on the boat. She's been knocked down with food poisoning for days."

"All these weeks I'm counting down to get to see this damn island. And boom, I get here and end up worshipping porcelain."

"Oh, no," Kelsey said, her sympathy honest. She'd gotten food poisoning a few years ago and the misery had been second only to detoxing from heroin.

"Oh, well," Maile said, flipping her long bangs away from her face. "It was a helluva way to lose a few pounds, but at least I was able to get into this dress tonight without a crow bar."

Kelsey laughed.

A waiter stopped by and poured wine for everyone, iced tea for Kelsey. After Kade took a sip of his Chardonnay, he nodded at the other seats. "So what's with the empty table?"

Wyatt glanced at the few people still straggling in. "Who knows."

Kelsey frowned. She knew Wyatt wasn't saying anything because he didn't want to share her secrets in front of Maile, but both of them deserved to know. If Kade and Maile were going to sit with them, they needed to be aware it could affect how the others looked at them. She looked to Kade. "People talked. They know I'm not a debutante from down south. And my guess is that most are assuming I'm a hooker who Wyatt paid to come with him."

"Fuck," Kade said, scowling.

"So I won't be offended if y'all want to sit somewhere else. I don't want either of you suffering the social stink eye because of me. I know you're here for business connections."

Kade sniffed. "Screw that. Let them think what they want, judgmental bastards. Half of them probably think I'm fucking my assistant, so what does it matter?"

"That's acceptable, apparently," Wyatt said, leaning his elbows on the table. "But not being a trust fund baby? That's a cardinal sin."

"Mind if we join you?" a male voice asked.

Kelsey turned her head, surprised to see Ferris and Mrs. Pritchard standing there.

"Absolutely," Wyatt said, standing up to help Mrs. Pritchard with her chair.

Mrs. Pritchard made a show of arranging her elaborate sparkly gold dress before settling in her chair. She sent Kelsey a sly smile. "I overruled Ferris on the outfit tonight. I couldn't pass this one up. I feel like the sun."

Ferris patted his mother's shoulder before taking his seat. "She just wants everyone revolving around her."

Introductions were made all around the table, and Ferris made drink orders for him and his mom. Kelsey shifted in her seat, not sure how to approach the new visitors. They'd been friendly with each other since that first night and she'd grown to like the quirky mother and son, but she had no idea if either of them had heard the gossip or not. The thought of lying to them made her nauseous. They'd been nothing but kind to her, and now she felt like an impostor.

But before she could even formulate a plan, Mrs. Pritchard pinned her with those heavily shadowed eyes. "So the idiot mill is saying you're an escort. Please tell me which imbecile started that so I can hit them with my heavy purse."

Kelsey's throat went dry. "I, uh . . ."

Ferris put a gentle hand on his mom's wrist. "Mother, please."

She waved him off. "Don't manage me, Ferris. There's no one in this room who can convince me Wyatt paid Kelsey to sleep with him. First of all, have you seen Wyatt?"

Ferris coughed and went red at the same time.

"Exactly. As if he'd have to pay for a girl . . . or a guy," Mrs. Pritchard said with a curt shake of her head as she turned back to Kelsey and Wyatt. "And second of all, I see how you two look at each other." She tapped her temple then pointed at them. "I've been in the wedding business long enough to know when there are real feelings there."

Kelsey stared at her in stunned silence for a moment, then managed a feeble reply. "I'm not an escort."

"Of course not, darling," Mrs. Pritchard said kindly. "I didn't believe that for a moment."

"But I did lie. My last name is LeBreck, not Adams. I'm not from a wealthy family," Kelsey said, feeling compelled to be honest with the woman who'd shirked off gossip without doubt. "And I have things in my past I'm not proud of."

Mrs. Pritchard accepted her drink from the waiter and took a prim sip. "Darling, don't we all. I could make a fortune on blackmail with the stuff I know about the people in this room alone. Don't you let all that ugly talk get to you. People only whisper about others because they're afraid if they don't give the mill fodder, they'll end up getting whispered about."

Wyatt reached out for Mrs. Pritchard's hand and gave it a squeeze. "Thank you, Mrs. Pritchard. I remember why you were always my favorite mom on the block."

She blushed a bit at that. "Oh, stop it, you charming boy. And don't think that lets you off the hook. I still expect to get your business when you decide to marry this girl."

He barked a laugh. "I wouldn't think of calling anyone else."

Kelsey dragged her teeth over her bottom lip, a pang of emptiness echoing through her. Wyatt sounded so genuine when he said it. Like there really was this possibility in the future. He was a better liar than she gave him credit for.

But she was pulled from her thoughts when the spotlights at

the front of the room went on and the performer was introduced. A magician. Joy. Just what she needed tonight—more illusions.

The show went on for thirty minutes without incident. The guy was good. Kelsey would give him that. But her attention kept wandering to the people at the tables around her. As soon as she'd meet anyone's gaze, they'd avert their eyes. If Wyatt leaned over to whisper something to her, others would whisper, too. It was unnerving and frustrating and after a while, plain pissing her off. But she kept repeating Wyatt's words in her head. She would not show shame in front of these people. She would not give them the satisfaction of letting them know they were getting to her.

And right when she settled down a bit, feeling calmer and more steady, all had to get shot to hell in one simple request. "I need a volunteer for this next part. How about you, my lovely?"

Kelsey's focus snapped forward as the spotlight from up front swung and landed on her. She blinked into the bright light. "What?"

The magician was stepping to the far end of the stage, holding his hand out toward her. "Miss, would you mind being my next victim?"

The audience tittered, but Kelsey barely heard it over the pounding in her ears. She shook her head.

"Aw, come on," the magician cajoled, smiling wide. "I promise this won't hurt a bit. You even get a prize for volunteering."

She shook her head again.

"Maybe you should offer to pay her," an unidentified male voice in the back said. "I've heard that works with her."

The crowd laughed, but this time the sound had a knife edge to it, slicing right through Kelsey. Wyatt's head whipped around, his body bowing up beside her as he looked for whoever had made the snide remark. "Motherfu—"

She laid a hand on his forearm and pushed herself out of her chair. "It's fine. I'll do it."

Wyatt's attention swiveled her way. "Baby, you—"

But she was already moving forward like a wooden doll, one foot in front of the other, not thinking, just doing. Like she used to do when she'd walk up on that stage at the club. It wasn't really happening if you turned your mind off.

Once she made it to the stage, she went through the motions of the trick without seeing the people in the audience. The lights were bright and she was on autopilot. Manny the magician put her in a box and made her disappear. She'd wished it were more than a trick and that it had worked, that she'd spring up back in her apartment far away from all this scrutiny. But after a few moments of being "gone," Manny brought her back into the box and she reappeared in front of everyone. They clapped. But she knew it wasn't for her.

It was the finale of the show and he kept her on stage at his side as he wrapped things up. The house lights came on so Manny could see the audience, and Kelsey tried to keep her focus on the back wall, but soon found her attention drifting from table to table. Every kind of expression stared back at her—curiosity, sneers, judgmental glares. Andrew Carmichael's gaze held lewd interest. *Jackass.*

Each new face made her feel smaller and smaller, cast out. She had the urge to look down at her feet. But when she forced her eyes to her own table, she found nothing but kind smiles from her friends and a thumbs-up from Maile. And Wyatt . . . the way he was looking at her nearly buckled her knees. There was a combination of pride and something else in his expression, something she couldn't even absorb. But it straightened her spine nonetheless.

If he could look at her like that, with no reservations or fear, then she damn well could stand up in front of everyone and keep her head up. He was right. Who the fuck were these people anyway?

Manny put a hand on her shoulder. "And Kelsey, for being such a good sport, Mr. Carmichael has offered a prize of five thousand dollars to your favorite charity."

"Oh," she said. "Thanks."

The older man smiled. "Why don't you tell us the name of your preferred charity and why it's so important to you so that maybe these lovely people will want to donate as well?"

He handed her the microphone and Kelsey panicked for a moment. Charity? The only charitable donations she'd ever made were clothes to Goodwill and the occasional dollar dropped in the buckets of the homeless people who haunted the corners of her old neighborhood. But as she held the microphone, staring out at the crowd, a sense of calm determination welled up in her. She knew exactly the place she wanted for the donation.

She cleared her throat and brought the microphone closer to her mouth, only the slightest tremor in her hand. "I'd like the money donated to the Women's Crisis Center of Dallas." She smoothed her lipstick, building her courage for the why part. "Because they help women when they have nowhere else to turn. And because they helped me."

Manny's dark brown eyes were soft as he took the microphone back. "Thank you, Kelsey. That sounds like a very worthy recipient."

She nodded, clasping her shaking hands in front of her. So there it was. Out there on her own terms. If those souls in the crowd wanted to judge her or her past, so be it. She was done hiding it.

Time to own it.

TWENTY-FIVE

Wyatt propped his head on his hand, staring down at a vision he didn't think he'd ever get the pleasure of seeing. He glanced at the clock. Six A.M.

She was still here. Kelsey had made it the whole night without sneaking off to the couch. Warmth moved up through his chest, lifting a smile on his lips. He brushed a lock of her hair off her cheek, fanning it across the pillow with the rest of her blonde mane. She was beautiful always, but never had he been so taken with anyone as when she had stood on that stage last night, her chin tipped upward as she'd chosen her charity. She'd silenced a whole room of backbiters, making them look like assholes in the classiest way possible.

Afterward, others had come up to them, apologized for assuming things, had asked Kelsey questions. She'd answered some, politely deflected others. Some partygoers had still ignored them, but that was fine by Wyatt. It showed him exactly the kind of people they were. What mattered to him most was that Kelsey had held her head high and hadn't shown any fear or shame. His girl had balls. He'd never been more proud to be by someone's side in his life.

And in that moment, he'd finally accepted one simple fact he'd been fighting since the first time he touched her. He'd fallen for her. Hard and fast and without doubt.

It scared the ever-loving shit out of him.

It was exactly what he told her wouldn't happen.

She was still young.

Still sweet.

It was even messier than he imagined.

But that didn't make it any less true.

Now he was stuck with having no idea what to do with all this . . . love.

Kelsey moaned in her sleep, a low, sexy sound that had his body rousing to attention. He moved his hand away from her hair.

"Wyatt," she murmured, a begging note in her tone, but her eyes still closed with slumber. "Yes. *Please.* I need you . . ."

She shifted beneath the thin sheet, and Wyatt watched in rapt awe as her hand slid down her belly, over her navel, down down down . . .

Oh, blessed blessed Lord. He must've done something really good in a former life.

Kelsey blinked in the gauzy pink light, her brain still hovering in that space between sleep and consciousness. Warmth enveloped her body, and she snuggled deeper into it, hoping to fall back into the erotic dream she'd been having. She'd been on a ship, held captive by a dark-haired pirate with a surprising Southern accent. He'd tied her to the plank instead of making her walk it and had gone about torturing her with his talented tongue and long fingers, making her come over and over again while the waves crashed against the side of the ship beneath her.

But before she could slip back into dreamland, a hand drifted along her stomach and nudged between her legs. She gasped softly as the fingers moved along her arousal-slicked skin. God, how was she so wet?

"Mmm, now that's the best early morning wake-up call I could imagine," Wyatt murmured, his voice clogged with sleep and sexy as shit. "Erotic moans and you already warm and wet. Must've been some dream."

Her eyes fluttered open to find the wispy curtains of their cabana blowing gently along the open windows. The barest amount of pre-dawn light filtered in, reminding her where she was. Not her apartment. Not alone. But on an island with her real-life pirate spooning and stroking her. And she hadn't woken up all night. She hadn't snuck out of bed. Her heartbeat ticked up a notch. "A great dream."

"Tell me about it."

She smiled, even though he couldn't see her. "It was just my normal hot dreams about the starting lineup of the Cowboys."

"Damn. Guess I'm going to have to work extra hard to get your mind off a whole team then," he said, sliding his fingers along her already throbbing clit, coaxing a moan from her.

She arched into his touch, nestling her ass against him, his hard length already like steel between them. "They've got nothing on you, sir."

He groaned and grabbed the underside of her knee, drawing her top leg into her chest and opening her to him. "You calling me that does it to me every fucking time, love. And all those sounds you were just making in your sleep. *Fuck.* I've been hard as stone for twenty minutes, but I couldn't stop listening to you, watching you." He cupped her breast, giving her nipple a soft tug. "Do you know you touch yourself in your sleep?"

She let out a soft puff of breath as the tug became more of a delicious pinch. "No."

"Or that you called my name? Begging me to make you come?" He ran his tongue over the shell of her ear. "You sounded so desperate, love, like you hadn't been touched in eons."

Her cheeks turned pink at that. Even after all the time together, she hadn't gotten enough of him. She'd searched him out in her sleep as well. "I've never been good with moderation, sir. When I like something, I want it all the time."

"Mmm," he murmured, giving her shoulder a soft bite. "This is an addiction I'll gladly endorse. Especially when I share the same one."

Without another word, he shifted his position, and braced a hand on the bottom of her thigh, holding it toward her chest. Then he was pushing inside her, her body offering no resistance. She moaned at the sudden feeling of fullness, at how hot he felt inside her.

"You feel so fucking amazing," he ground out, his hips rocking forward and burying deep. "Like cashmere against me, love."

His name fell past her lips, a sort of protest with no spine behind it. She'd had something to say, but when he moved his hand around the backside of her thigh, finding her swollen nub, she couldn't grab onto the fleeting thought.

He teased her clit with skillful fingers and fucked her with long, lazy strokes. Every fiber in her being seemed to wake up. Like water coming to a boil and bubbles popping at the surface. Bubbles of want, ache, desperation. She squirmed against him, trying to encourage him to take her hard, to charge toward the top of the hill.

"No, love," he admonished. "Not this time. I want to fuck you slow, want to feel every little clench of your pussy around me."

Her sex did exactly that at his words, his voice alone able to trigger seemingly involuntary responses.

"Watch the window. I promise you, you'll get what you want by the time the sun comes up."

The sun? He was going to make her wait . . . He gave her clit a quick flick, and she let out a little cry, a knot of bliss hovering just out of her reach, so ready to unravel. But he seemed to know exactly how far he could take her without going over. He went back to the soft strokes, his cock still sliding in and out with that deliciously tortuous pace. She shuddered against him, her pleasure like the tide outside—ebbing and flowing from sweetly sensual to maddeningly intense moment to moment.

And for some reason that combination had her chest tightening and inexplicable tears threatening. This wasn't like anything she'd ever experienced. It wasn't fucking. This was . . . romantic. It felt like what she'd imagined making love to be. And the realization had her thoughts twisting and curving, colliding, and confusing her. "Wyatt."

But he didn't respond. His hair tickled her as he kissed along the back of her shoulder, sucked at her neck, murmured things to her about how beautiful she was, how sexy, how perfect. And she couldn't muster up the will to make him stop. She wanted this. Wanted to get lost in him. In the fantasy.

By the time the sun cut golden beams across the wood floors, Kelsey was pleading in soft words. Wyatt had flipped her onto her back and was braced above her now, his eyes burning into hers as he moved inside her. Every inch of her begged for release. The hard points of her nipples he'd sucked and licked throbbed. Her thighs quivered. And her pussy gripped him with every thrust as if trying to coax out his release before he was ready.

"Tell me what you want, love," he said, his tone tender but his gaze intense, seeking.

He'd asked her this before, and she'd given him the dirty answer. But this time she could only manage the stark, terrifying truth. "I want *you*."

He smiled then, a slow, curling thing that seemed to shine light on dark places inside her and he dropped to his elbows, taking her mouth in a fevered kiss. She reached up, gliding her fingers through his hair, and opening to him. His tongue stroked hers in time to his rocking hips, devouring her and any thoughts she'd been hanging onto. He was inside her—in her body, in her mouth, and in her head. She was consumed. Soaring.

Her nails dug into Wyatt's shoulders and he groaned into their kiss, his muscles going taut as her own orgasm slammed into her. She held on to him, her body almost convulsing with the sheer force of it all. She broke off the kiss with a sharp cry, but right as she sucked in a breath, his lips were back on her. His mouth making love to her as much as any other part of him.

Her orgasm wouldn't relent, as if it wanted to get its money's worth after the long buildup. She arched against him, riding the pulsing pleasure and dragging him to his own edge. Finally, he quivered against her, biting her lip, and falling into his own release. He pumped inside her with forceful, moaning thrusts, all that measured self-control melting away.

He was so beautiful like that—a wild, masculine animal, the man behind the polish. She loved his quiet side, the person he was in the world. But this was a sight that yanked the breath from her chest. Suddenly, she felt a ridiculous surge of jealousy toward anyone who had ever seen him this way.

Wyatt stilled inside her and opened his eyes, his brows lowering briefly at her expression. "You okay?"

She smiled. "I'd say so."

"Mmm." After one last lingering kiss, Wyatt slipped out of her and rolled to the side, his flat belly rising and falling with fading exertion. "Good morning."

"Helluva wakeup call."

"I'd say. You sure you're okay? You looked a little mad just now." He shifted onto his side, propping on his elbow and peering over at her.

She would've blushed if her face wasn't already hot from

orgasm. "You're too observant, Mr. Austin. I was just having a girl moment."

He smirked. "Oh, do tell."

She sighed. How much should she reveal? She didn't want him to think she was getting all possessive on him, but he'd see through bullshit if she tried. "I had a passing moment of jealousy toward all the other women who've seen you like this. A brief hormonal brain fart."

He laughed and reached out to brush her hair away from her forehead. "No need to be jealous, love. Not many have seen me like this."

She rolled her eyes. "Yeah, okay. And I lost my virginity last week."

"No," he said, tapping a finger under her chin. "I mean, like *this*."

She rolled to her side to face him, but before she could ask him what he meant, a trickle of warm fluid slid over her thigh. A rush of anxiety went through her. "Oh, shit."

He frowned. "What's wrong?"

She swallowed hard, stealing herself for his reaction. When they'd discussed limits, she'd seen his expression at the thought of unprotected sex with her. And who could blame him? An unplanned pregnancy with someone like him could get a girl a big pile of cash. "We didn't use a condom. Wyatt, I'm sorry, I didn't think of it. And then everything was feeling so good, I kind of forgot. But I promise I'm on the pill and you've seen my medi—"

"Shh," he said, brushing a thumb over her lip and catching a drop of blood there from his earlier bite. "I wanted you without any barriers this morning. And you told me you were protected from pregnancy. I trust you."

His expression was so open, so relaxed and accepting that panic mainlined right through her veins. "Wyatt, what are you doing?"

"What?"

But she'd already seen the shift in him yesterday, the way he'd talked to her, held her. Tender. Caring. She'd thought it'd been part of the whole crazy day, an aftereffect of all that stress. And she could handle a lot. There wasn't much he could do to her physically that she couldn't deal with. But this—this could annihilate her.

She sat up, hugging a pillow to her chest. "Don't do that. Don't look at me like I mean something to you."

He pushed himself upward, turning toward her on the bed. "What the fuck are you talking about? Of course you mean something to me. You think I'm putting on a goddamned song and dance show for you? Why do you think I asked for more time with you yesterday?"

"A month, Wyatt. Don't give me the forever eyes."

"Kelsey—"

"Don't," she repeated. Her throat went tight, and she wished he wasn't so close. She couldn't think with him staring at her with those naked blue eyes. "That's not what this is. It's not what it's supposed to be. No romance, Wyatt. No sweet pillow talk."

"I love you."

"*What?*" The trap door fell right out from beneath her. She pulled her knees to her chest and pressed her forehead to the top of them, barely resisting covering her ears. *No. No. No.* "Don't do this, Wyatt. *Please.* I can't—"

He sighed. "You can't, what? Handle it? Love me back? Deal?"

"You don't love me. Don't say that."

"Don't tell me what I do and don't feel, Kelsey," he said, anger leaking into his tone as he reached over and grabbed for the robe he'd hung on the bedpost. "Believe me. This wasn't my plan either. But I'm not going to sit hear and lie about how I feel."

"Love? That's bullshit and you know it. You barely know me.

Yes, this week has been fun and I enjoy being with you. But we can't do this for real."

"Why the hell not?"

She looked at him, disbelief coursing through her. "You want to go through what we did last night every time you take me somewhere? Get those looks? I will never fit into this world. And even if you don't see it yet, I'm just a shiny, new toy for you—something different and exciting. As soon as the novelty wears off, I'll be the next Gwen. Only with a nice check in the bank so you don't have to feel so guilty."

A thundercloud crossed over his expression. "So this is what you're going to do, Kelsey? This is your life plan—push away anyone who could care about you so you can't ever get hurt?"

Her vision went blurry with tears. "You told me not to let you hurt me. You *told* me. This will hurt me. You said yourself you're no good for me. I deserve better than becoming another Saturday night special. Don't pretend that's not what this would become."

He scowled. "How the fuck am I supposed to know what this could become? But you're not even willing to see where it could go? To feel whatever we feel and go from there? I care about *you*, dammit. Not just fucking you. *Being* with you. I'm old enough to know the difference. Are you?"

"I guess not." She laced her hands behind her neck, still sitting in the fetal position, tears tracking down her cheeks. "I can't do this."

"You're going to sit there and pretend you don't feel something for me, too?"

"This is what I do, Wyatt," she said, lifting her head and meeting his eyes, her heart splintering at his guarded expression. "I fall too fast. It doesn't matter what I feel for you. Every time I've trusted my heart in my life, it led to nothing good. I'm addicted to relationships. And what you're offering me right now is the like the biggest, purest dose of heroin I could imagine."

He sat on the edge of the bed, but didn't reach for her. "Baby, you are not that girl anymore. Your heart wasn't telling you lies back then, the drugs and addiction were. Look at me."

She forced herself to meet his eyes.

"You're telling me you felt like this with those other guys? The boy who didn't take you to prom? The dudes who fed you pills and alcohol and pushed you on stage when you were just a fucking kid? The guy who put you on the Miller brothers' radar?"

"Please." She shook her head, wishing he would stop. His questions pushed at her brain, making everything scramble—her thoughts, her emotions, her fears. Of course that's not how this felt. How she felt about Wyatt was different than . . . everything. It was too much. It was all too much. "I can't deal with this right now."

He jaw flexed, his teeth obviously pressed hard against each other, but he didn't look away. "You want a drink, Kelsey?"

She inhaled a sharp breath. "*What?*"

"You want a drink? Simple question. There's a whole bottle of tequila in the cabinet." She stared at him in horror as he got up and strode over to the bar, uncapping the bottle and pouring a healthy shot. He stalked back toward the bed, the golden liquid sloshing in the high ball glass, and plunked it down on the bedside table. "Do you need salt. I'm sure we have that, too."

"Have you lost your fucking mind?"

"Maybe." He crossed his arms, staring down at her with ice chip eyes. "So, salt?"

"No!" She scrambled off the other side of the bed, pulling the sheet around herself and squaring off with him. "I don't want a goddamned drink. Why the hell would I—"

He smiled. Fucking smiled.

Then she realized what he'd done.

She put her hand to her forehead, her brain feeling like it was going to explode behind her eyes. "Jesus, Wyatt."

"Get in front of the bed," he said simply. "On your knees."

She blinked, her mind spinning so fast she could barely understand English, but her body complied before her executive functioning caught up. She found herself lowering to the ground without an ounce of hesitation, the sheet still tangled around her.

He stepped around the corner of the bed and sat down on the edge of it, taking her face in his hands. "It's okay if you don't love me back yet. It's okay that you're scared. But you are no longer allowed to use the excuse that you aren't strong enough or good enough to try something with me. Because that is utter bullshit."

Her throat went dry, her heart tattooing her ribcage. Maybe she was finally strong enough to handle emotional upheavals, but anxiety wrapped around her ribcage and squeezed. She didn't know how to be in a real relationship without sabotaging things. Without getting needy and clingy with the guy. Without getting wild and jealous. Without losing her own way while trying to be what the guy wanted. "I don't know how to be normal. The closer we get, the more I want to run."

He leaned over and pressed a kiss to her forehead. "Then I guess I'll have to be faster than you."

"You deserve better than that," she whispered.

"You're right. I do." His palms spanned the side of her head and he tilted her face upward. "And so do you. You want to spend your whole life running? Pushing away the good things because you're afraid they'll disappear?"

"They always do," she said, the knot in her throat like a steel fist.

The sympathy that crossed his features busted something open inside her. He shouldn't care this much. She hadn't earned that emotion on his face, that . . . love. She didn't even know if she was stable enough to exist on her own yet, much less as half of something else. Wyatt had already suffered through a relationship with a girl who'd used him as her emotional crutch. Kelsey refused to be that kind of albatross to anyone.

"I need to go home, Wyatt."

"Kelsey." His voice was a plea.

She met his eyes, letting all the emotion drain from her body until only the echo of loss pounded through her, and she said the one request she knew would do it. "I need space."

At that, those three simple words, his gaze clouded over, his expression closing. His hands lowered to his side in defeat. "I'll call for the boat."

TWENTY-SIX

The smells and sounds were the same. The clicking keyboards, the ringing phones, the scent of the carpet cleaner the weekend crew used. Even Wyatt's desk was exactly as he'd left it, everything in its place. His assistant had placed a stack of messages on top of his desk calendar, arranged first by urgency then by date they were received. Everything the way he liked it. Routine. Predictable. Safe. These four walls had been sanctuary for more years than not. Yet, as Wyatt sat in his desk chair, staring out the row of windows, he simply felt lost.

The day outside was bright despite the chill, but the tint on the building's windows gave everything on the other side a gray hue, reflecting Wyatt's mood back at him. He'd spent yesterday digging through files and combing through reports, not exactly sure he wanted to see what was there, but finding what had been hiding in them anyway. A goddamned nightmare tucked in a seemingly innocuous row of numbers.

And now nothing would ever be the same.

Cary, his assistant, breezed into his office, the smell of coffee alerting Wyatt of his presence. Cary cleared his throat in that practiced way he had to let Wyatt know he was no longer alone. "Mr. Austin, so good to have you back. I brought you coffee from a new place today. Hope you don't mind. The other was out of the kind you like."

"Thanks. I'm sure it'll be fine." Wyatt spun in his chair to face Cary.

Cary looked down at the steno pad in his hand. "So you have Mrs. Caracas coming in at ten. She wants to shift some investments around. Then I have Mr. Bristol in after lunch—he's ranting about the big loss he took last week." He rolled his eyes. "As if you didn't warn him that it was a shit move. And—"

Wyatt held up his hand. "Just send the schedule to my email. And cancel anything I have for the rest of the week."

Cary's eyes widened to panicked-deer mode. "What? But you have—"

"I don't care," Wyatt said, cutting him off, but not having the energy to explain further. "I'm going meet with my father in a few minutes. We aren't to be interrupted."

Cary clamped his jaw and nodded. "Yes, sir."

Wyatt grabbed a folder off his desk and walked over to Cary, putting a hand on his shoulder when he reached him. "Thank you for keeping the ship afloat while I was gone. I know your position isn't an easy one and that I can be a prick to deal with sometimes. You've done a great job."

Cary looked stunned, as if Wyatt had spoken it in a foreign language, but he quickly found his composure. "Thank you, sir."

Wyatt left him behind and headed toward his father's office. It was a walk he'd made thousands of times. But never before had he carried the dread he did today. He still had a sliver of hope he was wrong, but his gut never lied. And his gut was screaming foul.

He strode past his father's assistant, giving her a curt response when she attempted to thwart him from walking in unannounced, and opened his father's office door. His dad was on the phone when Wyatt walked in but he waved him in anyway. Wyatt shut the door behind him and took a seat in the palatial space that the rest of the staff secretly referred to as the Oval Office.

His father wrapped up his conversation after a few minutes, then hung up the phone, sending Wyatt a smile. "Welcome back, son."

"Thanks."

He leaned back in his chair and folded his hands over his stomach. "Looks like you got some sun."

Flashes of running through the waves with Kelsey flickered through Wyatt's mind, a painful reminder of what he no longer had now that he was back in this gray fog of a building. "Well, it was a beach vacation."

His father chuckled. "I'm impressed you spent that much time outside. I heard you got more than a suntan, though. Saw the email about Belle Pritchard. And I just got off the phone with Andrew Carmichael a few minutes ago. Seems you made quite an impression on him."

Wyatt's gaze narrowed. "What the hell is he doing calling you?"

"He's ready to work with us. Said he needs a risk-taker and you proved yourself to be one last week." A beaming smile broke through. "I have to tell you, son. I wasn't sure you could pull it off. But color me impressed. You're not as socially inept as I thought. Maybe I've raised a true CEO after all."

"I'm not accepting his business," Wyatt said flatly.

His father sat up straighter, deep lines digging into his forehead. "You sure as hell will. I've already confirmed with him."

Wyatt took the manila folder from his lap and tossed it onto his father's desk. "Tell me you're not laundering money for your clients."

His dad blinked, once, twice.

Wyatt leaned forward and opened the folder, pointing hard at the report on top, the red circles he'd made around certain transactions. His tone was lethal when he spoke again. "Fucking tell me that you are *not* putting this company, its employees, your family, and *me* at risk for goddamned prison."

"Where'd you get these?"

Wyatt made a disgusted sound. "What the hell does that matter? You thought you could hide it forever? Get your minions to doctor reports before they got to me without me noticing the inconsistencies?"

His dad's jaw twitched.

"Tell me it isn't true, Dad. Look me in the fucking face and tell me."

"Don't make demands on me, son," his father said coolly. "Especially when you already know the answer."

Hearing him admit it was even worse than Wyatt thought. A part of him really had been hoping someone else was responsible. That he hadn't been so blatantly betrayed by his own father. Wyatt's temper burned through him, the need to punch something coursing through him. "You put everyone at risk, Dad. *Me.* I'm your goddamned son! This company is supposed to be mine one day, and you were going to hand me a fucking time bomb? All these years, I've been the one to stand by you even when you acted like an asshole. And *this* is how you were going to reward me? Do you know how much I've given up to be this guy for you?"

He scoffed. "How much *you've* give up? I've spent my life molding you into who you are, giving you everything you needed to be successful. Without me—"

"I'd probably have a fucking life," Wyatt finished bitterly. "I wouldn't be sitting in some office for fourteen hours a day and thinking I'm making some kind of difference, when all I've been doing is supporting a sham and criminal."

His father's face went full red now, his composure slipping. "Don't give me some Pollyanna bullshit, Wyatt. This business is a good one and a smart one. You're naive if you think the other companies aren't doing the exact same thing. To land the big fish, you have to make some concessions, and helping them wash a little money is a minor one."

"Launder a little money?" he bit out. "Do you even care where that dirty cash might be coming from? Drugs? Slave trade? Hey, it's okay if some little girl gets sold into prostitution as long as you get your big client, right?"

"Don't be dramatic."

"Ha! Dramatic? You're lucky I'm not fucking climbing across this desk and shaking you," he seethed. "I want it stopped. Immediately. We need to drop the clients who don't want to be completely above board."

His dad sniffed. "That'd be half my list. Not a fucking chance."

Wyatt was so disgusted at the off-handed reply and his father's smugness, he could barely stand to be in the room anymore. All these years, he'd looked to this office like the brass ring, the ultimate sign he'd captured that goal, that his inertia hadn't been thwarted. But now the idea of it made his skin go cold.

Wyatt rose. "You fix it. Or I'll blow the whistle."

His dad shot to his feet. "How can you be so stupid? You do that and we lose everything."

Wyatt gave his own derisive sniff. "Lucky for me, you've taught me how to invest well. I don't need family money anymore. I've got loads of my own."

"Son—" There was honest fear in his voice now.

"Clean it up. Starting today." Wyatt walked to the door, grabbing the handle and then looking over his shoulder. "And find another CEO replacement to groom. I've got better things to do."

His father's eyes went round. "What?"

"I quit."

Wyatt walked out and didn't look back.

TWENTY-SEVEN

two weeks later

"You're giving her *space*?" Jace asked, plunking the stack of erotic books he'd been organizing for a display on the table next to him. "Why the fuck did you agree to that?"

Wyatt absently flipped through one of the novels Jace had put out, not seeing the words. He couldn't seem to focus on anything these days. "Because I know how it feels to be on the other end of that request. Mia tried to guilt me into staying with her when I needed out. I refuse to put that pressure on someone else. Maybe we're not ready for each other."

"Dude, she's scared."

Wyatt gave him a thank-you-Captain-Obvious glare. "Don't you think I fucking know that? Hell, I'm terrified, too. I don't know how to have a relationship. Have you seen my track record?"

Jace smirked. "A string of women who probably couldn't name one personal thing about you except the size of your dick and bank account?"

Wyatt shrugged. "Well, can't blame them there, both are pretty memorable."

Jace's jaw fell in mock amazement. "What? The genius makes a joke? Grab your canned goods, world, the apocalypse is imminent."

Wyatt threw the book at him, and Jace ducked, letting the thing crash into a shelf of lubricants behind him. Jace looked over his shoulder, laughing. "Clean up, aisle three!"

"I'm being serious," Wyatt said, smiling despite his statement. It felt good to joke around with his little brother, to not have that tension between them anymore. For the first time in his life, Wyatt felt like he had someone he could truly confide in, someone who had his back. "The only real relationship I was ever in ended up with the girl I cared about killing herself *because of me*."

Jace sighed. "Not because of you, bro. People break up every day. More goes into that decision to take your own life than losing your boyfriend. Mia needed help—help a twenty-one-year-old kid wasn't capable of giving. We all have moments we wish we could go back and handle differently. God, I still don't know how Evan ever gave me another chance after the stupid ass decisions I made when we were teenagers. Talk about ruining someone's life."

Wyatt looked up at the ceiling, shaking his head. "Even if I can convince Kelsey to give things a chance, I can't give her any guarantees beyond I love her and want it to work."

"Fuck, that's all any of us can do. Promise to try and be willing to make sacrifices. Are you willing to do that?"

"Of course."

Jace eyed him. "Even if that means working less hours and putting something besides work first for a change?"

Wyatt huffed a bitter laugh and walked over to the front counter, sitting on it. "That won't be a problem. I quit."

"Sure you did. I really would be stocking up on canned goods if that were true." He squatted down to pick up the bottles of lube that had rolled to the floor.

"Then grab some corn and peas, brother, because I told Dad to go fuck himself."

Jace stood, his green eyes wide, his task forgotten. "You're shitting me."

Wyatt rubbed the bridge of his nose beneath his glasses, exhausted all of a sudden. "I found out some things on the trip and confronted Dad. Turns out he's been quietly laundering money for some of his bigger clients for years. He would doctor the reports before they got to me because he knew I'd pick up on it."

"Holy fuck."

"I didn't want to believe it. But not only did he not deny it, he wanted me to take on Andrew Carmichael as a client and do the same for him. Like I'd put my neck on the fucking line and risk prison for that prick."

"Christ. So you just quit? After all the time you've put in there?"

Wyatt released a breath. He thought he'd feel empty walking away from that building, grieve the years he'd put in only to give it all up. But all he'd felt when he stepped out into the sunshine in the middle of a Monday afternoon was . . . freedom. And possibility. The only sadness that had punctured him had been when he'd walked past the Sugarcane Cafe and didn't see his pretty blonde waitress inside.

"I'm making Dad buy out my portion of the company and clean up his shit. A few of my clients will come with me, and I'll continue to advise them. But I'm going to put most of my focus on the venture capitalist thing instead."

"Wow," Jace said, leaning against the shelf, looking genuinely awed. "So now you have all the time in the world."

"I don't even want to admit how many movies I've watched in the last two weeks." Romantic ones to torture himself. Depressing ones to wallow. And blow-'em-up ones to forget all the others. *Fucking pathetic.*

Jace crossed his arms over his chest, compassion overtaking his normally cocky expression. "Don't give up on her, man. Go get her."

Wyatt groaned. "She doesn't want to be gotten."

"Bullshit. How many of those movies lining your shelves have you watched where the guy lets the girl he loves walk away? I saw Kelsey at The Ranch this weekend. She looks miserable, dude. This is the time for grand gestures and fucking boom boxes held over your head outside her window."

Wyatt crossed his arms and gave Jace a come-on-now look.

"What? I love the shit out of that movie. Hated that song he played though."

"Didn't you let Evan leave last year?"

He scowled. "I didn't have a choice at the time. But as soon as she was back in town, you can bet your ass I went full out."

"And what, pray tell, was your grand gesture?"

Jace shrugged, his eyes sparkling with the apparent memory. "It may or may not have involved illegal use of a cop uniform and breaking a few laws. But it doesn't matter what mine was because you need to figure out what's right for Kelsey. Show her what you can give her that no one else can."

Wyatt scrubbed his hands over his face, wondering if the end of the world really was near because his little brother was starting to make sense. But the thought of Kelsey sad, even for a moment, had his lungs squeezing tight and the wheels of invention turning in his head. He peered over at Jace and hopped off the counter. "Cancel any plans you have this weekend. I'm going to need your help."

Jace's grin went wide.

TWENTY-EIGHT

Kelsey set her phone down in the grass, staring at the screen, still not sure she'd heard correctly. The detective who had helped her with the Miller brothers had just called to tell her that Howie Miller wouldn't bother her anymore. The entire D-Town operation had been exposed over the weekend, including players from the bottom rungs all the way to the top dog—a guy with known ties to a drug trafficking ring in Houston. Apparently, an anonymous citizen had hired top-notch private investigators to track Howie's steps for the last few weeks and had gotten one of the players to turn against the group and give up vital information. None of the gang would be getting out of prison for a very long time.

She couldn't even process that good news. She was safe. *Safe.* She wouldn't have to leave.

A shadow crossed over the patch of grass she'd been sightlessly staring at, and cowboy boots appeared in her peripheral vision. Kelsey tilted her head up to find Grant eclipsing the sun.

He lowered himself, sitting back on his haunches and tilting his hat upward. "They called you."

She blinked, the statement stunning her. "*You* did this?"

His mouth lifted at the corner. "Nah, I wish I could take credit for the idea, but I just helped someone get in touch with a few old military buddies of mine. I knew they'd come through, though."

Someone. "Wyatt."

"He set it up before you left for the trip. He wanted you to be able to come home without worries."

She shook her head, the hollow ache that had been a constant presence since she'd gotten back from the trip seemed to yawn even wider. "I don't even know what to do with that."

Grant gave her knee a squeeze. "You do what you want, darlin'. You can go back to your life. Get your old job back, go to school."

She certainly could, though she wouldn't need the job for the money. She had a two-hundred-and-fifty-thousand-dollar check in her cabin. Wyatt apparently wasn't so great at math because he'd added an extra zero. She couldn't bring herself to cash it though.

She forced a smile for Grant, knowing that was the appropriate response to the situation. But all the things she'd been so happy with only a few weeks ago, the existence she'd been so desperate to hold on to, now seemed painted in colorless strokes in her mind—a faded version of her happy ending. "Thanks, Grant. Really. I can't even tell you how much it means that you helped."

"Anytime, darlin'." He put a hand out to her and pulled her to her feet as he rose. "But that's not why I came out here to talk to you."

"Oh?"

He cocked his head toward the main house at The Ranch. "I know you stopped taking clients, but there's a certain college football player in there who says he really needs to see you. What do you want me to tell him?"

She frowned. "Hawk's here?"

"Yeah, apparently he took it upon himself to drive out here when the receptionist told him you weren't taking appointments."

She stuck her hands in the back pockets of her jeans, staring up at the house. If Hawk had gone through all that trouble, something must be wrong. No way could she walk away from that guy if he needed her. "I'll go see him."

Grant smiled. "Kid got to you, huh?"

She sighed, a sound she found herself making a lot lately. "He's a good guy with a good heart. I just wish I could take away all that shame he carries around with him, make his life a little easier."

Grant laid his arm over her shoulder and guided her toward the house. "You know, darlin', I think I was wrong. Caring that much about your sub, wanting to take away his pain through pain . . . you do have a true domme's will in you."

She leaned into his shoulder, the big brother vibe from Grant unfamiliar but welcome. "Too bad I have a submissive heart."

He opened the door for her with a sympathetic smile. "That's not a bad thing, Kelsey. It's a beautiful gift. You just have to make sure you put it in the right hands."

She looked away, unable to let her mind go there. "What room is he in?"

"Dungeon B. And be warned, he didn't come alone."

"What do you mean?"

"You should probably see for yourself."

Uh-oh. Kelsey made her way up to the second floor, not even bothering to stop by the locker room to change and grab her gear. She usually never let her clients see her in street clothes, but the way Hawk had come here unannounced and with a guest needed to be discussed first. It wasn't like him to push the rules like that. But when she looked through the viewing window of Dungeon B, she forgot all about discussing the rules.

Hawk sat on one of the benches aligned along the far wall, his head bowed. Next to him was a pretty dark-eyed girl with hair down to her waist. She was gripping Hawk's hand so hard her knuckles were pale, but her expression was pure determination. *Oh, shit. This can't be good.*

Kelsey turned the knob and walked in, drawing their attention her way. Some combination of relief and desperation crossed Hawk's face, but the girl's hard expression fell instantly. Her lips pressed together as if she were fighting tears. She turned to Hawk with a choked whisper. "You could've told me she was so pretty. *Goddammit*, Hawk."

"Baby," he said, shaking his head miserably. "It's not about that."

Kelsey took a deep breath. "Hawk, would you like to tell me what's going on?"

He raked a hand through his already messy hair and stood. "I'm sorry"—he swallowed hard and glanced back at his girl—"Mistress."

The girl winced like she'd been slapped.

"I know I shouldn't have come like this, but Christina, she—"

"I demanded he show me." Christina rose and brushed invisible lint off her khaki skirt before looking up, as if biding time and building courage to speak more. "He tried to break up with me, and I wanted to know why."

"Oh, Hawk," Kelsey said softly.

"He loves me. I know he does and he wanted to just . . . end it." Christina's voice caught on the last two words.

Hawk shook his head, his eyes bloodshot. "I wasn't going to tell her, but she deserved to know why. I'm not good for her. I'm fucked up."

Kelsey didn't think, but instead reacted. Her hand came up and smacked Hawk right across the face, the sound reverberating in the small space. "*Do not* call yourself that."

Christina gasped and Hawk blinked, his pupils going big, his submissiveness kicking in whether he wanted it to or not. Face slapping was one of his kink buttons. "I'm so sorry, Mistress."

Christina stalked over, grabbing Hawk's arm, and shooting Kelsey the coldest, most hateful look she'd ever seen on such a sweet-looking girl. "You crazy bitch! You *hit* him! I'm—"

Christina lunged forward like she was going to return the favor, but Hawk held her back. "Baby, don't . . . This . . . That's what this is. I—I need to be hurt sometimes."

"The hell you do!"

He pressed his lips to Christina's hair as he held her, the anguish on his face breaking Kelsey's heart into little fragments. "That's why I need to let you go, Chris. I'm . . ." Kelsey watched him as he searched for a word that wouldn't get another correction. "I'm different. I crave this, and that's not going to go away. You deserve better."

The words hit Kelsey with the force of a kick to the sternum. She'd said the same thing to Wyatt just a few weeks ago. Had given the same "I'm fucked up" speech that had earned Hawk a slap. She was such a goddamned hypocrite.

Christina pulled back from Hawk, her dark eyes going shiny. "I *have* better. I have you. And I'm not going to give that up just because you're . . . whatever this is."

"Baby," Hawk pleaded.

But Christina was already turning toward Kelsey, her shoulders squaring and chin lifting, shaky bravado but impressive nonetheless. "Let her show me."

"What?" Hawk asked, looking horrified.

Christina put her hands on her hips and faced Hawk. She looked so damn prim—a proper Southern sorority girl—but Kelsey recognized steel will when she saw it. "You want to crawl on your knees for a woman, want to be beaten on, called names? Then you damn well better be doing it for me and not some blonde with bigger boobs than mine."

Hawk's eyes went wide. "What?"

Christina looked to Kelsey, ignoring Hawk's question. "Can you teach me? Show me how to give him what he needs?"

Kelsey raised her eyebrows, a little stunned, but a lot impressed by this girl. "That's up to Hawk."

"Chris, you don't know what this is, how . . . ugly and brutal it can seem," Hawk said, but there was a note of hope in his voice.

"Shut up." Christina stepped in front of Hawk and put her hands on his shoulders, pushing onto her tiptoes to reach, and exerted pressure. Without hesitation he went down to his knees before her. This big brute of a guy falling to a little slip of a girl. Kelsey didn't think she'd ever seen anything so beautiful. Christina touched Hawk's stubbled cheek. "I love you, you jerk. No part of you will ever be ugly to me. I don't care if I don't know much about this. I'm willing to learn. I'm tougher than you think."

Hawk, who had never cried in Kelsey's sessions, no matter how much pain she dished out, teared up. Salty warmth touched Kelsey's cheek, too. The willingness of this girl to simply accept Hawk, regardless of the complications involved, was humbling. Christina loved him.

And Kelsey realized, as she stood there watching, that this was what love looked like. Not a picture perfect "normal." Not neat corners and the absence of baggage. But acceptance of it all and a willingness to face it all together. To embrace the ugly.

Kelsey leaned back against the wall, the weight of that realization making her want to slide to the floor.

"I love you, too," Hawk said, pressing his cheek to Christina's chest. "Baby, I love you so much. Thank you."

Christina stroked his hair and smiled down at him. "If I'm being honest, the idea of you tied up and following my directions is past the level of super hot."

"Really?" he asked, his voice full of wonder.

Christina gripped his hair with surprising strength and yanked his head upward so he could see her face. "But I swear to God, if you keep going to some other woman for what you need, I'm going to string you up by your balls and beat the shit out of you."

"God, Chris." Hawk's eyes glazed over a bit at that, and Kelsey had to hold back a chuckle. The girl had no idea how much she was turning her boyfriend on right now. Hawk looked toward Kelsey. "Would you be willing to train her, Mistress? I know you're not taking clients any—"

"I'm not taking paying clients anymore," Kelsey said, pushing off the wall and smiling. "But this I'll do for free." She looked to Christina. "As long as your new mistress here is willing to share the room with me for a little while."

Christina backed away from Hawk and eyed Kelsey. "You never slept with him?"

"He wouldn't have done that to you, hon. He told me every session how in love with you he was." Kelsey put her hand to her throat, rubbing the spot where Wyatt had collared her in his tender grip. "And I'm in love with someone else."

Hawk's gaze flitted her way, and he gave her the biggest, broadest smile she'd ever seen him wear.

Christina held out her hand to Kelsey. "Then we've got a deal. Make me a badass bitch."

Kelsey laughed and shook her hand. "Oh, Hawk, you're in trouble."

He leaned forward and grabbed Christina by the waist, dragging her down to him. "No, I'm in heaven."

Kelsey smiled for the two of them, keeping her own melancholy off her face. She was glad Hawk was in heaven.

Maybe it was time for her to step out of her own hell.

TWENTY-NINE

"I have a bridal emergency."

Kelsey hit the speaker phone button and set her phone in her car's cup holder. "Talk to me."

"Where are you?" Brynn asked.

Kelsey glanced at the mile marker as it whizzed by. "Uh, probably like thirty minutes outside of town. I'm moving back into my apartment this afternoon."

"Ooh, so I know I'm being a total pain, but would you possibly be willing to put that on hold for tonight? I'm freaking out about the bridesmaid's dress I chose, and I need you to try another one on for me. They have to be ordered by tomorrow if I'm going to make the switch and have them in time."

Kelsey rolled her eyes, but couldn't help but smile. *Brides.* They were their own species. "Anything for you, B. Where do I need to go?"

Brynn gave her directions to the shop, and Kelsey hung up and sagged into her seat. She'd been hoping to go home tonight and get settled in, maybe come up with a way to call Wyatt and thank him for what he did with Howie Miller. But that would have to wait. And perhaps it was for the best. She wasn't sure if she had the right words for Wyatt yet. What she'd said to him to end it had been the lowest move. To even reference what had happened to him in the past had been cruel and cowardly on her part. She wouldn't blame him if he didn't take her call.

Kelsey parked in front of the dress shop a little while later and headed in to find her sister. Brynn was talking to one of the employees when Kelsey walked in, and Kelsey gave a little wave. Brynn excused herself and hurried over to Kelsey, giving her a big hug. "I'm so glad you made it. And God, it feels like I haven't seen you in forever. You're so tan."

Kelsey laughed. "Being on an island vacation will do that to a girl."

Brynn tilted her head in a way that said she saw right through Kelsey's smile. "Things went okay?"

"Oh, you know, a little swimming, a lot of sex, a bit of a broken heart, but I'm still in one sober piece, so there's that."

"Aww, honey." She gave her another squeeze. "I'm sorry."

Kelsey waved her sympathy away. "We're not here to boo-hoo about me. I'm here for the fun stuff. Get me in this dress that's stolen your heart."

Brynn clapped her hands together with glee. "I think you're going to love it. It's a fifties vintage."

"Sweet, I'm already sold. I love fifties style." Kelsey followed Brynn to the dressing area with a grin, her sister's enthusiasm contagious.

Brynn reached into one of the unoccupied rooms and brought out the dress.

"Oh, my God," Kelsey breathed, taking the hanger from her and holding the dress out, instantly in love. It was gorgeous, strapless, and ruby red. The fitted bodice gave it a sexy flirtiness, but the skirt of gathered tulle layers was pure vintage perfection. It was exactly the type of dress she would've picked for herself. "I want to marry this dress. If it doesn't fit, I'll go on a liquid diet before the wedding."

Brynn laughed. "I don't think that'll be necessary. But let's try it on."

They went into the dressing room, and Brynn fussed over her and helped her get it on, tugging everything into the right place and adjusting as needed. Finally, Brynn looked her up and down and nodded. "Turn around."

Kelsey spun around and stared at her reflection in the mirror. Her boobs were plumped up by the bodice, the waist cut at just the right place, and the tulle skirt hit her right past her knee. She did a little twirl. "It fits!"

Brynn pressed a hand to her chest like a proud mom. "It looks like it was made for you."

"So we're good, right? This is the one?" Kelsey asked, turning to her and rocking on the balls of her feet.

Brynn bit her lip. "Would you mind staying for a few more minutes? They have their hair and makeup person doing demos tonight and I want to see how everything will work together."

Kelsey stared at her, amused. "You're serious?"

She shrugged, a little sheepish. "I'm a perfectionist."

"You're nuts, but I love you. And sure."

Half an hour later, Kelsey's hair was in an intricate up-do and her makeup had been applied with expert skill, bringing out the blue in her eyes and the angle of her cheekbones but not looking overdone. Kelsey stood on the center platform between a trio of mirrors. "So, now do we have a winner, bride-to-be?"

"I'd say so," said a familiar voice.

Kelsey spun around so fast, she almost knocked herself right off her heels.

Wyatt stood at the entryway of the dressing area. *In a full tuxedo.* He smiled that dimpled smile of his, looking like a movie star who'd just stepped off the red carpet. "You look amazing, Kelsey."

Her tongue was like a dry sponge lodged in her mouth. She forced herself to breathe, to swallow. "What are you doing here?"

He grasped his hands behind him, a little tentative. "I thought maybe you'd let me give you a bit of normal tonight. Make up for something you deserved but never got."

She stepped down from the platform, her heart like a bass drum in her ears. "I don't understand."

He walked over to her with measured steps like he was afraid she was going to run away if he moved too fast. But he never took his eyes off hers. He stopped an arm's length away and pulled something from behind his back. "Kelsey LeBreck, would you go to prom with me?"

Her gaze dropped to the clear box in his hand and the delicate red and white corsage contained within. "*Prom?*"

He opened the box, pulled out the wrist corsage, and took her hand. "Just say yes, love."

She didn't understand what was going on. Thoughts were firing in her head at hyper-speed, but none were making any sense. Prom. Wyatt. Corsage. Wyatt. Dress. *Wyatt.* None of it mattered except the Wyatt part. Having him this close again, seeing the hint of mischief in his eyes, hearing that low, cajoling voice, she could only do one thing. She said yes.

He gave her the full wattage of his smile, kissed her hand, then slid the corsage over her wrist. "Thank you. I even have the white horse this time."

She took his arm, wondering if she'd actually fallen asleep in the dressing room or hit her head on a sharp object. Maybe she was having some weird drug flashback. "This isn't my dress. We can't walk out—"

"It is and we can."

"What?"

But he didn't answer; he simply kept moving forward. On their way to the door, Kelsey scanned the store for Brynn, but she was nowhere to be found. Reality finally clicked into place. Her sister—normally the world's worst liar—had duped her? "Brynn knew about this?"

"That sister of yours is like a barracuda when it comes to protecting you, but you were right—she's also a hopeless romantic."

Holy shit. It'd all been a ruse? She shook her head, stunned. "But I told you I wasn't."

"You used to be. Maybe I can change your mind again. And if not . . ." Wyatt grabbed her hand and laced his fingers with hers, then pulled his expression into a fiercely serious one. "Come with me if you want to live."

She stared at him for a second, then let out an embarrassing snort laugh. "Okay, you're right, *Terminator 2* won't exactly work here."

"Guess you'll have to settle for my way, then." He smiled and she thought he might kiss her, but then he seemed to think better of it and led her outside. At the curb, a horse-drawn carriage awaited them.

"You've got to be kidding me," she blurted, unable to hold back her reaction.

Wyatt patted the horse's brown mane, the corner of his mouth lifting. "Okay, so he's not white, but I promise, he's very noble."

She put her hand to her forehead, almost giddy with how wonderfully bizarre this man was. "He's perfect."

You're perfect.

Wyatt helped her into the carriage and then climbed in next to her. "Ready?"

"Yes." And she was. Finally.

The moonlight gilded the grass in Wyatt's backyard, mixing with the glow from the white sparkle lights that had been hung from all the trees, and retro pop music drifted across the wide expanse of property. A temporary dance floor had been assembled in the middle of the yard and tables lined the edges of it, each with candles flickering in their centers. And Kelsey and Wyatt weren't alone.

Familiar faces, all glammed out in prom dresses and tuxes, filled the tables: Jace, Andre, and Evan; Charli and Grant; her sister and Reid; and Kade and Janessa, another domme from The Ranch. It was the school dance she never had, only more lovely and filled with people she actually cared about. Kelsey turned to Wyatt, and he offered a ghost of a smile, a shimmer of vulnerability in his eyes like he was still scared she was going to bail.

"I can't believe you did all this."

He pushed an escaped lock of hair behind her ear. "I wanted to give you something you never had. I know this is over the top and that I told you I would give you space. But I've spent my career knowing how to spot a good bet. And we're a good bet, Kelsey. I don't want to walk away from that. I don't want to walk away from *you*."

Her eyes closed, and she breathed in his words, absorbing them, feeling the truth behind them. When she opened her eyes again, all the confusion and fear that always tried to shroud her happy moments fell away like dead leaves. She stepped into his space, sliding her arms around his waist. This was Wyatt. Running faster. Like he promised. And finally, she wanted nothing more than to be caught. "Take me to prom. Sir."

He let out a long breath as if he'd been holding it for weeks and looked down at her, cradling her face in his hands and brushing away tears she hadn't realized she'd shed. "I want to give you the world, Kelsey."

She pressed her cheek into his palm, smiling, feeling as if she was exactly where she was supposed to be. "I don't need the world. Just you. I love you."

The pleasure that broke across his face nearly had her crying again, but he cut off that reaction by leaning down and capturing her mouth in a long, lingering kiss. Sweet and tender, the taste of him was like water after a trip through the desert. God, how had she ever thought she could live without this, without him? All the times in her life she'd thought she'd been in love seemed like ridiculous playacting now. This soaring happiness inside, this trust that they could work through whatever came their way—that was what love felt like.

Wyatt reached down and lifted her up, never breaking the kiss as he wrapped her legs around him. She looped her arms around his neck and kissed him back hard, letting all the ugly stuff that had pushed its way between them fade to the back of her mind. She was strong enough for this. She deserved a chance at happy.

She deserved him.

Applause and a lewd whistle came from their left. She and Wyatt broke away from the kiss and turned their heads to find everyone on their feet. Her cheeks went hot. "Sorta forgot we had an audience."

Wyatt grinned and set her on her feet to face everyone.

"Aren't y'all supposed to break out into a synchronized dance number now?" Kelsey called out. "I've watched those movies. That's what happens at prom, right?"

Jace grinned from the center of the crowd. "I tried to get these bastards to pull off that number from *Footloose*, but Andre kept stepping on my feet."

Kelsey tipped her head back, laughing, and Wyatt picked her up again, spinning her toward the dance floor. "Let's get this started. Because there's only one thing better than prom."

Her feet touched the ground, and he tugged her against him as a new song began. "What's that?"

His grin turned wicked. "Losing your virginity afterward."

EPILOGUE

eight months later

Wyatt clicked through to a different report, scrolling through the last two years of numbers for a tech company he was considering investing in, but the numbers were blurring at the edges. He pushed his glasses atop his head and rubbed his eyes. He'd worked right through dinner and suddenly he felt both brain dead and famished. He wasn't used to this kind of late-night schedule anymore.

Kelsey had told him she'd be studying with a group at the culinary institute tonight and wouldn't be home until late. Apparently, soufflé baking was kicking all their asses. But he was determined to stay awake so he could see her before bed. He had a surprise for her he couldn't wait to share. He stretched his arms above his head and yawned, the sound echoing off the walls of his home office, and leaned back in his chair, closing his eyes for a minute.

Maybe just a little power nap.

"Egg white omelet with spinach and cheddar and two slices of turkey bacon, extra crispy," a soft voice said. "Would you like coffee with that, Mr. Austin?"

Wyatt's eyes snapped open, and he pulled his glasses back down. Kelsey, like a vision from a dream he was on the verge of having, smiled and set a plate in front of him, leaning over far enough so that he saw straight down her top—her waitress top. *Oh, fuck, yes.*

He cleared his throat, trying to find his voice. "Coffee sounds fantastic."

She set his mug down and straightened, giving him the full view of her outfit. She hadn't worked at the Sugarcane again after the day with Howie Miller, but apparently she'd kept the outfit he'd fantasized about one too many times. But instead of tennis shoes, she was wearing the highest, sexiest white leather boots he'd ever seen. And her long blonde hair was in that ponytail he loved so much. All his blood rushed straight south, and any remnants of exhaustion drained right out of him.

"Working too hard, I see," she said, a mischievous smile touching her glossed lips.

"No. I believe I'm sleeping . . . and dreaming."

She placed her palms flat on the desk and brushed her lips against his. "Not asleep."

He slid a hand along her waist and pulled her down until she was straddling his lap. "This outfit always drove me crazy. I defiled every part of it in my fantasies while I was sitting in that booth."

"You're a naughty man, Wyatt Austin," Kelsey said, bending down and kissing him. "And a hard one."

She wiggled her ass against him, drawing a shudder from him. "Hey, hot girl on lap. What else am I supposed to do?"

She smiled and undulated her hips, dragging her body along the length of his shaft and sending darts of *fuck yeah* through all his good parts.

"Definitely not sleeping" he said, groaning as his erection

swelled to full force. He slid his hand beneath her panties and brushed her smooth, damp skin. "You're good at this lap stuff, love."

She smirked. "No shit. I used to get paid for it and everything. Though, I would've cut off a guy's balls if he tried to do what you're doing right now."

He ran the pad of his thumb over her slippery nub, and her eyelids went half-mast. "I would've stolen you off that stage, would've never let any man you didn't want near you looking at you that way, touching you. I'm jealous that any of those scumbags got to see you like this."

"Never like this, sir. Let me show you what I never showed them," she said, leaning down to nip at his bottom lip. "I'm asking permission to take a little bit of control tonight."

His eyebrows crept upward. She'd never shown any inclination to dominate him in all these months. Though, he had set up a few scenes at The Ranch where he'd watched her dominate a male sub then fucked her while the other guy enjoyed the view. He knew that Kelsey wasn't a full switch, but dominance did feed something inside her and he didn't want to deny her that. Plus, he found it impossibly hot watching her manage someone else, knowing that at the end of it all, she'd kneel down and give up all that power to him.

He wasn't sure he was capable of playing submissive even for a little while. But for her, he'd give anything a try. "What'd you have in mind, love?"

She slid off his lap and went to his laptop. She pulled her iPod from her pocket and plugged it in. She turned to him and smiled, her fingers teasing at the top button on her blouse. "So I couldn't find my cheerleader outfit to fulfill your exact high school fantasy, but I hope this will fit the bill."

"Oh, love, nothing's hotter than you in this little waitress getup."

"Good." She let the first button slide through. "Then let me dance for you."

His tongue stuck to the roof of his mouth at the thought. Knowing Kelsey had stripped for a living put a pit in his stomach. He hated that she'd had to sell herself like that. But he'd be a lying bastard if he said he hadn't thought about how fucking sexy she must've looked up there on that stage. How it must've felt to be one of those guys she turned her pretty blue eyes on.

"Baby, you don't have to—I know—" Logical speech alluded him.

Her lips curled in a slow, knowing smile. "You can't even talk you're so turned on."

He tilted his head back against his chair. "I'm a dirty, perverted excuse for a boyfriend."

"Exactly how I like you." She moved forward, sauntering on those heels like she was in flats, and moved his plate and coffee to the credenza on the far side of the office. Then she stepped back in front of his desk, her eyes meeting his. "You're not allowed to touch me. Yet. But you have permission to touch yourself if the spirit moves you."

He rubbed his lips together. "Yes, ma'am."

She turned back to his laptop and hit a button.

"Dirty! Rotten! Filthy! Stinkin'!" A loud drumbeat filled the wireless speakers around the room.

Wyatt stared at her then burst out laughing. "Tell me you didn't."

She grinned as the grinding guitar of Warrant's "Cherry Pie" started. "Hey, I wanted this to be authentic. This song was big the years you were in high school. God, you're old by the way."

He gave her leg a little smack and she laughed.

"Plus . . ." She shoved the computer aside and put a booted foot on top of the desk, hoisting herself up with ease. "It's a song about pastry. How could I resist?"

Wyatt shook his head, staring up in awe. Gorgeous *and* a wicked sense of humor. "I'm the luckiest fucker alive."

"You are." She put the toe of her boot in the center of his chest and pushed, sending his chair rolling backward so that he had the best view possible, then she met his gaze head-on—no shame, no closing her eyes and pretending she was somewhere else—and began to move to the beat.

Her fingers flicked open the next button of her blouse, but Wyatt couldn't pull away from her eyes. He was transfixed by what he saw there. Despite the tongue-and-cheek song and the playful outfit, this was more than a little sexy fun. This was her gift to him. She was showing him what those other guys had never seen, what she'd never given any other man—her trust, her heart, the soul of the girl behind the seductress.

She was beautiful.

And whole.

Strong.

She slipped her shirt off her shoulders and snaked her way down to eye level with him, dropping the blouse around his neck. The scent of her perfume surrounded him—perfume and maybe the faintest hint of maple syrup forever trapped in the uniform. He inhaled deeply and smiled. Then she was working her way back upward again, turning her back to him and dancing in fluid motion as she peeked coyly at him over her shoulder and released the front hook of her bra. The lacy bit of material dropped off her shoulders, hitting the desk. She cupped her breasts, still hidden from his view, and tipped her head back as she let out a little *mmm*.

"You're so fucking sexy, love," he said, his fingers flexing. "It's killing me not to touch you."

She spun slowly around again, giving him the full sight of her teasing her nipples until they were flushed and hard in the golden lamplight of the room. To keep himself from reaching out for her, he unbuttoned his slacks and took his cock in his hand, giving it a slow stroke. She smiled down at him and ran the tip of her tongue over her bottom lip.

"Tease," he said, smirking.

"Oh, no, for you, I always deliver on my promises," she said, lifting up her skirt and giving him a peek at the skimpy lace thong she wore beneath.

"Take them off," he whispered, his words gruff.

"Can't resist giving commands, huh?"

She stepped to the side of the desk closest to him, putting him near eye level with the apex of her thighs, then hooked her fingers in the sides of her panties. He barely resisted begging. Maybe he *could* have a submissive moment. She rolled her hips and dragged the wisp of lace down her legs. Her sweet, sexy scent hit him, sending his head spinning and his patience waning. God, he needed to touch her, taste her.

Kelsey kicked off the panties, then lowered herself down and climbed off the desk. She stood before him in only that little skirt and those fuck-me boots. "I think you've earned a lap dance, sir."

"I tip well."

With a smile of illicit promise, she trailed her hands up his legs and brought her breasts right in front of his mouth, dancing and teasing him with every beat of the music. He moved his hand away from his cock and let the edges of her skirt brush his length with each sway of her hips. He was lost in her, absolutely fucking lost. The house could burn down around them and there was no way he was leaving this spot.

Kelsey braced her hands on his thighs and with a wicked spark in her eyes, worked her way down between his knees. A few strands of her ponytail danced over his crotch, heaven marking a path over his skin. All semblance of self-control left him. He grabbed a fistful of her ponytail, and she gasped.

"On your knees, love," he said, his voice hoarse with need.

She complied without protest, her body sinking down to the floor. "Yes, sir."

He took her hair in his fist and wound her long ponytail around his cock, the golden strands like spun silk against him. He groaned at the sight he'd imagined so many times. She kept her head bowed, letting him use her however he wished, and put her hand over his, helping him with the first silken stroke. The nape of her neck was bared to him as their hands moved in tandem, sliding her soft locks against him. He stared at that expanse of skin, an ache digging into his chest.

She gripped his knee, still covered by his slacks, and the sight of her bare left ring finger only deepened the pang. But he had to be patient with her. He didn't want to overwhelm her with how sure he was in his love for her, how far he saw it stretched out before them. He reached out with his free hand and traced a line over her neck. "I want to collar you, Kelsey."

Her hand stilled against him and he let her ponytail slide through his fingers, then lifted her face to him. Her cheeks were flushed with desire, but her eyes were wide and clear. "I have a collar, sir."

"Yes, a generic one I bought before I really knew you. I want you to wear *my* collar. I want a ceremony."

Without hesitation or any of the fears he worried would come to the surface again, she brought his hand to her mouth, kissing his palm. "There's nothing I want more than to be yours, Wyatt."

His entire body swelled with emotion.

"God, say that again, love." She did and he pulled her onto his lap, taking her mouth in a heated kiss and sliding inside her.

———

Wyatt stole Kelsey's thoughts with the kiss, and everything inside her tightened and quivered as he thrust into her. She moaned into his mouth, the sheer bliss of having him filling her, claiming her, was a sensation that never got old. He'd been an epic fail in the sub role, but that had only turned her on more. She loved that intensity that overtook him when he couldn't hold back the need to dominate her.

And now he wanted to collar her. For real. She knew he'd held back from putting any pressures on their relationship because he didn't want to freak her out. But the thought of being tied to him in that way no longer put terror in her heart. Love was a risk. Happiness was never a guarantee. But like he'd said that night at the prom, they were a good bet.

For the first time in her life, *she* was a good bet.

And she was ready to jump without a parachute.

He pulled back from the kiss and took her nipple in his mouth, sucking and biting and sending rapid, rolling pleasure through her. She gripped his shoulders hard, riding him and the sensation of it all even as heavy words formed on her lips. He pressed his fingers against her clit, stroking and teasing with each rock of her hips. Her nails dug into his skin.

"You want to come, love?" he asked, kissing and nibbling her neck.

"I want to get married."

Everything halted. Wyatt lifted his head, his eyes shocked behind his glasses. "What?"

Panic gripped her. *Shit. Shit. Shit.* Maybe she'd read his signs wrong. Maybe she was assuming things she shouldn't. "I mean—"

He pressed his fingers against her mouth. "Don't you dare take it back."

She squeezed her eyes shut, mortified.

"Look at me."

She took a deep breath and forced her eyes open. He let his hand fall from her lips and she started babbling. "Oh, my God, I can't believe I just said that. You must think I've lost my mind. Of course we can't get married. We've only been seeing each other for eight months and what would people think and—"

"I would marry you tomorrow," he said without a hint of hesitation in his voice.

She blinked.

Dimples appeared, and he lifted her onto the desk, laying her out beneath him. "In fact, how about next month? I already had two plane tickets to Paris I was going to surprise you with. Thought you'd like to visit the mecca of all things pastry."

She stared at him. "You're taking me to France?"

He pressed a kiss to her parted lips. "No, now I'm *marrying* you in France. If you'll have me."

"Wyatt . . ." Everything inside her went still, quiet, as she wrapped her mind around what he was saying. She saw their future roll out before her. A life filled with shared laughter and dorky movie references and long mornings in bed.

And hot, kinky sex.

Her normal. Their normal.

"Just say yes," he said softly.

She smiled, remembering his request from prom. And this time the word was even easier to say. "Yes."

He cradled her cheek in his palm and rocked into her. "Come for me, my love. We've got a life to plan."

She wrapped her arms around his neck and dragged him down for a kiss, crying out in bliss as they fell over the edge together.

She'd been wrong. So very wrong.

Reality kicked the shit out of fantasy.

Keep reading for an excerpt from the next
Loving on the Edge novel by Roni Loren

NEED YOU TONIGHT

Available soon from Heat Books

Someone's naked ass is on my imported marble counter-tops. That was Tessa's first thought when she walked into her kitchen that warm Tuesday afternoon. Not, *Why is Doug home this early?* Or, *Why does he have his pants around his ankles?* And most definitely not *Why is my best friend moaning like an injured cat?* Nope. Tessa's brain couldn't absorb those things just yet. Instead all she could think about was how there was a butt crack sliding along the spot where she'd chopped strawberries for breakfast.

The two occupants in the kitchen didn't even notice they were no longer alone, apparently too caught up in their counter defiling to bother. God, were they *that* oblivious and swept up in passion? It's not like she'd been particularly quiet walking in. And she'd slept with the man who'd dropped trou in this little tableau for the last ten years. She knew he didn't inspire losing yourself to the moment. But maybe he saved his good tricks for Tuesday afternoons when he fucked the woman Tessa would've trusted her life with before today.

Tessa cleared her throat, attempting to draw their attention, but all that greeted her was the sound of Doug telling that *lying bitch* how hot she was. Rage washed through Tessa in a slow, powerful roll, boiling up and over until she was shaking with it. She calmly set down her purse next to the fruit bowl and wrapped her hand around a large navel orange. Without pausing to reflect, she lifted the fruit and launched it right at her husband's head.

It went whizzing past him without notice, sailing into the living room, but she couldn't stop herself now. She picked up another and hurled it even harder. This one hit him right on the ear with a fat thud.

"*What the fuck?*" Doug's hand went up to his ear, and he swiveled his head her way. "Shit."

The traitor on the counter opened her eyes then, her gaze going wide.

But Tessa kept throwing. Oranges, a grapefruit, apples. It was as if some other force had possessed her. Fruit whizzed across the kitchen, pelting both of them as they scrambled to get up and pull their clothes around themselves.

"Ow, Tessa, stop it! What the fuck is wrong with you?" Doug roared as he yanked at his pants with one hand while trying to fend off flying fruit with the other.

"What is wrong with *me*? *Me?!*" Tessa shouted, knowing she sounded like a lunatic but unable to stop herself.

"Tessa, honey," Marilyn said, hands out in front of her, blouse still hanging open. "Let's just calm down, okay?"

Tessa pinned her former best friend with a glare. "Did you just *dare* speak to me?"

"Marilyn, sweetheart," Doug said softly, putting a hand on her elbow and blocking her from Tessa with his body. "Why don't you get out of here? I'll deal with her."

Sweetheart? Deal with her? Loud, crashing bells were going off in Tessa's head. She was glad the knife block was out of reach because she wasn't sure she could trust herself in that moment.

Marilyn nodded after a quick, worried glance at Tessa, then hurried through the living room toward the sliding glass doors that led to the pool area and a backyard exit. Apparently, she knew better than to try to walk by Tessa to get to the front door. Wise move. Because Tessa was ready to throw down, Jerry Springer style.

With a tired sigh, Doug turned back to Tessa, his fly still unbuttoned and his cock still half-mast behind the material. The bastard hadn't even lost his erection. In fact, he looked more annoyed that he'd been interrupted than ashamed of what he'd done. Tessa's fist balled. "You lying, cheating asshole."

He pulled on his dress shirt and looked around the carnage of busted fruit on the floor. "Call the maid and have her come in early to clean this up. It'll draw ants if it sits too long. I've got to get back to work."

Tessa blinked, almost too stunned to speak. "That's what you have to say for yourself?"

"You don't want to hear what I have to say." He adjusted his cuffs like it was any other day of getting ready for work and not like the whole foundation of their marriage had just shattered beneath them.

"Oh, no. I really do," she said, seething.

His mouth curled in condescension. "Fine. You want to hear that I need something on the side? That you don't satisfy all of my needs?"

"Your *needs*?" If she'd had another piece of citrus to throw, she would've reached for it then. How many nights had she put all she had into pleasing him even when he hadn't put half the effort toward her? How many times had she donned expensive lingerie trying to catch his eye? She'd been willing to do *anything* for him. She'd loved him.

And he'd been screwing around on her the whole time. With her *best friend*. The thought almost doubled her over. She reached out and grabbed the edge of the counter.

"Look, you're upset. I get it. But, Tessa, it's just sex. I don't love them, and I'm not going to leave you for any of them. They're not a threat to you."

"You have the nerve to talk to me about love right now?" she asked, her throat trying to close. *Them*. So it was more than just Marilyn. She wondered if Marilyn knew she was just the tramp in the Tuesday slot on his calendar. "You're disgusting."

His lips curved back into that patronizing smirk he was so good at. "And you're boring in bed and my intellectual inferior, but I've learned to live with it. At least you're nice to look at now that you've gotten your gym routine back on course."

The hateful words knocked the breath right out of her. Doug had said mean things to her before in the heat of the moment. They'd been together since high school, so of course they'd had their fights. He could be critical beyond reason, always watching that she didn't eat too many calories or go outdoors without makeup or say the wrong thing in public. She'd tolerated it because she knew how concerned he was about image in his business. And she'd comforted herself with those moments when he was sweet and indulgent with her behind closed doors. He had the capacity to make her feel like a princess. And even though those times had grown few and far between over the last five years, she'd had no idea his opinion of her had sunk so low. Boring in bed. Inferior. Stupid.

God, is that what he told the women he cheated on her with? My wife isn't too bright, and she's clueless in the sack.

She grabbed her purse, her stomach threatening to toss up all its contents. She couldn't stand here for another second and look at his smarmy face, smell the scent of sex in the air. "Go to hell, Doug. I hope you're happy with your college-educated whores. Now you won't have to worry about me getting in the way."

He scoffed. "Come on, Tessa. Stop being melodramatic. You're not going to divorce me. Your life and everything in it exist because of me. Leave, and it all goes away. You're going to give up all this just because I like a novel fuck every now and then? Please." He grabbed his wallet and flipped a piece of plastic her way. "Take the credit card. Go punish me by buying something useless and extravagant—you're good at that—and we'll move on."

The credit card landed at her feet, and she had the urge to spear its platinum face with the heel of her Jimmy Choo pump. He was right. If she left him, every bit of her lifestyle would disappear in a poof. From the clothes on her back to the oranges she'd just hurled at him—all of it was funded by him. There'd be no way to prove his affair in court, not with the legal demons he could afford to hire. And she'd signed a pre-nup. She'd be left with a pittance of alimony. All the comfort and security she'd worked toward her whole life would be gone. She'd be back where she started all those years ago—a nobody with nothing.

Alone. With no money of her own and only a high-school education to her name.

She bent and picked up the card from the floor, turning it in her fingers before dropping it in her purse.

Doug smiled, satisfied. Victorious.

Without another word, she turned on her heels and calmly walked back out to her Mercedes. When she made it into town, she bought the two most extravagant things she could think of.

The services of an attorney.

And a plane ticket home.

It'd be the last of Doug Barrett's money she'd ever spend.

ONE

"Hold up. Why are you buying condoms? You said this was an emergency stop." Tessa snatched the box of Trojans from Sam's fingertips and held them up like Exhibit A.

Sam sent her an innocent look, one that Tessa had seen her use rather effectively on both sets of foster parents she'd shared with Sam. "What? I'm out. And we may need them."

"You may need condoms," Tessa repeated. "For a *cooking* class."

Sam grabbed another box from the rack. "*We* may need them. I'll get some for you, too. You never know who we might meet."

Tessa groaned and looked up at the buzzing fluorescent lights of the drugstore. Sam's ability to look for dating opportunities around every corner never failed to amaze Tessa. "We're not going to meet anyone. It's a cooking class. It's going to be married couples, women, and gay men."

Which is exactly why Tessa had agreed to go. After months of Sam trying to drag her out to bars or clubs on Friday nights to get her over that "dickwad ex-husband," finally her friend had come up with something that didn't make Tessa's stomach turn and her body break out into a cold sweat. But now, as she took in Sam's snug skirt and high heels, Tessa's dread was growing. She'd thought Sam had simply chosen to dress up because the class was being held at one of the swankiest restaurants in Dallas. But now the puzzle pieces were locking together into a new picture.

"Straight men like to cook, too," Sam pointed out as she strolled away from the prophylactics aisle toward the cosmetics section. "Particularly when it's a Perfect Match meet-up event."

Tessa's shoe squeaked on the floor as she halted mid-stride. "Sam, you'd better be screwing with me."

Sam grabbed a lip gloss off a rack and held the colored cap next to Tessa's mouth, frowned, then picked up a different color. "I'm not screwing with you. I'm *helping* you. My friend is the receptionist at the local Perfect Match office. She offered to sneak us onto the list because the event wasn't full. How could I pass it up? It was like fate tapping my shoulder. You want to scratch items off your list. This will accomplish that and maybe get you a date as a bonus. Two for the price of one."

"Learning to cook is on my list. Dating is not. Dating is actually diametrically opposed to the whole spirit of the list."

"Diametrically? Wow, someone's getting A's in her night classes." Sam gave her a teasing smile and dropped the lip gloss into her hand basket. "And if I'm not mistaken, one of the items you have on that sacred to-do list of yours is to tackle being 'boring in bed.' How exactly do you plan to fix that one without actually coming into contact with the opposite sex?"

A guy perusing greeting cards across the aisle gave them a sideways glance and smirked. Tessa's face heated. "Could you at least try to keep your voice down while discussing my sex life?"

"What sex life?" Sam replied, not bothering to lower her voice. "This is exactly why we're going tonight. You need to loosen up. Be open to a world of infinite possibilities. And by possibilities, I mean hot men."

"Ugh." She should've never let Sam see her stupid list. It'd been something she'd written down in those first few weeks after she'd left Doug and her life in Atlanta. She'd landed in Dallas with no plan, no place to stay, no job. All she'd had was her suitcase and a head filled with all the critical things Doug had said to her over the course of their marriage and that final day in the kitchen.

He'd said she was nothing without him.

And as she'd sat in Sam's guest room one night, trying to put together a resume to apply for jobs and feeling sorry for herself, she'd realized the bastard had been right on some level. Since she'd met Doug in high school, her entire existence had been centered around being who he wanted her to be. Being what *everyone* wanted her to be. For Doug, it was the doting girlfriend. For her classmates, it was the bubbly, popular cheerleader. For her foster parents, it was the girl who never broke the rules and went to church with them every Sunday.

She'd been a master chameleon without ever realizing it. It'd kept her from being moved to yet another home. It'd kept her safe from the vicious bullying in high school. It'd given her a way to secure a future with a man who would take care of her. She'd never be that little girl left alone and scared again.

Only the whole plan had been built out of Popsicle sticks. She'd counted on someone else for her happiness and security. A fatal mistake. How had she ever let herself be so stupid as to trust someone again? Her mother had said she'd always be there, and look how that had turned out.

As Tessa had stared at that blinking cursor, she'd made a decision. Never would she let herself depend on anyone else again. She would survive on her own. She'd done it for years as a kid.

She could do it now. And she wouldn't just make it through; she'd transform. Thrive. She'd vowed that by the end of the year, a resume of her life would no longer be a stark blank page. She would take those insults Doug had hurled at her and use them as fuel, not just to find a job but to tackle every facet of her life. She'd prove that she was more than the trophy wife she'd let herself become.

But that plan had not included dating. Sex, maybe. Eventually. She didn't plan to enter the convent and abstain for the rest of her life. But dating and getting any emotional entanglements would only send her sliding backward. "Sam, I'm not ready to date. You know that."

Sam sighed and linked her arm with Tessa's, leading her to the register. "So just come for the food and cooking lesson then. The whole point of these meet-ups is that it's a no-pressure environment. And we're getting sangria and a fancy meal *for free*. How long has it been since you've had a chance to eat in a restaurant that doesn't serve food wrapped in greasy paper?"

Tessa groaned. "Don't remind me."

One of the main reasons she was interested in cooking classes in the first place was because she missed the delicious meals Doug's housekeeper used to prepare for them and all the gourmet restaurants she and Doug had gone to regularly. If she had to eat another bowl of canned soup, she might stab herself with a spoon. But she didn't have the income to fund nice restaurants anymore. So if she wanted to eat something that wasn't frozen or canned, she was going to have to learn how to cook it herself.

Sam swiped her credit card and took her bag from the cashier. "Exactly. Barcelona is one of the hottest restaurants around. This is your chance for a major treat. The only sacrifice is that you'll have to make small talk with a stranger who happens to have a penis. Big deal."

Tessa sighed, her ability to fight against Sam's hopeful gaze crumbling. Sam had good intentions, even if they were misguided. And really, what was a little awkward small talk with someone Tessa would never see again when there was free sangria to be had? "You're lucky I'm a sucker for tapas."

Sam's face broke into a grin, and she pulled out the lip gloss to give it to Tessa. "Gloss up, babe. Let's go cook some shrimp and break some hearts."

When Tessa walked through the doors of Barcelona, it was like walking through a portal to a world she wasn't a native of anymore. Soft Spanish music played, the scent of exotic spices drifted through the air, and the saffron-colored walls flickered with the dancing light of candlelit tables. Every detail screamed trendy elegance and money. As did most of the guests sitting at the tables. She could almost see her old self sitting among them, wineglass in hand, diamonds sparkling at her throat, her husband sitting across from her telling her about the latest acquisition he was working on. Anyone looking at them would've been envious.

But seeing the image in her mind's eye now showed a picture that was warped and tarnished. An illusion. The conversation would've been one-sided because Tessa had never understood Doug's business speak. The diamond choker around her neck would've probably been a guilt gift he'd given her after one of his affairs. And the wine would've been her attempt at getting in the mood for the lackluster sex they'd have later that night.

She didn't miss this world.

And she didn't miss that woman.

"Hello, ladies, do you have a reservation?" the host asked.

Sam stepped forward. "We're here for the cooking class."

"Ah, yes," he said, his smile welcoming. "Follow me. You'll be in the banquet room."

The host led them through the main dining area and then

through a short hallway and another set of doors. The banquet room looked much like the other side of the restaurant, but the lights weren't as low and there were tables set up around the perimeter with cooking equipment and little bowls of ingredients. In the center of the room, there were smaller, more intimate tables where they'd presumably eat their meal after learning how to prepare it. Pitchers of sangria gleamed ruby red on each table. A number of people were already sitting at the small tables, mingling and drinking. The tinkling sounds of nervous, first-date laughter mixed in with the music.

Tessa's stomach did a flip, and she almost turned to leave. Sam put a hand on Tessa's arm, as if reading her unspoken intention, and guided her forward. "Don't chicken out now."

A man with a clipboard near the entrance grinned brightly. "Welcome to the meet-up ladies. I'm Jim, your event liaison for the night. Names?"

"I'm Samantha Dunbar, and this is Tessa McAllen."

Jim scanned the clipboard, nodding. "Ms. Dunbar, your perfect match is Cory Heath, table five. He's already here if you'd like to head over and say hi. We're letting everyone chat and enjoy their drinks for a few minutes before the class starts. Break the ice, you know?"

"Sure," Sam said, peeking over at the dark-haired guy at table five, scanning him from head to loafer. "Sounds good."

But Tessa's brain snagged. "Wait a second. I thought we were just mingling with everyone?"

Jim smiled. "Oh, no, ma'am. Perfect Match is full service. We took the profile you sent us and matched you up with someone compatible for the evening. No use wasting time on people you have nothing in common with, right?"

"The *profile* I sent in?" Tessa asked, shooting daggers at Sam.

Sam sent her a please-don't-kill-me look and gave Tessa's hand a squeeze. "Just try to have a good time, okay? I promise, it's no big deal. It'll be fun."

With that, Sam hurried off toward her "perfect match." Tessa had to fight hard not to lose it right there. Not only was she going to have to manage a date with a stranger, but said stranger would be under the impression that they'd been matched together. And God only knew what Sam had put in Tessa's profile. She cringed at the thought.

Jim was scanning his list again, and Tessa smoothed the front of her dress. She hadn't thought to put much effort into her outfit tonight. This was supposed to be a cooking class, after all. So she'd simply stayed in the black wrap dress she'd worn to work. But now she felt plain and out of place. Everyone else had put on their A-game ensemble for date night.

God, why was she even worrying about it? *This isn't a real date.* She'd been trained by Doug to look her best at all times because you never knew who you'd run into, and sometimes that old urge was hard to shake. But she wasn't here to impress anyone. She was here to drink sangria and to learn how to cook. That's it.

The door opened behind her as more people came in.

"Ms. McAllen?" Jim asked, a small frown curving his thin lips as he lifted his gaze from the clipboard. "Do you have your confirmation number with you? You're not showing on my list."

"My what?" She automatically put her hand on her purse, but knew she had nothing of the sort in there. "No. My friend set all this up for us both."

"Hmm." Jim tapped his pencil on the clipboard. "Well, I'm not showing you on here, which means we don't have confirmation of your payment. If you'd like to pay the fee now, we can let you stay for the class. Then if you find your confirmation, we'll refund you. But since you weren't on the list, we won't have a match set up for you. You'd just be staying for the cooking portion unless we have any other walk-ins."

No match sounded like a fantastic idea. Maybe this was a blessing in disguise. "How much is it?"

"Two hundred dollars."

A gasp escaped her lips. Two hundred dollars? She should've expected it, but the number still caught her off guard. And it was a number she couldn't fund. "I'm sorry. I'll just have to find out what happened to my original fee and do this another time. Maybe I can talk to my friend and see if she has the information."

He smiled kindly, but she saw it in his eyes. He knew she was bailing because she didn't have the money. "Of course."

Shame tried to edge in, heating her cheeks. But she swallowed it back. She would not get teary over missing some stupid cooking class. She took a step to head toward Sam's table, hoping that even though they were technically party crashers, her friend had some magical confirmation number. But before she could move forward, a warm hand touched her elbow.

"I'll cover the fee."

The rich timbre of the man's voice rolled over Tessa like sun-heated ocean water. She stiffened at the contact and her body's unexpected visceral reaction. She spun around, her gaze going up, up, up, and finally colliding with clear blue eyes and a face made for Greek sculpture. Her brain forgot to form words.

"I'd hate for you to miss one of the best meals of your life because of a computer glitch," the man said, a ghost of a smile touching his lips.

Tessa simply stared back. The way he held her gaze had her thoughts scattering and her brain reaching for some memory she couldn't quite grab hold of. She shook her head, breaking the gaze and trying to clear her head. *No.* This stranger was offering to pay two hundred dollars for her to eat. She knew how that worked. She'd played that game before. "Really, that's very kind of you to offer. But I'll just come back another time."

He pulled his wallet from his pocket, pulled two crisp bills from it, and handed it to Jim. "I insist. And it's no problem. I'm sure they'll pay me back when they find your original reservation."

Tessa shook her head again, even though her mind was already fast-forwarding and picturing how decadent it would be to sit and sip sangrias with this stranger. But she couldn't fall into her old habits and let him pay her way. It didn't matter that he was gorgeous or that he didn't seem to mind or that he was wearing a watch that said two hundred dollars was a drop in the bucket for him. "I'm sorry. I can't take your money."

Before the stranger could protest, she moved past him and the few people waiting behind them to head for the door. She needed to get out—now. She knew it was ridiculous, but she had the sudden urge to cry, to scream, to pound on something. All she'd wanted tonight was to relax and have a fun girl's night with Sam. Instead, she'd been reminded of the life she used to have, how feeble her bank account was now, and how fucked up she was when it came to men.

She moved through the hallway that led back to the main dining room at a rapid clip, hoping to reach the parking lot before the tears broke free, but a hand touched her shoulder. "Hey, hold up."

The quiet command of his voice and the gentleness of the touch had her halting her step before she could think better of it. She closed her eyes, took a breath, and turned around, speech prepared. But when she saw the genuine concern on his face, her words got stuck in her throat.

He tucked his hands in his pockets, the move pulling his black dress shirt snug across what looked to be long, lean muscles beneath. His eyes scanned hers. "Are you okay? I didn't mean to chase you off."

She put her hand to her too-hot forehead, trying to catch her breath and center herself. "I'm sorry. It wasn't you. I'm fine. This night just isn't working out like I thought it would."

"Expected to meet your perfect match?"

She made a sound that was some mixture of a snort, a sob, and a laugh. "Oh my God. Hardly. What a joke that is. A perfect match."

His mouth lifted at the corner, his blue eyes sparkling with a hint of amusement. "So you're telling me you paid two hundred dollars to attend something you don't buy into?"

"I didn't pay," she admitted. "A friend told me she'd get me on the list. And I—I wanted to learn to cook and to taste the food."

He chuckled and glanced back at the closed door. "A party crasher. How scandalous."

His low laugh was like a gust of summer air across her nerve endings, reminding her of someone long ago. Someone she hadn't had to be a chameleon for. She found herself smiling, her dour mood lifting. "That's me. A scandal a minute. And now I'm causing more. I'm sure your perfect match date is anxiously awaiting you inside."

"Nah, I don't believe in perfect matches either. Just instant attraction." He stepped closer and the air in the room seemed to thicken, warm. "So answer me one question. Are you leaving because you were opposed to the money or to me?"

She blinked, caught off guard by the question and his nearness. "What?"

"You came out here tonight to take a class and have a nice meal. I was happy to help you do that. So, did you turn down my offer because you think the money comes with strings or are you just opposed to spending the evening with me?"

"I—" She wet her lips. The way he'd said *spend the evening with me* had her mind conjuring pictures of him braced over her, his blond hair mussed, his eyes heated, and that sensual mouth whispering dirty things to her. Her thighs clenched, and she tried to come up with something to say that wasn't *God, you're beautiful, please push me up against this wall and make me forget my name.* "I can't accept the money."

That answer seemed to please him. "And me?"

She couldn't tell if it was the warm, smoky spices from the restaurant mixing in, but even the scent of him was exotic and dangerous, tempting. She wanted to bury her face in the open collar of his shirt and inhale. All her resolve seemed to disintegrate in the space between breaths. "I'm not opposed."

He reached out and pushed a stray lock of hair away from her face, the simple brush of fingers like lightning rods touching her skin. "So if I promised you I wouldn't pay a dime for the rest of the evening, would you agree to spend it with me?"

She swallowed hard, the notion almost too much for her psyche to absorb. She knew what he was offering wasn't simply dinner and a chat. There was a ripple of heat beneath each uttered word, a promise. Her body was on board with this plan, whether her good sense agreed or not. Already, she could feel the flush of arousal tightening her nipples and dampening her panties. She hadn't been touched by anyone other than Doug in years, and her experiences with him had always been underwhelming. Just being this close to this mystery man made everything inside her feel hot and alive. But it'd be stupid and reckless to say yes. She'd never had a one-night stand. She didn't even know if she was capable of it. Plus, what if she really was boring in bed?

She'd told herself that Doug had thrown that out there just to hurt her, but what if there was some truth to it? Her sexual history was brief since she'd gotten married so young. What if she hopped in bed with this guy and was completely out of her league?

"I can't leave. I'm my friend's ride," she said, her voice thready and breathless from him being so close.

His smile was slow, sexy. "I never said we had to leave."

She closed her eyes, his mere presence overwhelming her system and making her heart pound in her throat. "What do you mean?"

His breath brushed her ear. "Just take my hand, and I'll show you."

A shiver worked its way down her neck and along her skin. Every nerve ending screamed for his touch, all the years of pent-up frustration surging to the surface. She needed this escape, this release. She needed to feel like a woman again.

When she looked up at him finally, the pure confidence and interest shining there in his eyes had her nerves smoothing. She knew in that moment that this man would never allow her to be boring in bed. This was a man who got what he wanted. A man who wouldn't be afraid to tell her exactly what to do, how he liked it, and how he was going to have her.

Suddenly, she wasn't so interested in sangria anymore.

Or sitting in the car alone to have a good cry.

She reached out and let her hand slide into his.

Maybe she'd scratch something off her list tonight after all.

ABOUT THE AUTHOR

Roni Loren wrote her first romance novel at age fifteen when she discovered writing about boys was way easier than actually talking to them. Since then, her flirting skills haven't improved, but she likes to think her storytelling ability has. Though she'll forever be a New Orleans girl at heart, she now lives in Dallas with her husband and son. If she's not working on her latest sexy story, you can find her reading, watching reality television, or indulging in her unhealthy addiction to rock stars, er, rock concerts. Yeah, that's it. Visit her website: www.roniloren.com.